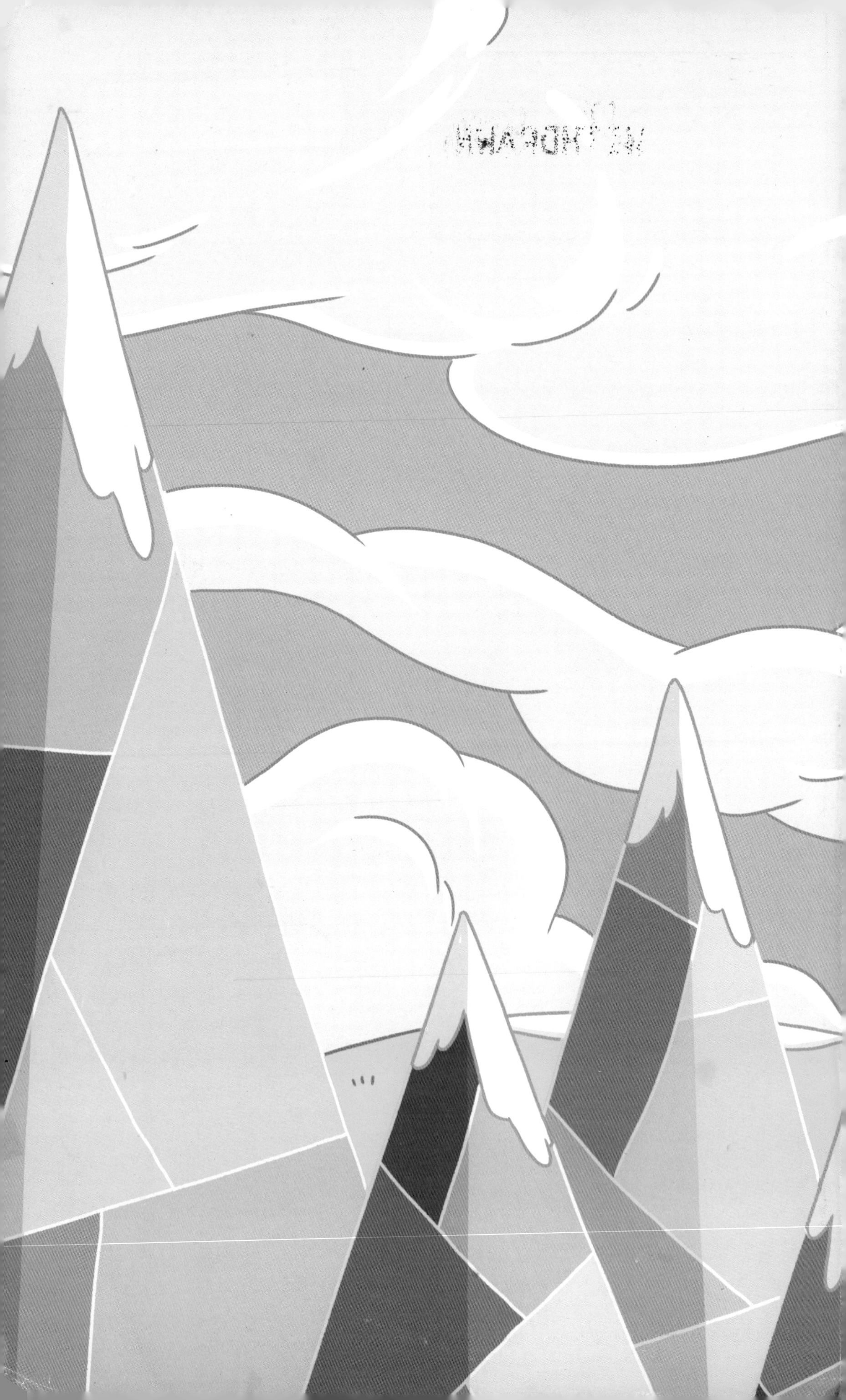

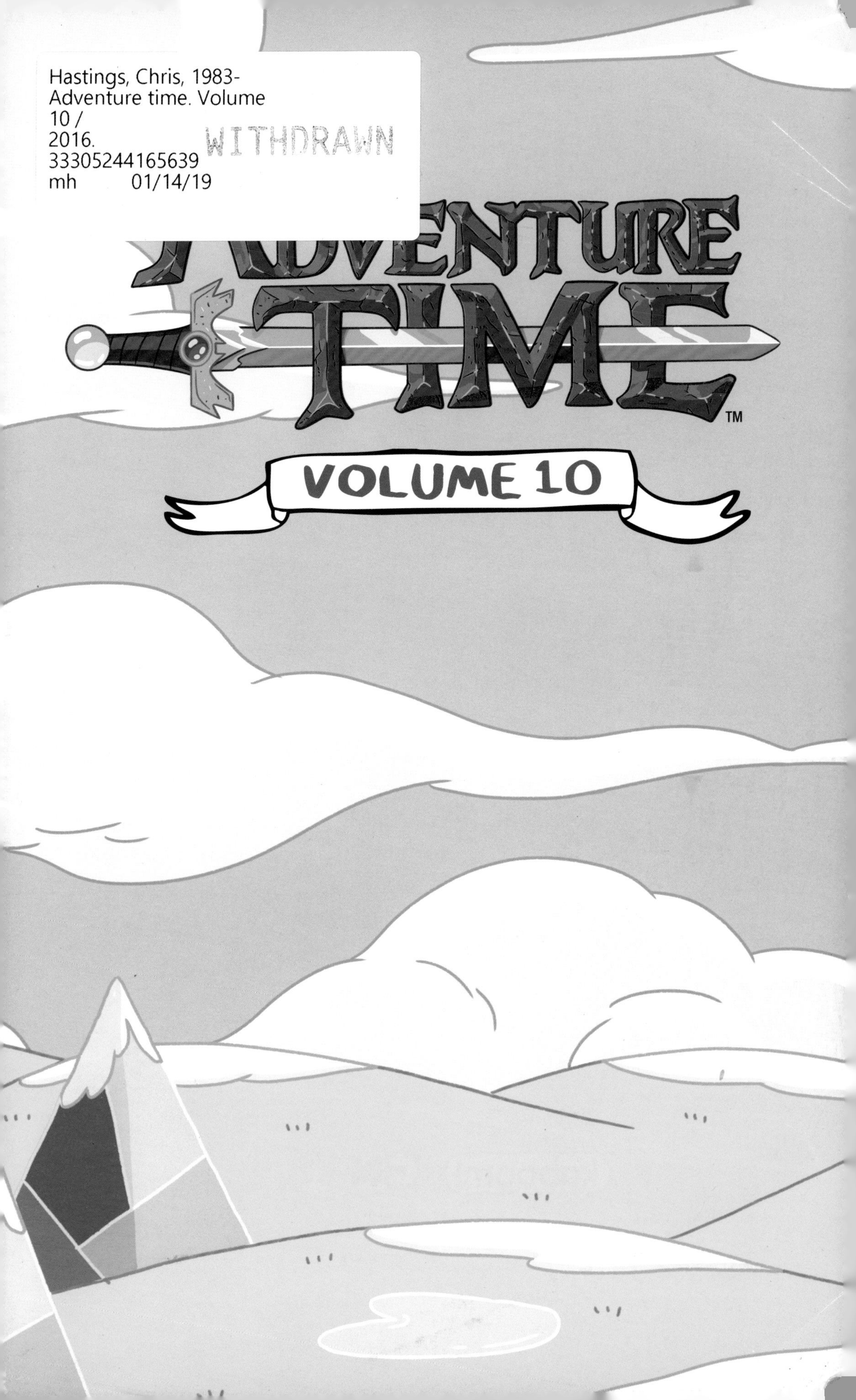
ADVENTURE TIME™
VOLUME 10

ROSS RICHIE CEO & Founder • MATT GAGNON Editor-in-Chief • FILIP SABLIK President of Publishing & Marketing • STEPHEN CHRISTY President of Development • LANCE KREITER VP of Licensing & Merchandising • PHIL BARBARO VP of Finance • BRYCE CARLSON Managing Editor • MEL CAYLO Marketing Manager • SCOTT NEWMAN Production Design Manager • IRENE BRADISH Operations Manager • SIERRA HAHN Senior Editor • DAFNA PLEBAN Editor, Talent Development • SHANNON WATTERS Editor • ERIC HARBURN Editor • WHITNEY LEOPARD Associate Editor • JASMINE AMIRI Associate Editor • CHRIS ROSA Associate Editor • ALEX GALER Associate Editor • CAMERON CHITTOCK Associate Editor • MARY GUMPORT Assistant Editor • MATTHEW LEVINE Assistant Editor • KELSEY DIETERICH Production Designer • JILLIAN CRAB Production Designer • MICHELLE ANKLEY Production Designer • GRACE PARK Production Design Assistant • AARON FERRARA Operations Coordinator • ELIZABETH LOUGHRIDGE Accounting Coordinator • STEPHANIE HOCUTT Social Media Coordinator • JOSÉ MEZA Sales Assistant • JAMES ARRIOLA Mailroom Assistant • HOLLY AITCHISON Operations Assistant • SAM KUSEK Direct Market Representative • AMBER PARKER Administrative Assistant

ADVENTURE TIME Volume Ten, November 2016. Published by KaBOOM!, a division of Boom Entertainment, Inc. ADVENTURE TIME, CARTOON NETWORK, the logos, and all related characters and elements are trademarks of and © Cartoon Network. (S16) Originally published in single magazine form as ADVENTURE TIME No. 45-49. © Cartoon Network. (S16) All rights reserved. KaBOOM!™ and the KaBOOM! logo are trademarks of Boom Entertainment, Inc., registered in various countries and categories. All characters, events, and institutions depicted herein are fictional. Any similarity between any of the names, characters, persons, events, and/or institutions in this publication to actual names, characters, and persons, whether living or dead, events, and/or institutions is unintended and purely coincidental. KaBOOM! does not read or accept unsolicited submissions of ideas, stories, or artwork.

A catalog record of this book is available from OCLC and from the KaBOOM! website, www.boom-studios.com, on the Librarians Page.

BOOM! Studios, 5670 Wilshire Boulevard, Suite 450, Los Angeles, CA 90036-5679. Printed in China. First Printing.
ISBN: 978-1-60886-909-1, eISBN: 978-1-61398-580-9

CREATED BY
Pendleton Ward

WRITTEN BY
Christopher Hastings

ILLUSTRATED BY
Zachary Sterling & Phil Murphy

ISSUE #45 COLORS BY
Chrystin Garland

ISSUE #46-49 COLORS BY
Maarta Laiho

ISSUES #45-48 LETTERS BY
Steve Wands

ISSUE #49 LETTERS BY
Warren Montgomery

COVER BY
Chris Houghton
COLORS BY **KASSANDRA HELLER**

DESIGNER
Grace Park

ASSOCIATE EDITOR
Whitney Leopard

EDITOR
Shannon Watters

With special thanks to
Marisa Marionakis, Rick Blanco, Jim Valeri, Curtis Lelash, Conrad
Montgomery, Meghan Bradley, Kelly Crews, Scott Malchus, Adam Muto
and the wonderful folks at Cartoon Network.

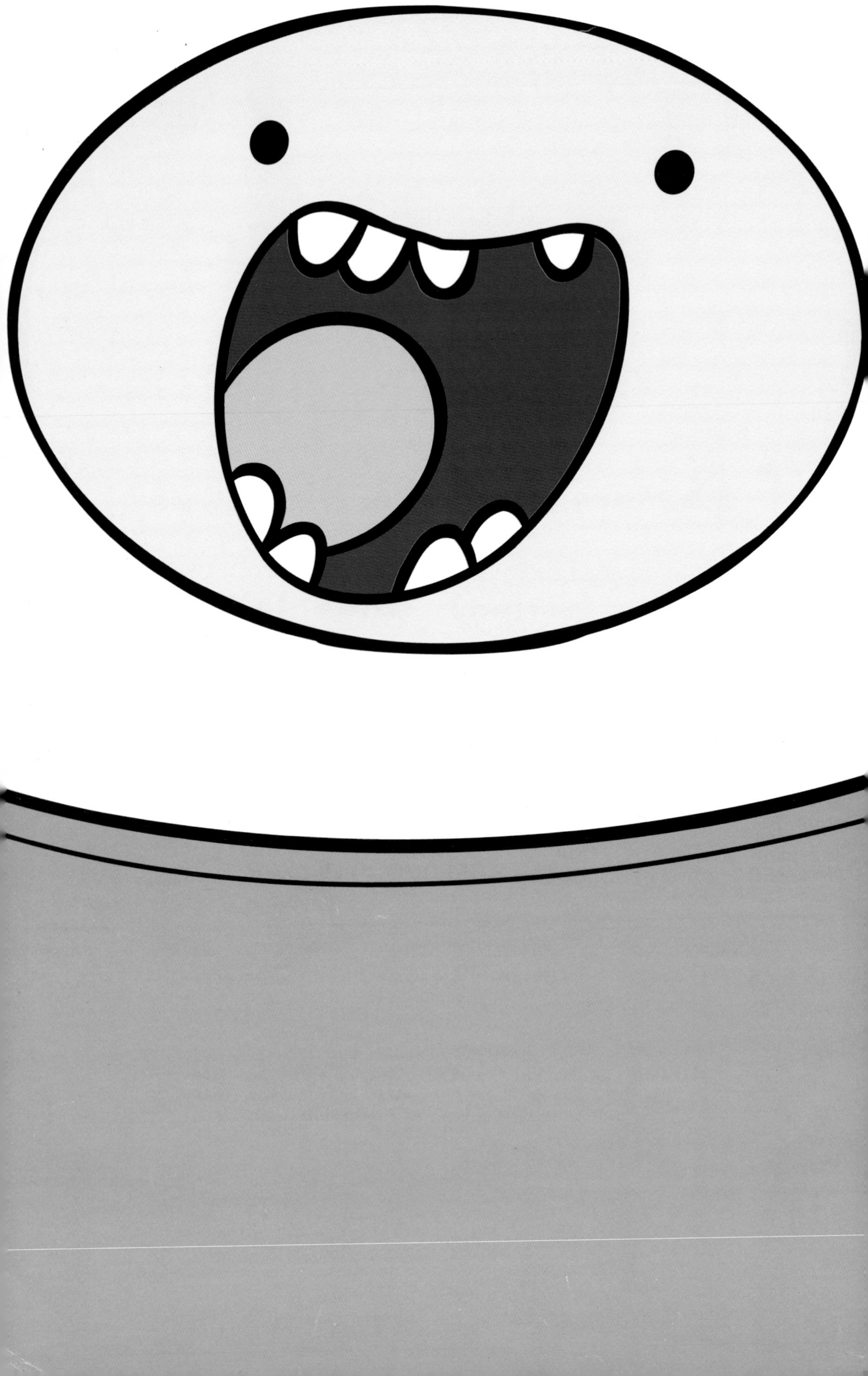

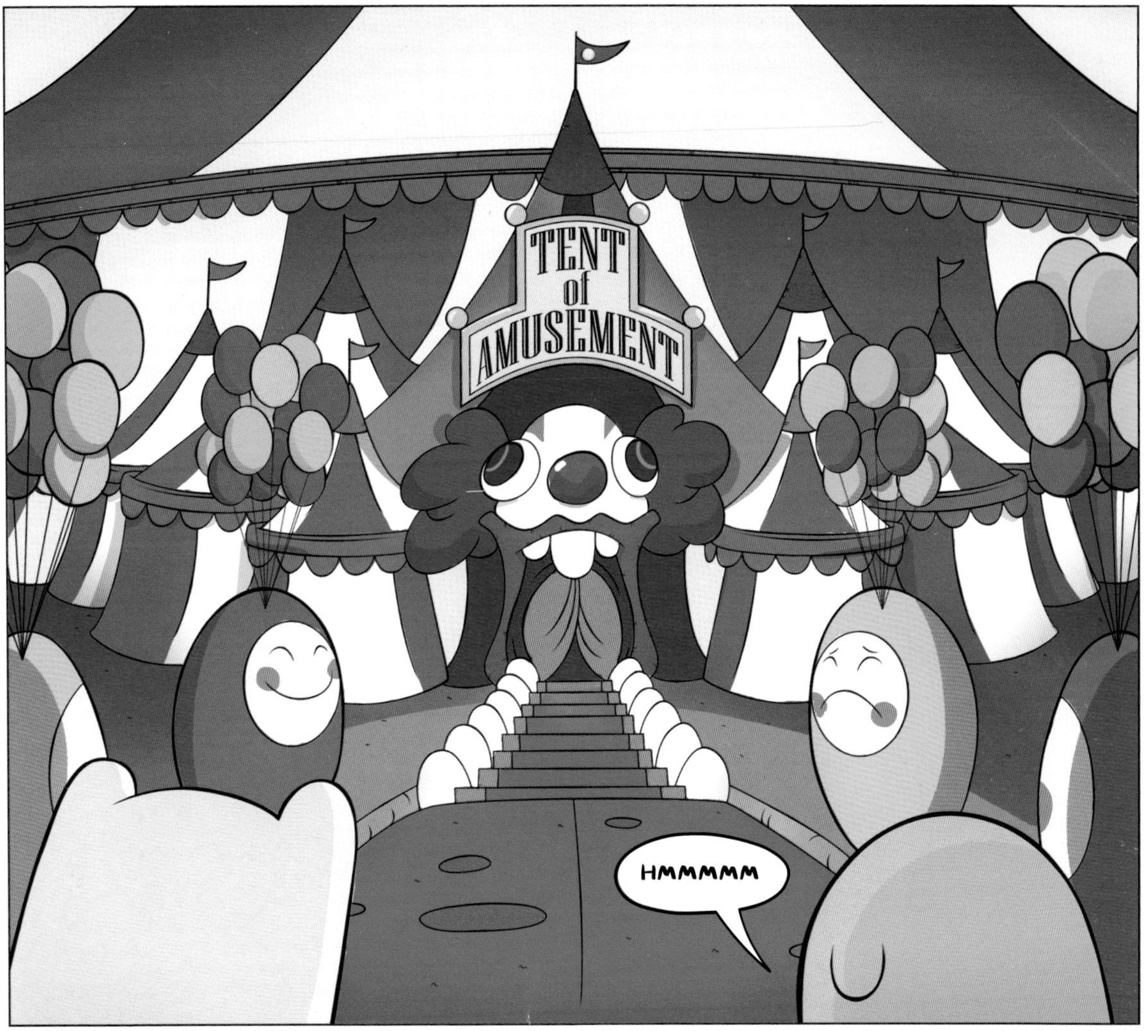
TENT of AMUSEMENT
HMMMMM

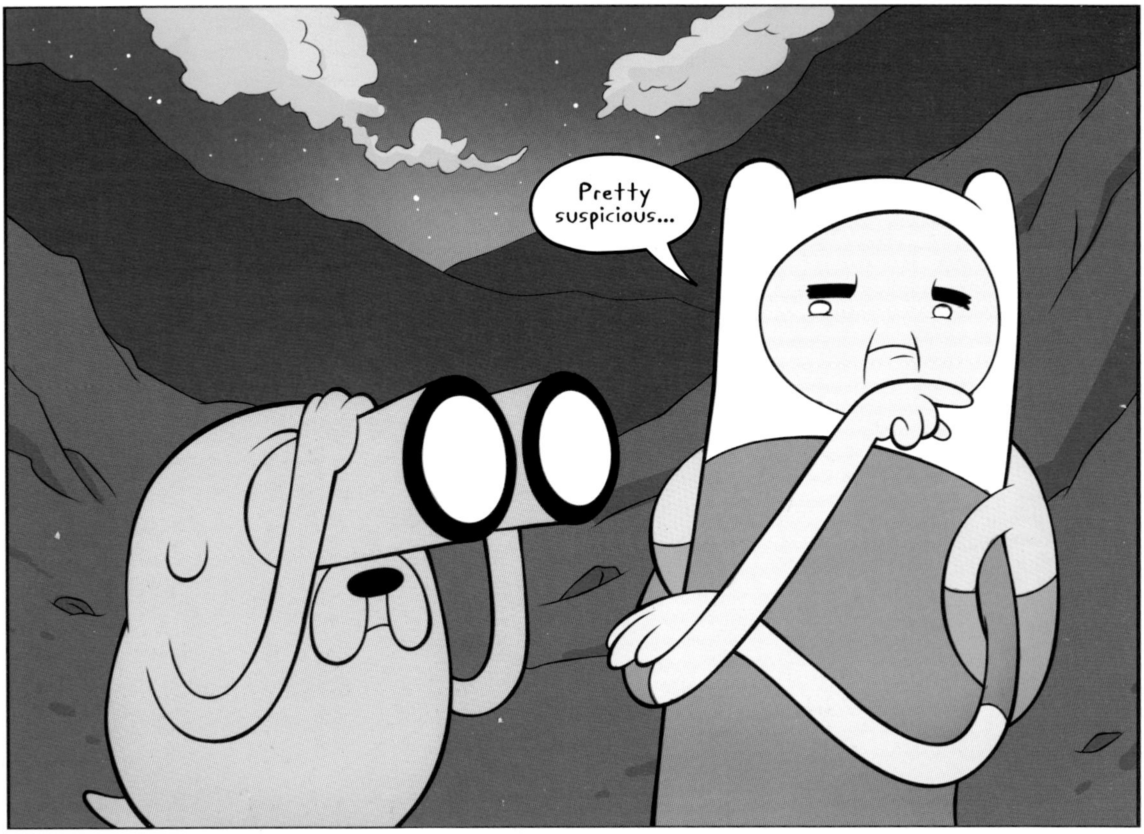
Pretty suspicious...

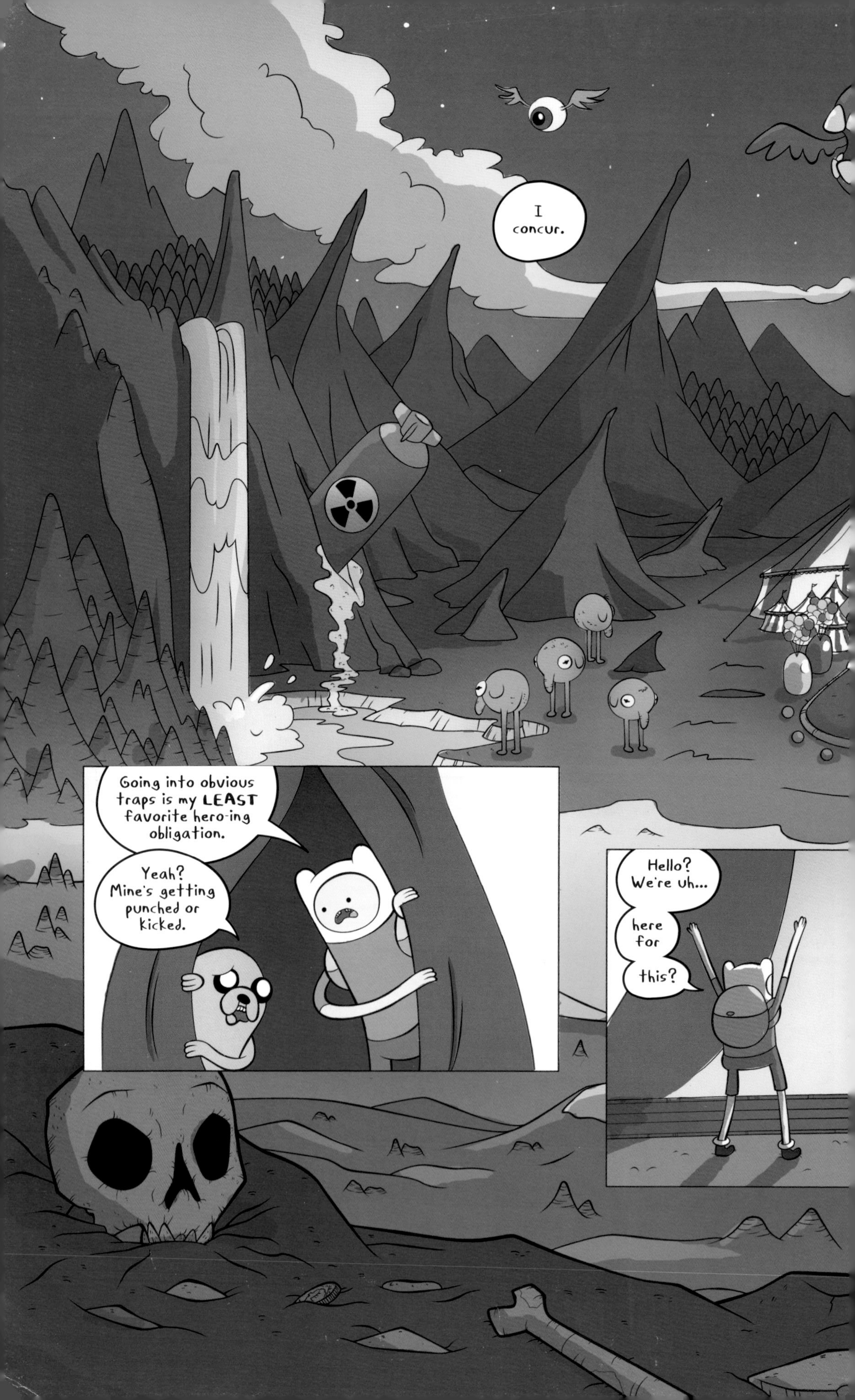
I concur.
Going into obvious traps is my LEAST favorite hero-ing obligation.
Yeah? Mine's getting punched or kicked.
Hello? We're uh...
here for
this?

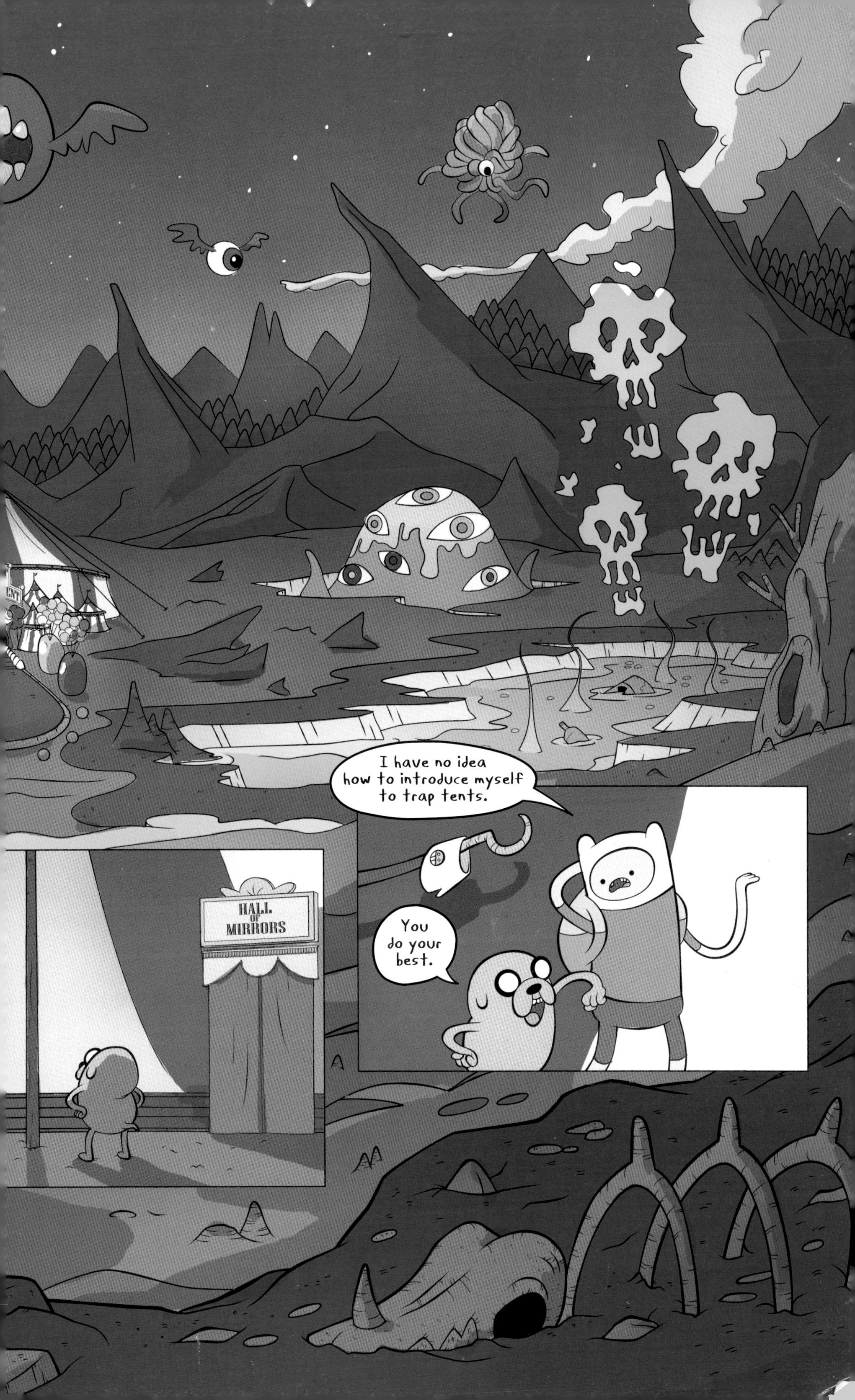
HALL OF MIRRORS
I have no idea how to introduce myself to trap tents.
You do your best.

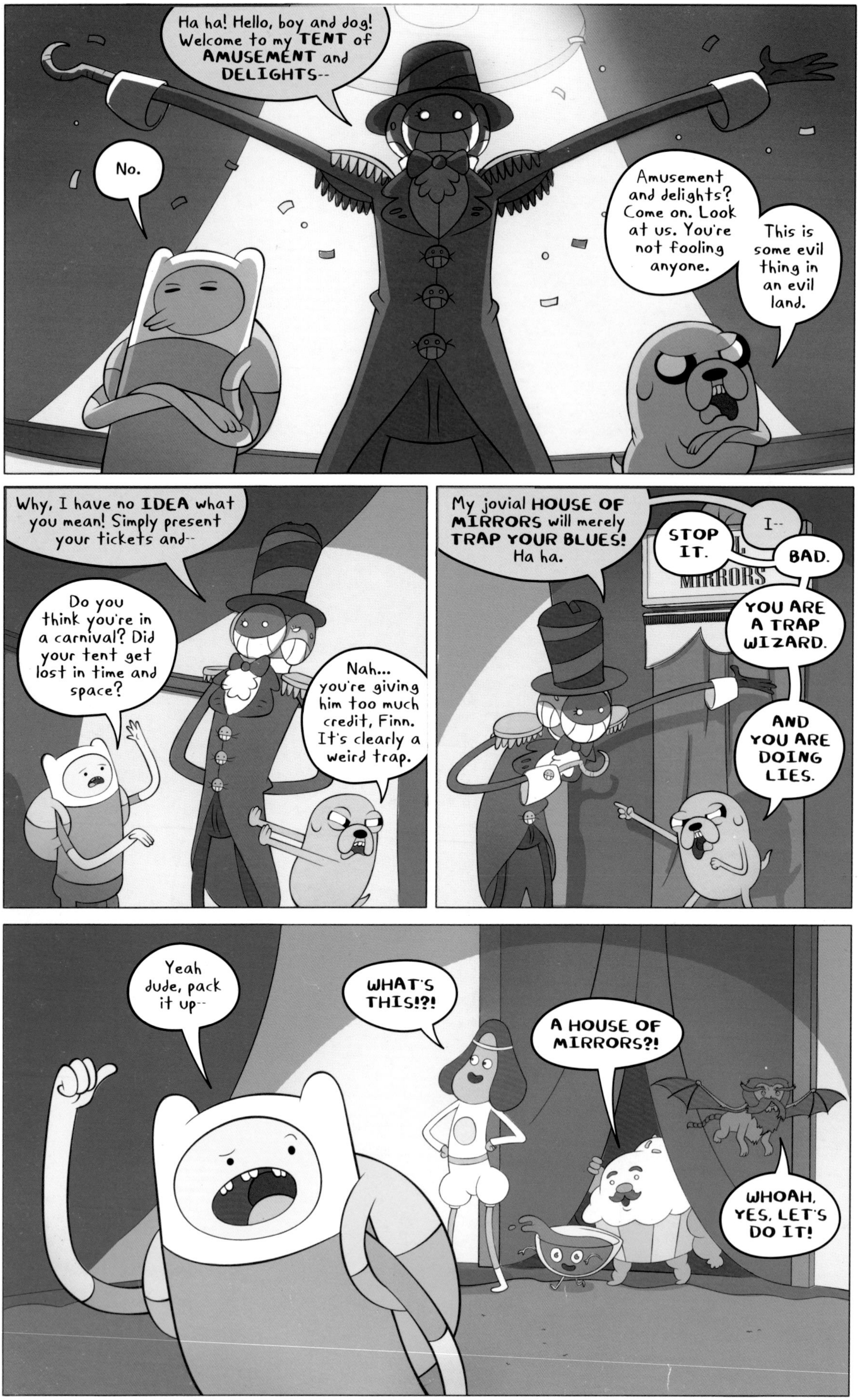

Ha ha! Hello, boy and dog! Welcome to my TENT of AMUSEMENT and DELIGHTS--
No.
Amusement and delights? Come on. Look at us. You're not fooling anyone.
This is some evil thing in an evil land.
Why, I have no IDEA what you mean! Simply present your tickets and--
Do you think you're in a carnival? Did your tent get lost in time and space?
Nah... you're giving him too much credit, Finn. It's clearly a weird trap.
My jovial HOUSE OF MIRRORS will merely TRAP YOUR BLUES! Ha ha.
I--
STOP IT.
BAD.
MIRRORS
YOU ARE A TRAP WIZARD.
AND YOU ARE DOING LIES.
Yeah dude, pack it up--
WHAT'S THIS!?!
A HOUSE OF MIRRORS?!
WHOAH, YES, LET'S DO IT!

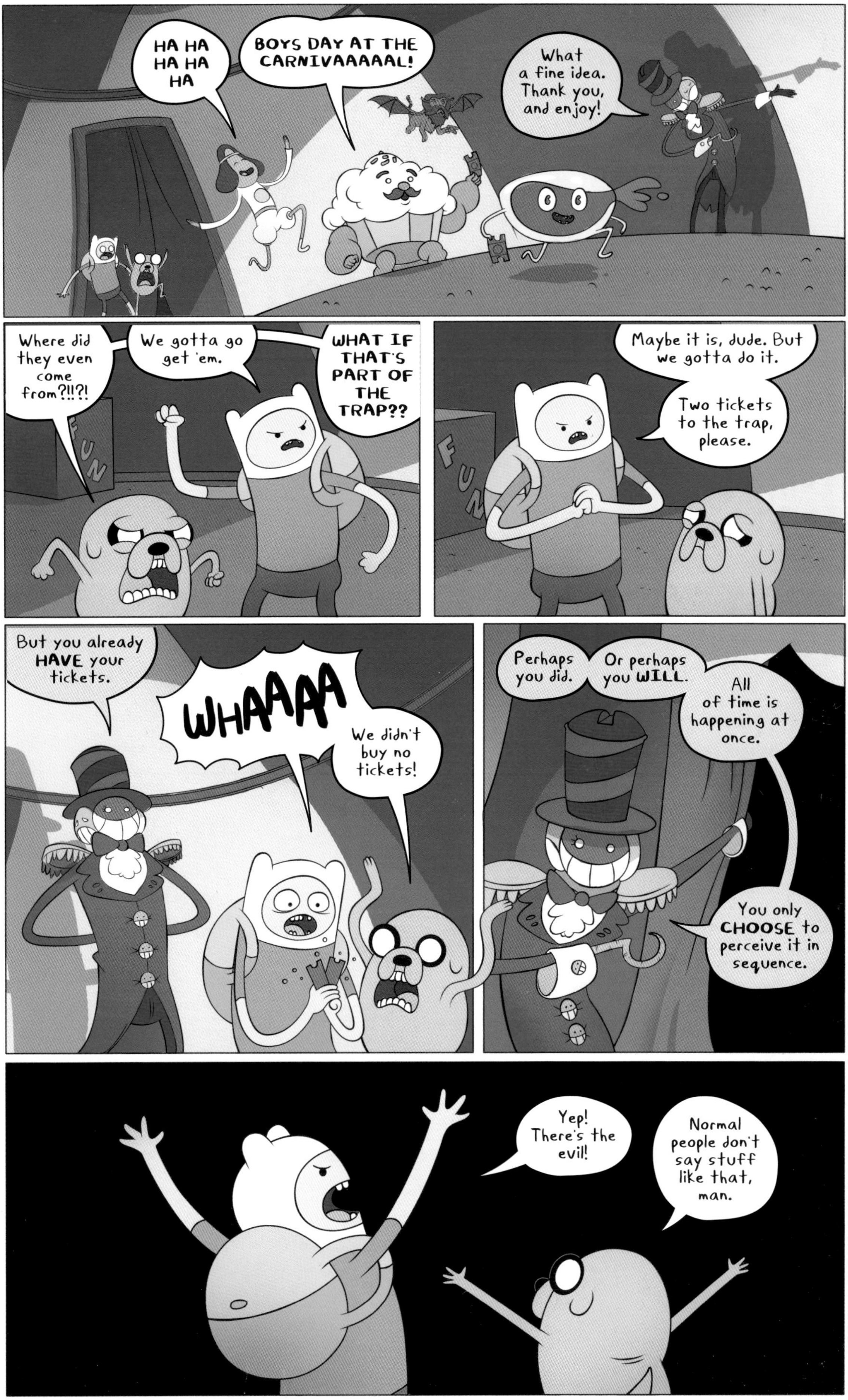
HA HA HA HA HA
BOYS DAY AT THE CARNIVAAAAAL!
What a fine idea. Thank you, and enjoy!
Where did they even come from?!!?!
We gotta go get 'em.
WHAT IF THAT'S PART OF THE TRAP??
Maybe it is, dude. But we gotta do it.
Two tickets to the trap, please.
FUN
But you already HAVE your tickets.
WHAAAAA
We didn't buy no tickets!
Perhaps you did.
Or perhaps you WILL.
All of time is happening at once.
You only CHOOSE to perceive it in sequence.
Yep! There's the evil!
Normal people don't say stuff like that, man.

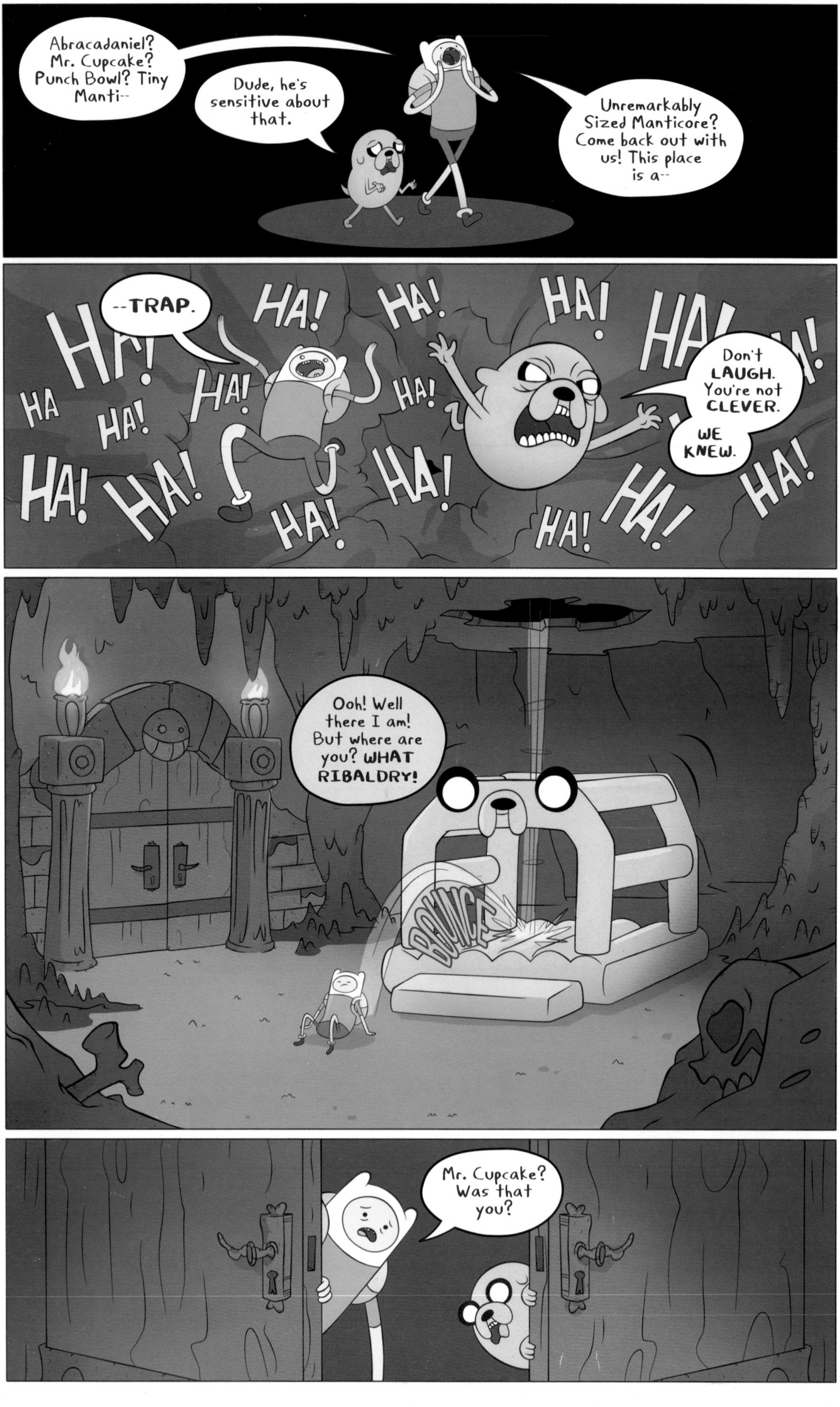
Abracadaniel? Mr. Cupcake? Punch Bowl? Tiny Manti--
Dude, he's sensitive about that.
Unremarkably Sized Manticore? Come back out with us! This place is a--
--TRAP.
HA! HA! HA! HA! HA! HA! HA! HA! HA! HA! HA! HA! HA! HA! HA! HA! HA! HA!
Don't LAUGH. You're not CLEVER.
WE KNEW.
Ooh! Well there I am! But where are you? WHAT RIBALDRY!
BOUNCE
Mr. Cupcake? Was that you?

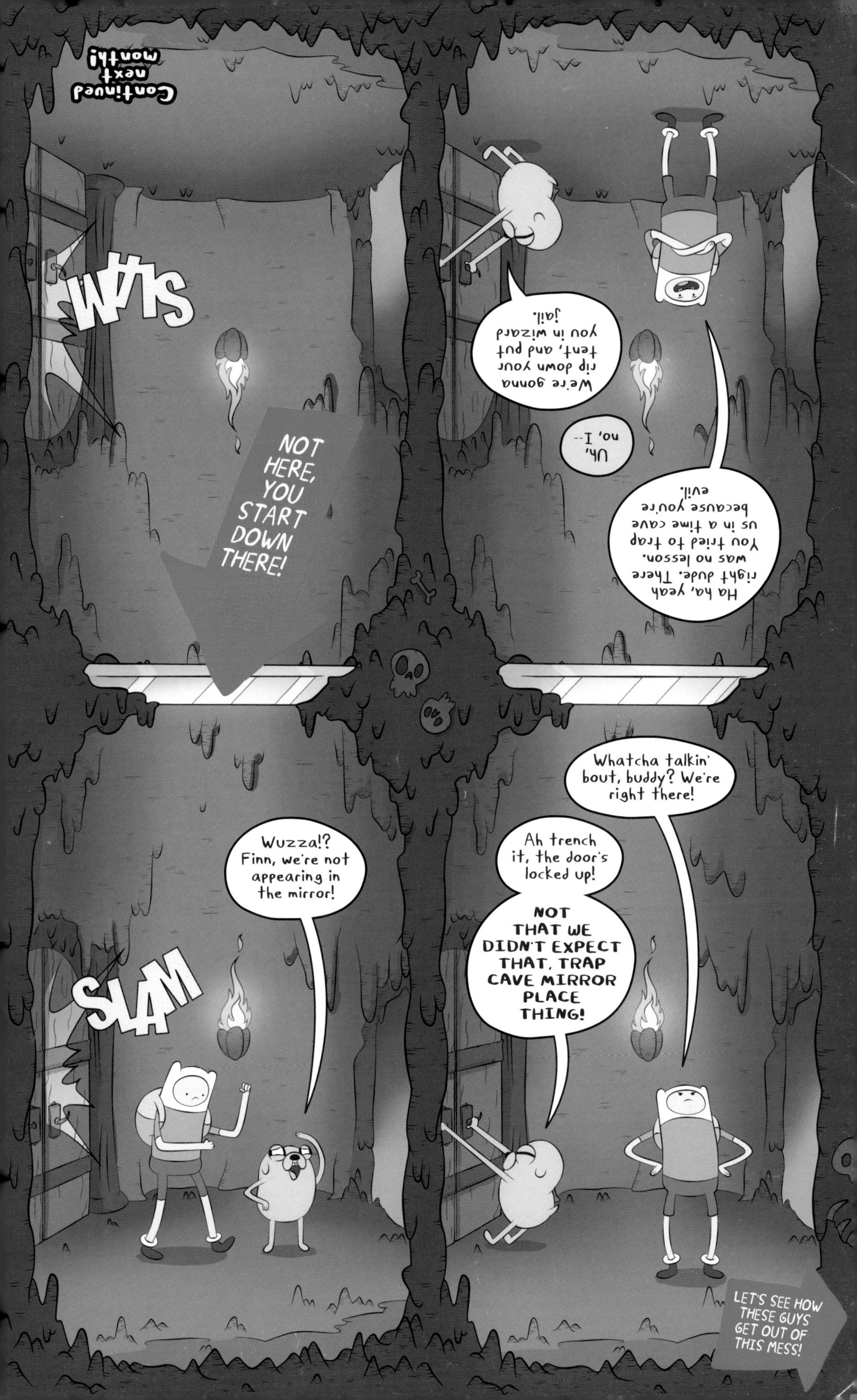

NOT HERE, YOU START DOWN THERE!
SLAM
Wuzza!? Finn, we're not appearing in the mirror!
Ah trench it, the door's locked up!
NOT THAT WE DIDN'T EXPECT THAT, TRAP CAVE MIRROR PLACE THING!
Whatcha talkin' bout, buddy? We're right there!
LET'S SEE HOW THESE GUYS GET OUT OF THIS MESS!
Ha ha, yeah right dude. There was no lesson. You tried to trap us in a time cave because you're evil.
Uh, no, I--
We're gonna rip down your tent, and put you in wizard jail.
SLAM
Continued next month!

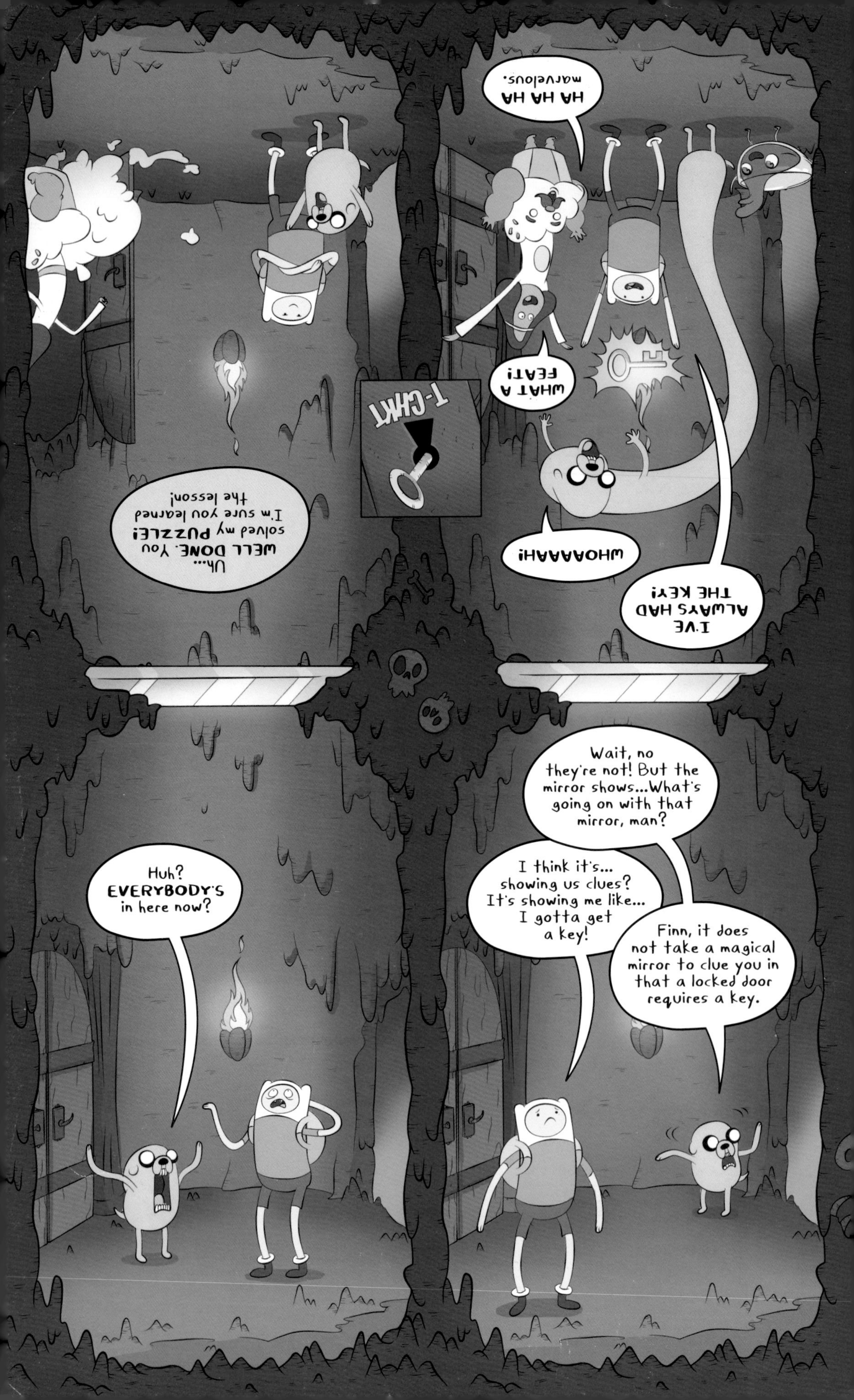
I'VE ALWAYS HAD THE KEY!
WHOAAAAH!
WHAT A FEAT!
HA HA HA marvelous.
T-CHKT
Uh... WELL DONE. You solved my PUZZLE! I'm sure you learned the lesson!
Huh? EVERYBODY'S in here now?
Wait, no they're not! But the mirror shows...What's going on with that mirror, man?
I think it's... showing us clues? It's showing me like... I gotta get a key!
Finn, it does not take a magical mirror to clue you in that a locked door requires a key.

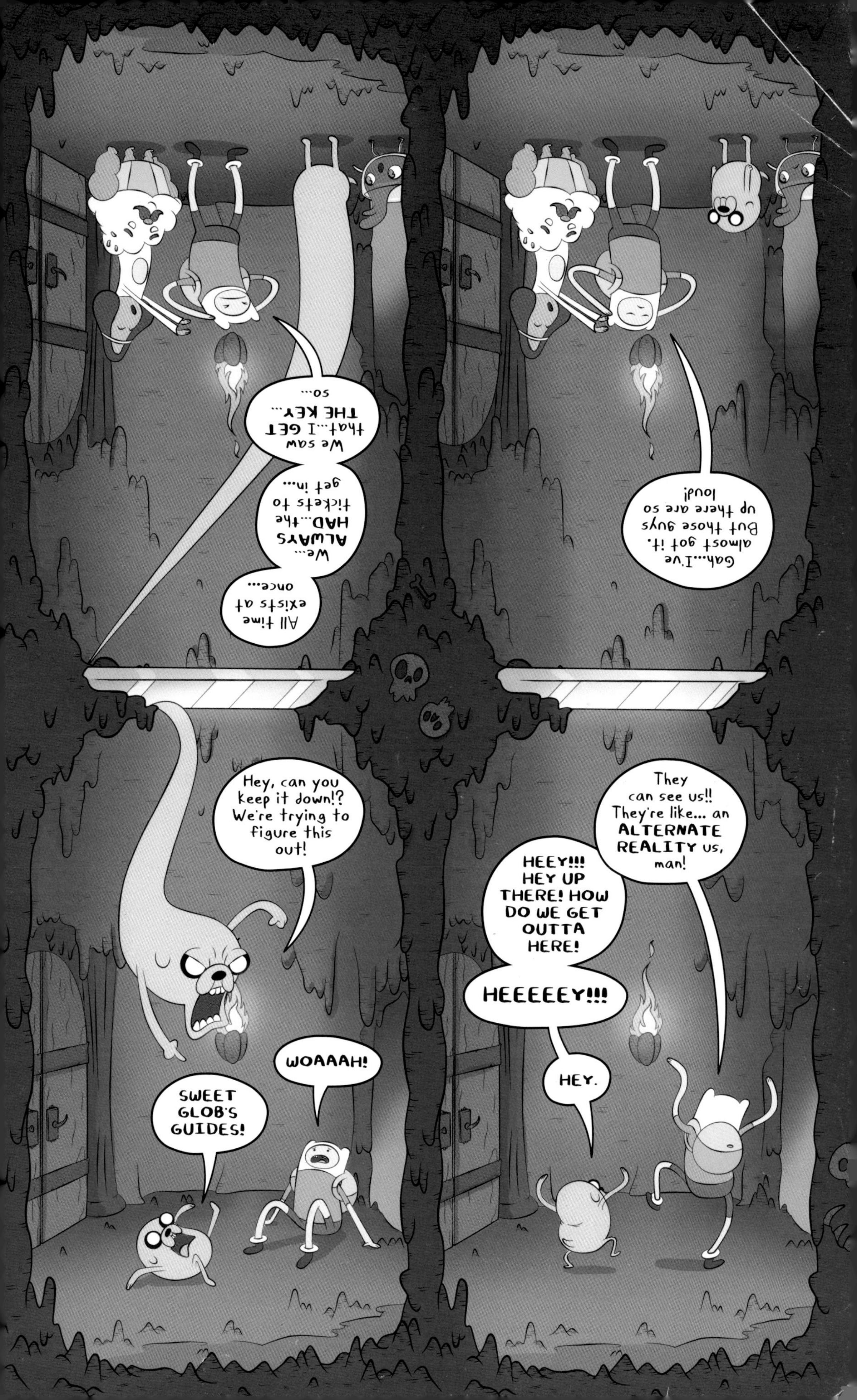
All time exists at once...
We... ALWAYS HAD...the tickets to get in...
We saw that...I GET THE KEY... so...
Gah...I've almost got it. But those guys up there are so loud!
Hey, can you keep it down!? We're trying to figure this out!
SWEET GLOB'S GUIDES!
WOAAAH!
HEEY!!! HEY UP THERE! HOW DO WE GET OUTTA HERE!
HEEEEEY!!!
HEY.
They can see us!! They're like... an ALTERNATE REALITY us, man!

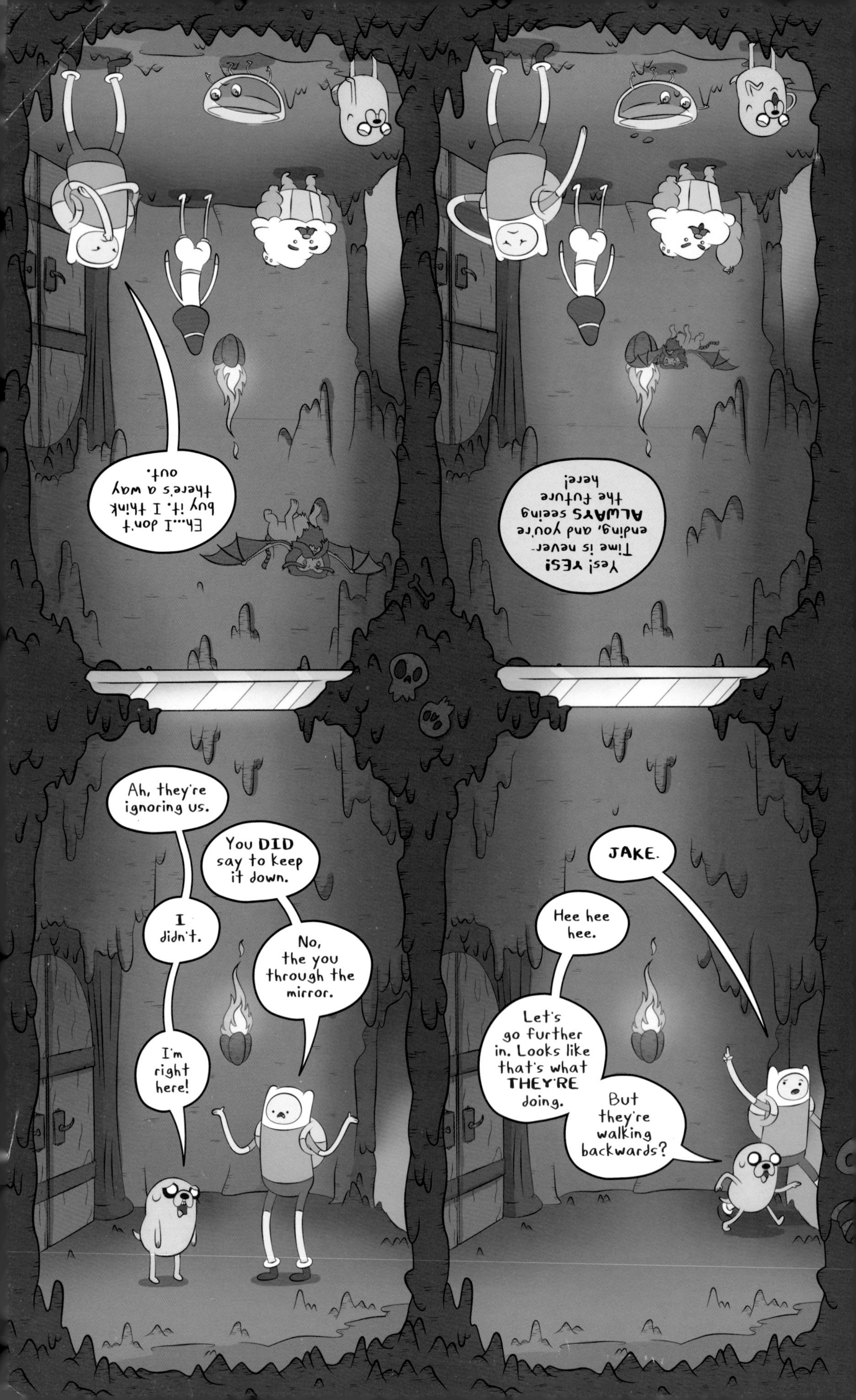

Eh...I don't buy it. I think there's a way out.
Yes! YES! Time is never-ending, and you're ALWAYS seeing the future here!
Ah, they're ignoring us.
You DID say to keep it down.
I didn't.
No, the you through the mirror.
I'm right here!
JAKE.
Hee hee hee.
Let's go further in. Looks like that's what THEY'RE doing.
But they're walking backwards?

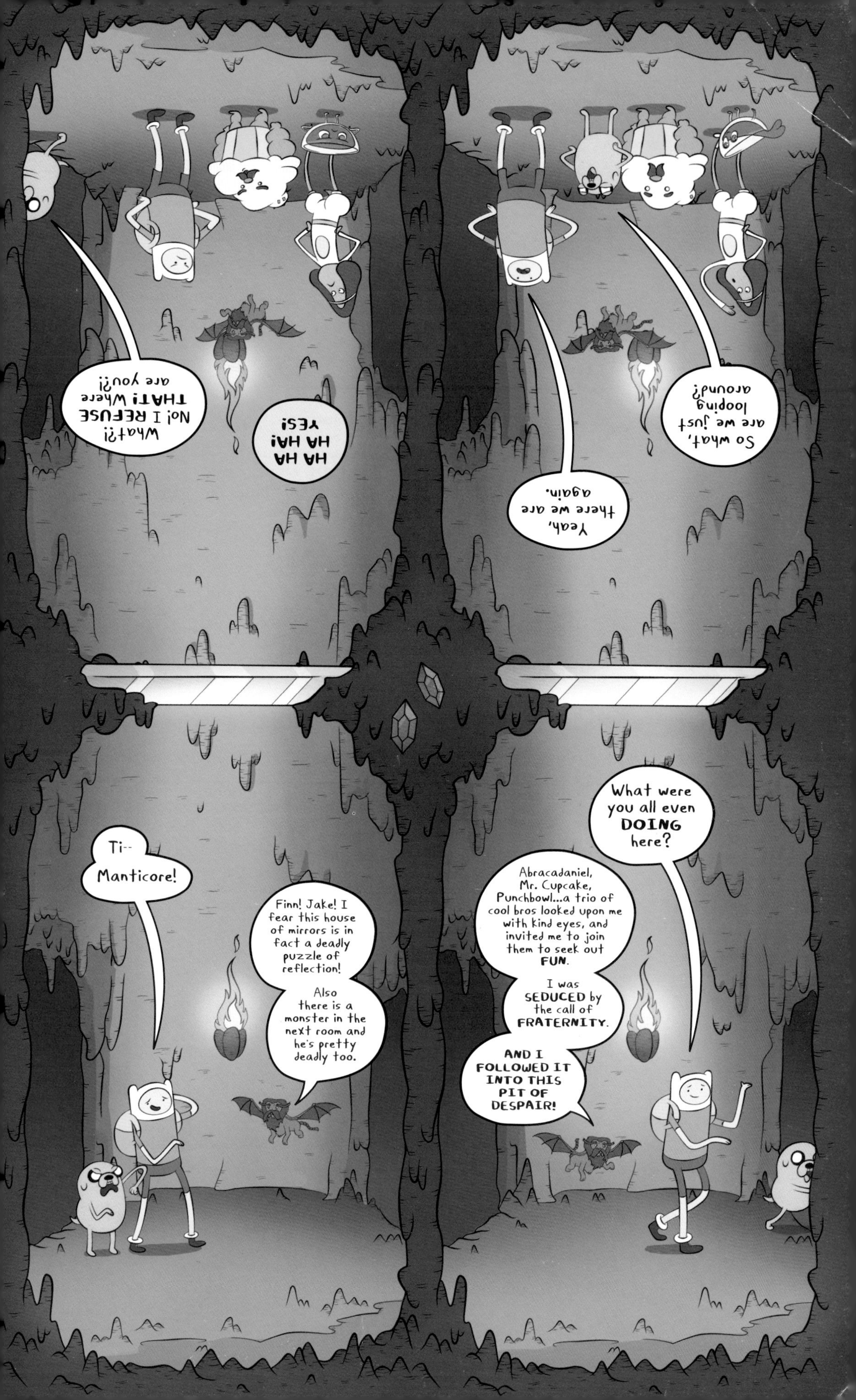

What?! No! I REFUSE THAT! Where are you?!
HA HA HA HA! YES!
So what, are we just looping around?
Yeah, there we are again.
Ti-- Manticore!
Finn! Jake! I fear this house of mirrors is in fact a deadly puzzle of reflection!
Also there is a monster in the next room and he's pretty deadly too.
What were you all even DOING here?
Abracadaniel, Mr. Cupcake, Punchbowl...a trio of cool bros looked upon me with kind eyes, and invited me to join them to seek out FUN.
I was SEDUCED by the call of FRATERNITY.
AND I FOLLOWED IT INTO THIS PIT OF DESPAIR!

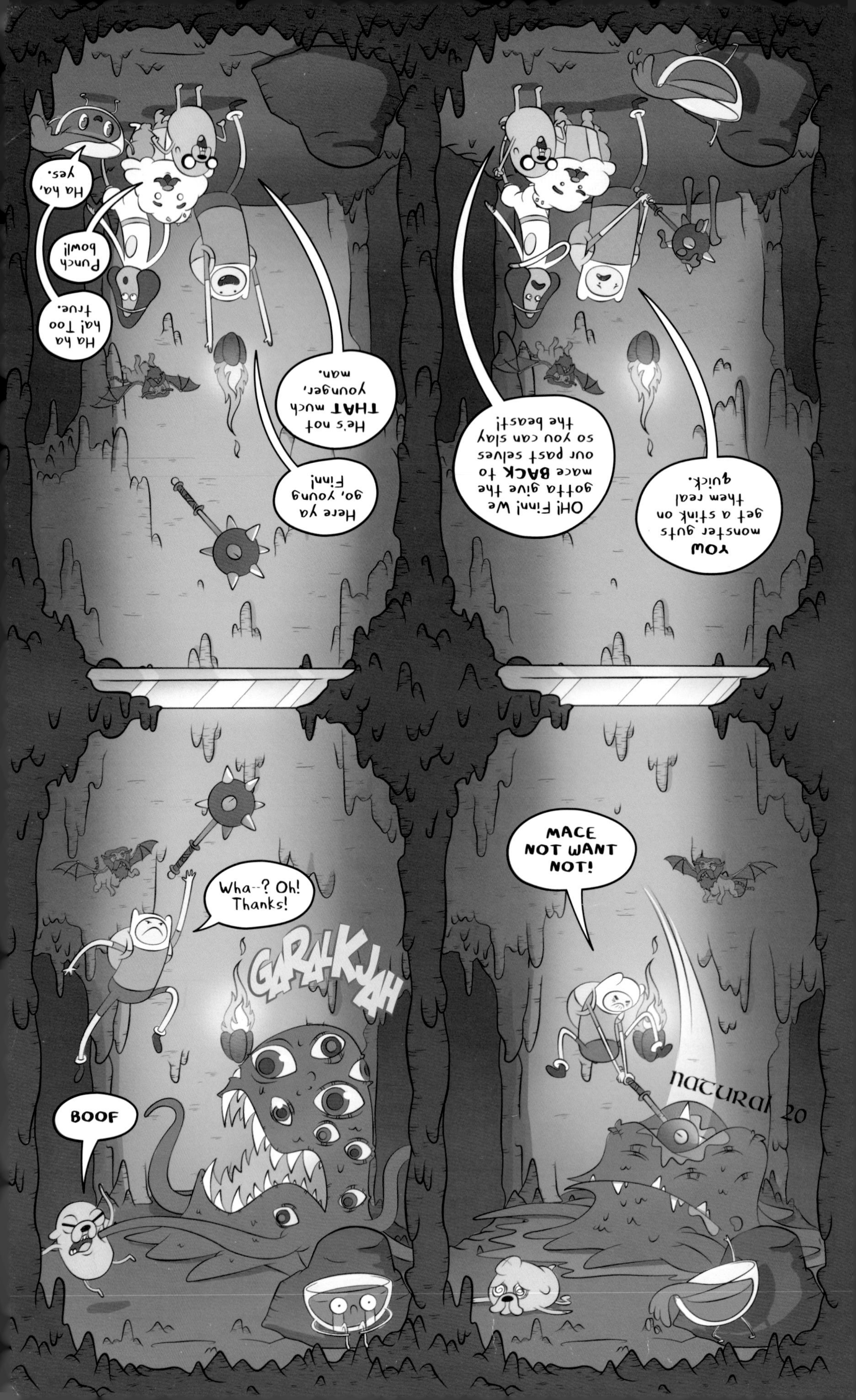

Here ya go, young Finn!
He's not THAT much younger, man.
Ha ha, yes.
Punch bowl!
Ha ha ha! Too true.
OH! Finn! We gotta give the mace BACK to our past selves so you can slay the beast!
YOU monster guts get a stink on them real quick.
Wha--? Oh! Thanks!
GARAKJAH
BOOF
MACE NOT WANT NOT!
NATURAL 20

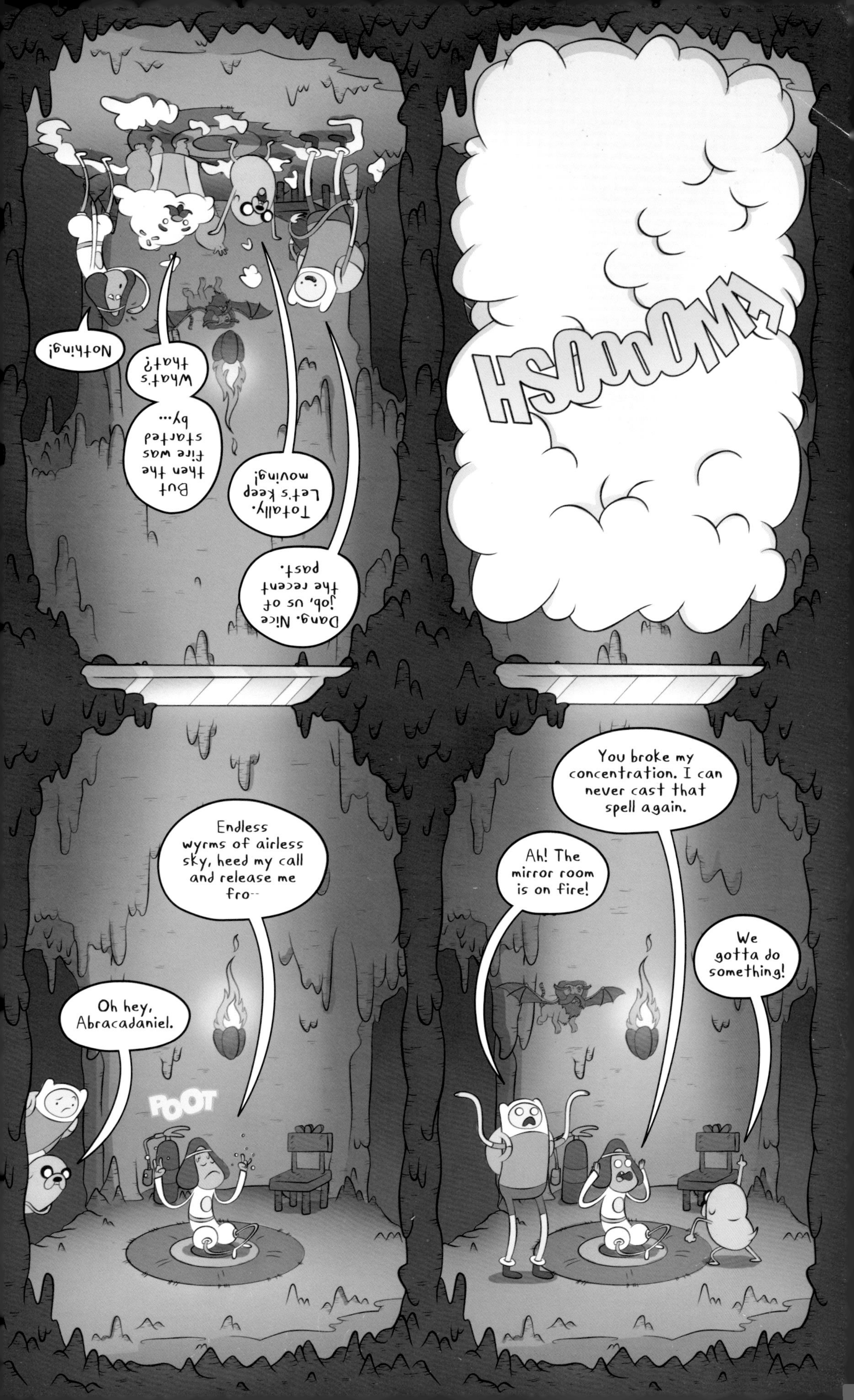
Dang. Nice job, us of the recent past.
Totally. Let's keep moving!
But then the fire was started by...
What's that?
Nothing!
WHOOOOSH
Endless wyrms of airless sky, heed my call and release me fro--
Oh hey, Abracadaniel.
POOT
You broke my concentration. I can never cast that spell again.
Ah! The mirror room is on fire!
We gotta do something!

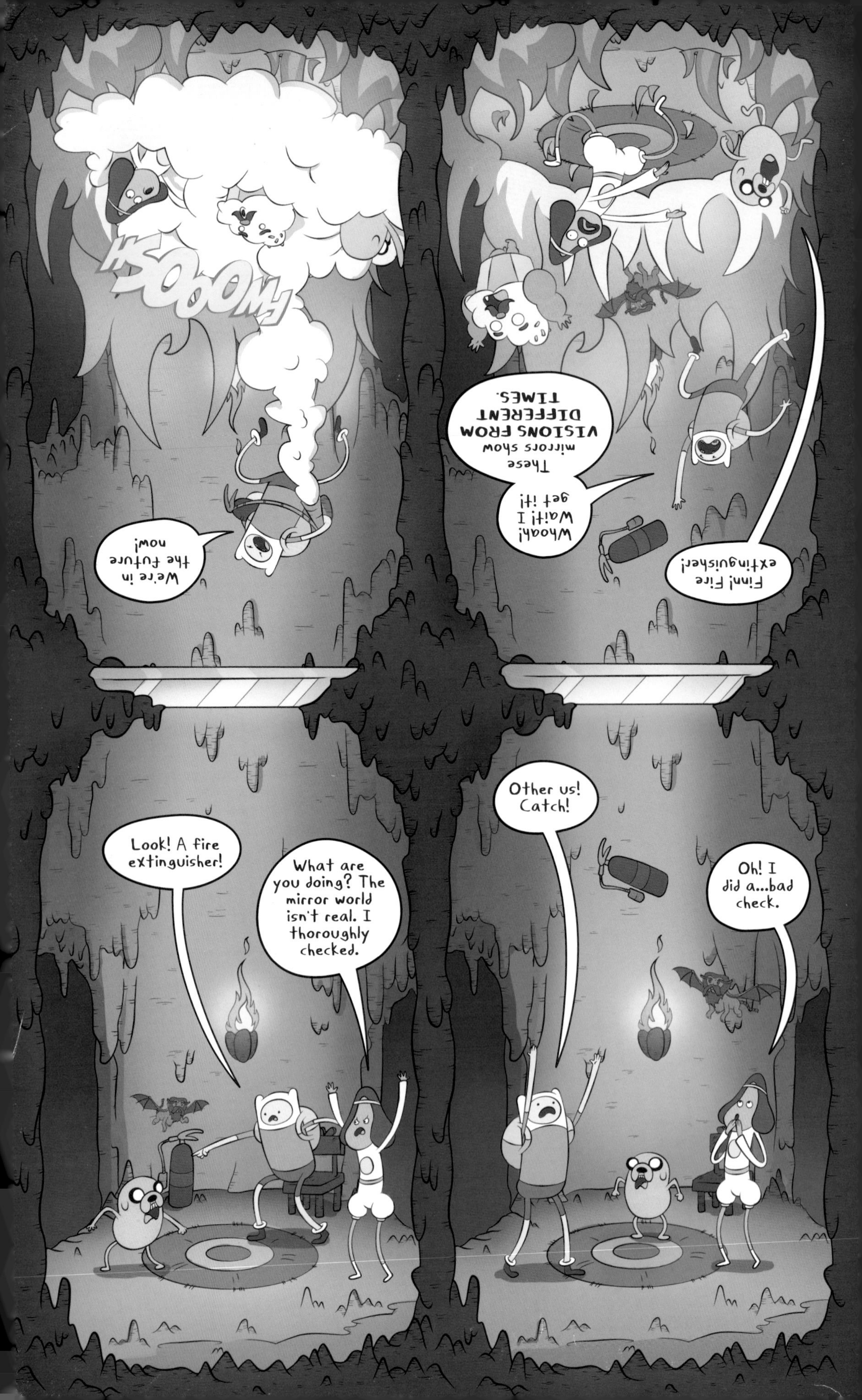
WHOOOSH
We're in the future now!
Whoah! Wait! I get it!
These mirrors show VISIONS FROM DIFFERENT TIMES.
Finn! Fire extinguisher!
Look! A fire extinguisher!
What are you doing? The mirror world isn't real. I thoroughly checked.
Other us! Catch!
Oh! I did a...bad check.

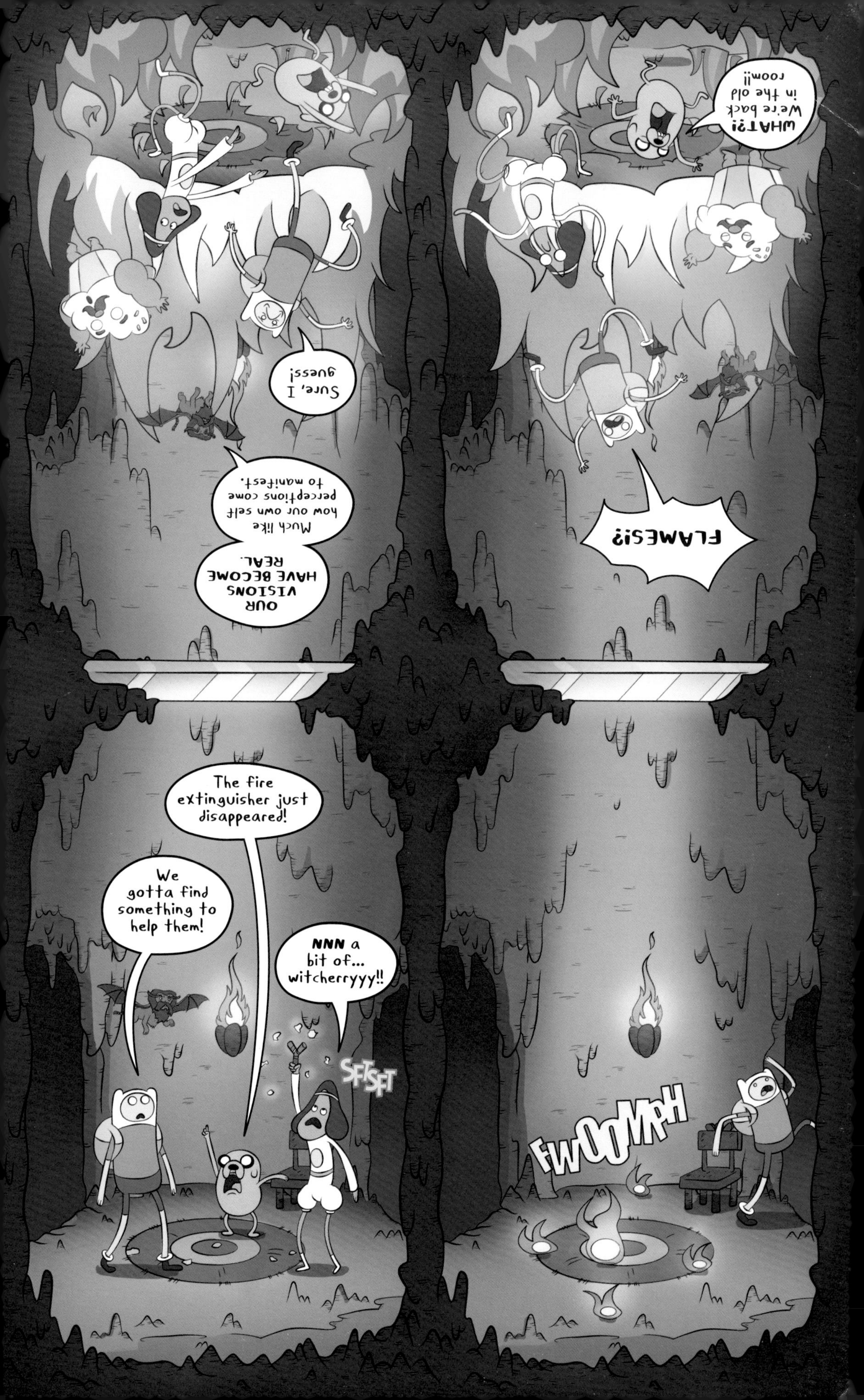

OUR VISIONS HAVE BECOME REAL.
Much like how our own self perceptions come to manifest.
Sure, I guess!
FLAMES?!
WHAT?! We're back in the old room!
The fire extinguisher just disappeared!
We gotta find something to help them!
NNN a bit of... witcherryyy!!
SFTSFT
FWOOMPH

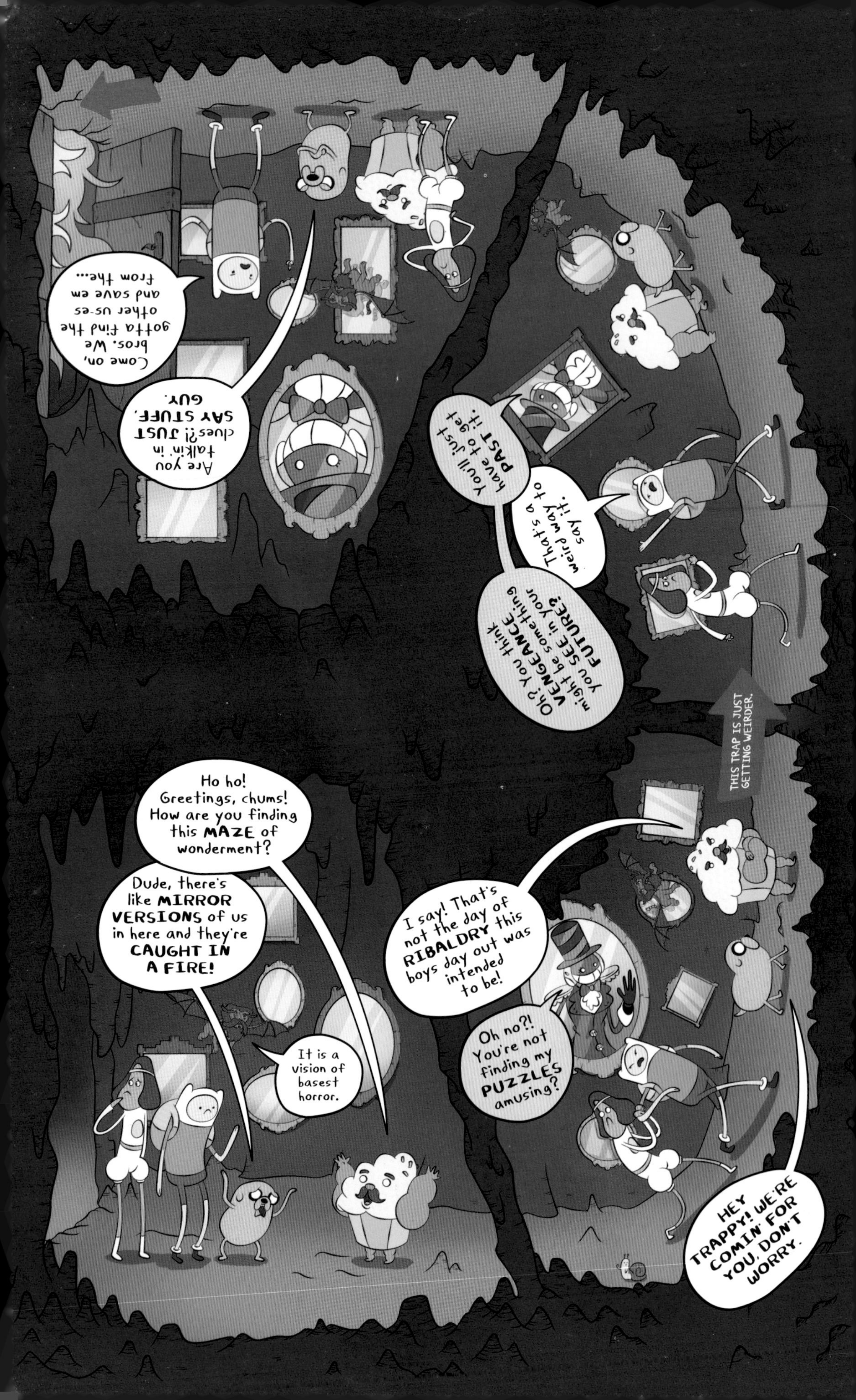

Ho ho! Greetings, chums! How are you finding this MAZE of wonderment?
Dude, there's like MIRROR VERSIONS of us in here and they're CAUGHT IN A FIRE!
It is a vision of basest horror.
I say! That's not the day of RIBALDRY this boys day out was intended to be!
Oh no?! You're not finding my PUZZLES amusing?
HEY TRAPPY! WE'RE COMIN' FOR YOU, DON'T WORRY.
THIS TRAP IS JUST GETTING WEIRDER.
Oh? You think VENGEANCE might be something you SEE in your FUTURE?
That's a weird way to say it.
You'll just have to get PAST it.
Are you talkin' in clues?! JUST SAY STUFF, GUY.
Come on, bros. We gotta find the other us-es and save em from the...

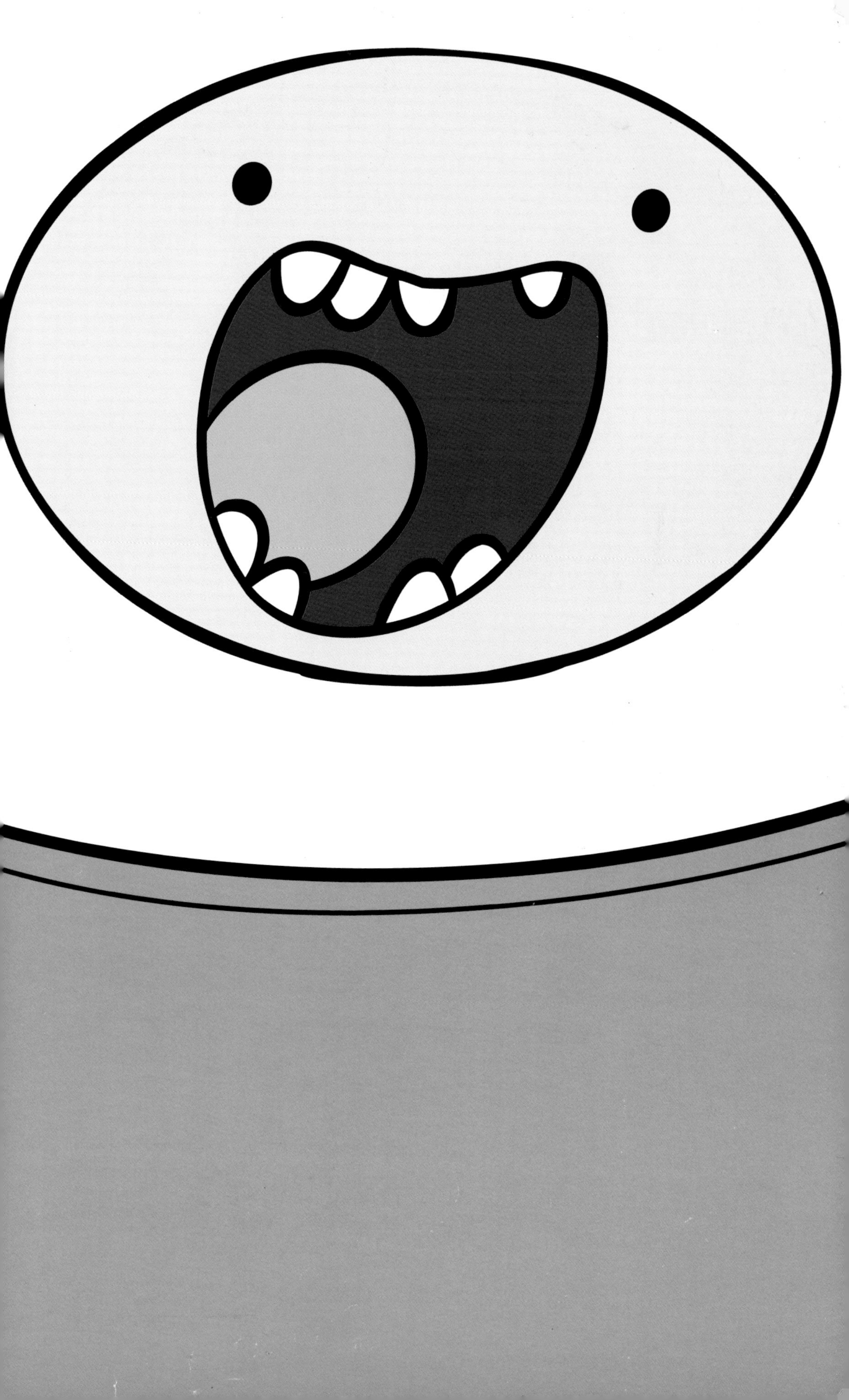

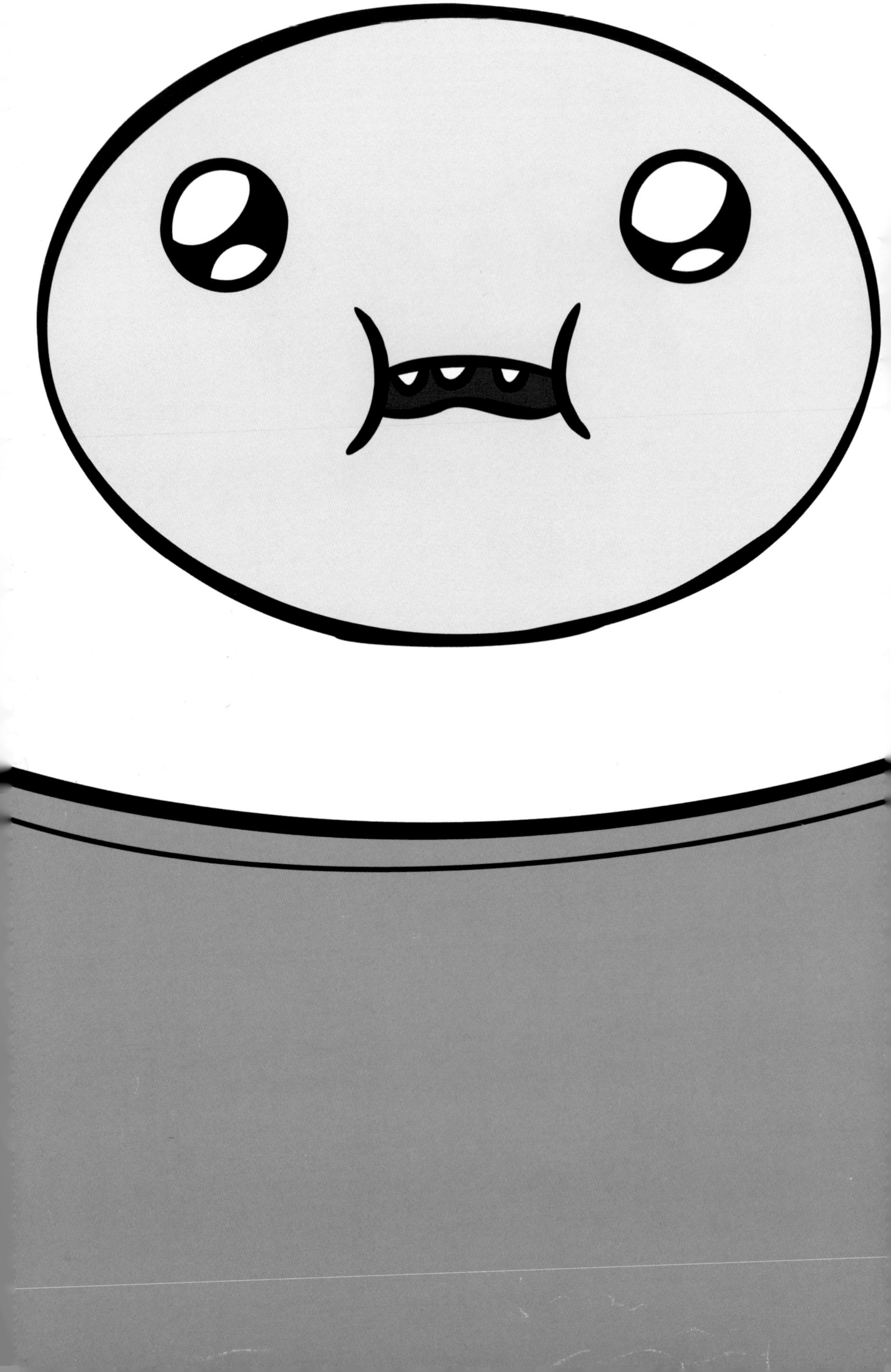

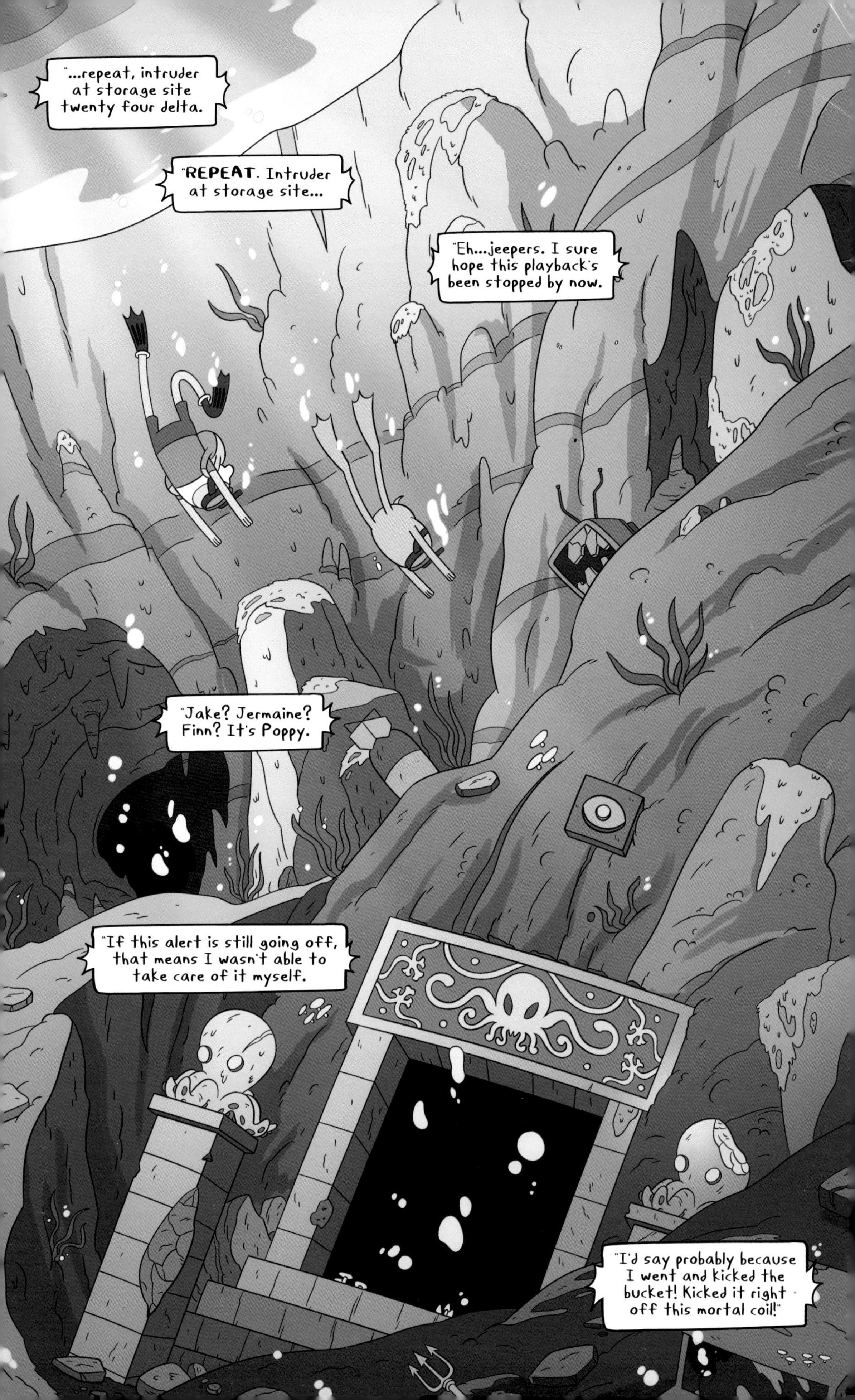
"...repeat, intruder at storage site twenty four delta.
"REPEAT. Intruder at storage site...
"Eh...jeepers. I sure hope this playback's been stopped by now.
"Jake? Jermaine? Finn? It's Poppy.
"If this alert is still going off, that means I wasn't able to take care of it myself.
"I'd say probably because I went and kicked the bucket! Kicked it right off this mortal coil!"

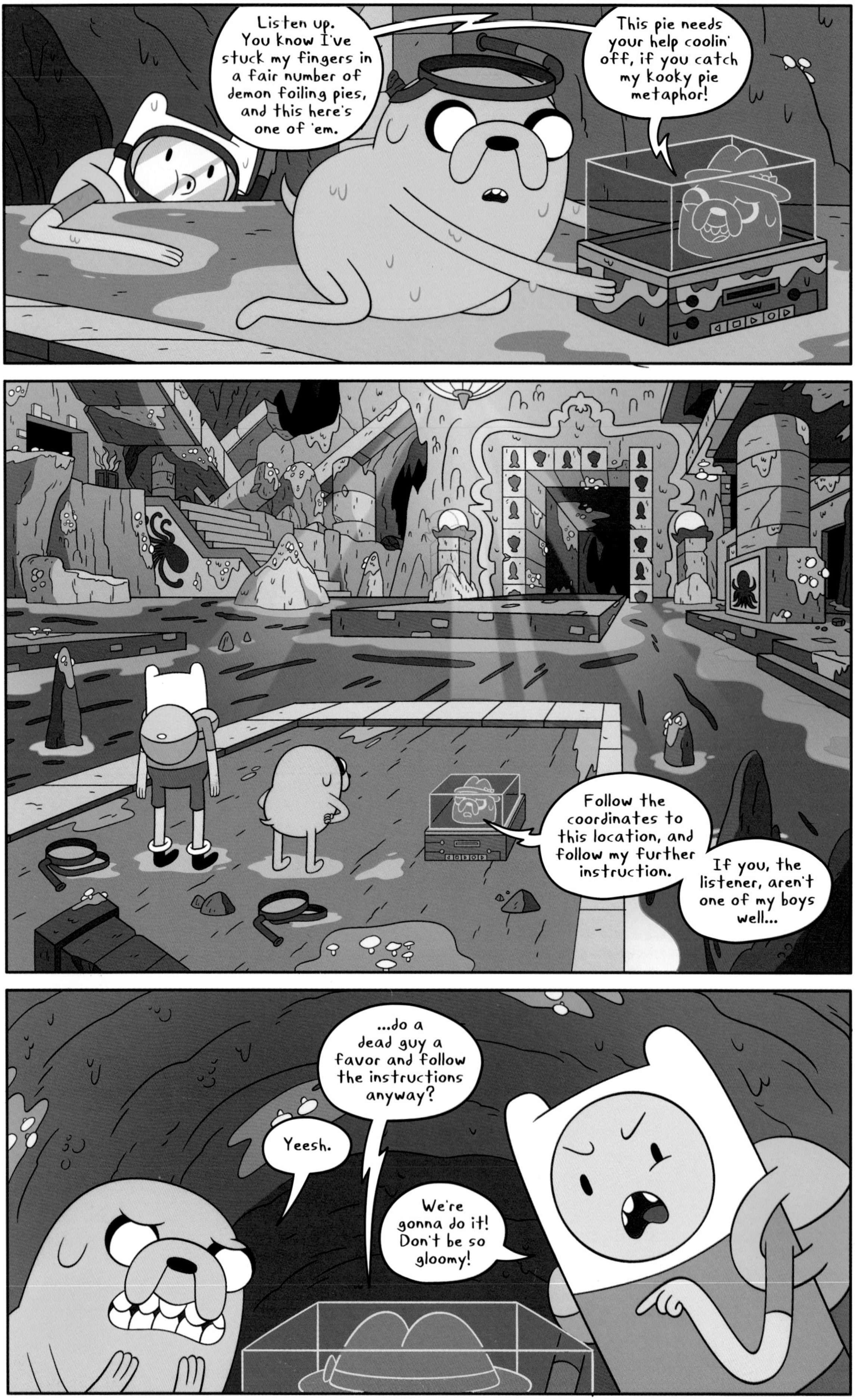
Listen up. You know I've stuck my fingers in a fair number of demon foiling pies, and this here's one of 'em.
This pie needs your help coolin' off, if you catch my kooky pie metaphor!
Follow the coordinates to this location, and follow my further instruction.
If you, the listener, aren't one of my boys well...
...do a dead guy a favor and follow the instructions anyway?
Yeesh.
We're gonna do it! Don't be so gloomy!

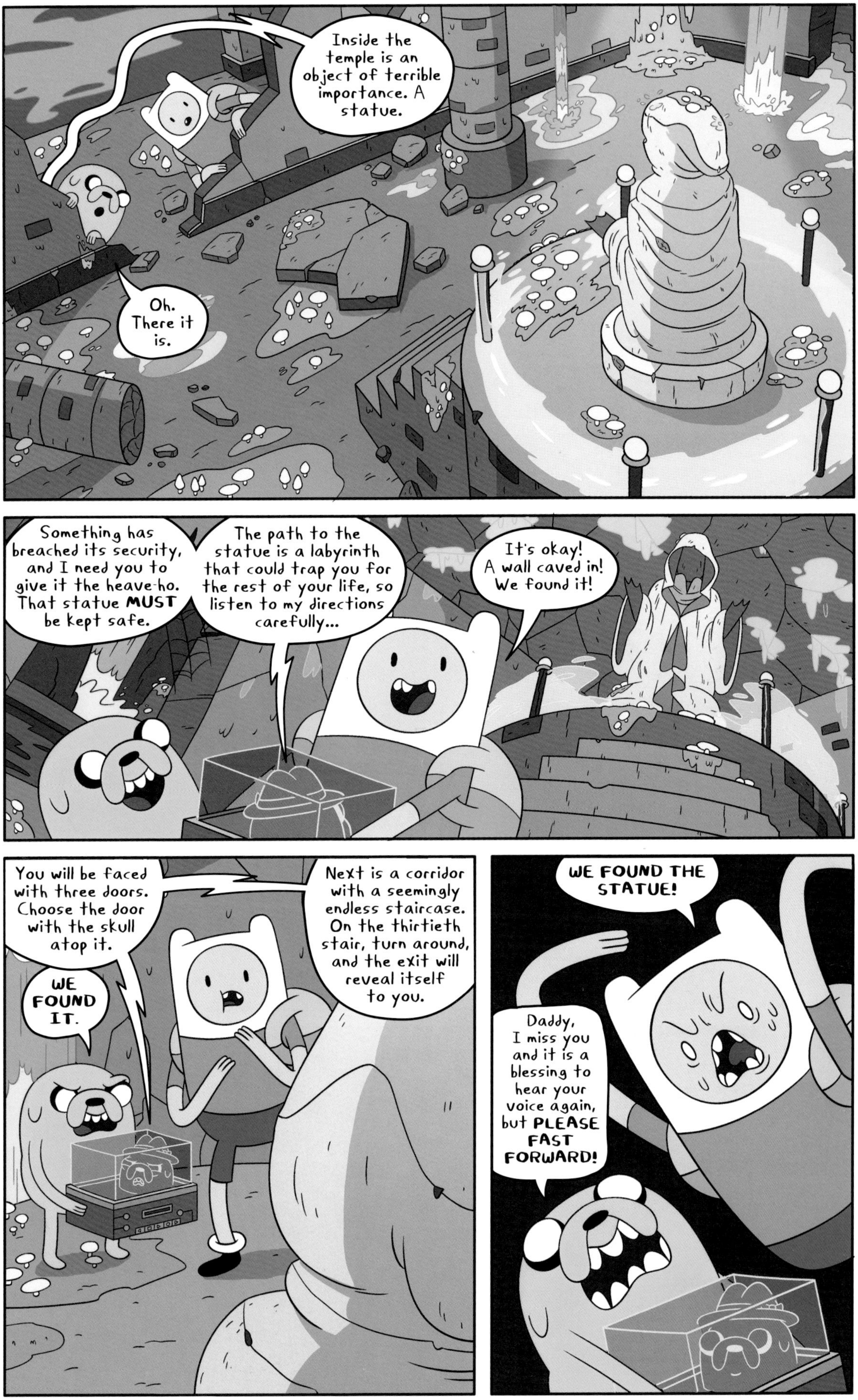
Inside the temple is an object of terrible importance. A statue.
Oh. There it is.
Something has breached its security, and I need you to give it the heave-ho. That statue **MUST** be kept safe.
The path to the statue is a labyrinth that could trap you for the rest of your life, so listen to my directions carefully...
It's okay! A wall caved in! We found it!
You will be faced with three doors. Choose the door with the skull atop it.
WE FOUND IT.
Next is a corridor with a seemingly endless staircase. On the thirtieth stair, turn around, and the exit will reveal itself to you.
WE FOUND THE STATUE!
Daddy, I miss you and it is a blessing to hear your voice again, but **PLEASE FAST FORWARD!**

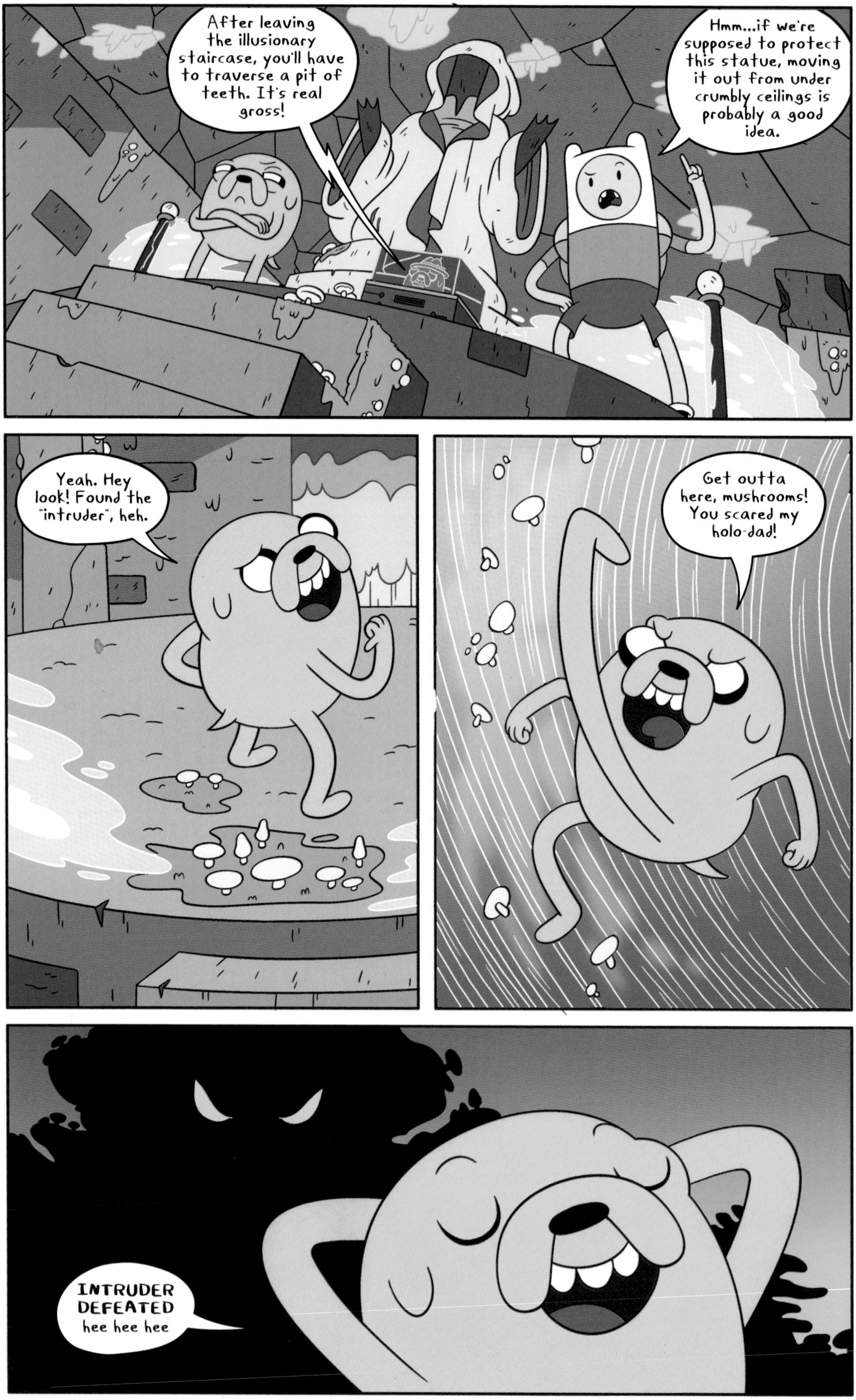
After leaving the illusionary staircase, you'll have to traverse a pit of teeth. It's real gross!
Hmm...if we're supposed to protect this statue, moving it out from under crumbly ceilings is probably a good idea.
Yeah. Hey look! Found the "intruder", heh.
Get outta here, mushrooms! You scared my holo-dad!
INTRUDER DEFEATED hee hee hee

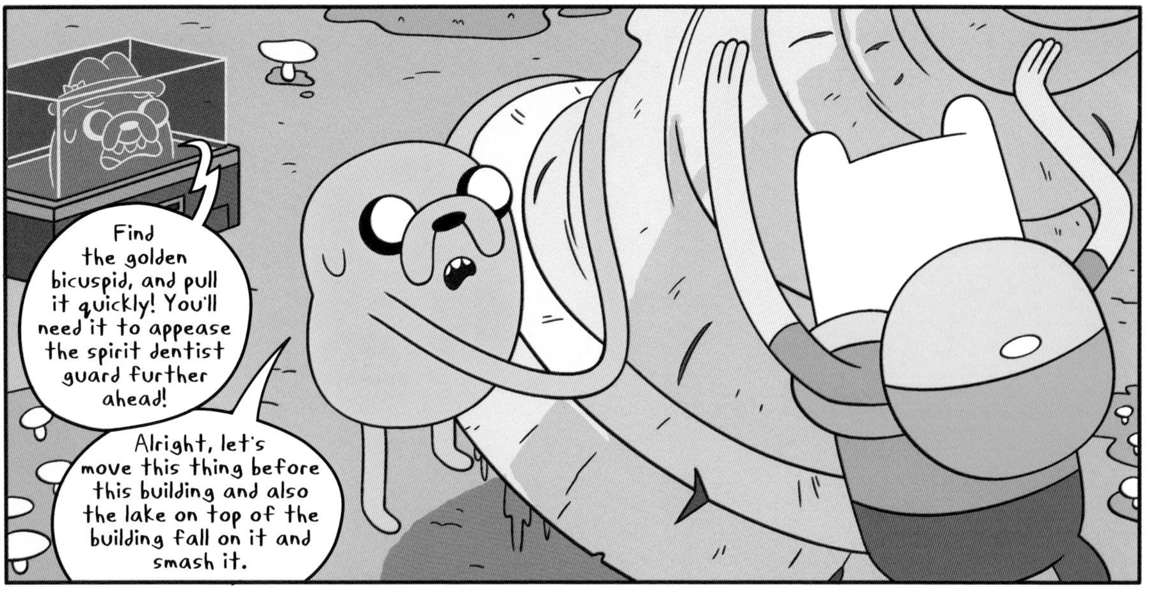
Find the golden bicuspid, and pull it quickly! You'll need it to appease the spirit dentist guard further ahead!
Alright, let's move this thing before this building and also the lake on top of the building fall on it and smash it.

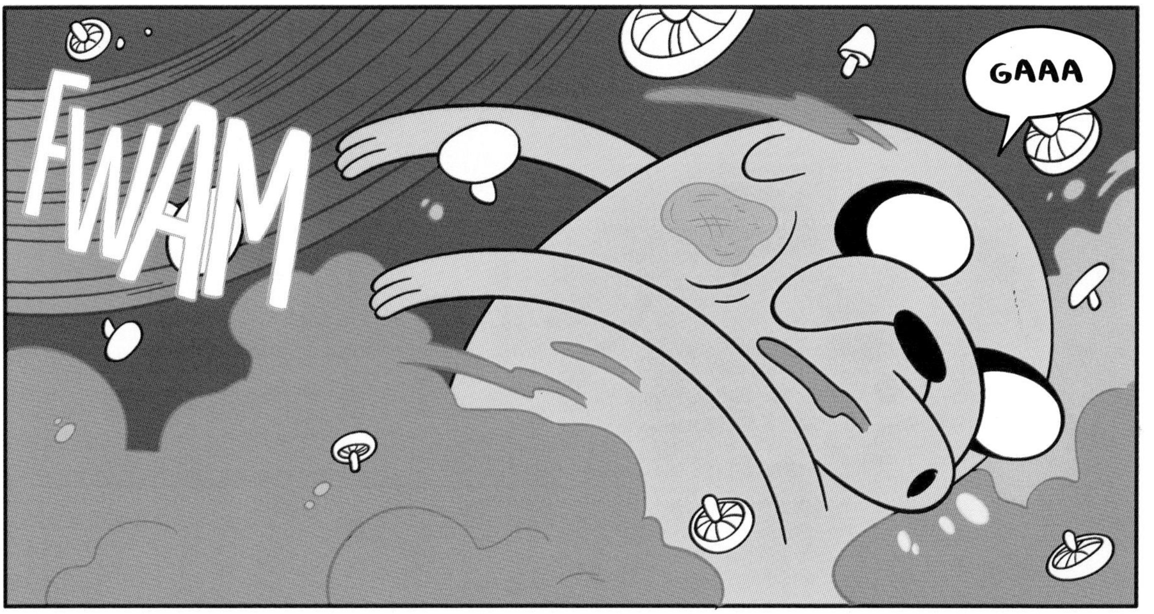
FWAM
GAAA

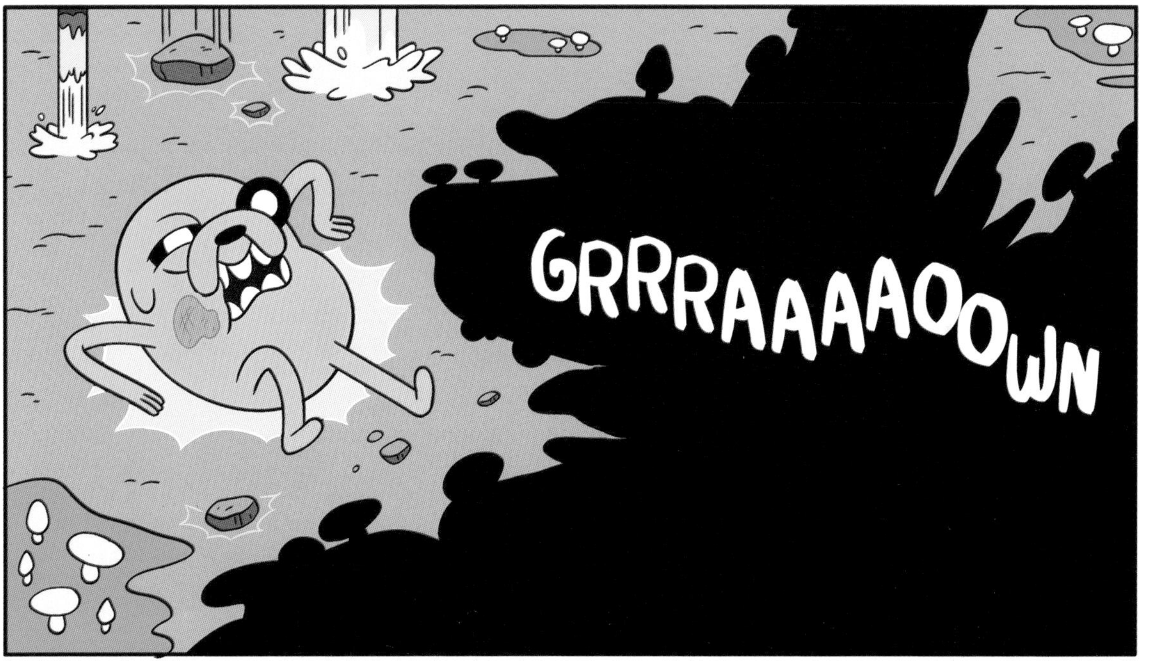
GRRRAAAAOOWN

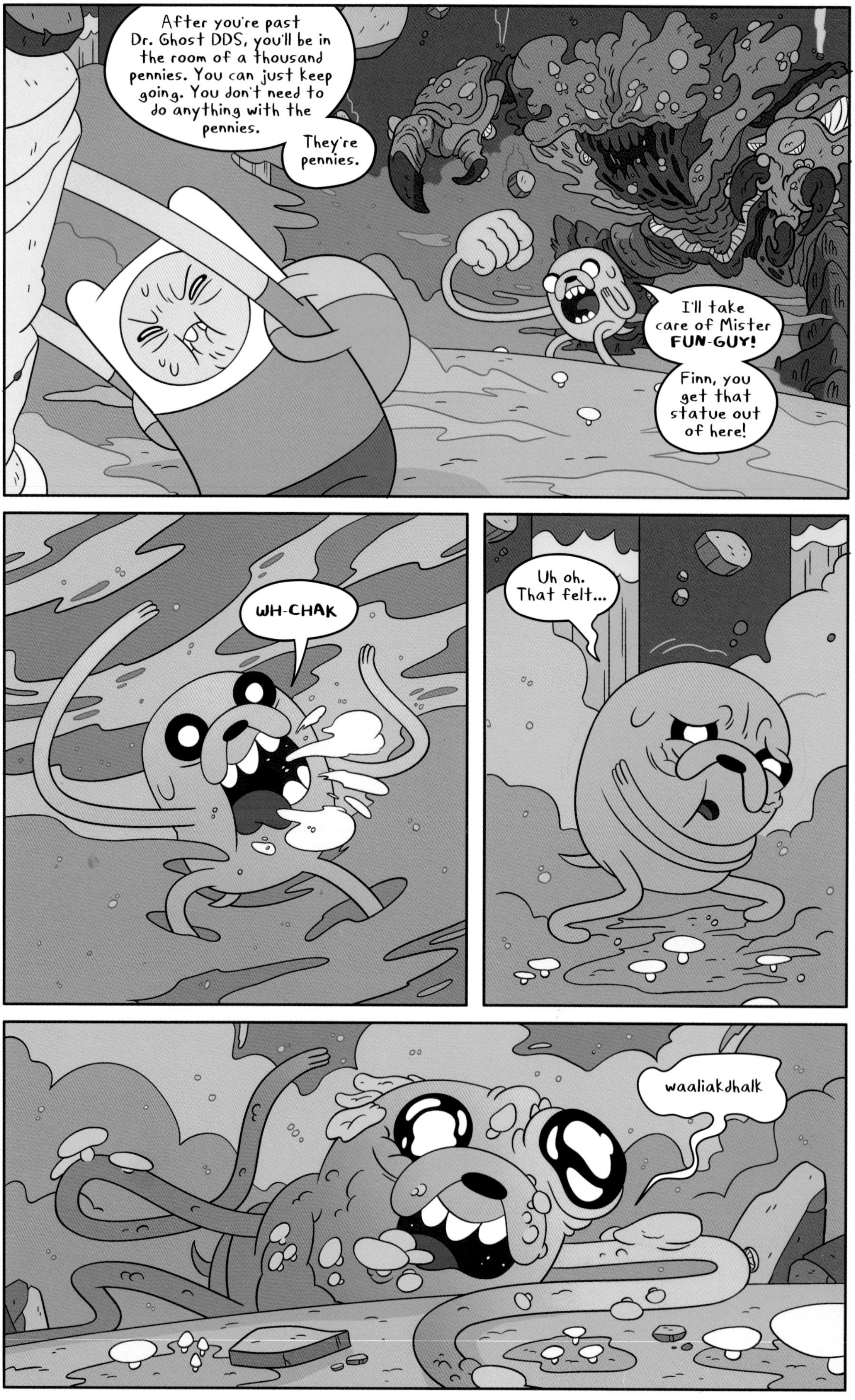
After you're past Dr. Ghost DDS, you'll be in the room of a thousand pennies. You can just keep going. You don't need to do anything with the pennies.
They're pennies.
I'll take care of Mister **FUN-GUY!**
Finn, you get that statue out of here!
WH-CHAK
Uh oh. That felt...
waaliakdhalk

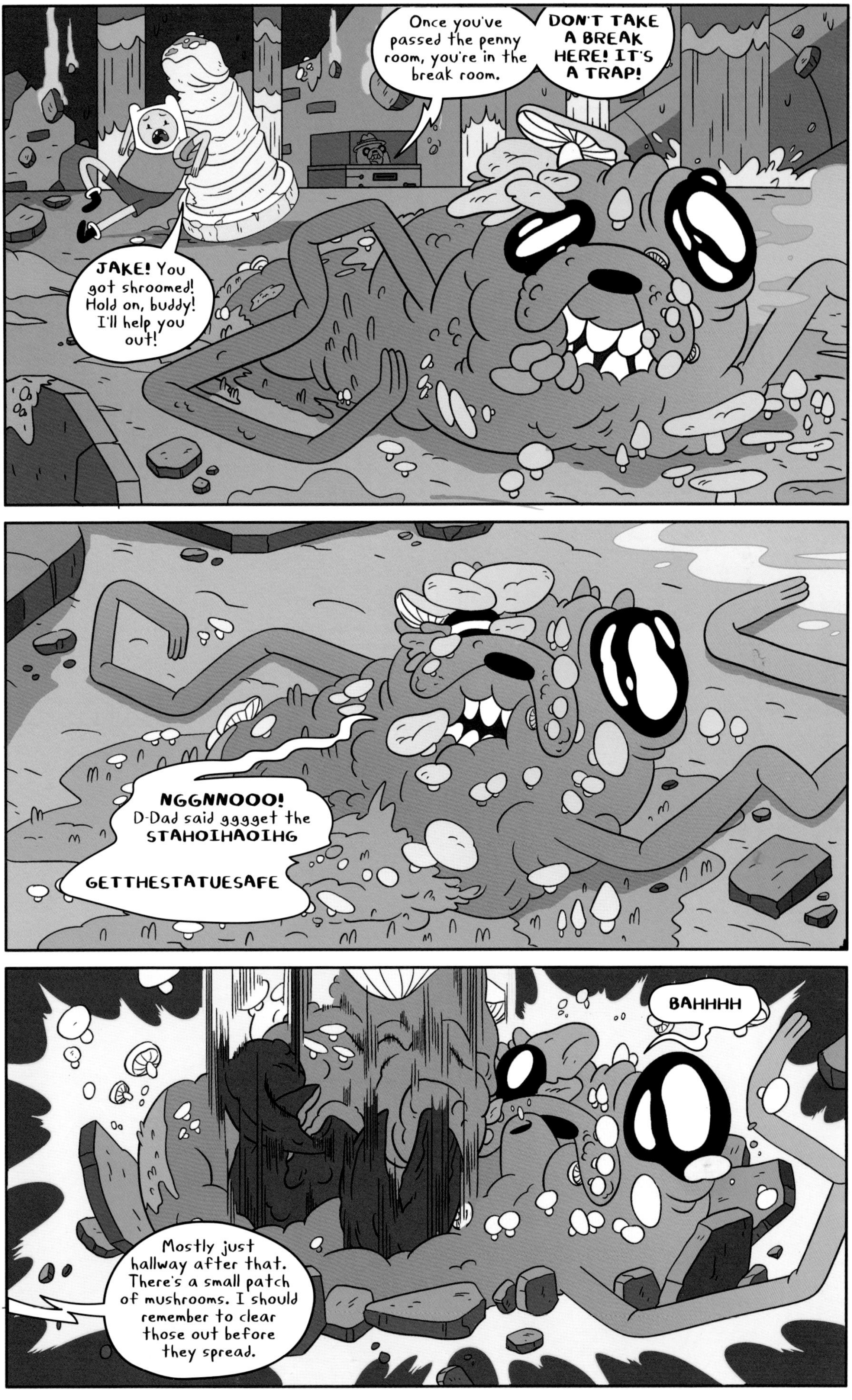
Once you've passed the penny room, you're in the break room.
DON'T TAKE A BREAK HERE! IT'S A TRAP!
JAKE! You got shroomed! Hold on, buddy! I'll help you out!
NGGNNOOO! D-Dad said ggggget the STAHOIHAOIHG
GETTHESTATUESAFE
BAHHHH
Mostly just hallway after that. There's a small patch of mushrooms. I should remember to clear those out before they spread.

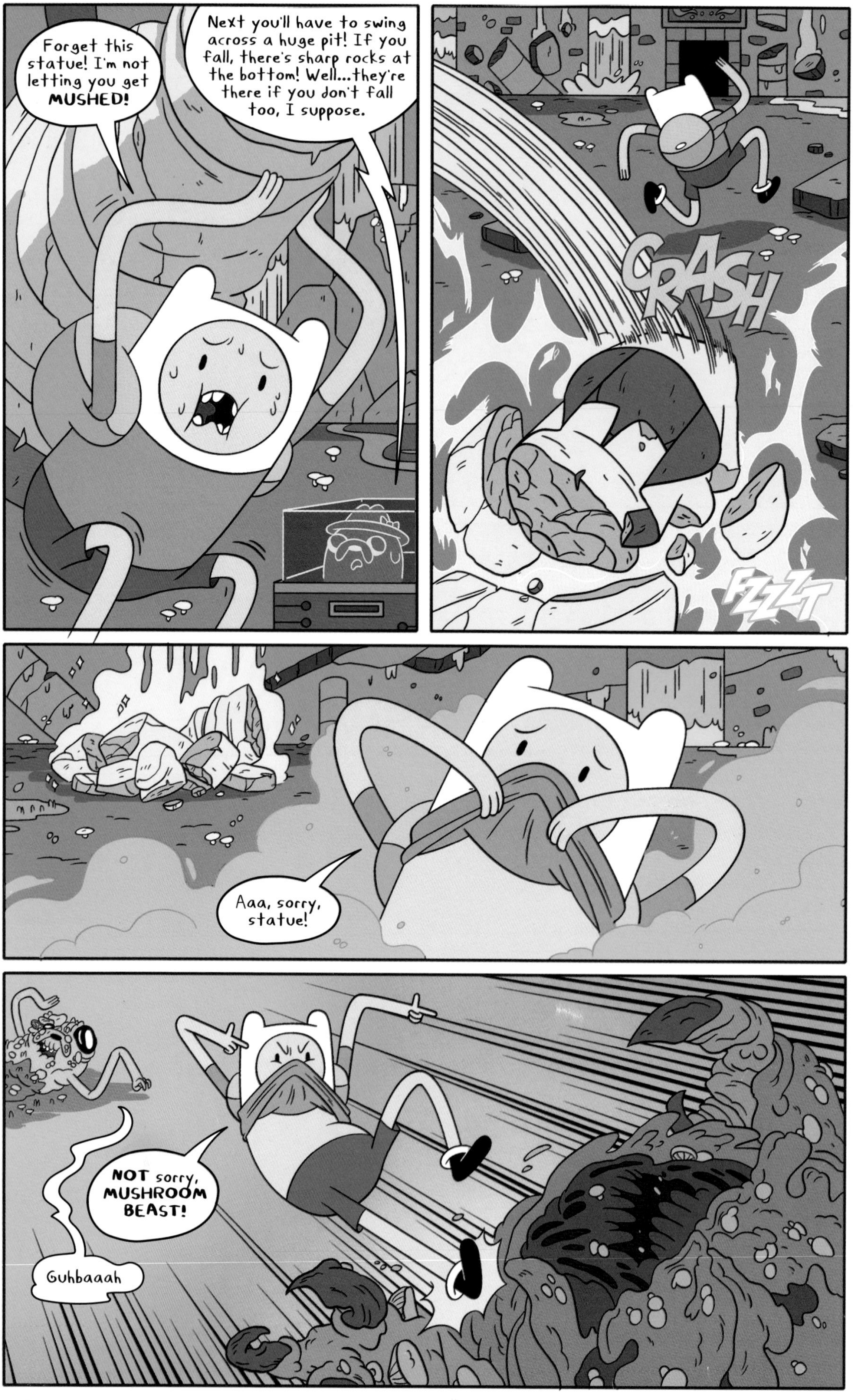
Forget this statue! I'm not letting you get MUSHED!
Next you'll have to swing across a huge pit! If you fall, there's sharp rocks at the bottom! Well...they're there if you don't fall too, I suppose.
CRASH
FZZZT
Aaa, sorry, statue!
NOT sorry, MUSHROOM BEAST!
Guhbaaah

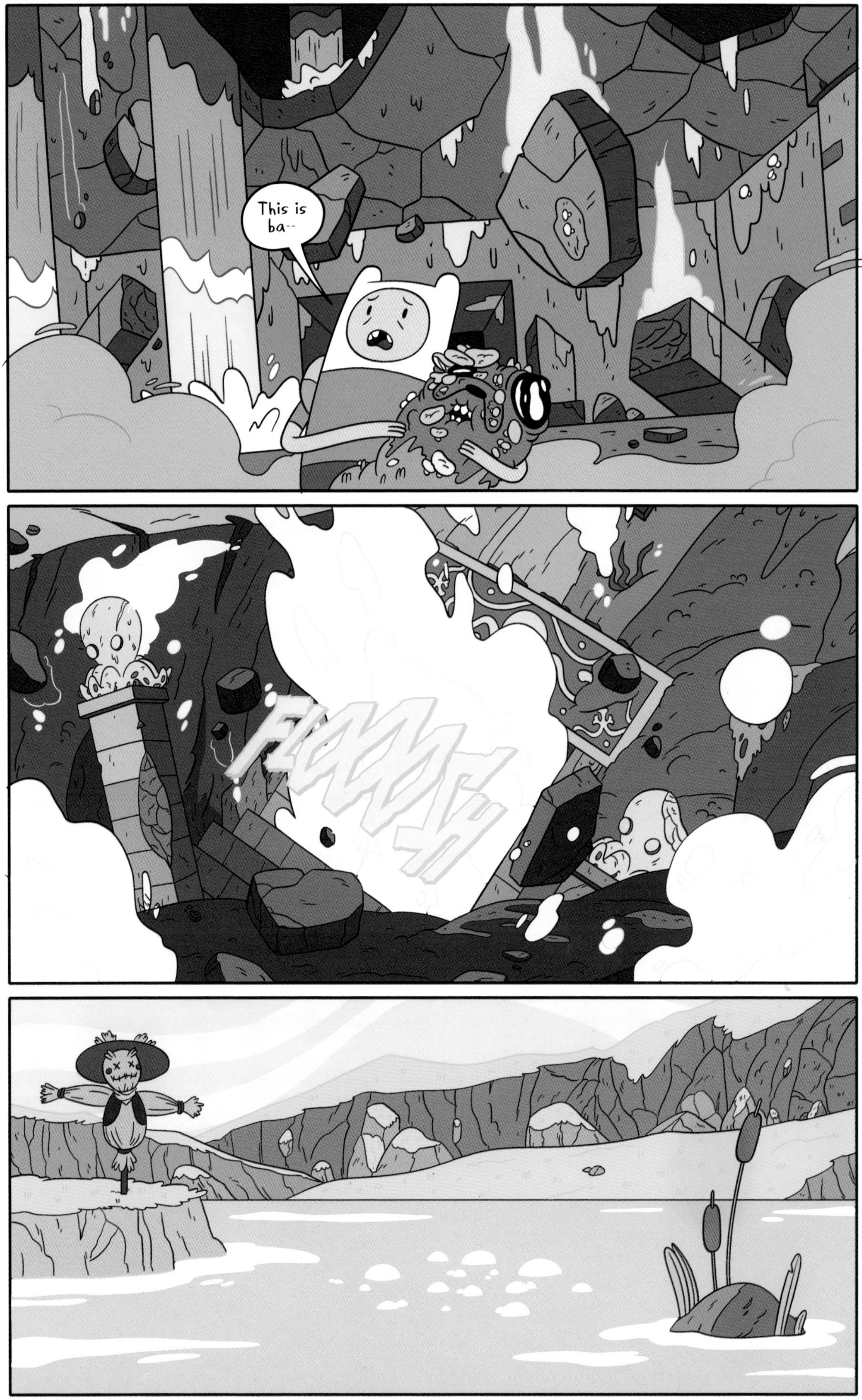
This is ba--
FLOOMPH

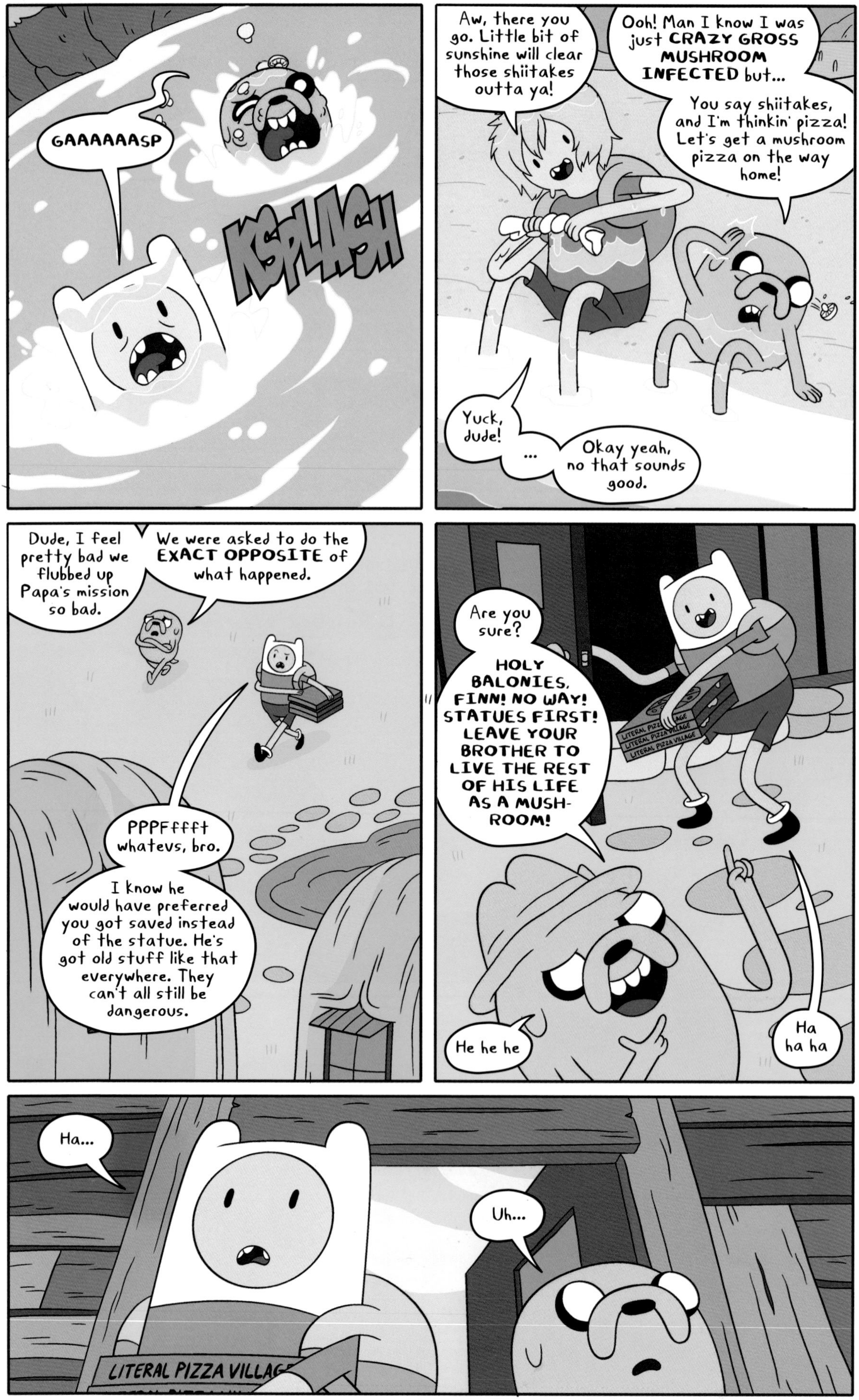
GAAAAAASP
KSPLASH
Aw, there you go. Little bit of sunshine will clear those shiitakes outta ya!
Ooh! Man I know I was just CRAZY GROSS MUSHROOM INFECTED but...
You say shiitakes, and I'm thinkin' pizza! Let's get a mushroom pizza on the way home!
Yuck, dude!
...
Okay yeah, no that sounds good.
Dude, I feel pretty bad we flubbed up Papa's mission so bad.
We were asked to do the EXACT OPPOSITE of what happened.
PPPFffft whatevs, bro.
I know he would have preferred you got saved instead of the statue. He's got old stuff like that everywhere. They can't all still be dangerous.
Are you sure?
HOLY BALONIES, FINN! NO WAY! STATUES FIRST! LEAVE YOUR BROTHER TO LIVE THE REST OF HIS LIFE AS A MUSH-ROOM!
LITERAL PIZZA VILLAGE
He he he
Ha ha ha
Ha...
Uh...
LITERAL PIZZA VILLAGE

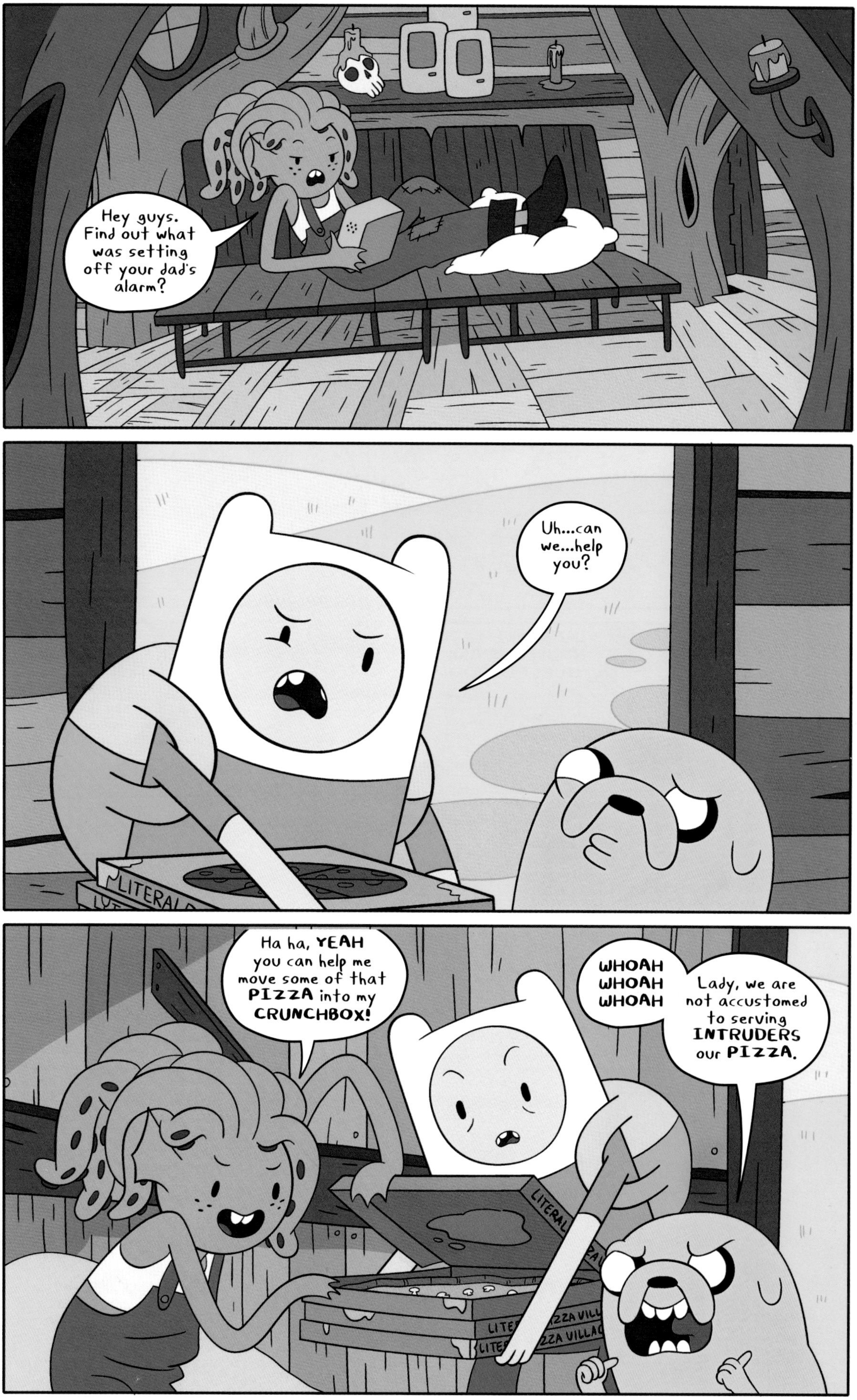
Hey guys. Find out what was setting off your dad's alarm?
Uh...can we...help you?
Ha ha, YEAH you can help me move some of that PIZZA into my CRUNCHBOX!
WHOAH WHOAH WHOAH
Lady, we are not accustomed to serving INTRUDERS our PIZZA.

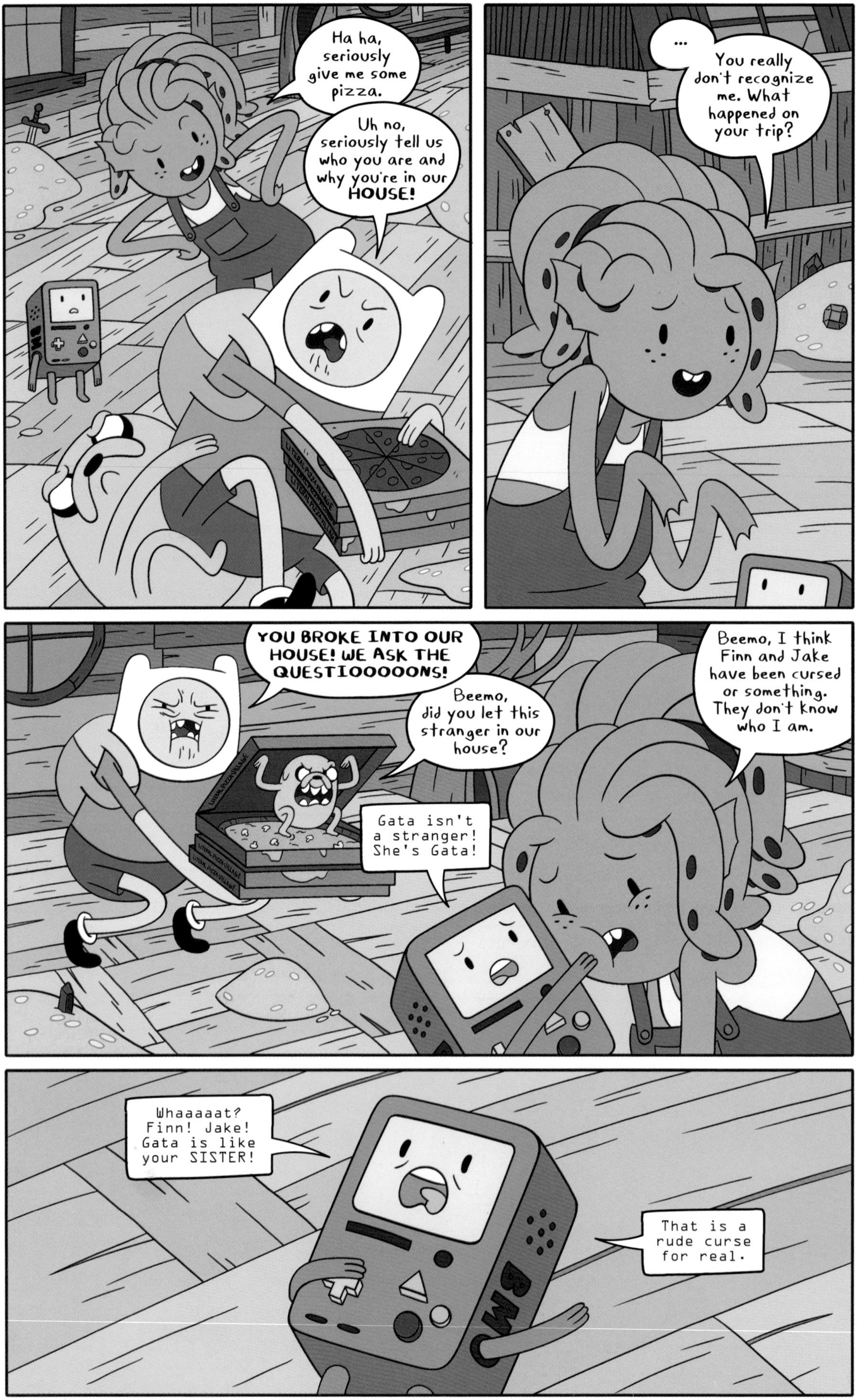
Ha ha, seriously give me some pizza.
Uh no, seriously tell us who you are and why you're in our **HOUSE!**
...
You really don't recognize me. What happened on your trip?
YOU BROKE INTO OUR HOUSE! WE ASK THE QUESTIOOOOONS!
Beemo, did you let this stranger in our house?
Gata isn't a stranger! She's Gata!
Beemo, I think Finn and Jake have been cursed or something. They don't know who I am.
Whaaaaat? Finn! Jake! Gata is like your SISTER!
That is a rude curse for real.

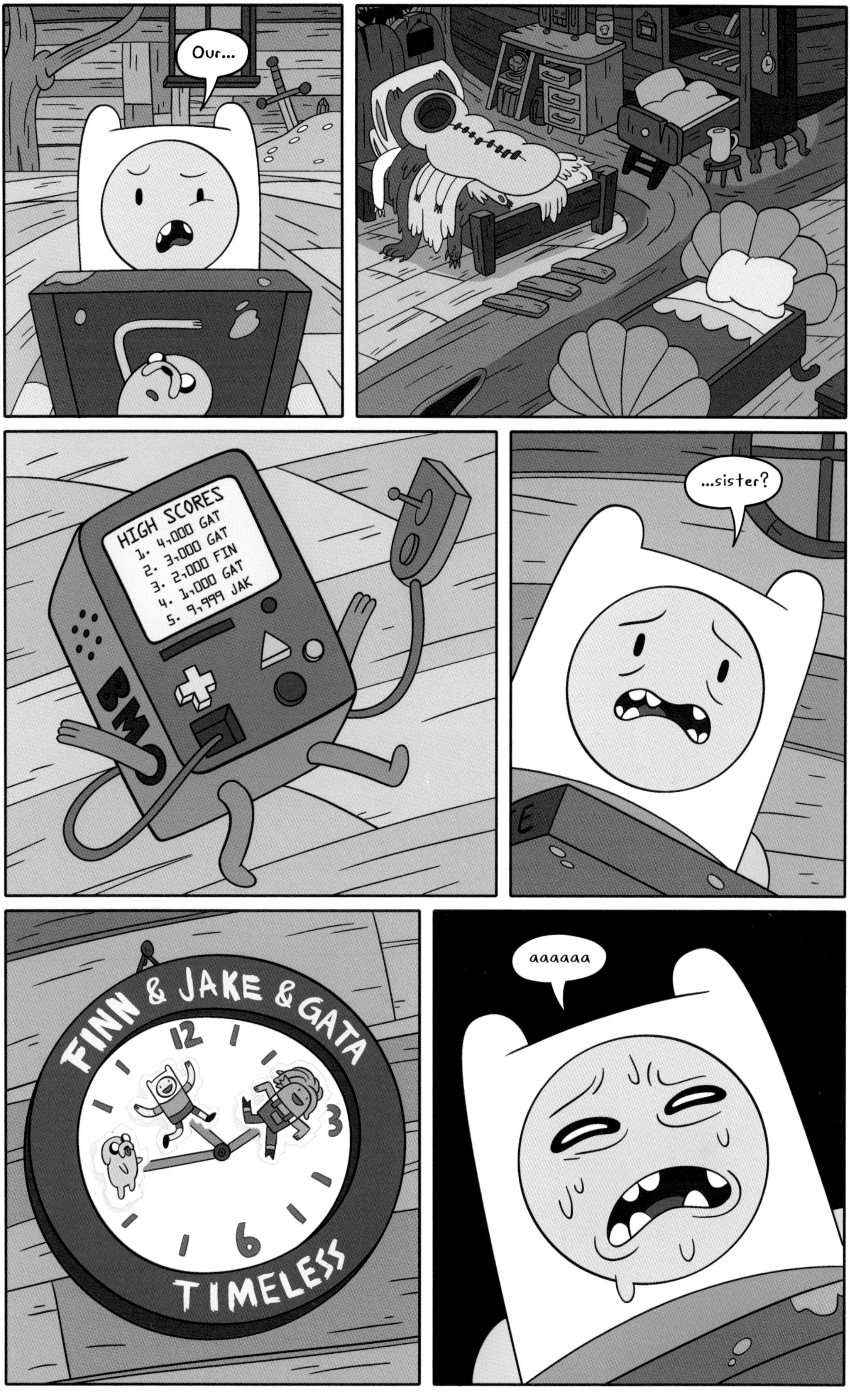

Our...
HIGH SCORES
1. 4,000 GAT
2. 3,000 GAT
3. 2,000 FIN
4. 1,000 GAT
5. 9,999 JAK
BMO
...sister?
FINN & JAKE & GATA
12
3
6
TIMELESS
aaaaaa

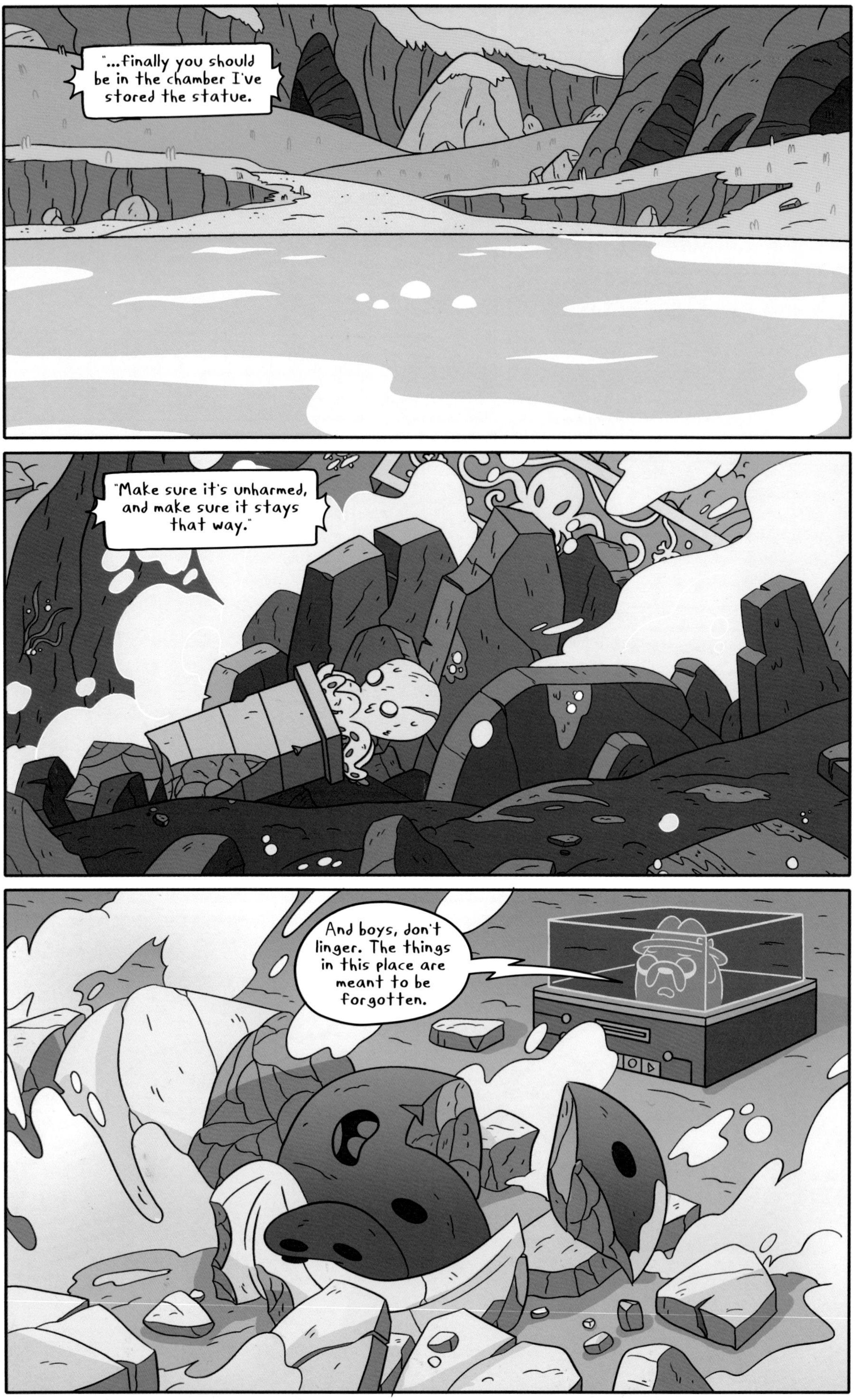
"...finally you should be in the chamber I've stored the statue.
"Make sure it's unharmed, and make sure it stays that way."
And boys, don't linger. The things in this place are meant to be forgotten.

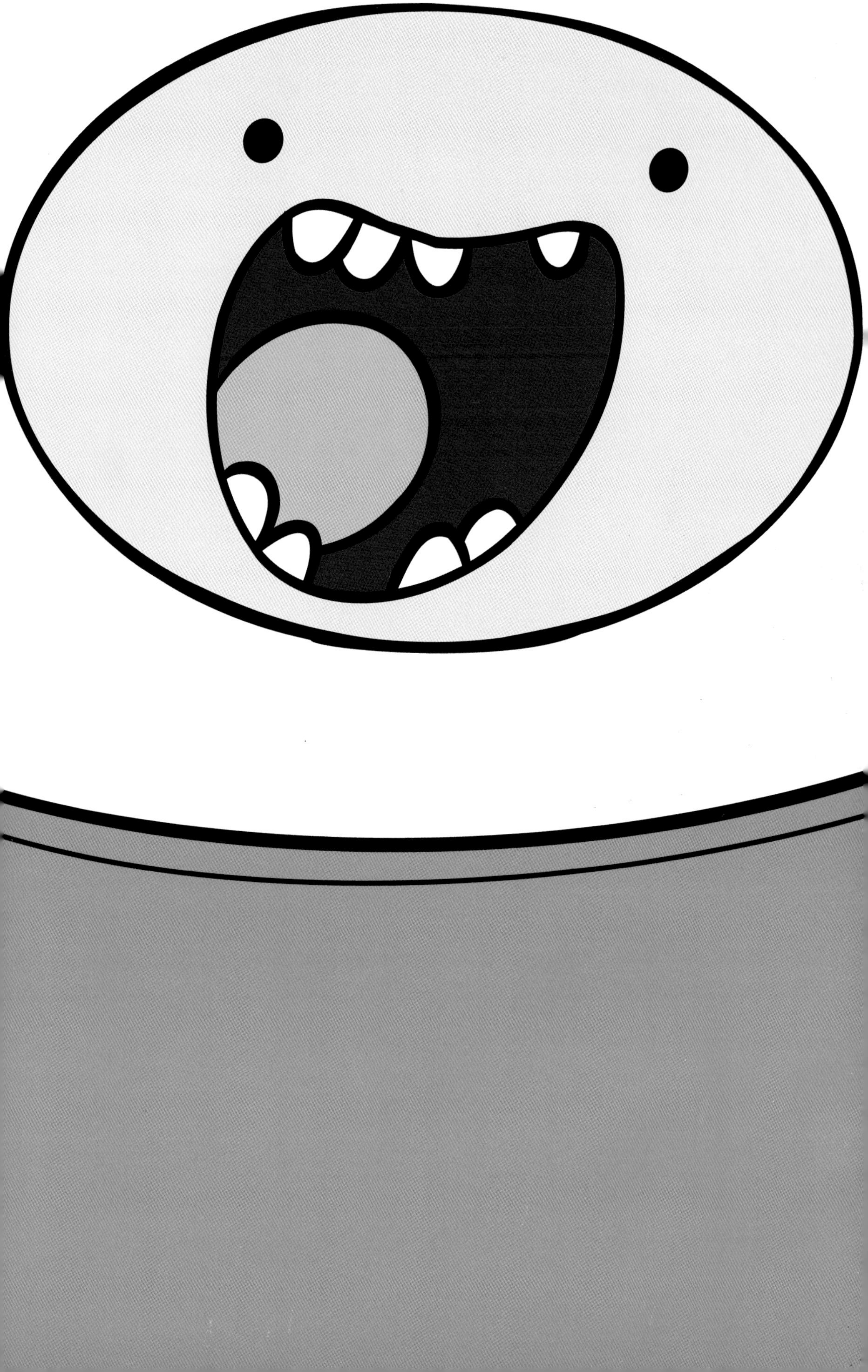

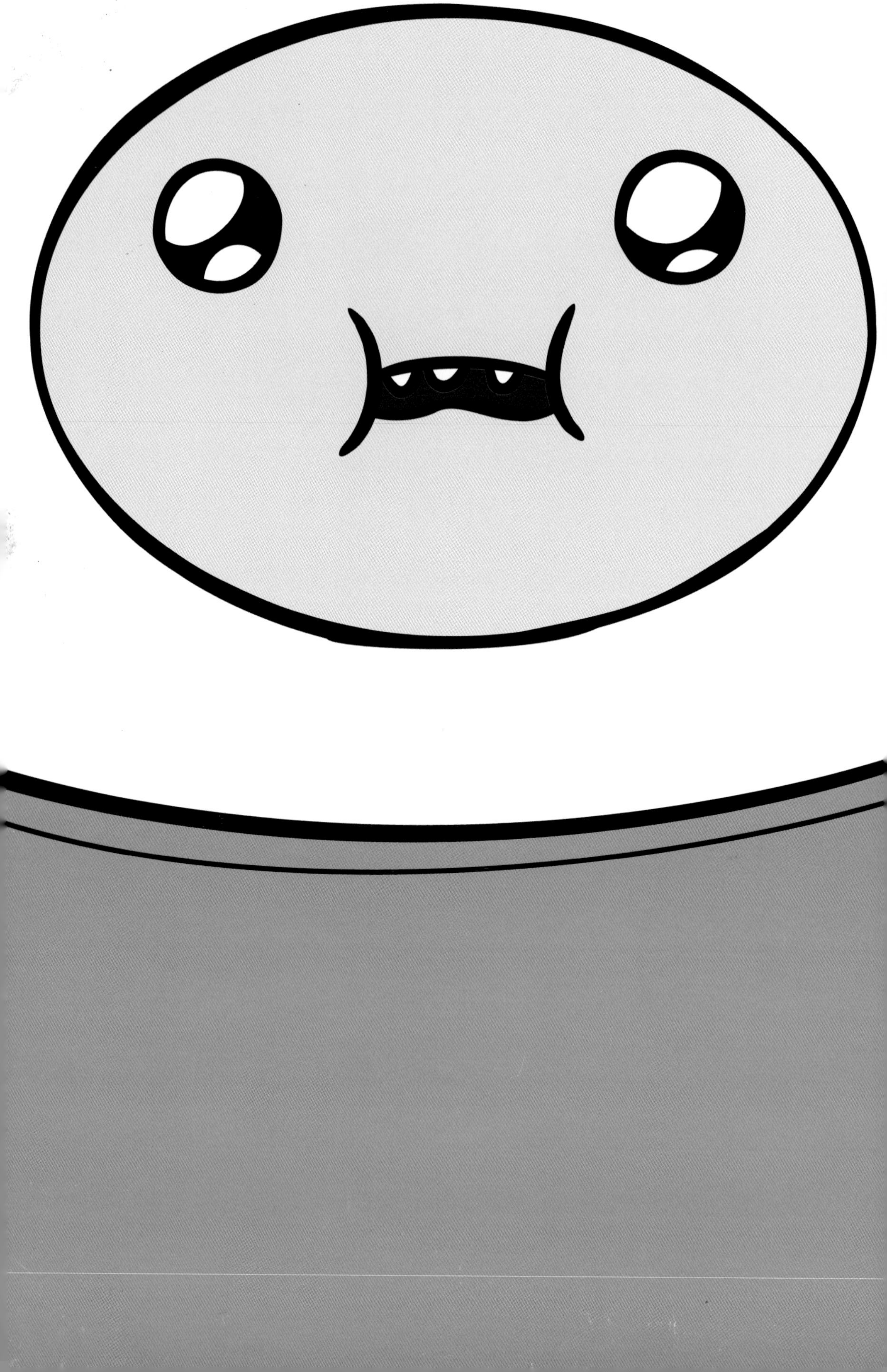

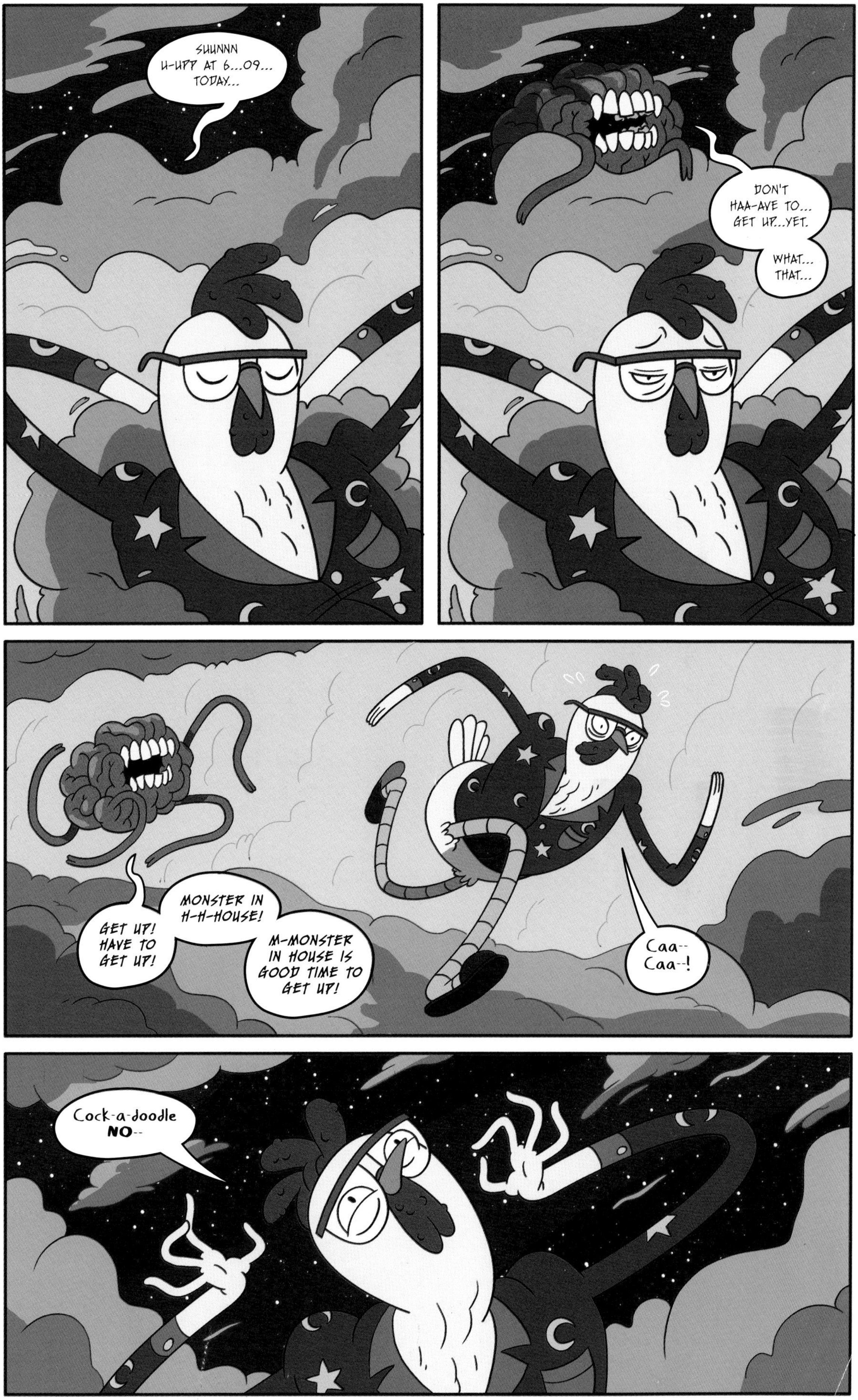
SHUNNN H-UPP AT 6...09... TODAY...
DON'T HAA-AVE TO... GET UP...YET.
WHAT... THAT...
GET UP! HAVE TO GET UP!
MONSTER IN H-H-HOUSE!
M-MONSTER IN HOUSE IS GOOD TIME TO GET UP!
Caa-- Caa--!
Cock-a-doodle NO--

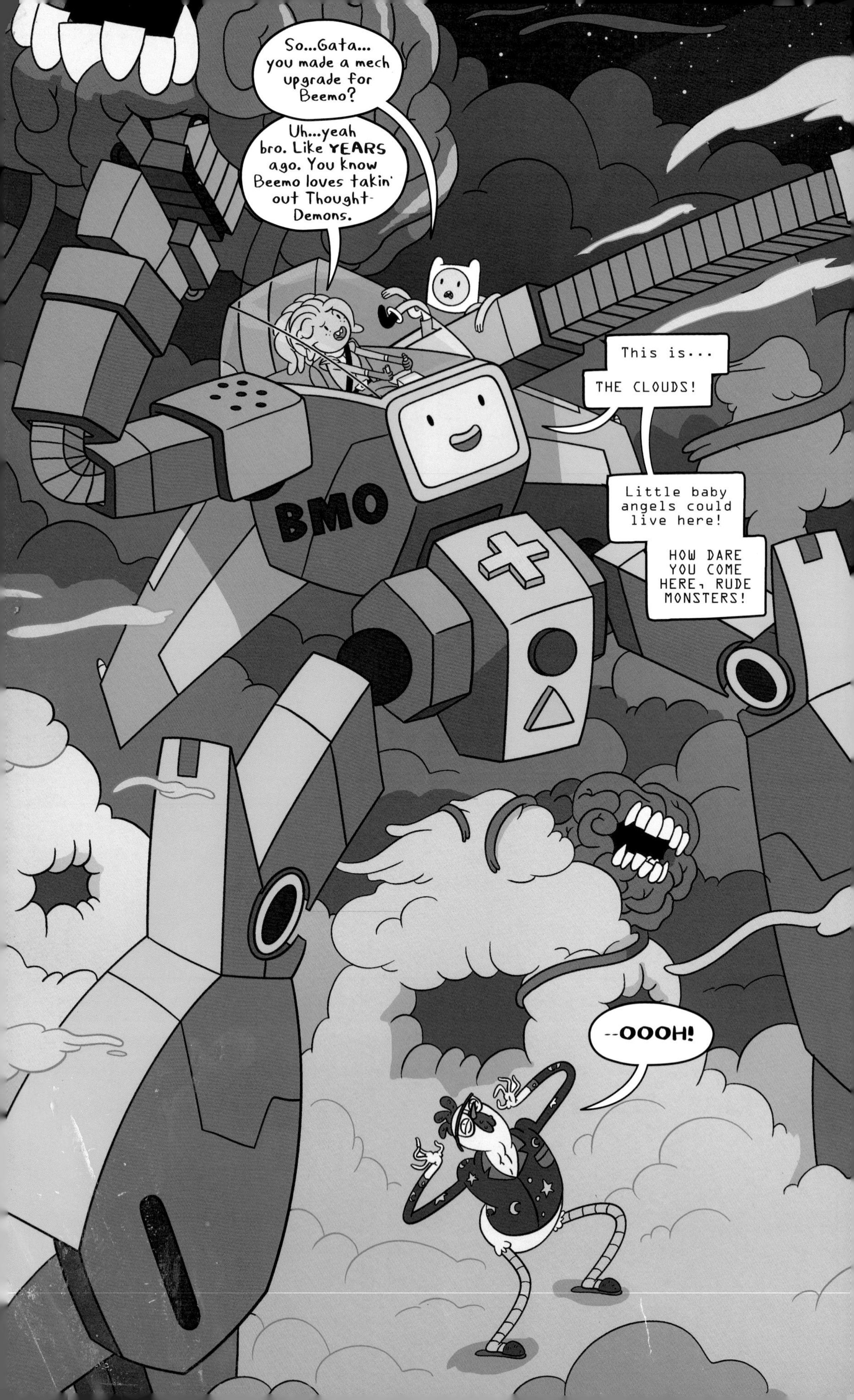
So...Gata... you made a mech upgrade for Beemo?
Uh...yeah bro. Like YEARS ago. You know Beemo loves takin' out Thought-Demons.
This is...
THE CLOUDS!
Little baby angels could live here!
HOW DARE YOU COME HERE, RUDE MONSTERS!
BMO
--OOOH!

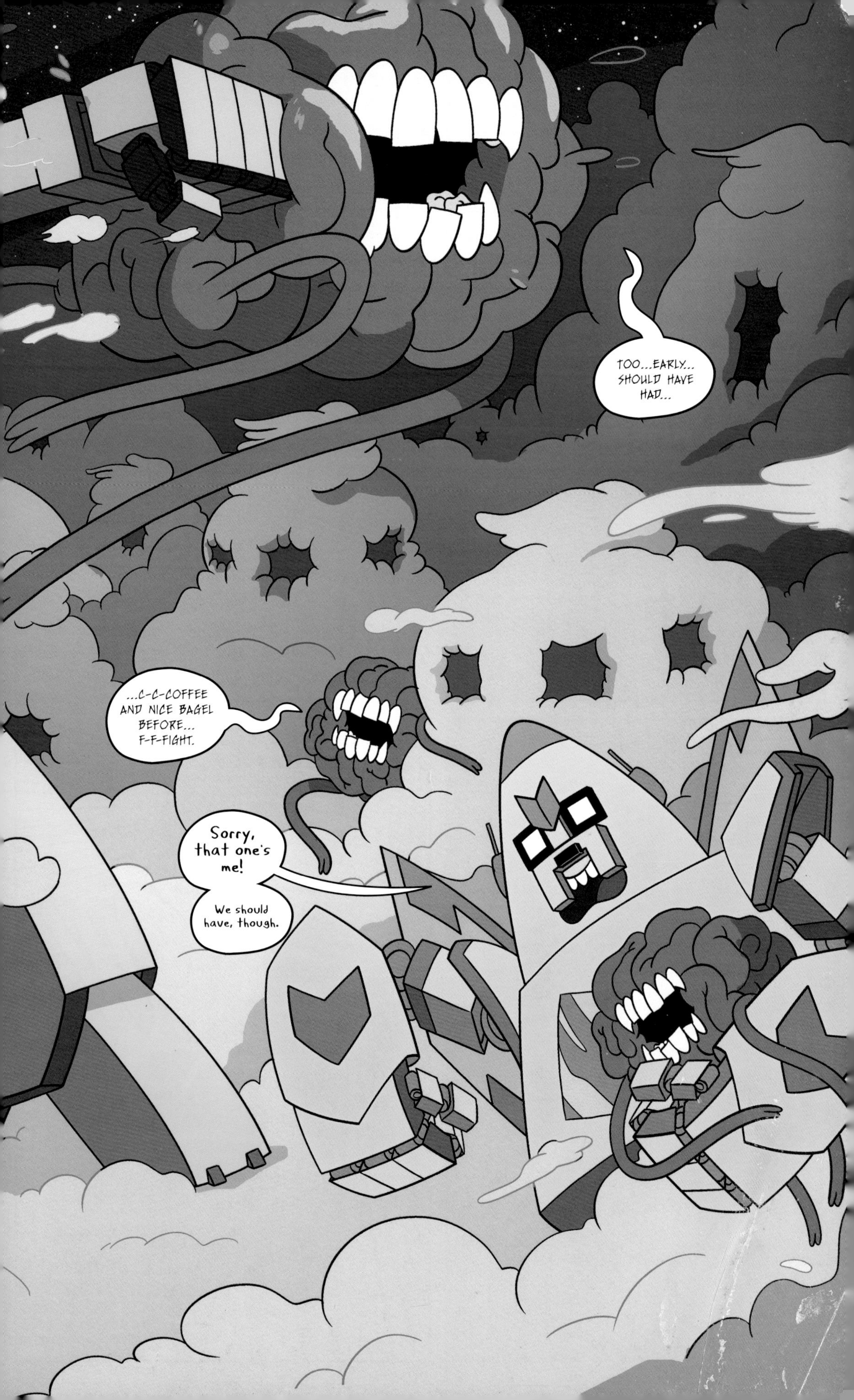
TOO...EARLY...
SHOULD HAVE
HAD...
...C-C-COFFEE
AND NICE BAGEL
BEFORE...
F-F-FIGHT.
Sorry, that one's me!
We should have, though.

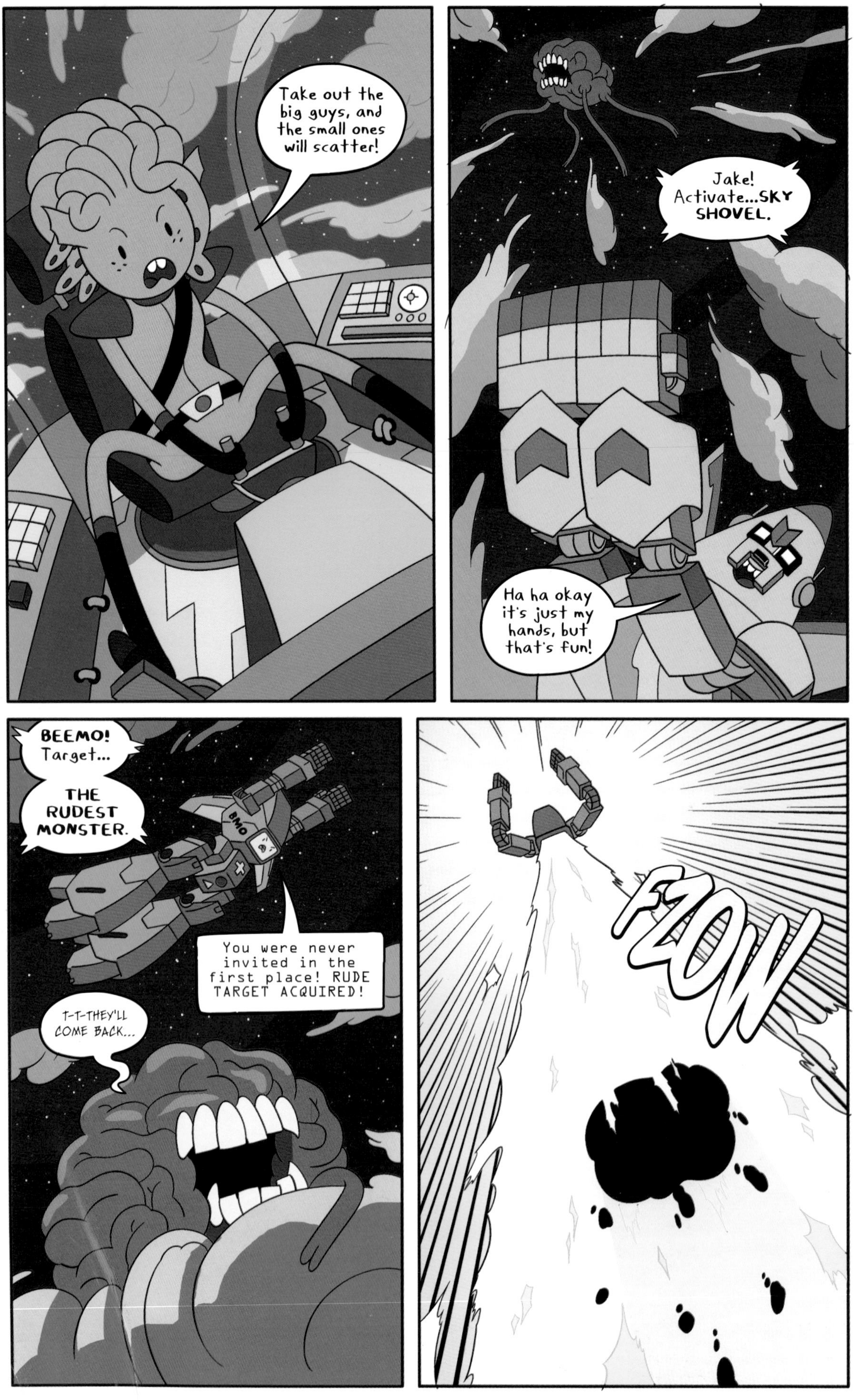
Take out the big guys, and the small ones will scatter!
Jake! Activate...SKY SHOVEL.
Ha ha okay it's just my hands, but that's fun!
BEEMO! Target...
THE RUDEST MONSTER.
BMO
You were never invited in the first place! RUDE TARGET ACQUIRED!
T-T-THEY'LL COME BACK...
FZOW

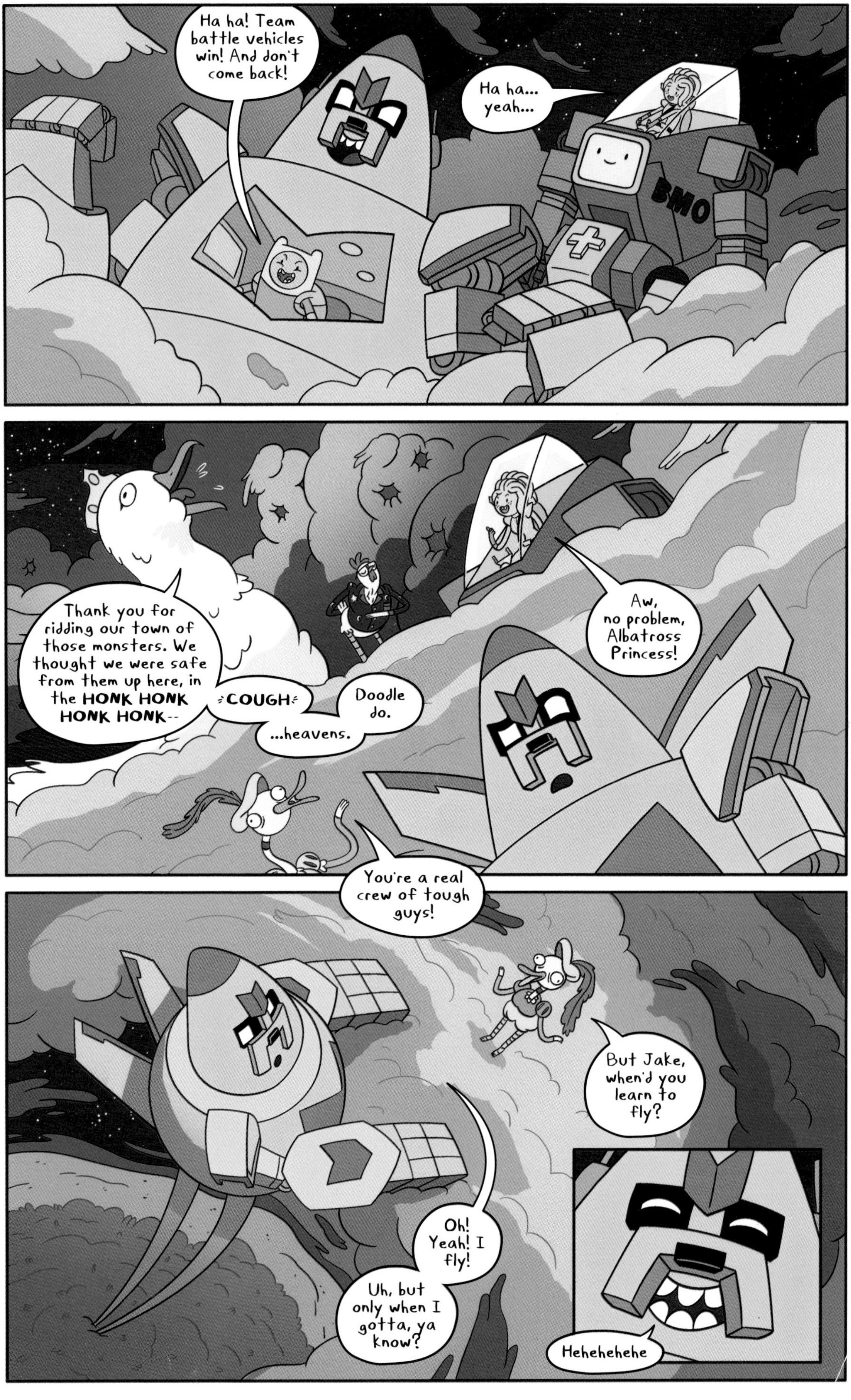

Ha ha! Team battle vehicles win! And don't come back!
Ha ha... yeah...
BMO
Thank you for ridding our town of those monsters. We thought we were safe from them up here, in the HONK HONK HONK HONK--
COUGH
...heavens.
Doodle do.
Aw, no problem, Albatross Princess!
You're a real crew of tough guys!
But Jake, when'd you learn to fly?
Oh! Yeah! I fly!
Uh, but only when I gotta, ya know?
Hehehehehe

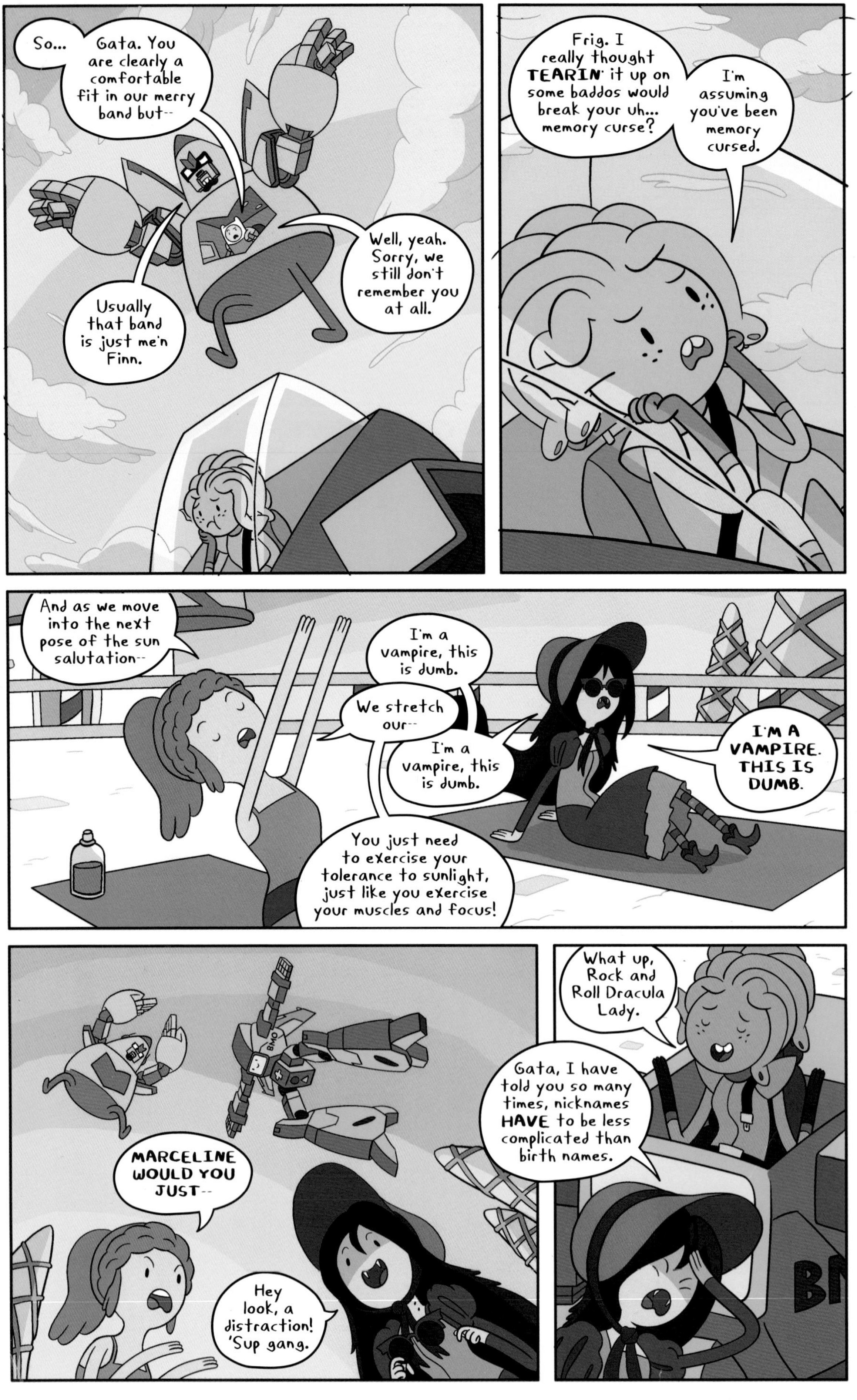
So...
Gata. You are clearly a comfortable fit in our merry band but--
Usually that band is just me'n Finn.
Well, yeah. Sorry, we still don't remember you at all.
Frig. I really thought TEARIN' it up on some baddos would break your uh... memory curse?
I'm assuming you've been memory cursed.
And as we move into the next pose of the sun salutation--
I'm a vampire, this is dumb.
We stretch our--
I'm a vampire, this is dumb.
I'M A VAMPIRE. THIS IS DUMB.
You just need to exercise your tolerance to sunlight, just like you exercise your muscles and focus!
MARCELINE WOULD YOU JUST--
Hey look, a distraction! 'Sup gang.
BMO
What up, Rock and Roll Dracula Lady.
Gata, I have told you so many times, nicknames HAVE to be less complicated than birth names.

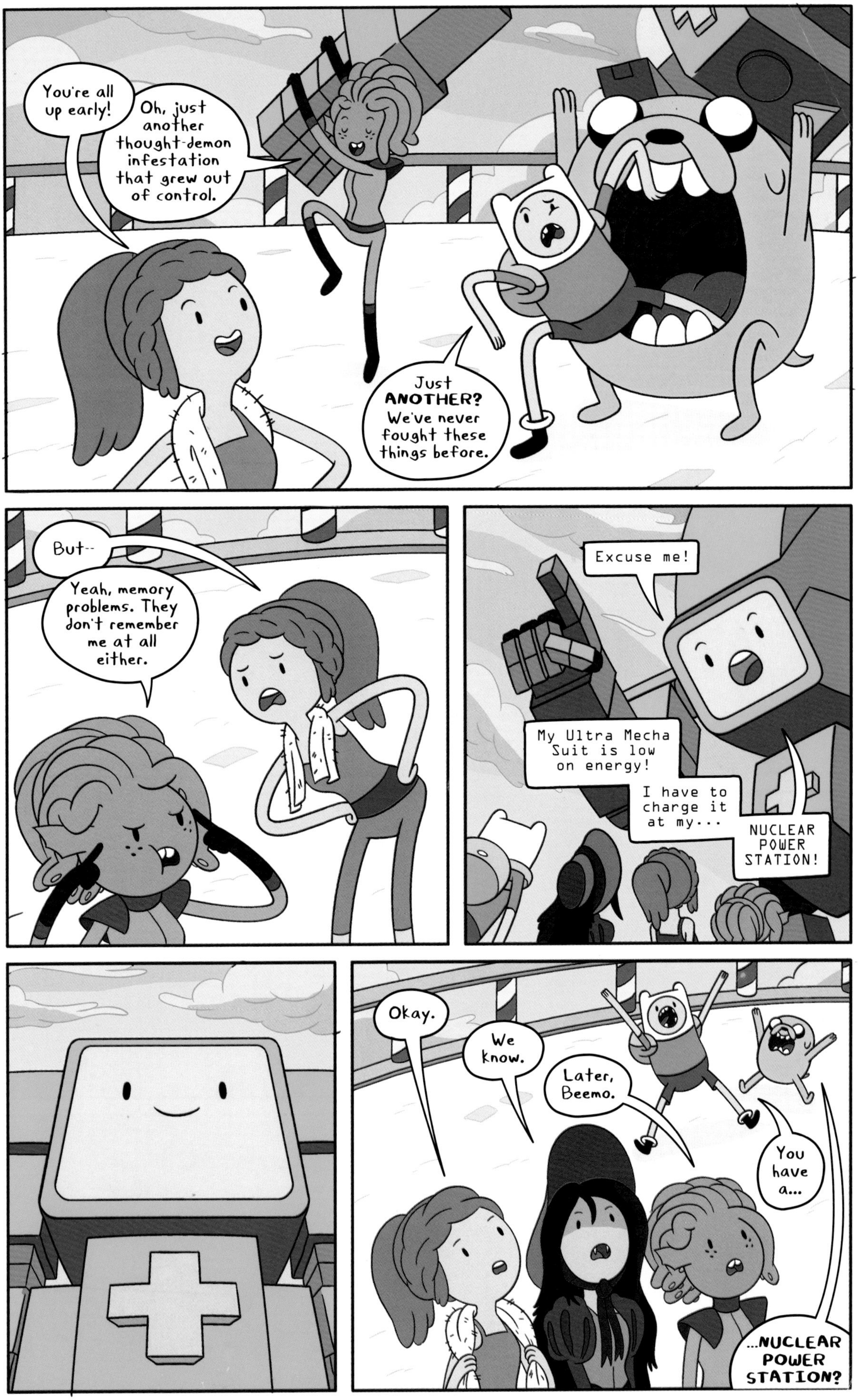
You're all up early!
Oh, just another thought-demon infestation that grew out of control.
Just **ANOTHER?** We've never fought these things before.
But--
Yeah, memory problems. They don't remember me at all either.
Excuse me!
My Ultra Mecha Suit is low on energy!
I have to charge it at my...
NUCLEAR POWER STATION!
Okay.
We know.
Later, Beemo.
You have a...
...NUCLEAR POWER STATION?

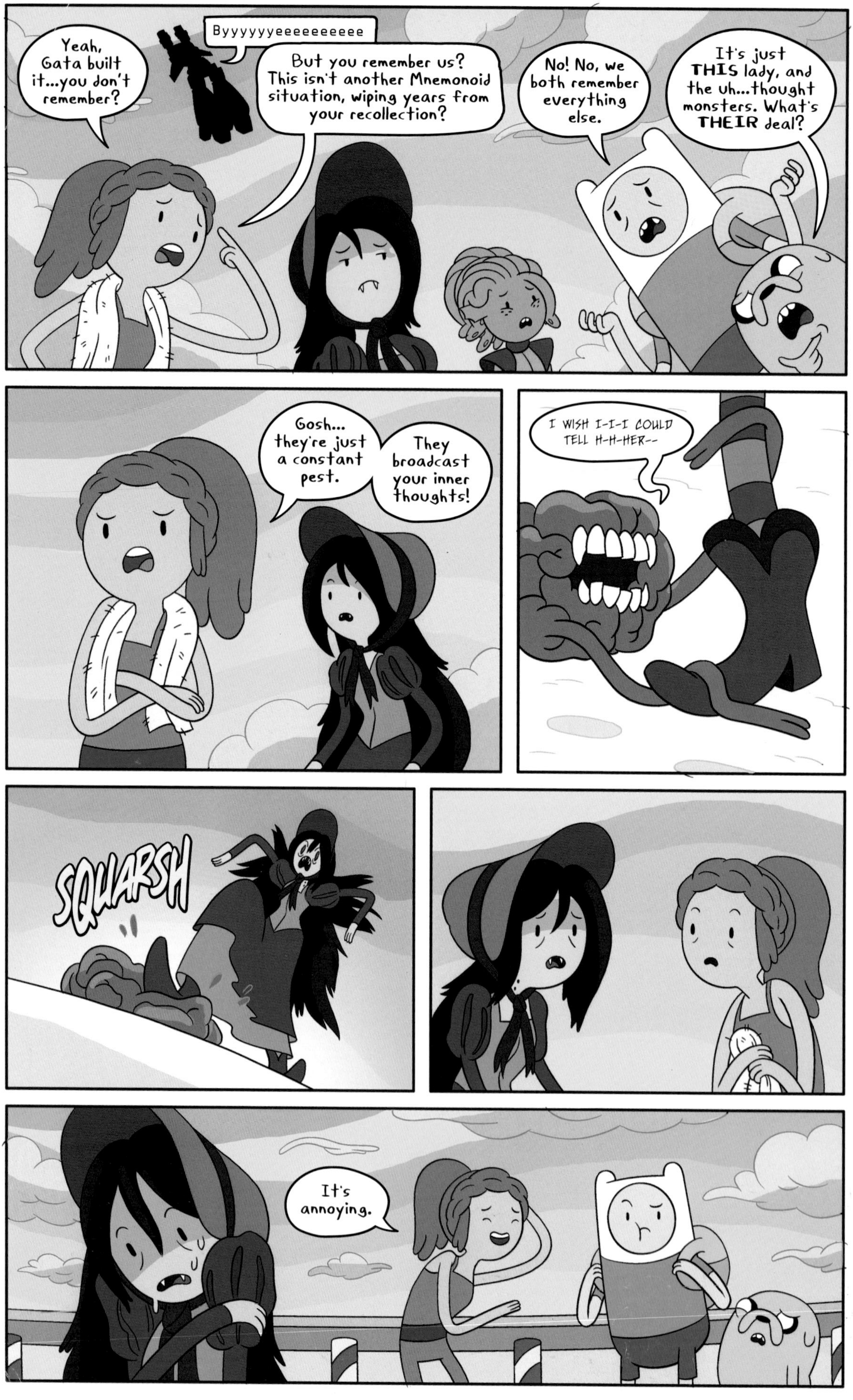
Yeah, Gata built it...you don't remember?
Byyyyyyeeeeeeeeee
But you remember us? This isn't another Mnemonoid situation, wiping years from your recollection?
No! No, we both remember everything else.
It's just THIS lady, and the uh...thought monsters. What's THEIR deal?
Gosh... they're just a constant pest.
They broadcast your inner thoughts!
I WISH I-I-I COULD TELL H-H-HER--
SQUARSH
It's annoying.

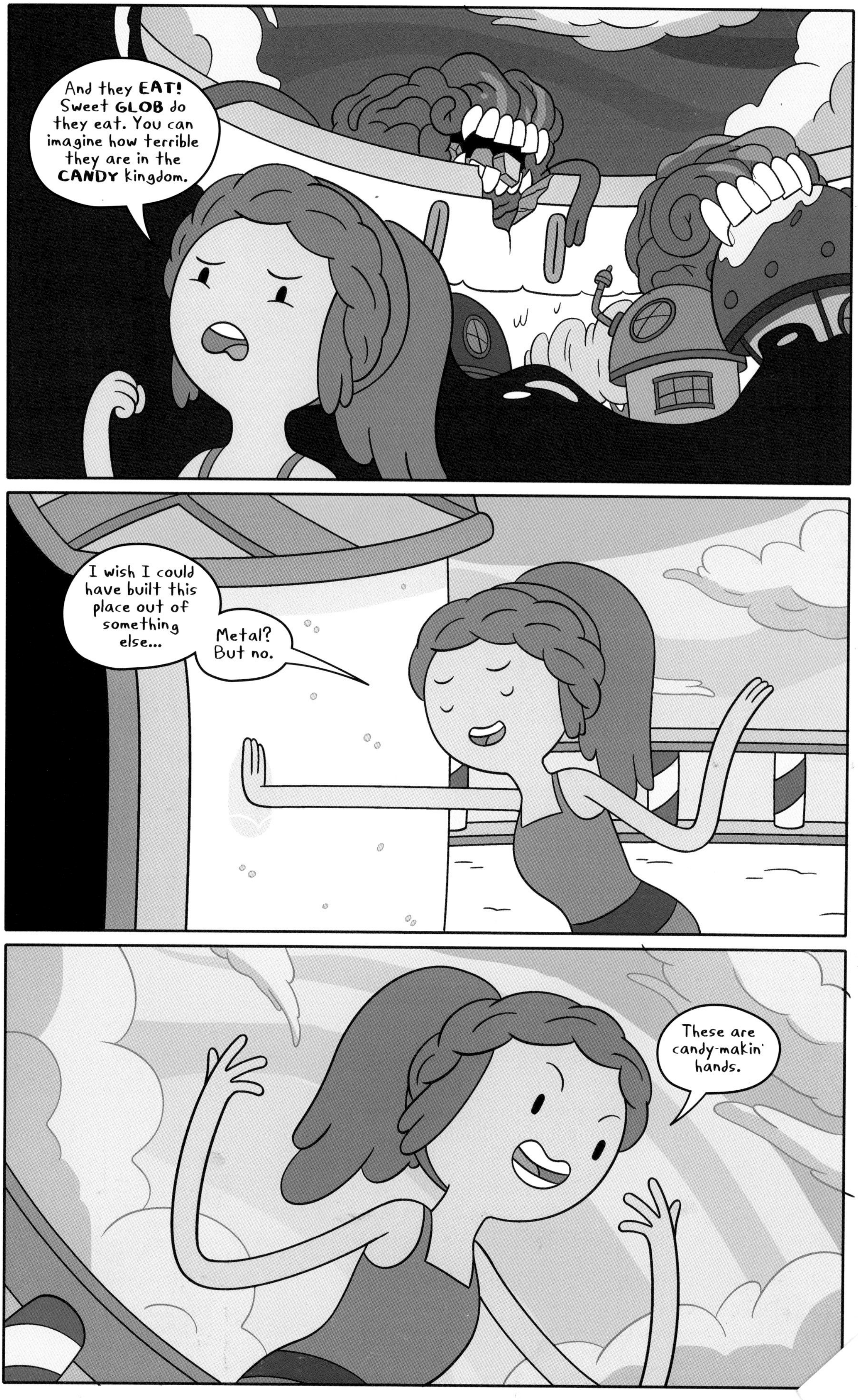
And they EAT! Sweet GLOB do they eat. You can imagine how terrible they are in the CANDY kingdom.
I wish I could have built this place out of something else...
Metal? But no.
These are candy-makin' hands.

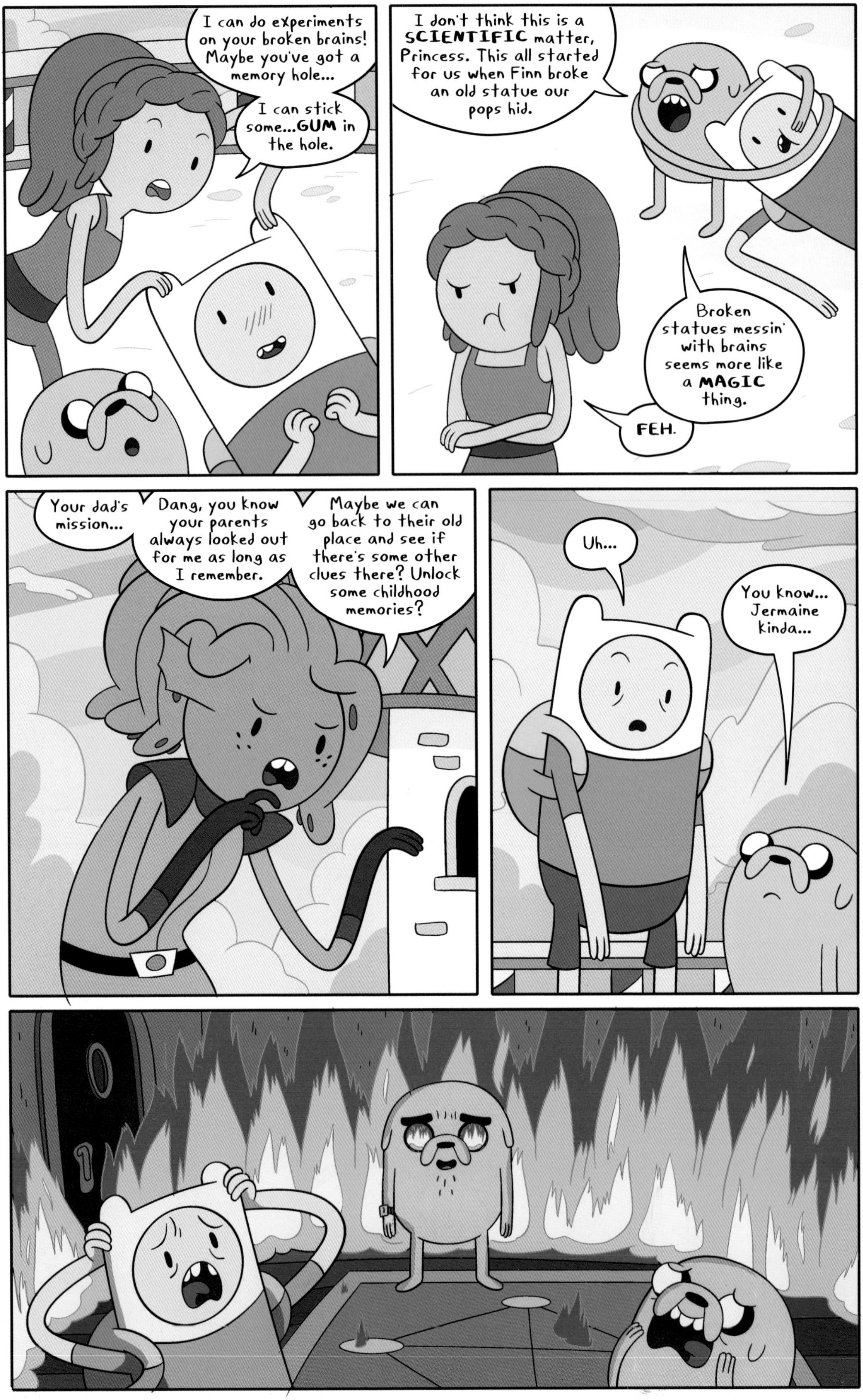
I can do experiments on your broken brains! Maybe you've got a memory hole...
I can stick some...GUM in the hole.
I don't think this is a SCIENTIFIC matter, Princess. This all started for us when Finn broke an old statue our pops hid.
Broken statues messin' with brains seems more like a MAGIC thing.
FEH.
Your dad's mission...
Dang, you know your parents always looked out for me as long as I remember.
Maybe we can go back to their old place and see if there's some other clues there? Unlock some childhood memories?
Uh...
You know... Jermaine kinda...

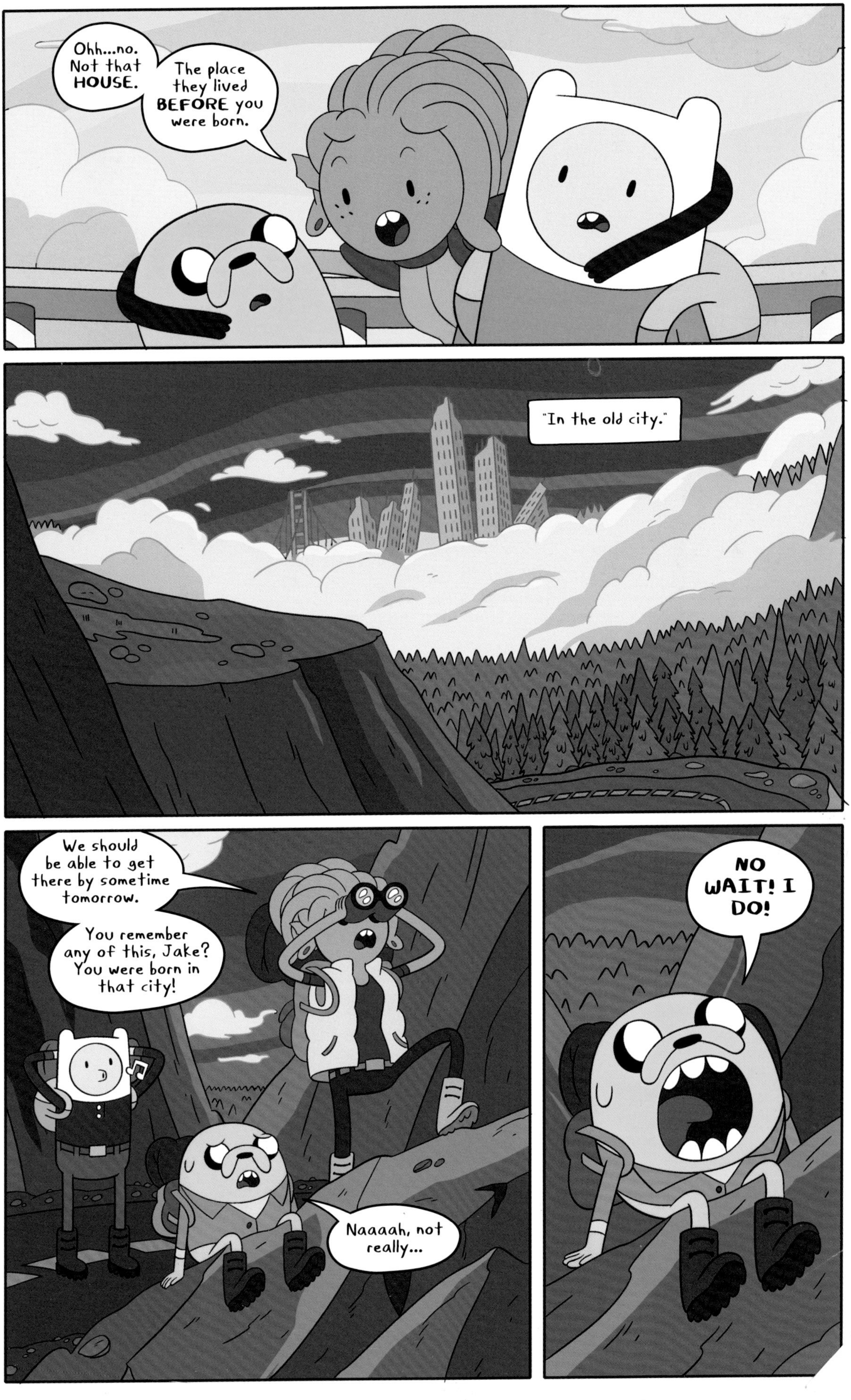
Ohh...no. Not that HOUSE.
The place they lived BEFORE you were born.
"In the old city."
We should be able to get there by sometime tomorrow.
You remember any of this, Jake? You were born in that city!
Naaaah, not really...
NO WAIT! I DO!

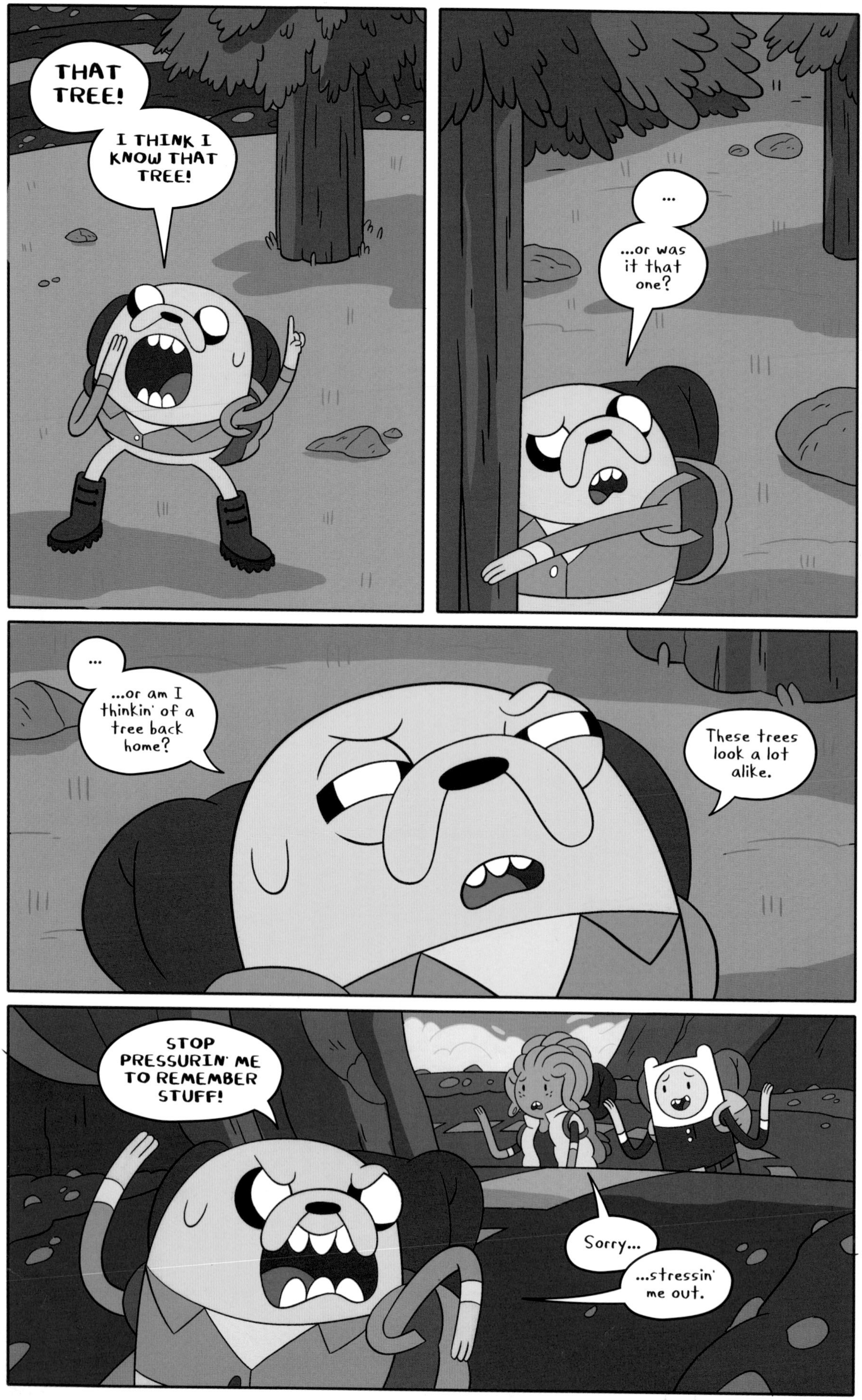
THAT TREE!
I THINK I KNOW THAT TREE!
...
...or was it that one?
...
...or am I thinkin' of a tree back home?
These trees look a lot alike.
STOP PRESSURIN' ME TO REMEMBER STUFF!
Sorry...
...stressin' me out.

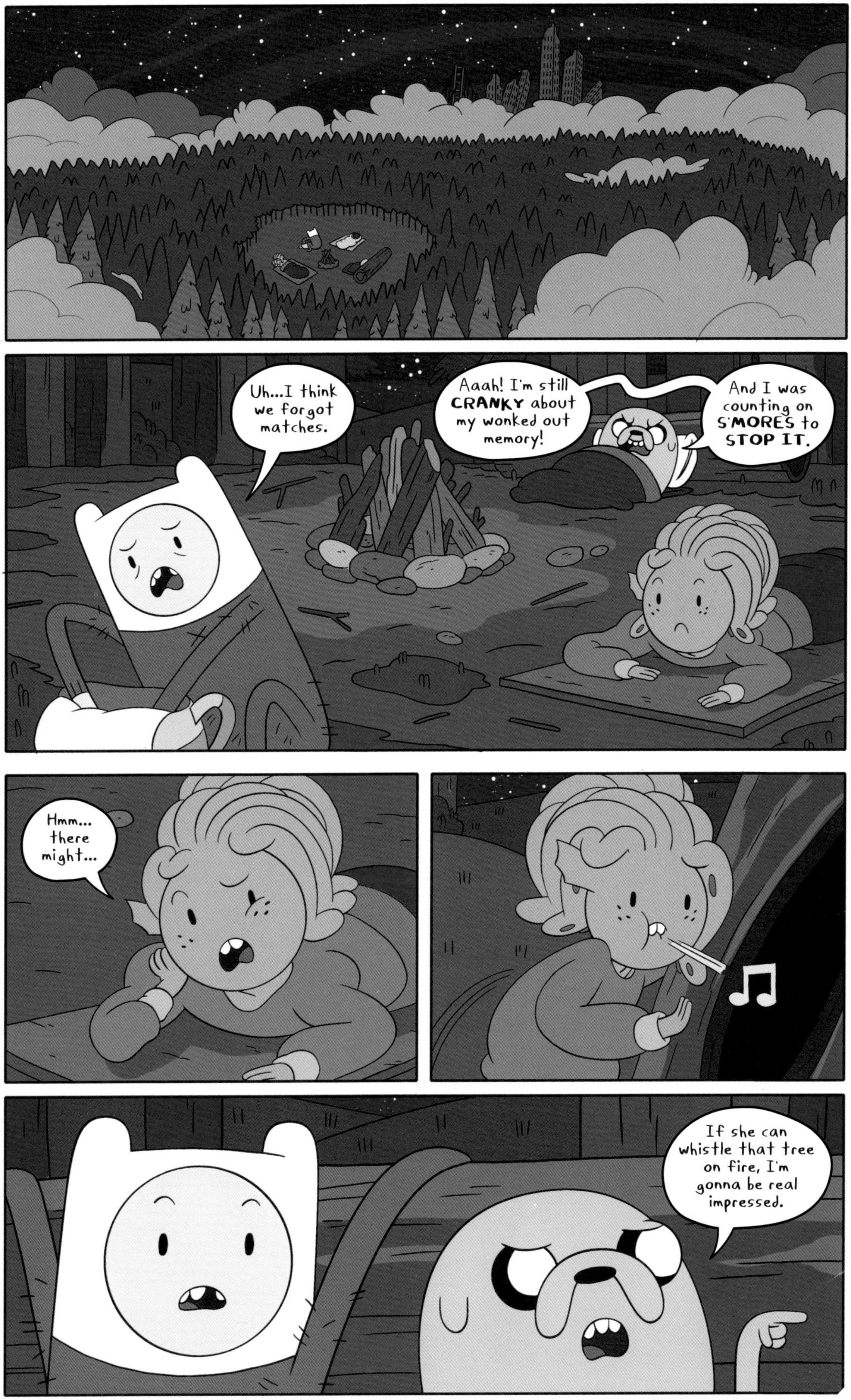

Uh...I think we forgot matches.
Aaah! I'm still CRANKY about my wonked out memory!
And I was counting on S'MORES to STOP IT.
Hmm... there might...
If she can whistle that tree on fire, I'm gonna be real impressed.

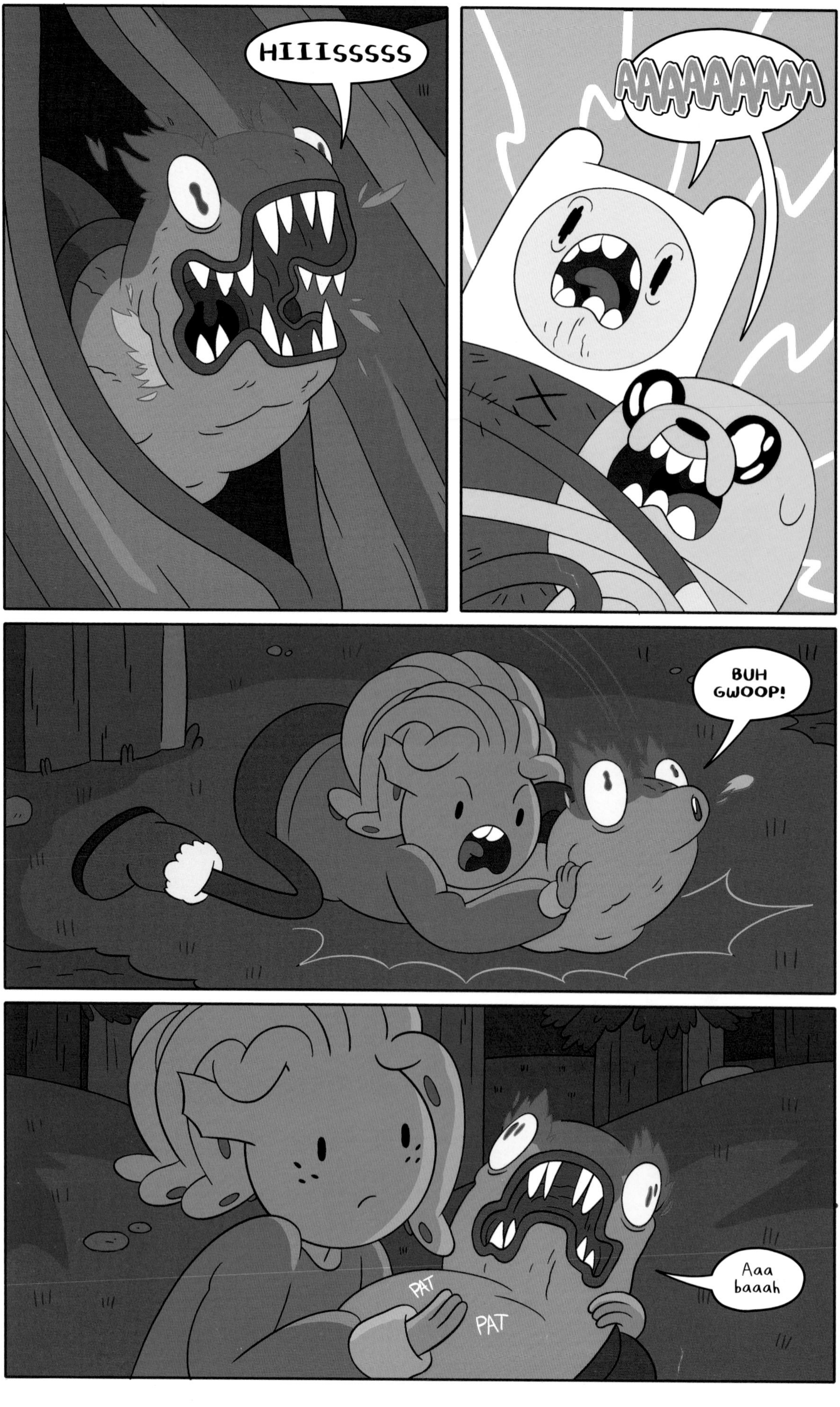
HIIISSSSS
AAAAAAAAA
BUH GWOOP!
PAT
PAT
Aaa baaah

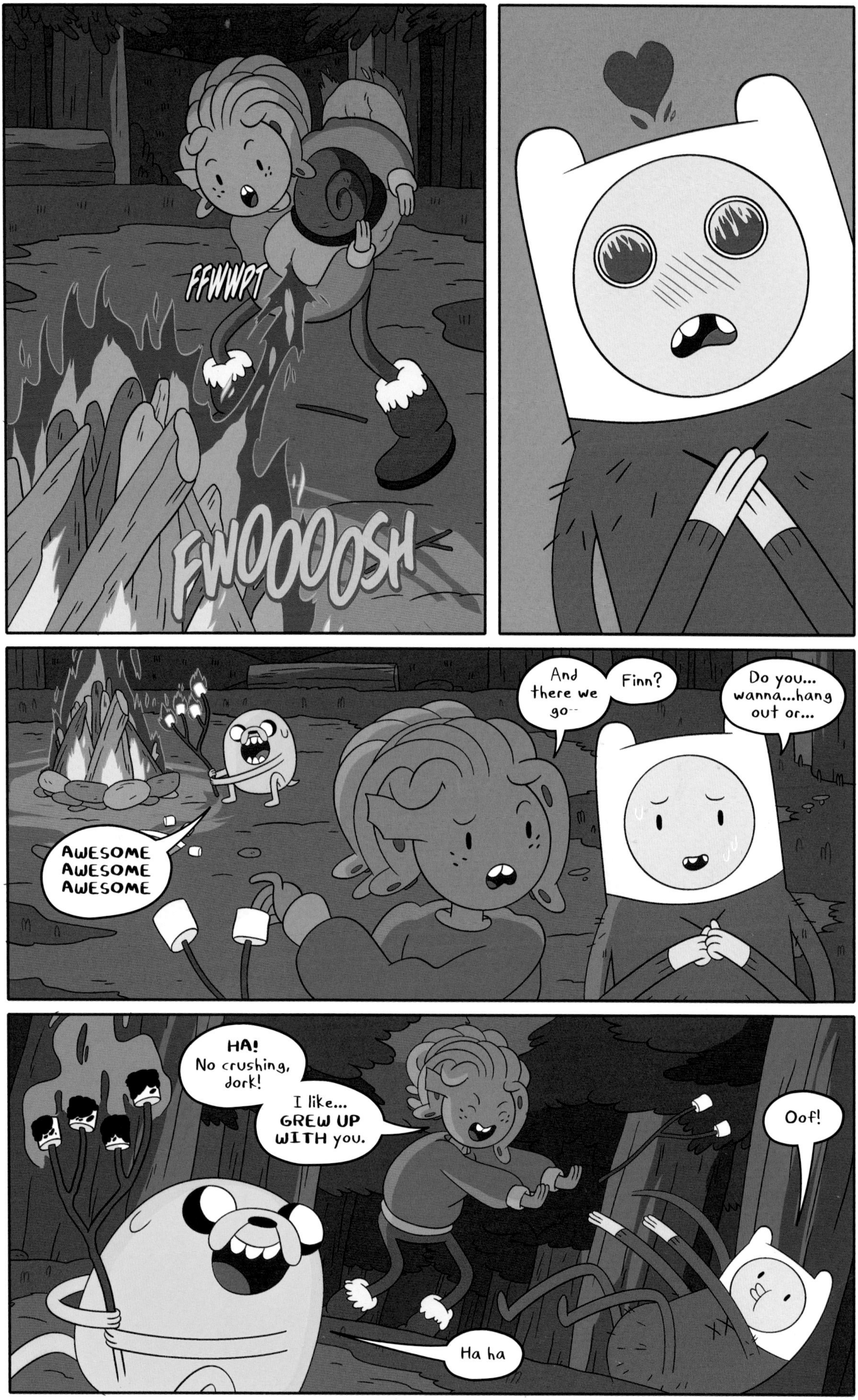
FFWWPT
FWOOOOSH
AWESOME AWESOME AWESOME
And there we go--
Finn?
Do you... wanna...hang out or...
HA! No crushing, dork!
I like... GREW UP WITH you.
Oof!
Ha ha

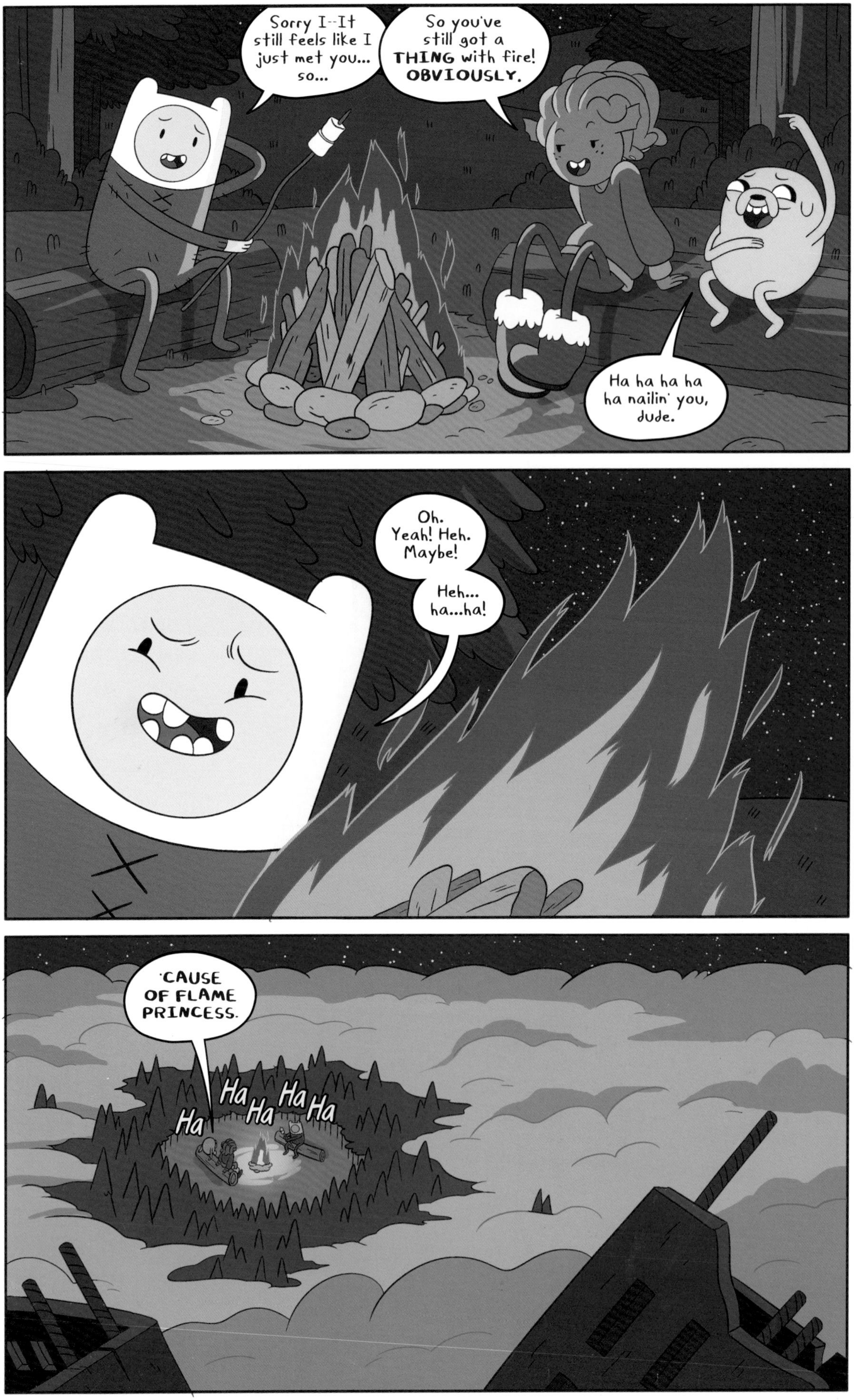
Sorry I--It still feels like I just met you... so...
So you've still got a THING with fire! OBVIOUSLY.
Ha ha ha ha ha nailin' you, dude.
Oh. Yeah! Heh. Maybe!
Heh... ha...ha!
'CAUSE OF FLAME PRINCESS.
Ha Ha Ha Ha Ha

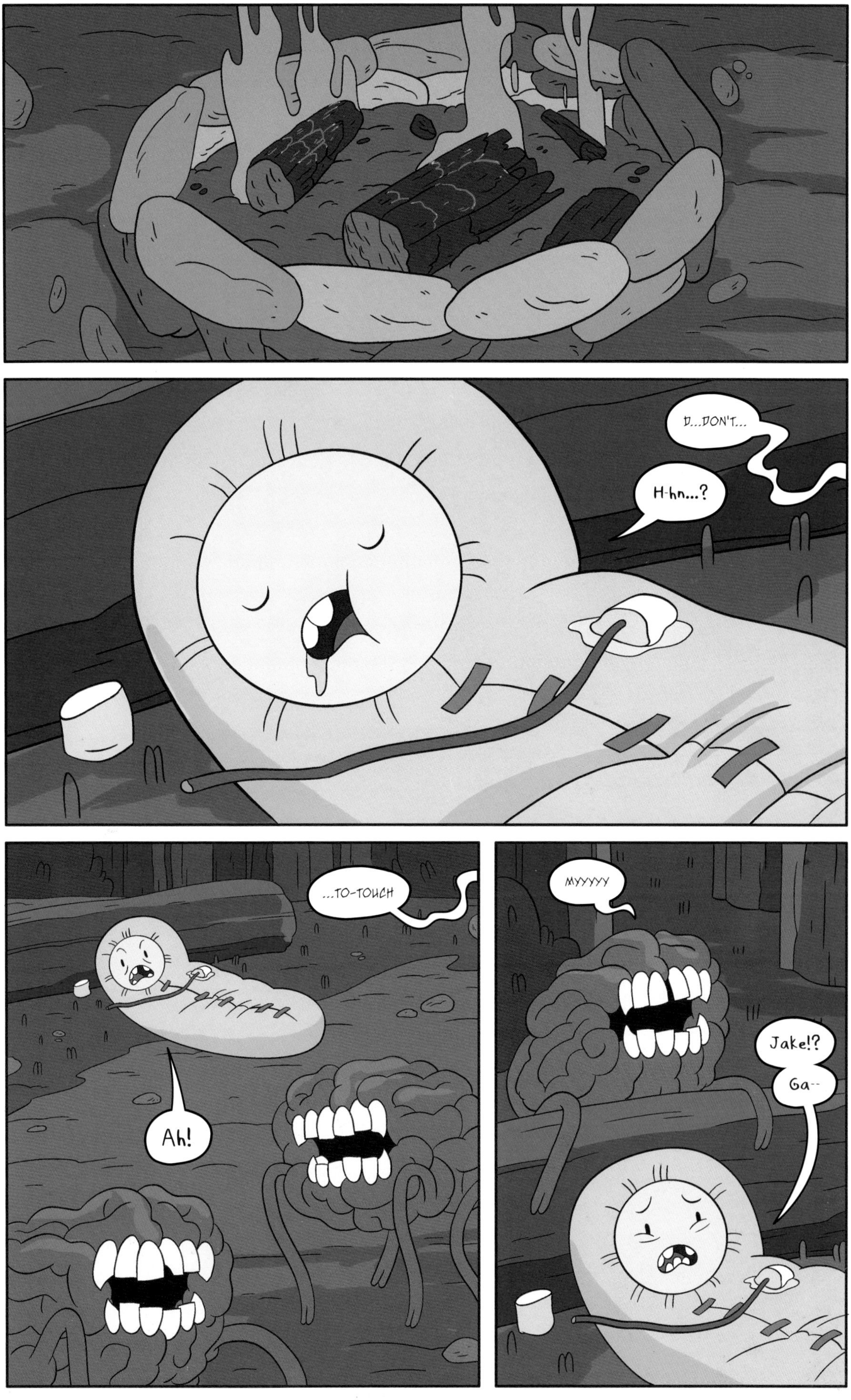
D...DON'T...
H-hn...?
...TO-TOUCH
Ah!
MYYYYY
Jake!?
Ga--

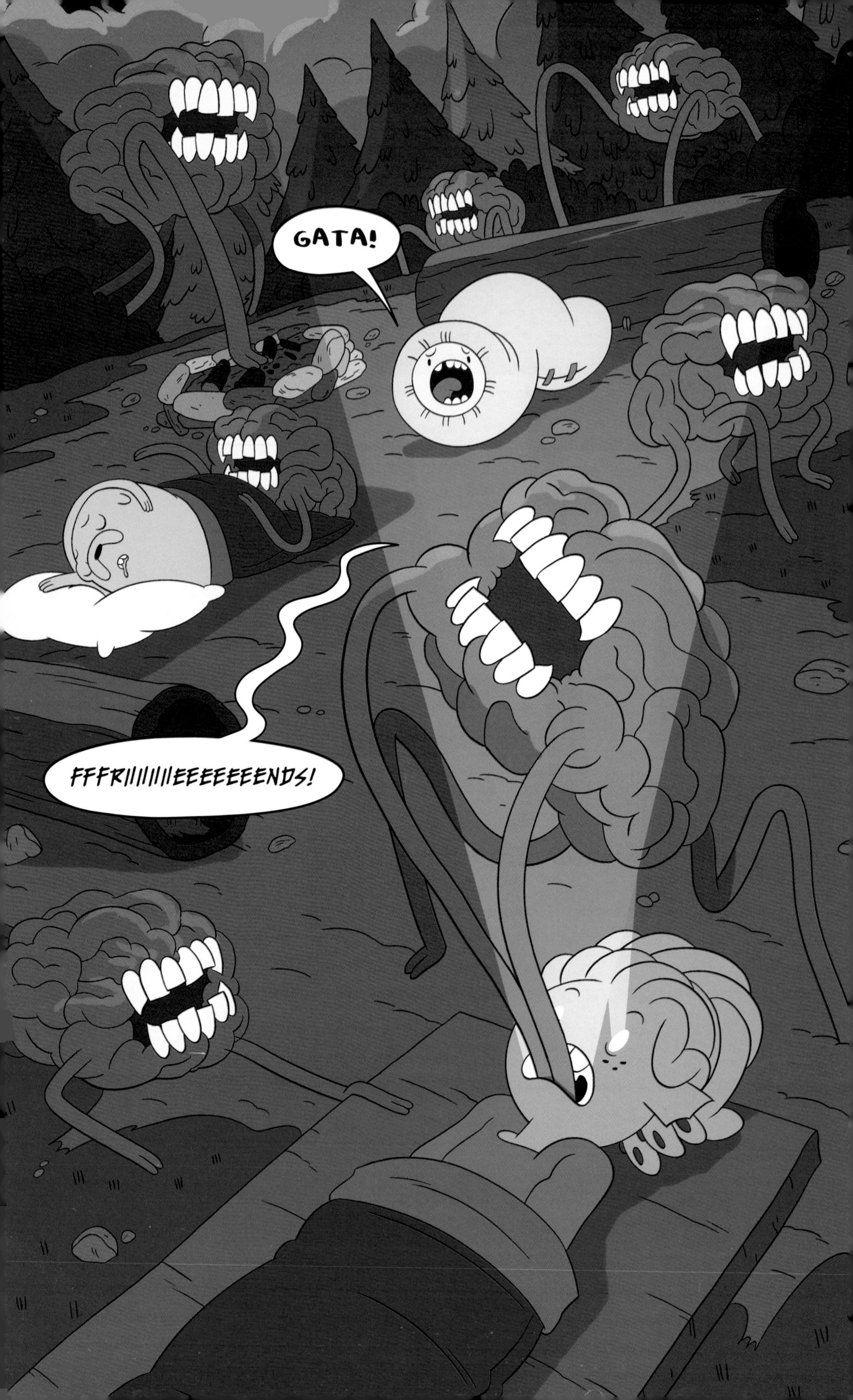
GATA!
FFFRIIIIIIIIEEEEEEEENDS!

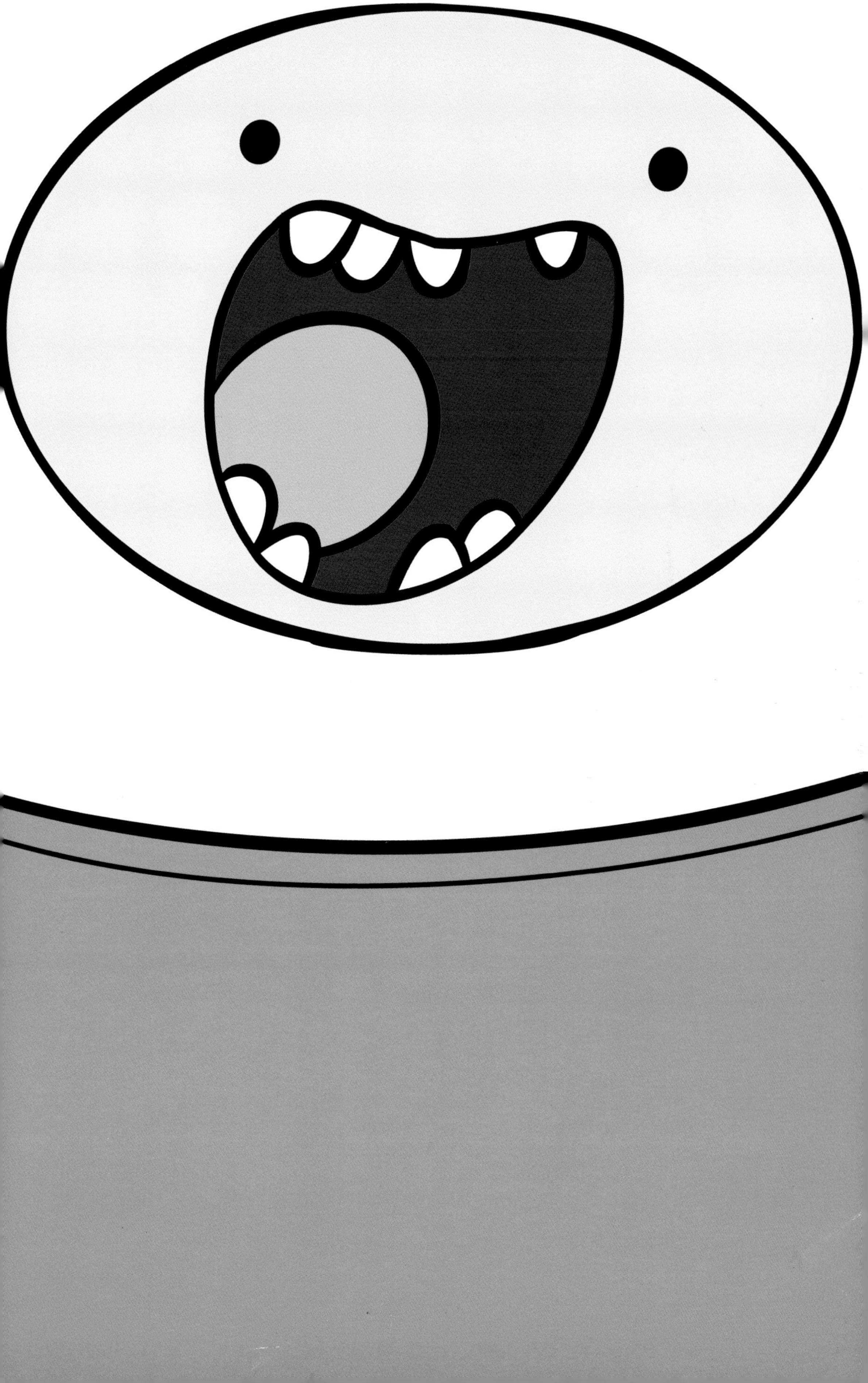

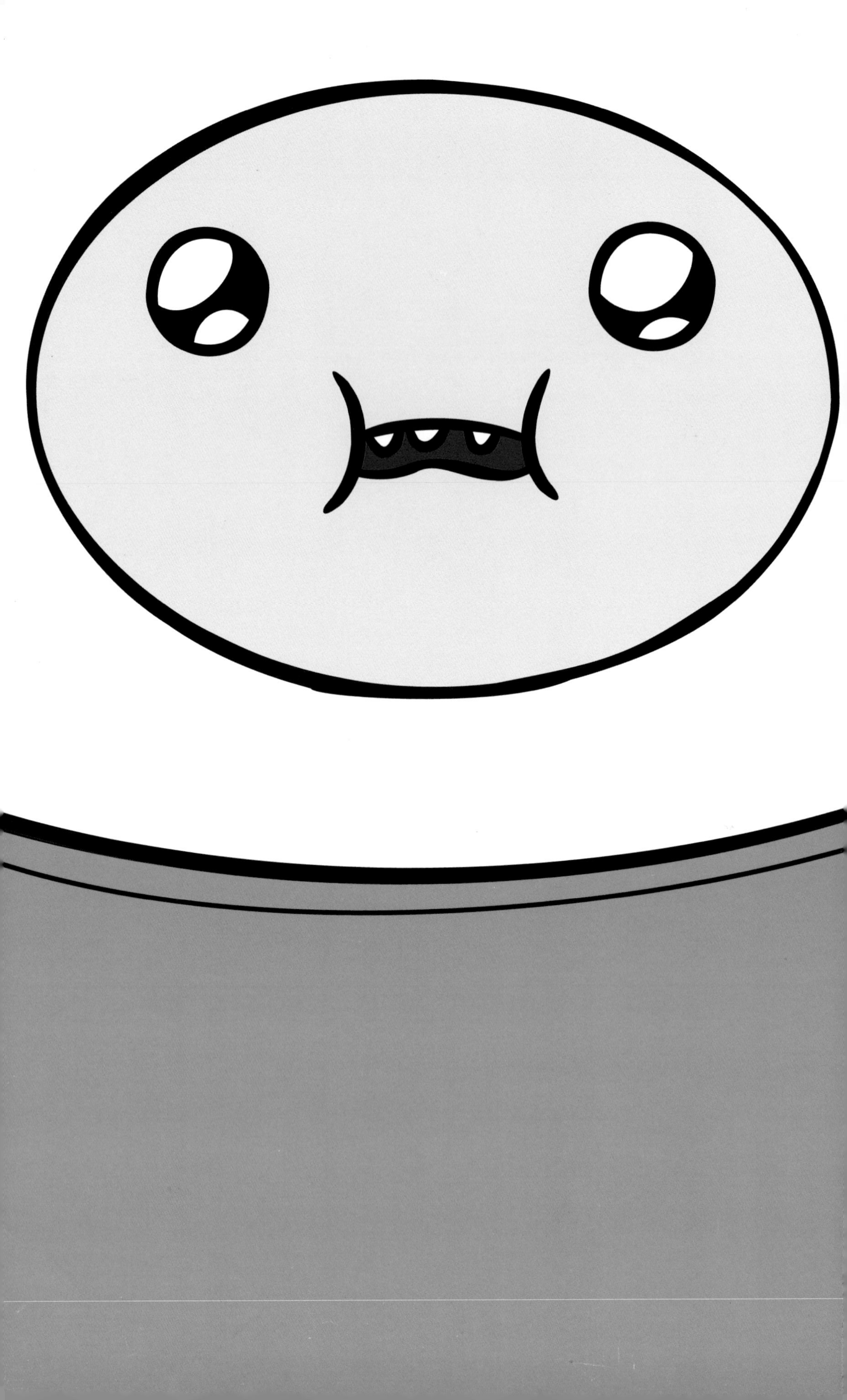

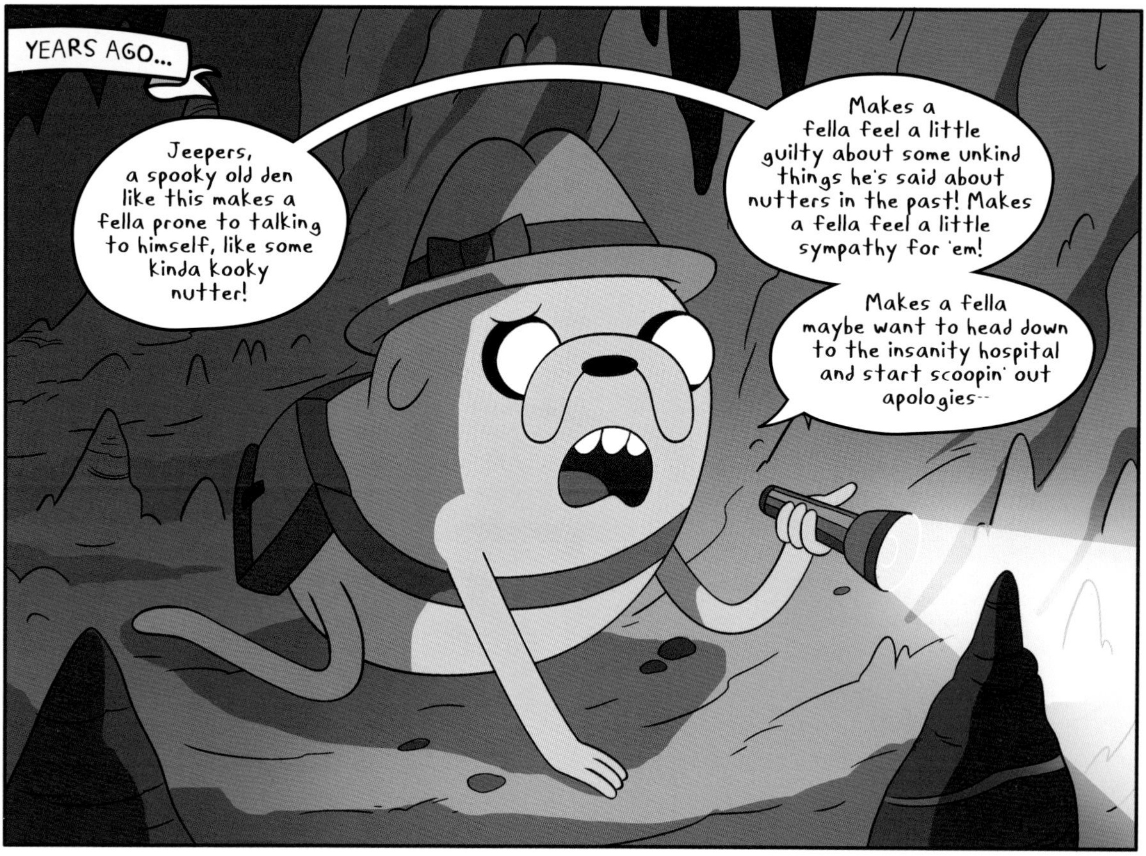
YEARS AGO...
Jeepers, a spooky old den like this makes a fella prone to talking to himself, like some kinda kooky nutter!
Makes a fella feel a little guilty about some unkind things he's said about nutters in the past! Makes a fella feel a little sympathy for 'em!
Makes a fella maybe want to head down to the insanity hospital and start scoopin' out apologies--

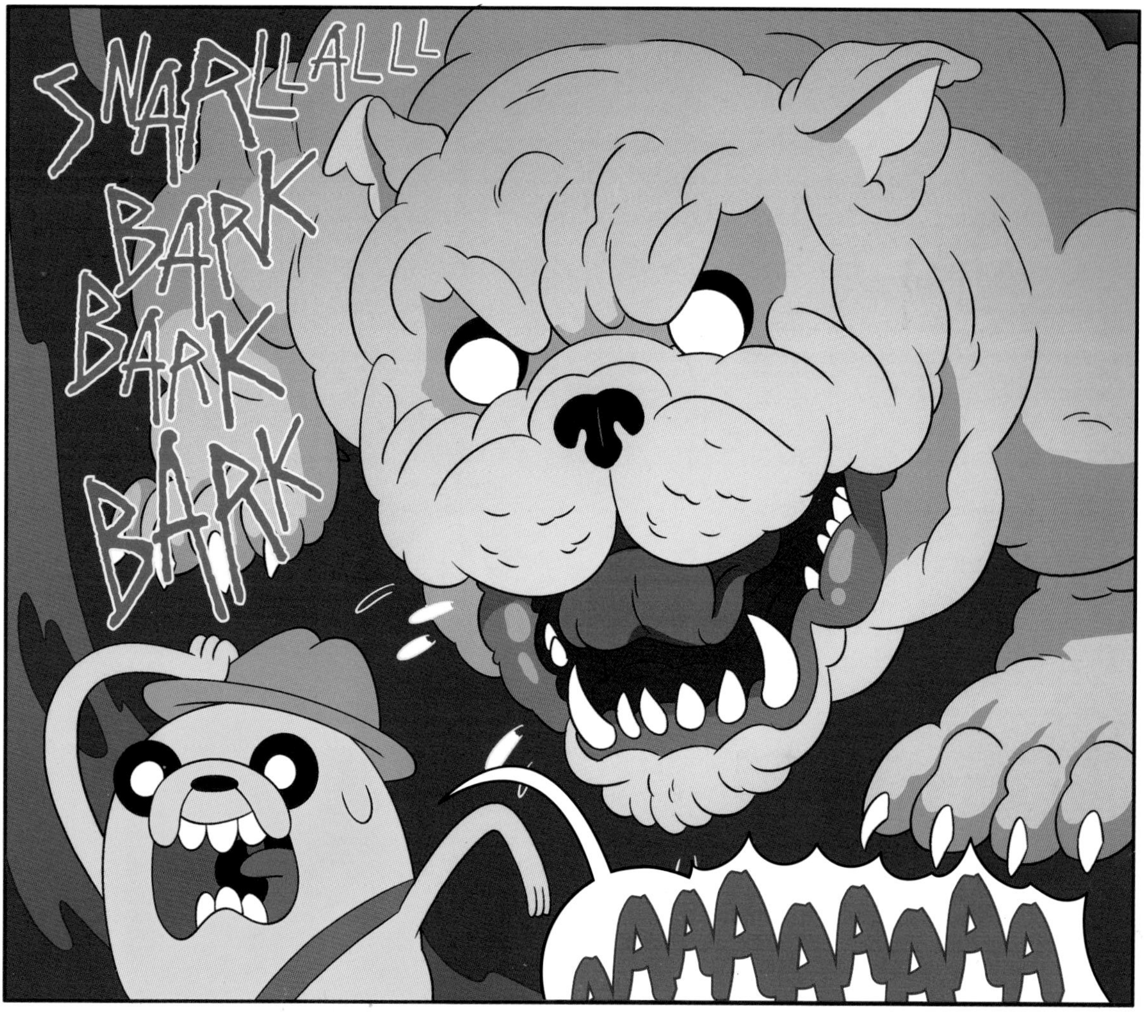
SNARLLALLL
BARK
BARK
BARK
AAAAAAAAA

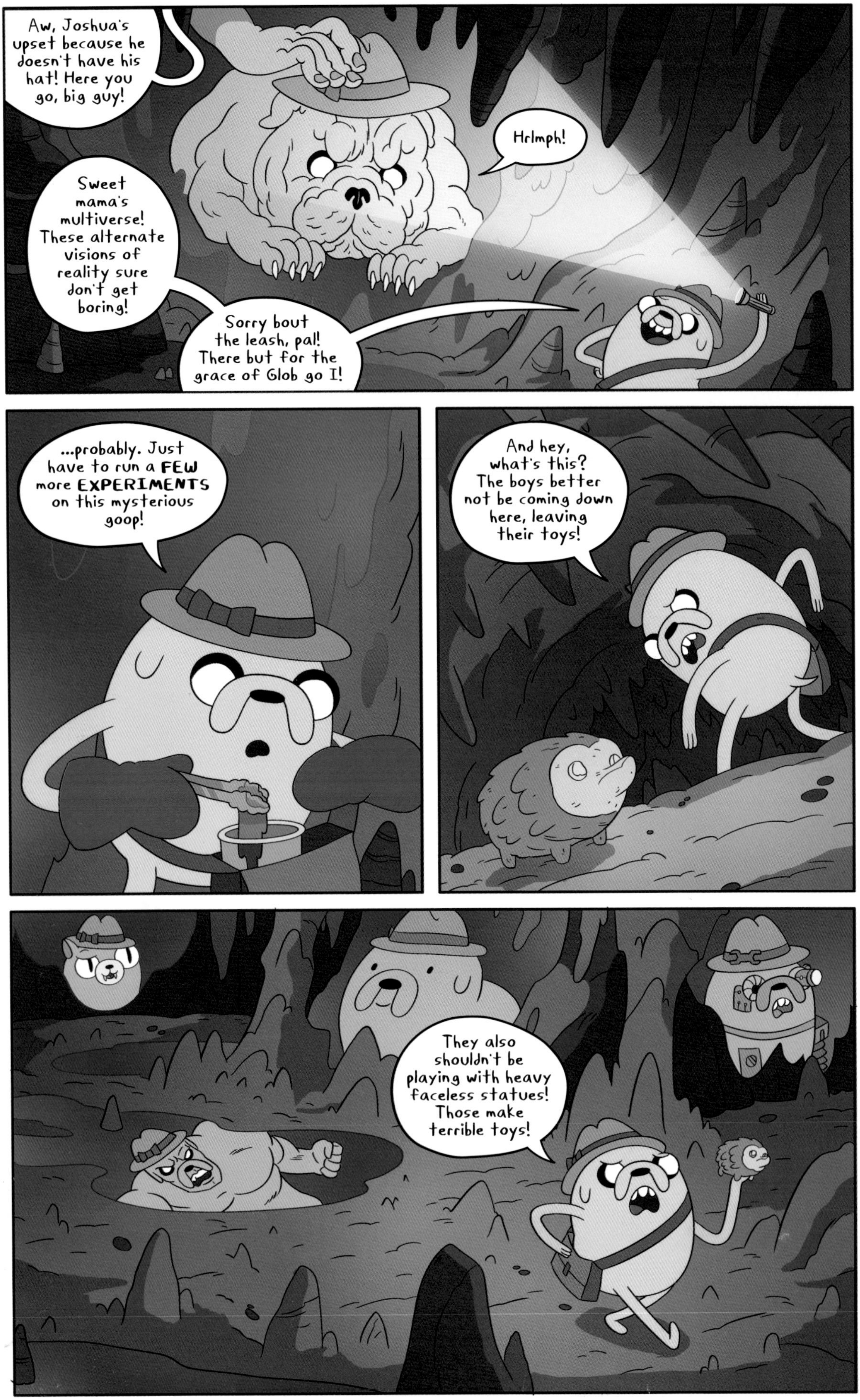
Aw, Joshua's upset because he doesn't have his hat! Here you go, big guy!
Hrlmph!
Sweet mama's multiverse! These alternate visions of reality sure don't get boring!
Sorry bout the leash, pal! There but for the grace of Glob go I!
...probably. Just have to run a FEW more EXPERIMENTS on this mysterious goop!
And hey, what's this? The boys better not be coming down here, leaving their toys!
They also shouldn't be playing with heavy faceless statues! Those make terrible toys!

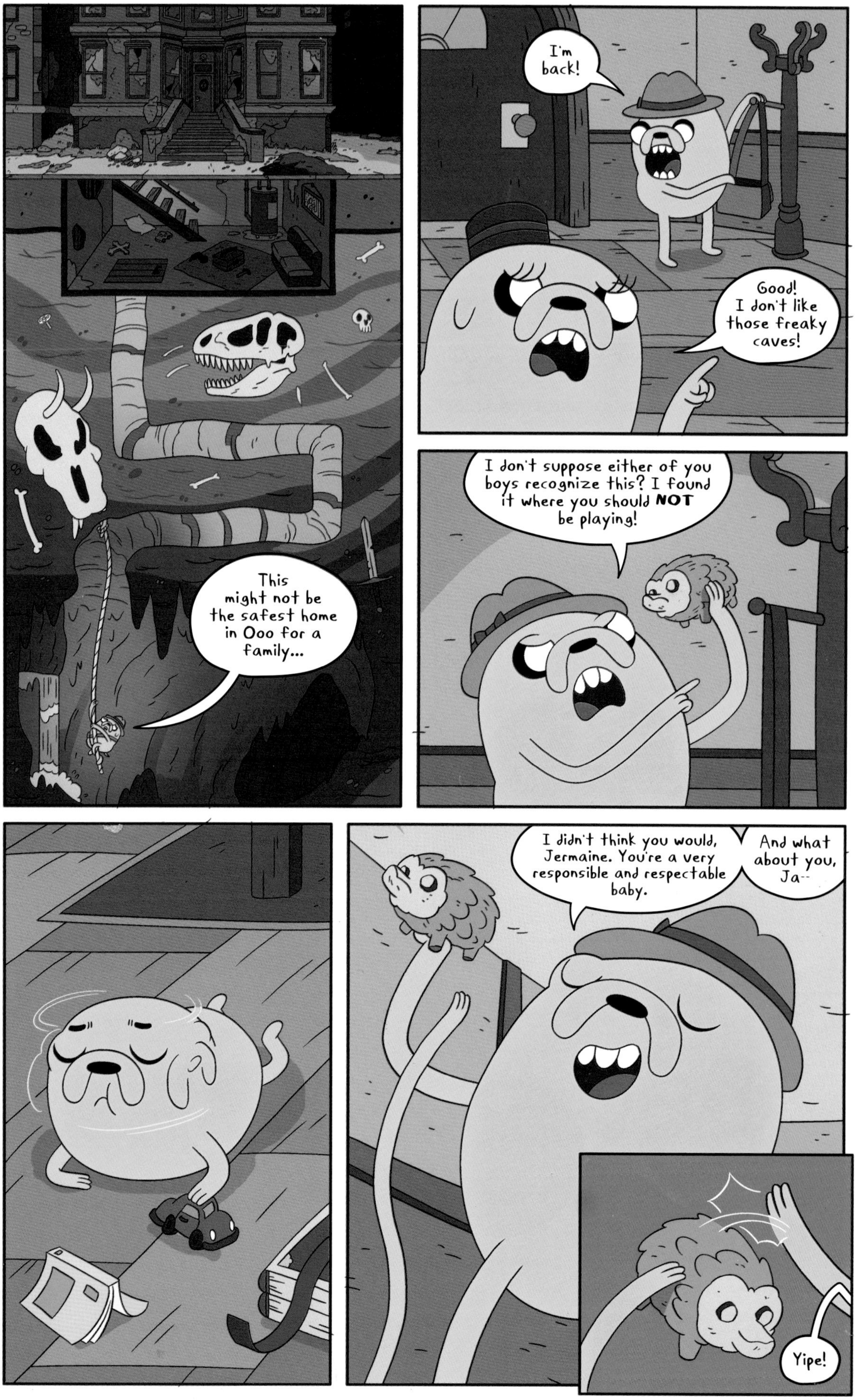
This might not be the safest home in Ooo for a family...
I'm back!
Good! I don't like those freaky caves!
I don't suppose either of you boys recognize this? I found it where you should NOT be playing!
I didn't think you would, Jermaine. You're a very responsible and respectable baby.
And what about you, Ja--
Yipe!

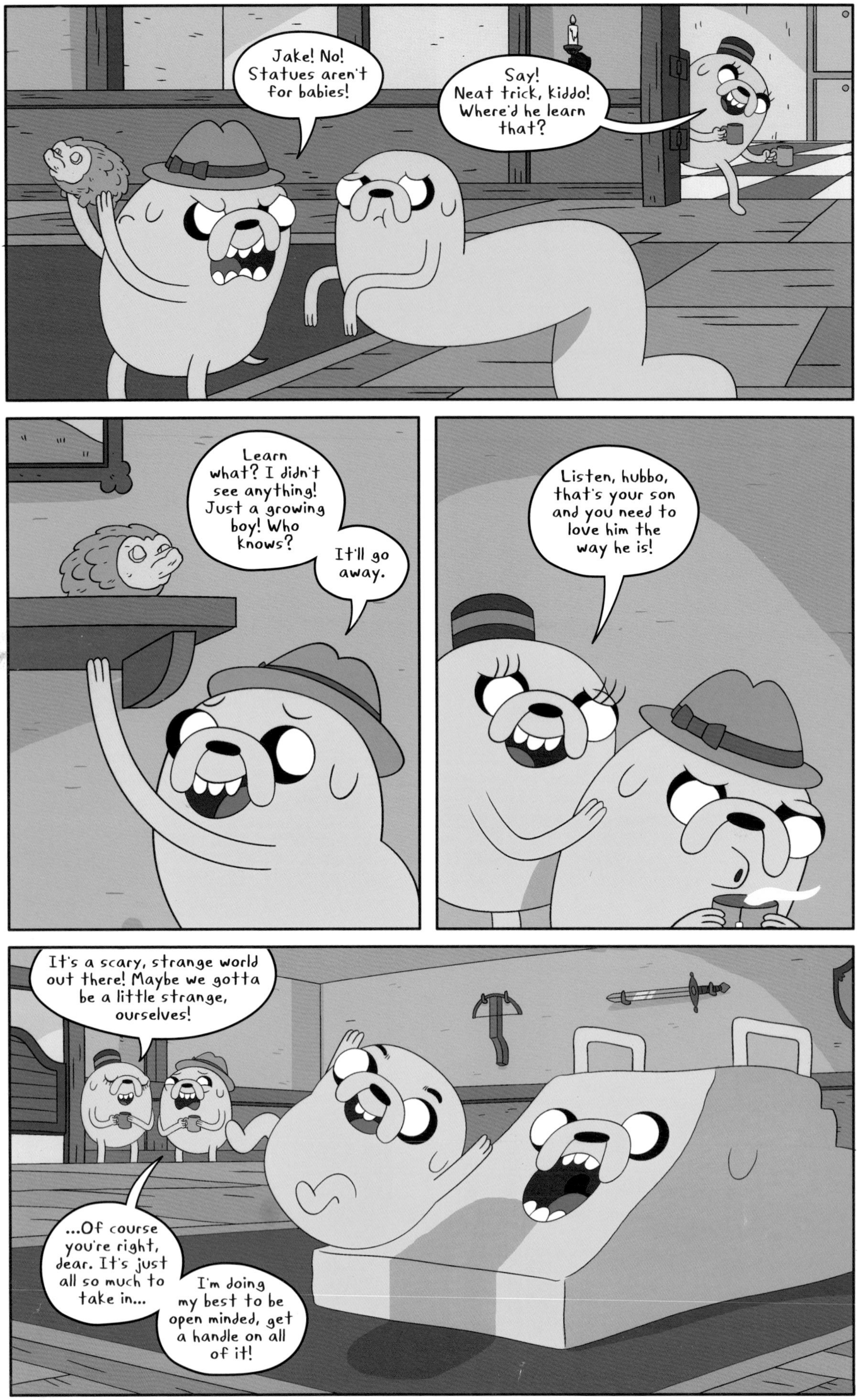
Jake! No! Statues aren't for babies!
Say! Neat trick, kiddo! Where'd he learn that?
Learn what? I didn't see anything! Just a growing boy! Who knows?
It'll go away.
Listen, hubbo, that's your son and you need to love him the way he is!
It's a scary, strange world out there! Maybe we gotta be a little strange, ourselves!
...Of course you're right, dear. It's just all so much to take in...
I'm doing my best to be open minded, get a handle on all of it!

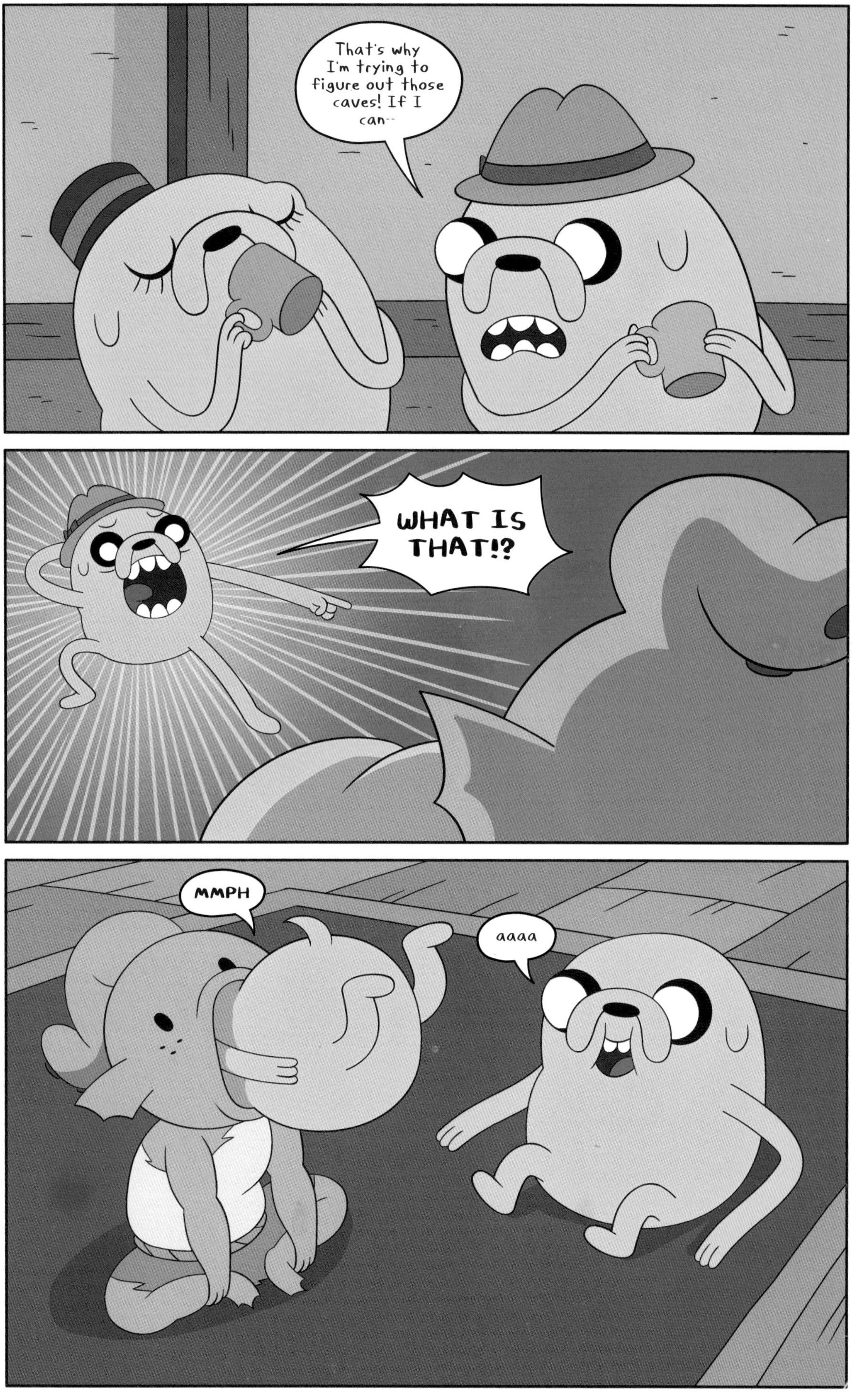
That's why I'm trying to figure out those caves! If I can--
WHAT IS THAT!?
MMPH
aaaa

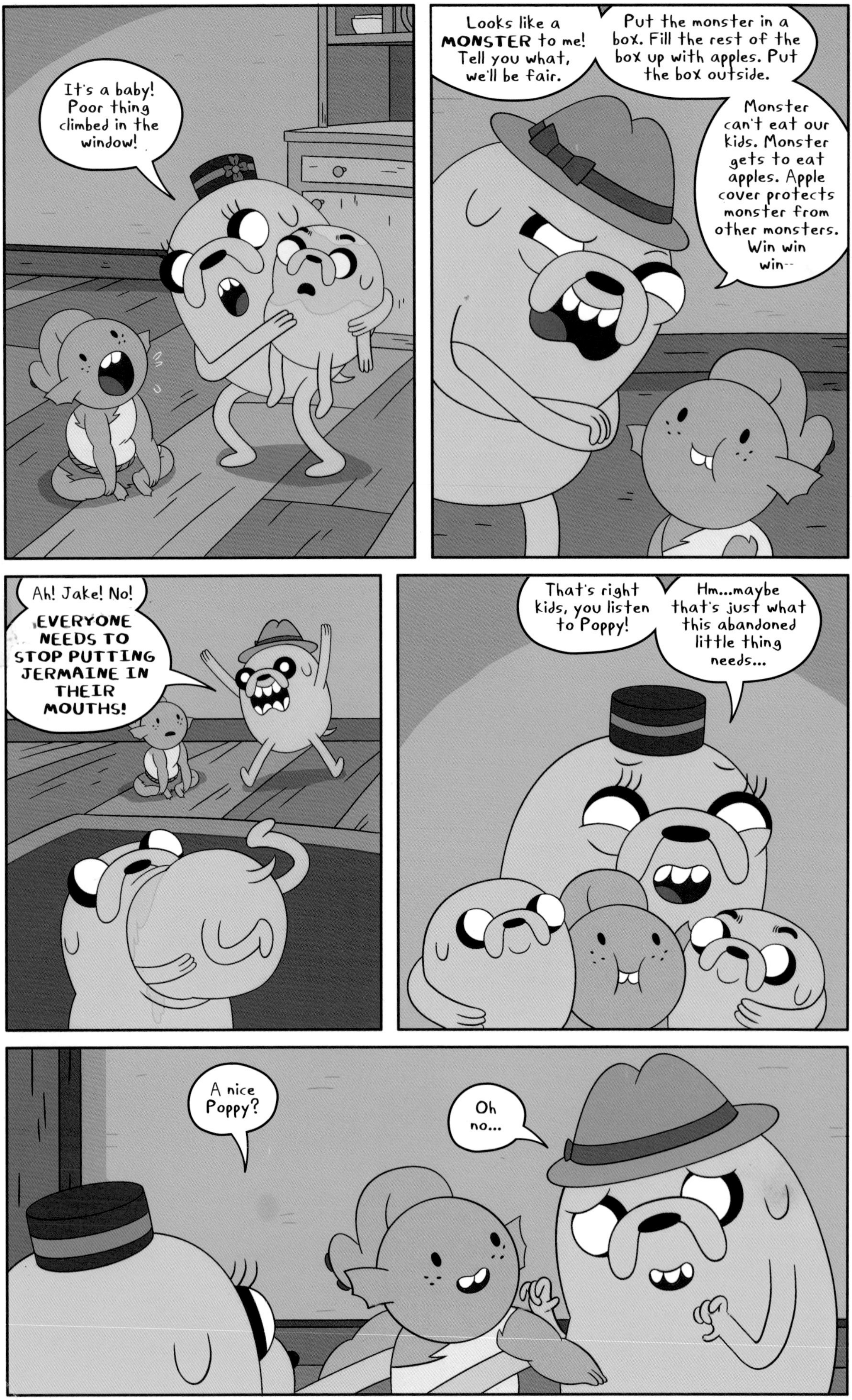
It's a baby! Poor thing climbed in the window!
Looks like a MONSTER to me! Tell you what, we'll be fair.
Put the monster in a box. Fill the rest of the box up with apples. Put the box outside.
Monster can't eat our kids. Monster gets to eat apples. Apple cover protects monster from other monsters. Win win win--
Ah! Jake! No!
EVERYONE NEEDS TO STOP PUTTING JERMAINE IN THEIR MOUTHS!
That's right kids, you listen to Poppy!
Hm...maybe that's just what this abandoned little thing needs...
A nice Poppy?
Oh no...

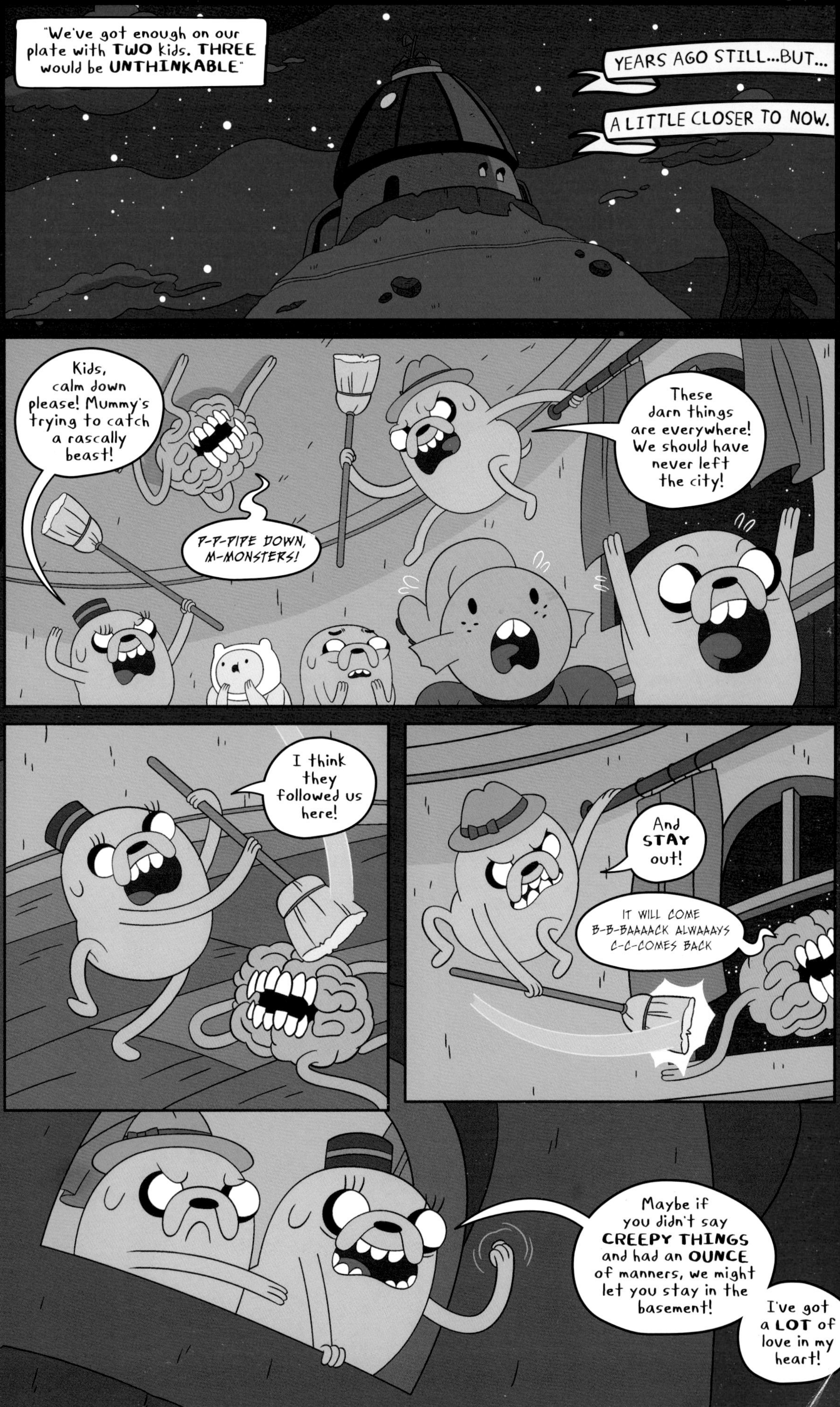

"We've got enough on our plate with TWO kids. THREE would be UNTHINKABLE"
YEARS AGO STILL...BUT...
A LITTLE CLOSER TO NOW.
Kids, calm down please! Mummy's trying to catch a rascally beast!
These darn things are everywhere! We should have never left the city!
P-P-PIPE DOWN, M-MONSTERS!
I think they followed us here!
And STAY out!
IT WILL COME B-B-BAAAACK ALWAAAYS C-C-COMES BACK
Maybe if you didn't say CREEPY THINGS and had an OUNCE of manners, we might let you stay in the basement!
I've got a LOT of love in my heart!

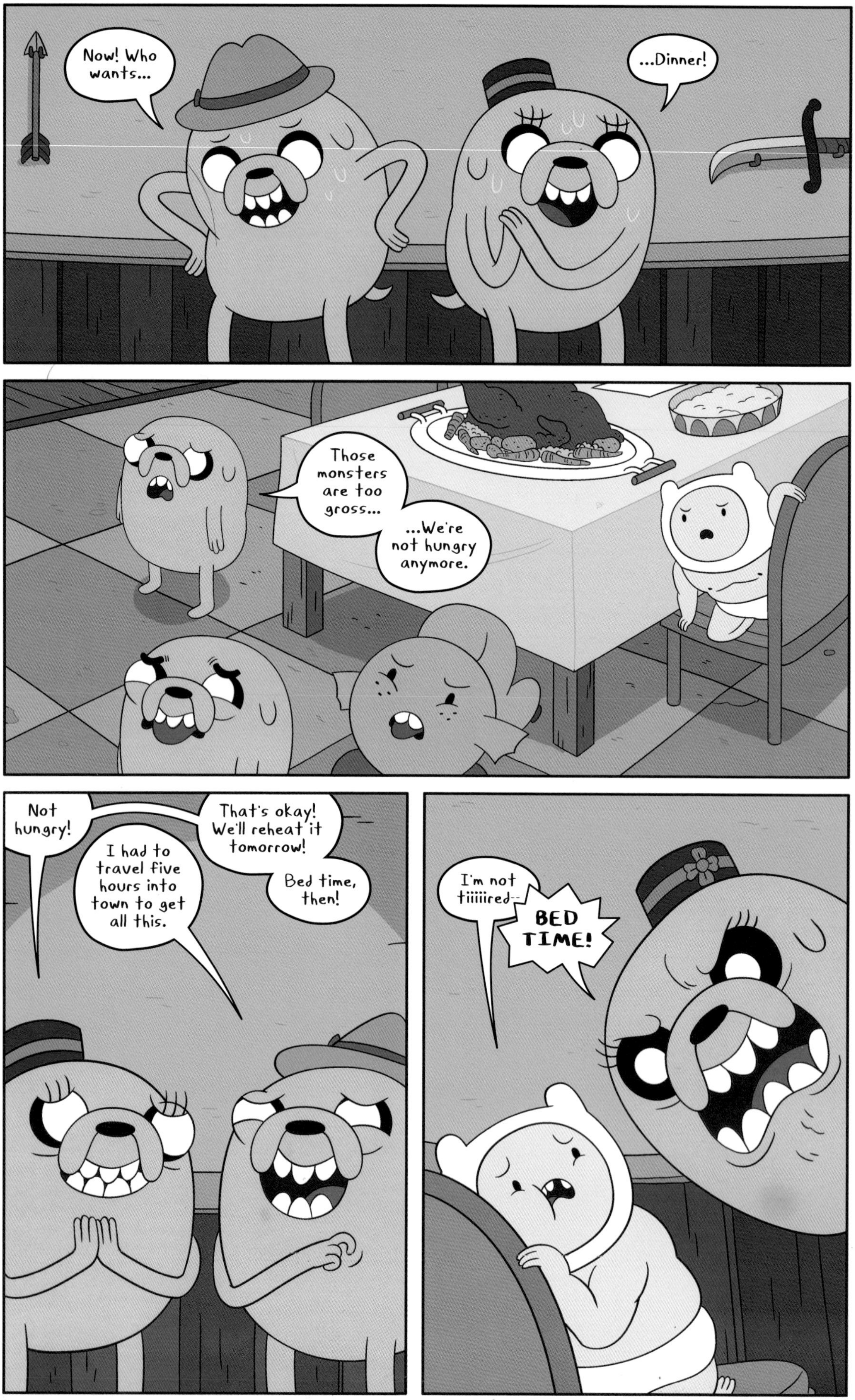
Now! Who wants...
...Dinner!
Those monsters are too gross...
...We're not hungry anymore.
Not hungry!
I had to travel five hours into town to get all this.
That's okay! We'll reheat it tomorrow!
Bed time, then!
I'm not tiiiiired--
BED TIME!

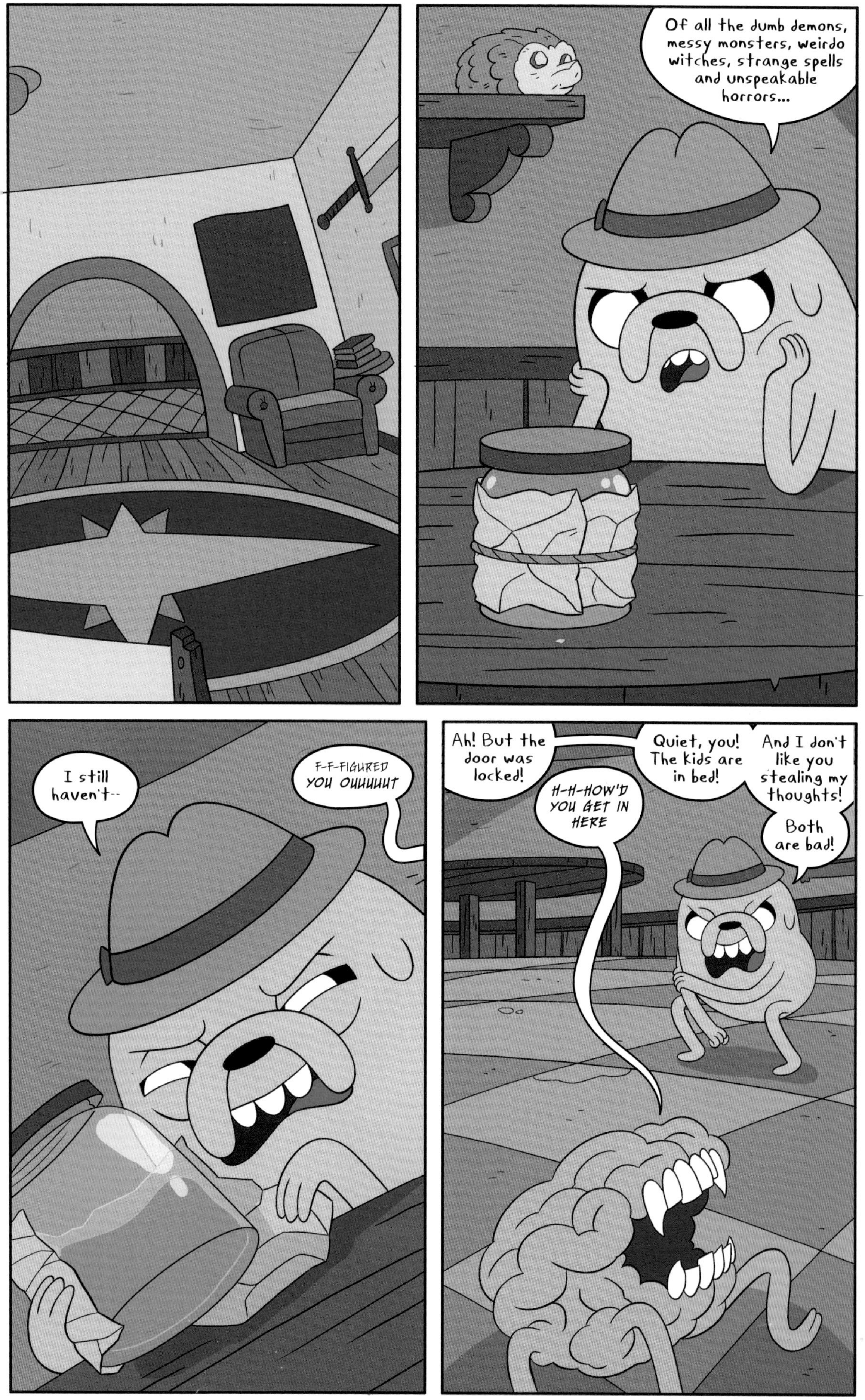
Of all the dumb demons, messy monsters, weirdo witches, strange spells and unspeakable horrors...
I still haven't--
F-F-FIGURED YOU OUUUUUT
Ah! But the door was locked!
H-H-HOW'D YOU GET IN HERE
Quiet, you! The kids are in bed!
And I don't like you stealing my thoughts!
Both are bad!

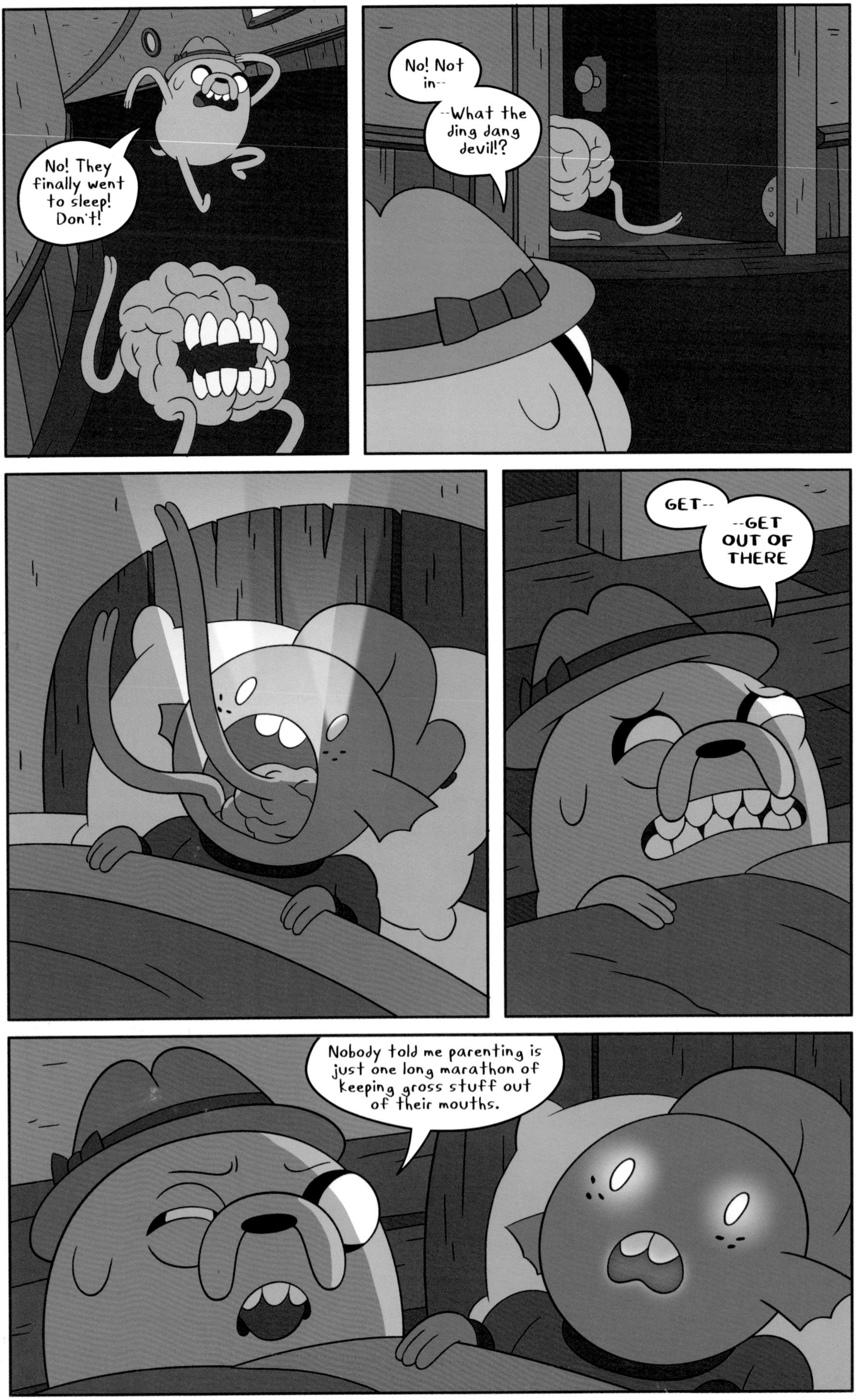
No! They finally went to sleep! Don't!
No! Not in--
--What the ding dang devil!?
GET--
--GET OUT OF THERE
Nobody told me parenting is just one long marathon of keeping gross stuff out of their mouths.

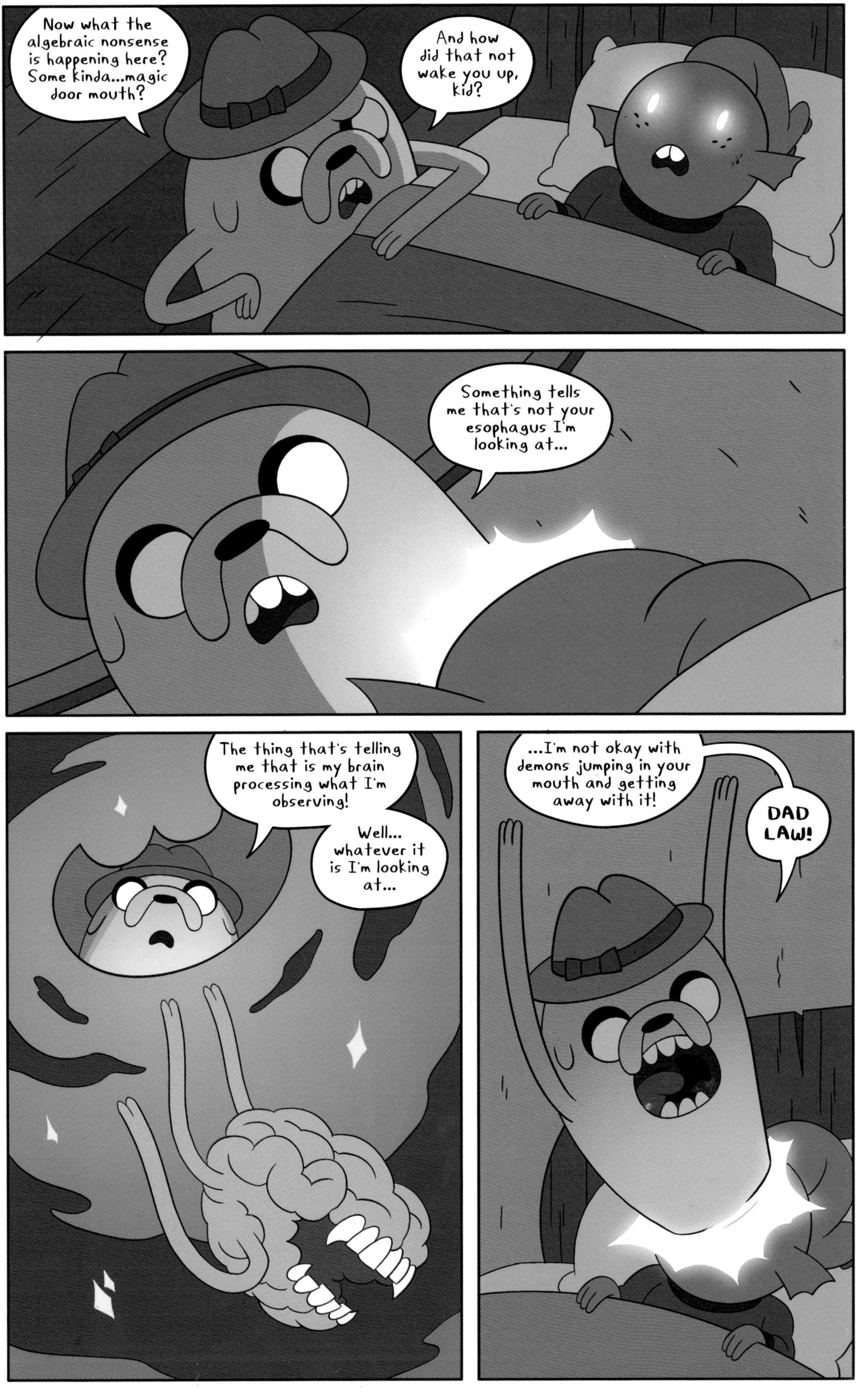

Now what the algebraic nonsense is happening here? Some kinda...magic door mouth?
And how did that not wake you up, kid?
Something tells me that's not your esophagus I'm looking at...
The thing that's telling me that is my brain processing what I'm observing!
Well... whatever it is I'm looking at...
...I'm not okay with demons jumping in your mouth and getting away with it!
DAD LAW!

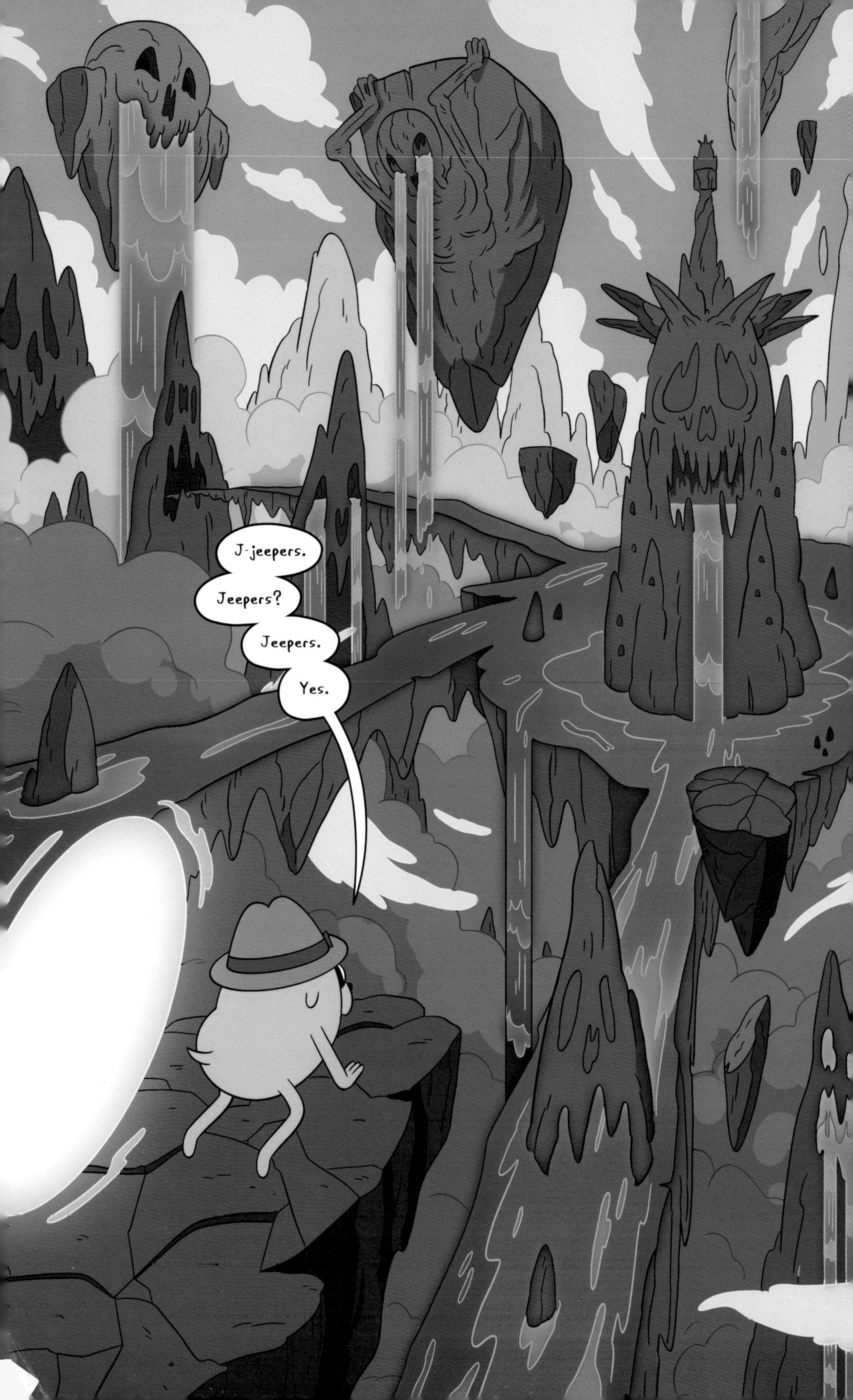
J-jeepers.
Jeepers?
Jeepers.
Yes.

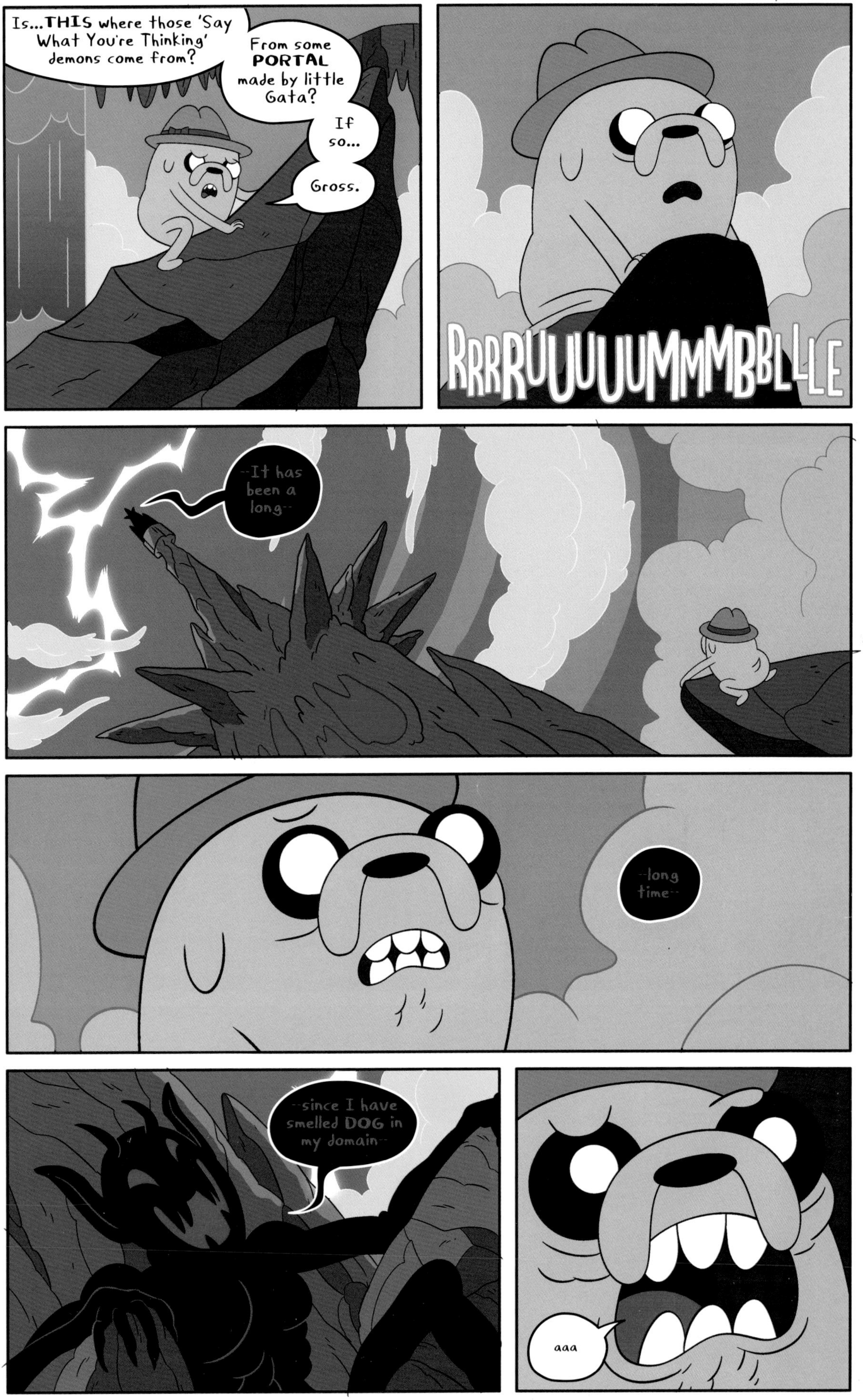
Is...THIS where those 'Say What You're Thinking' demons come from?
From some PORTAL made by little Gata?
If so...
Gross.
RRRRUUUUMMMBBLLLE
--It has been a long--
--long time--
--since I have smelled DOG in my domain--
aaa

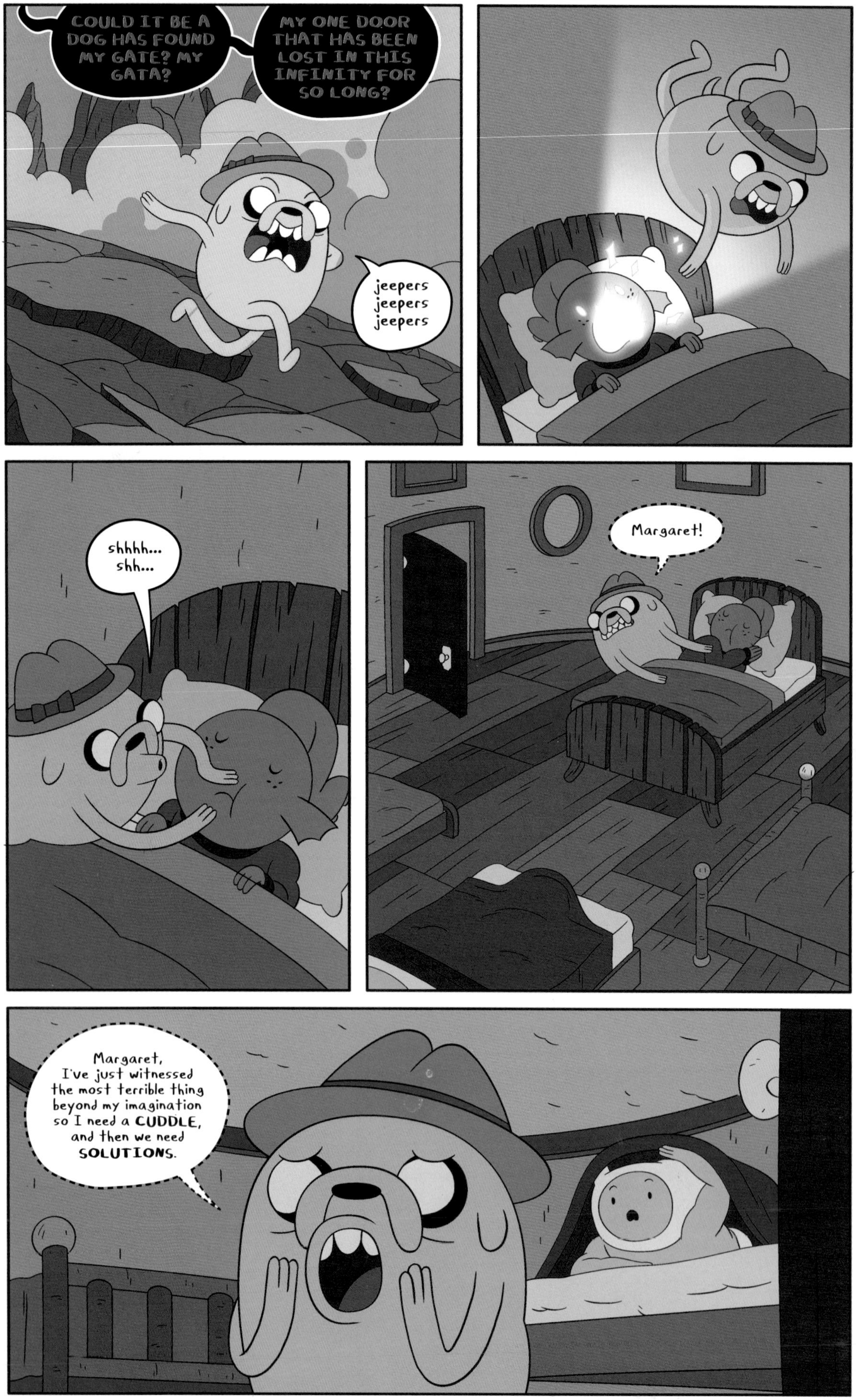
COULD IT BE A DOG HAS FOUND MY GATE? MY GATA?
MY ONE DOOR THAT HAS BEEN LOST IN THIS INFINITY FOR SO LONG?
jeepers jeepers jeepers
shhhh... shh...
Margaret!
Margaret, I've just witnessed the most terrible thing beyond my imagination so I need a CUDDLE, and then we need SOLUTIONS.

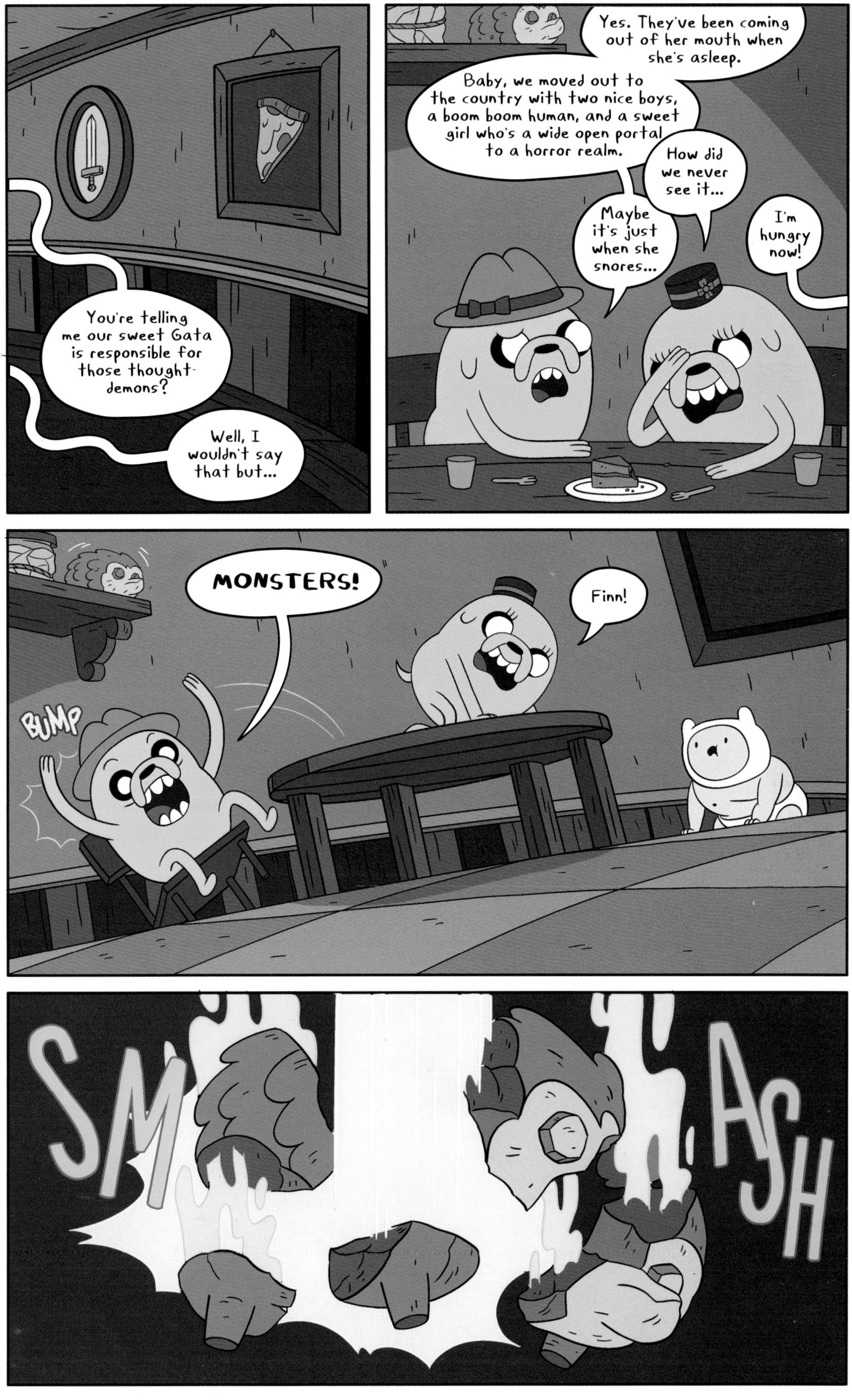
You're telling me our sweet Gata is responsible for those thought-demons?
Well, I wouldn't say that but...
Yes. They've been coming out of her mouth when she's asleep.
Baby, we moved out to the country with two nice boys, a boom boom human, and a sweet girl who's a wide open portal to a horror realm.
How did we never see it...
Maybe it's just when she snores...
I'm hungry now!
MONSTERS!
Finn!
BUMP
SMASH

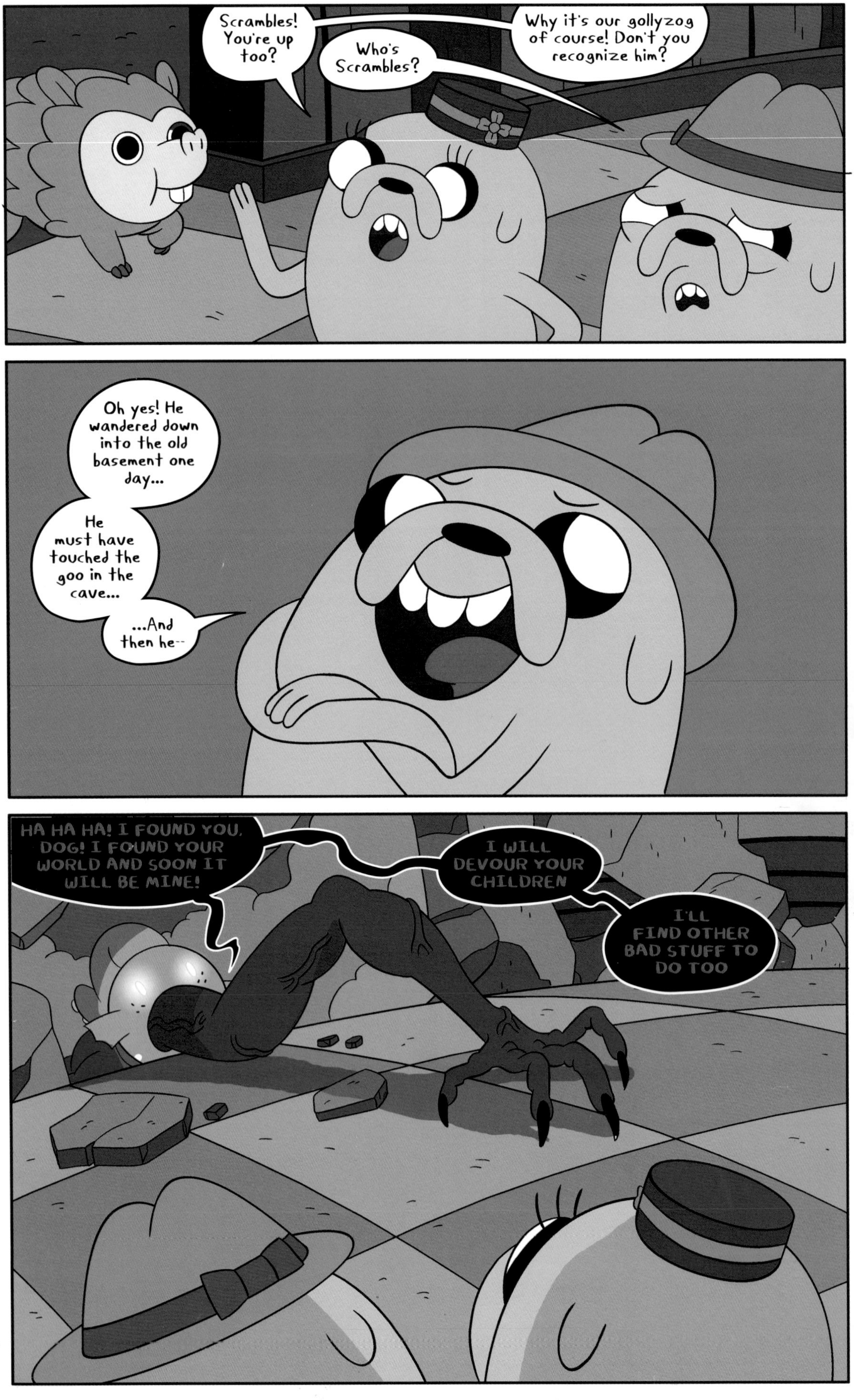
Scrambles! You're up too?
Who's Scrambles?
Why it's our gollyzog of course! Don't you recognize him?
Oh yes! He wandered down into the old basement one day...
He must have touched the goo in the cave...
...And then he--
HA HA HA! I FOUND YOU, DOG! I FOUND YOUR WORLD AND SOON IT WILL BE MINE!
I WILL DEVOUR YOUR CHILDREN
I'LL FIND OTHER BAD STUFF TO DO TOO

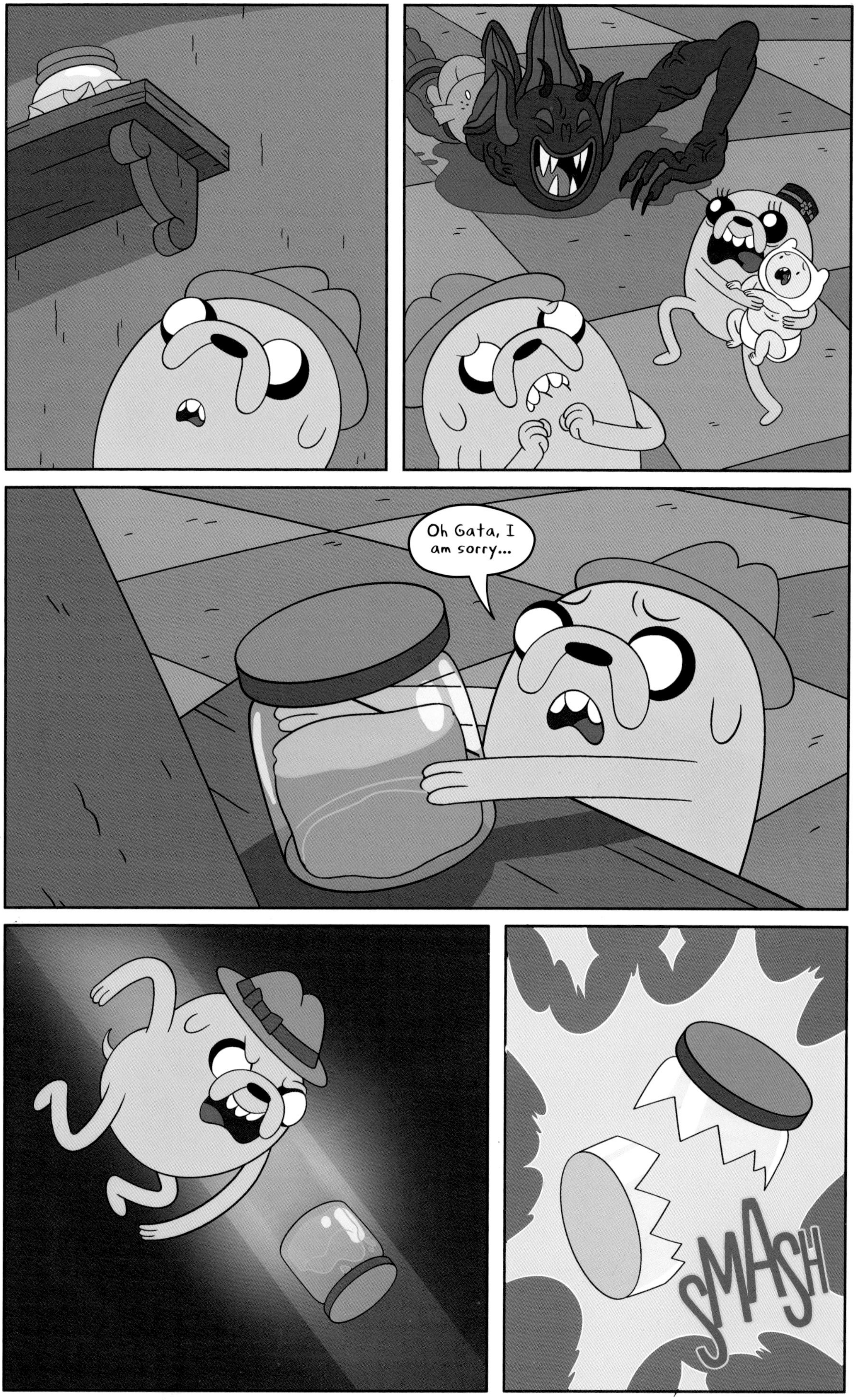
Oh Gata, I am sorry...
SMASH

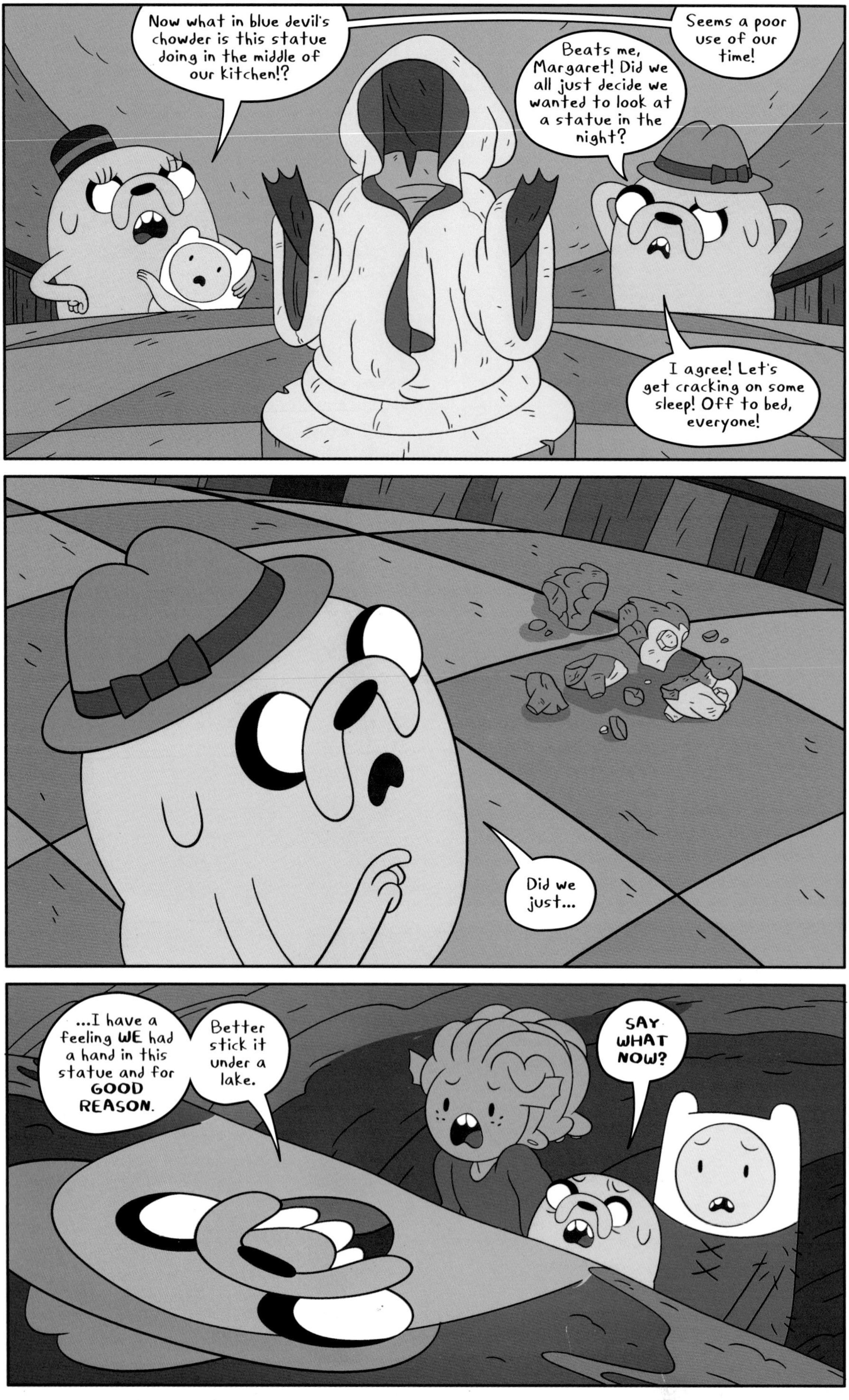
Now what in blue devil's chowder is this statue doing in the middle of our kitchen!?
Seems a poor use of our time!
Beats me, Margaret! Did we all just decide we wanted to look at a statue in the night?
I agree! Let's get cracking on some sleep! Off to bed, everyone!
Did we just...
...I have a feeling **WE** had a hand in this statue and for **GOOD REASON**.
Better stick it under a lake.
SAY WHAT NOW?

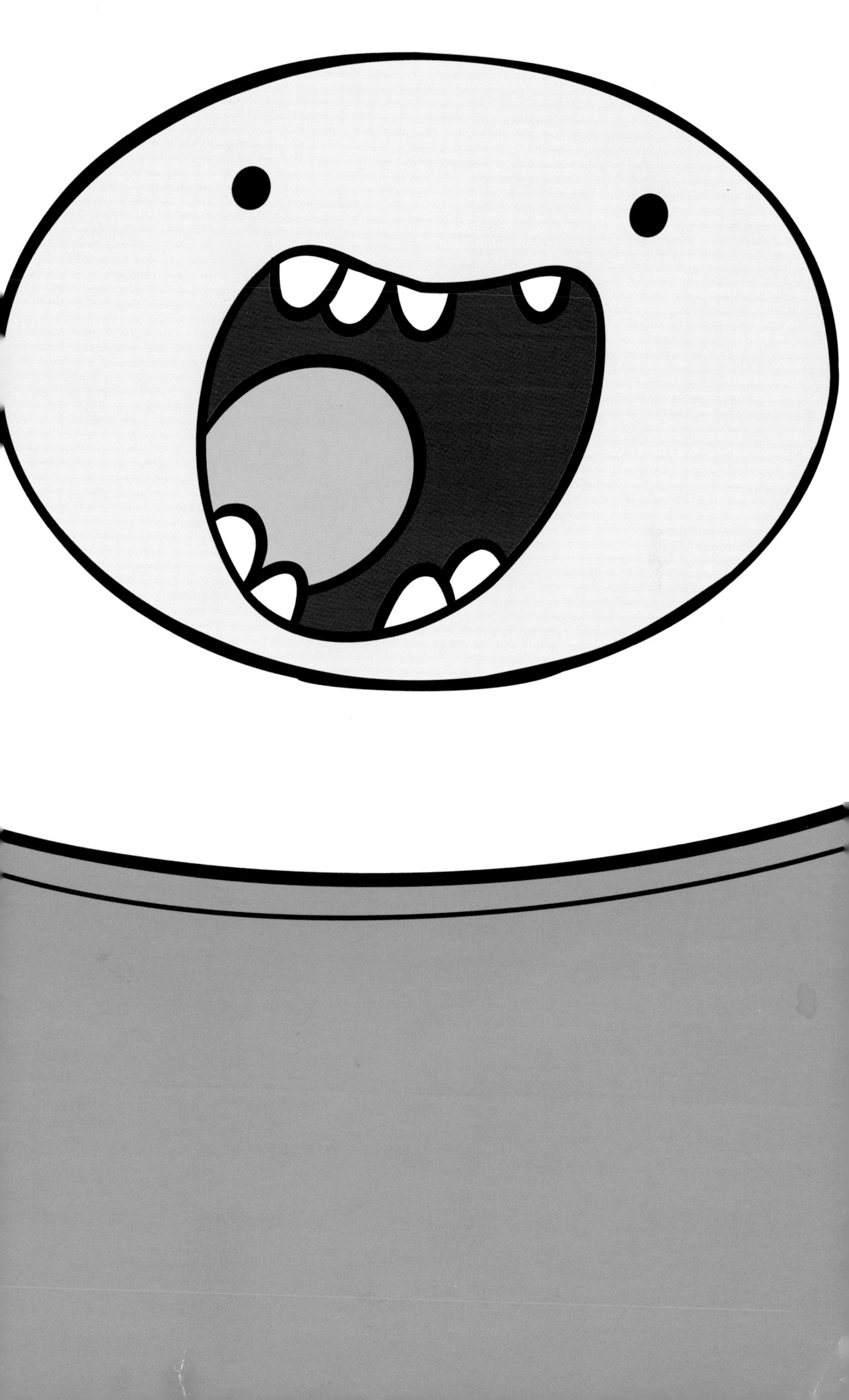

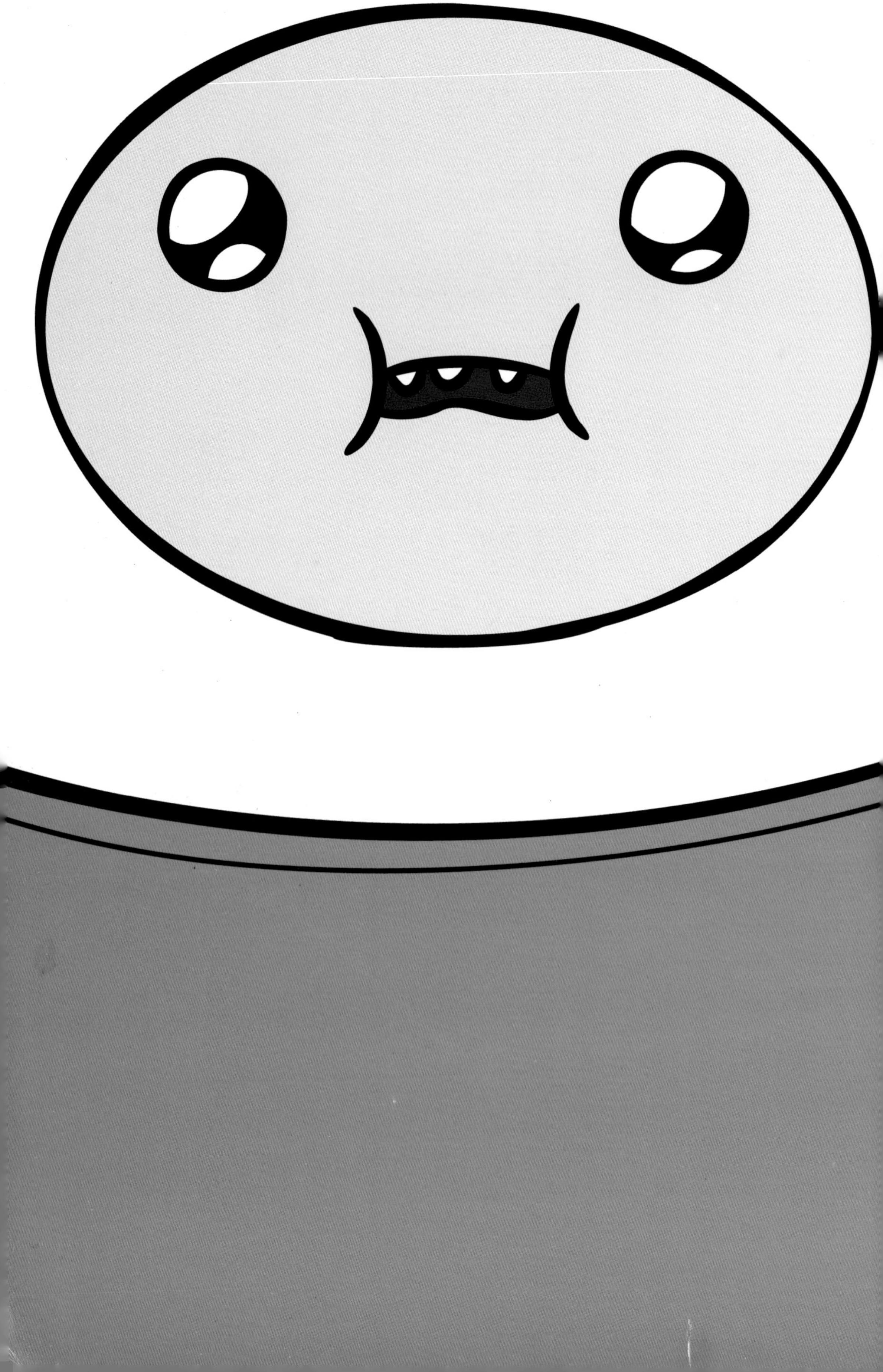

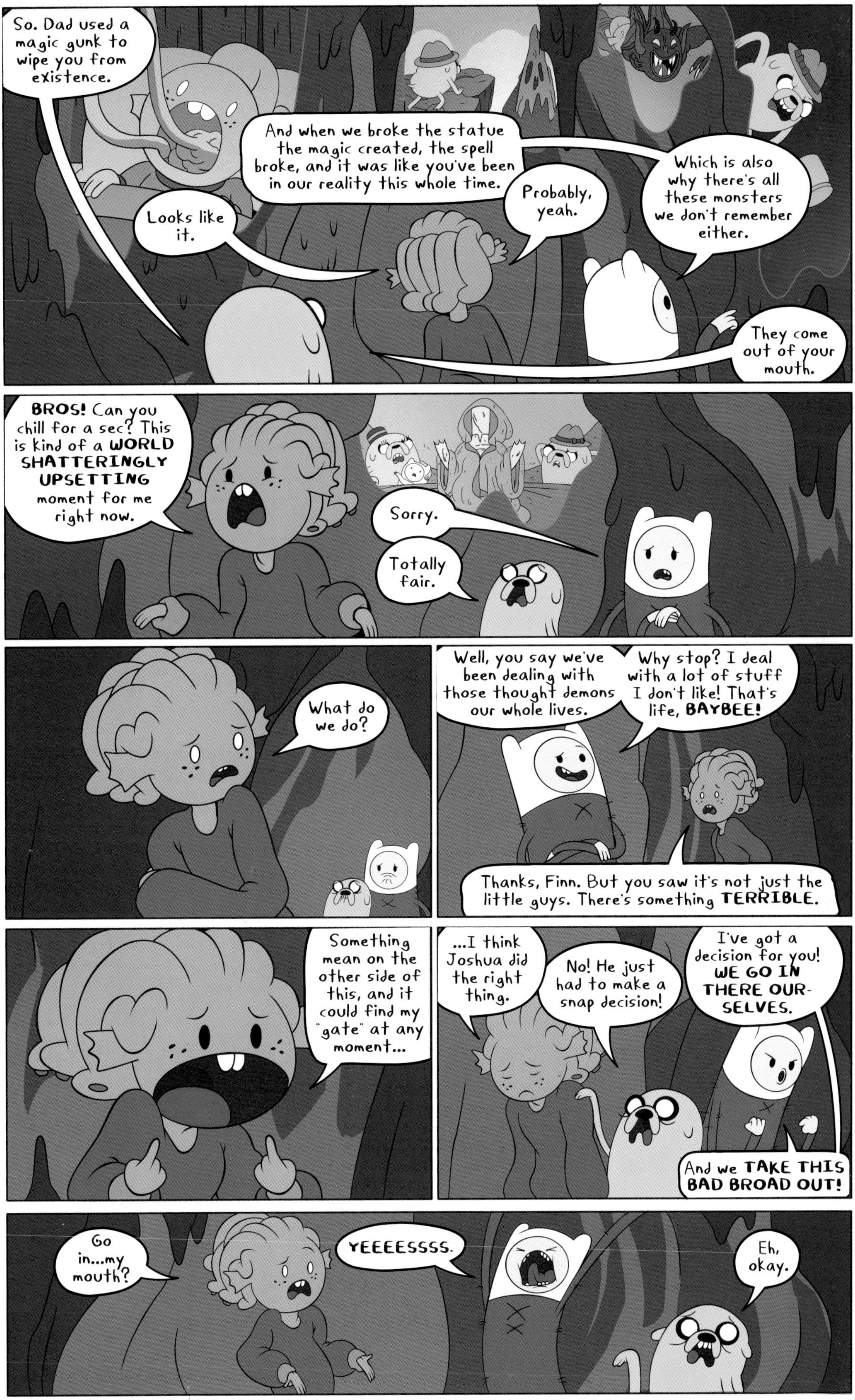

So. Dad used a magic gunk to wipe you from existence.
And when we broke the statue the magic created, the spell broke, and it was like you've been in our reality this whole time.
Looks like it.
Probably, yeah.
Which is also why there's all these monsters we don't remember either.
They come out of your mouth.
BROS! Can you chill for a sec? This is kind of a **WORLD SHATTERINGLY UPSETTING** moment for me right now.
Sorry.
Totally fair.
What do we do?
Well, you say we've been dealing with those thought demons our whole lives.
Why stop? I deal with a lot of stuff I don't like! That's life, **BAYBEE!**
Thanks, Finn. But you saw it's not just the little guys. There's something **TERRIBLE.**
Something mean on the other side of this, and it could find my "gate" at any moment...
...I think Joshua did the right thing.
No! He just had to make a snap decision!
I've got a decision for you! **WE GO IN THERE OURSELVES.**
And we **TAKE THIS BAD BROAD OUT!**
Go in...my mouth?
YEEEEESSSS.
Eh, okay.

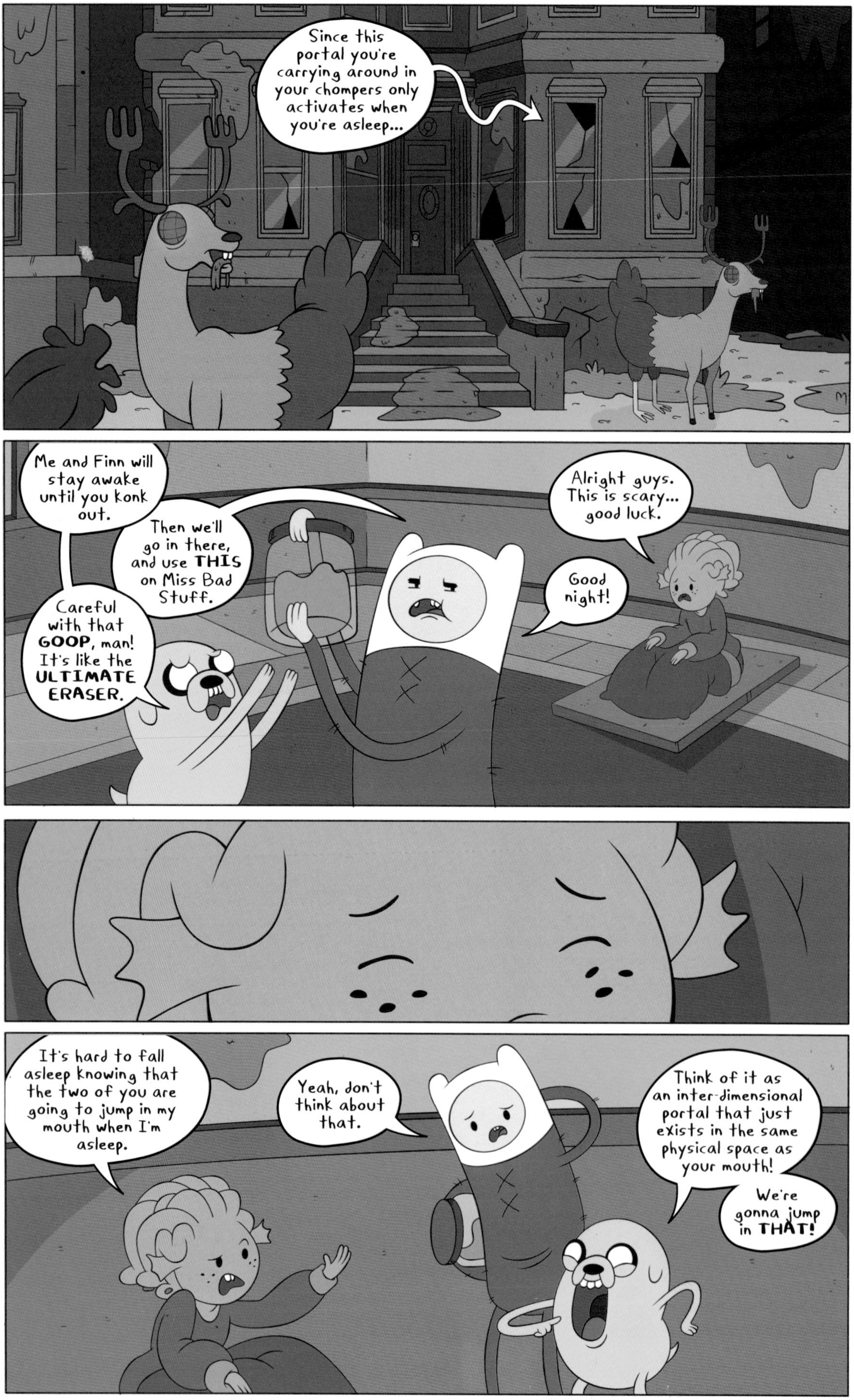
Since this portal you're carrying around in your chompers only activates when you're asleep...
Me and Finn will stay awake until you konk out.
Then we'll go in there, and use **THIS** on Miss Bad Stuff.
Careful with that **GOOP**, man! It's like the **ULTIMATE ERASER.**
Alright guys. This is scary... good luck.
Good night!
It's hard to fall asleep knowing that the two of you are going to jump in my mouth when I'm asleep.
Yeah, don't think about that.
Think of it as an inter-dimensional portal that just exists in the same physical space as your mouth!
We're gonna jump in **THAT!**

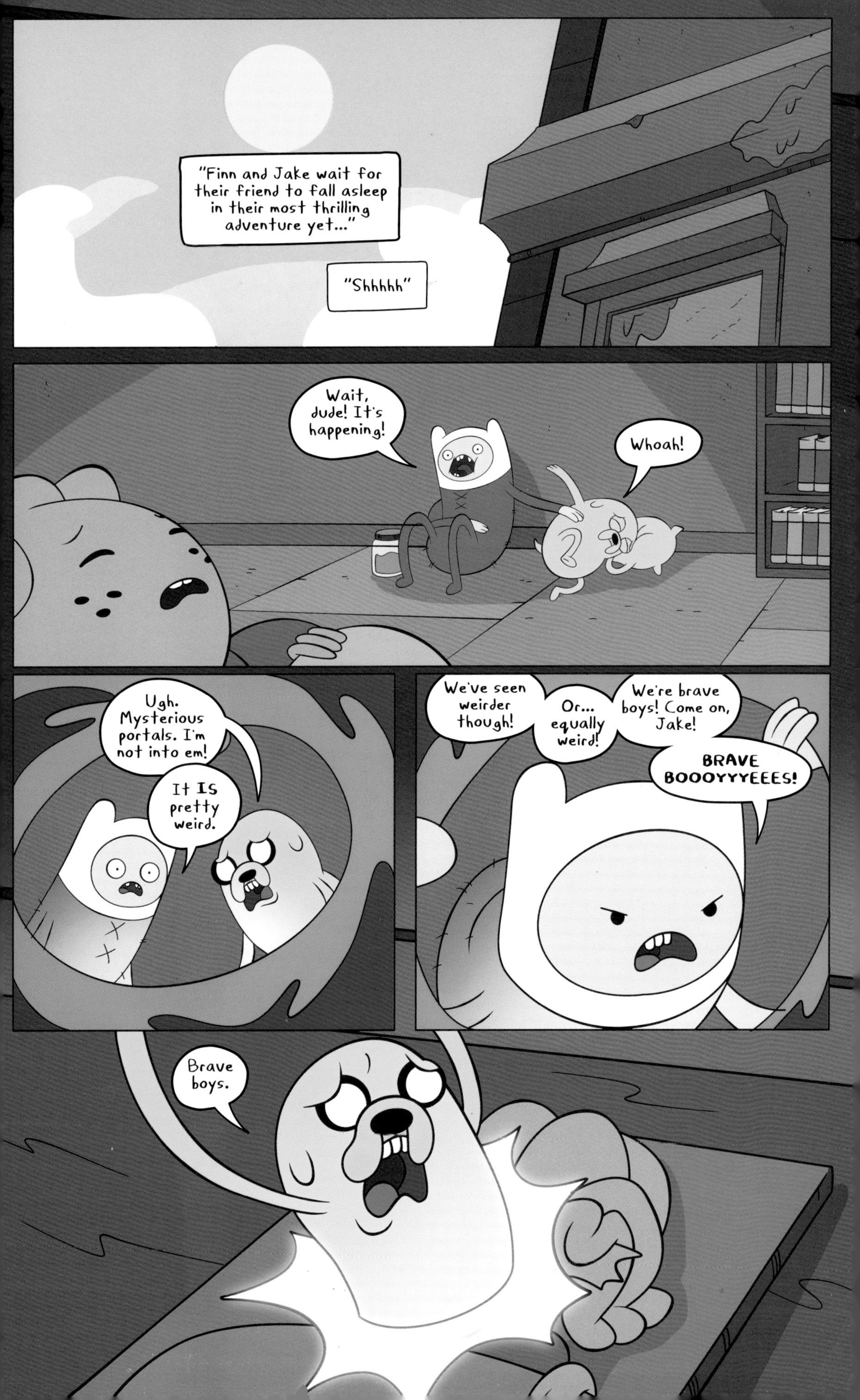
"Finn and Jake wait for their friend to fall asleep in their most thrilling adventure yet..."
"Shhhhh"
Wait, dude! It's happening!
Whoah!
Ugh. Mysterious portals. I'm not into em!
It IS pretty weird.
We've seen weirder though!
Or... equally weird!
We're brave boys! Come on, Jake!
BRAVE BOOOYYYEEES!
Brave boys.

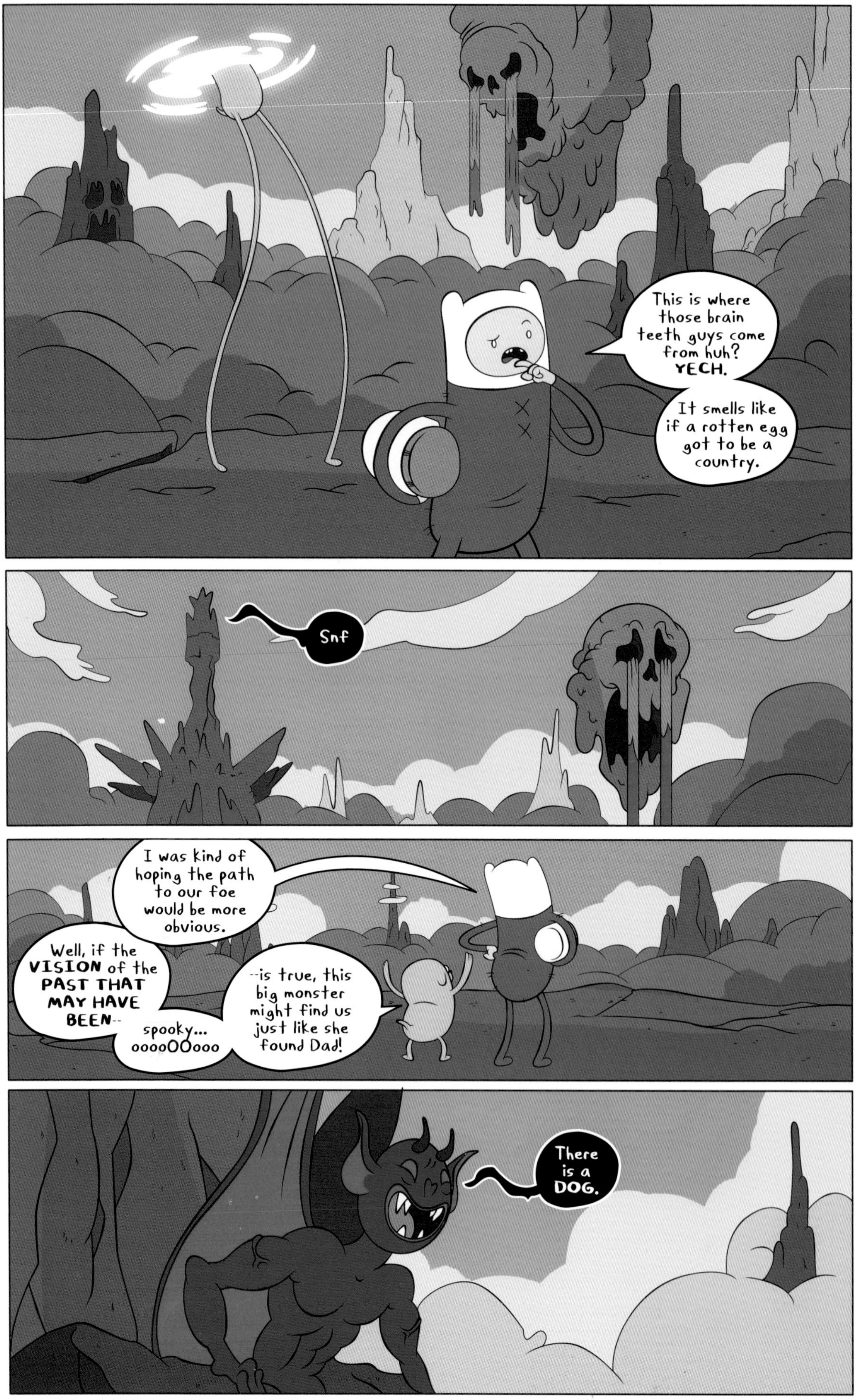
This is where those brain teeth guys come from huh? **YECH.**
It smells like if a rotten egg got to be a country.
Snf
I was kind of hoping the path to our foe would be more obvious.
Well, if the **VISION** of the **PAST THAT MAY HAVE BEEN**--
spooky... oooo0Oooo
--is true, this big monster might find us just like she found Dad!
There is a **DOG.**

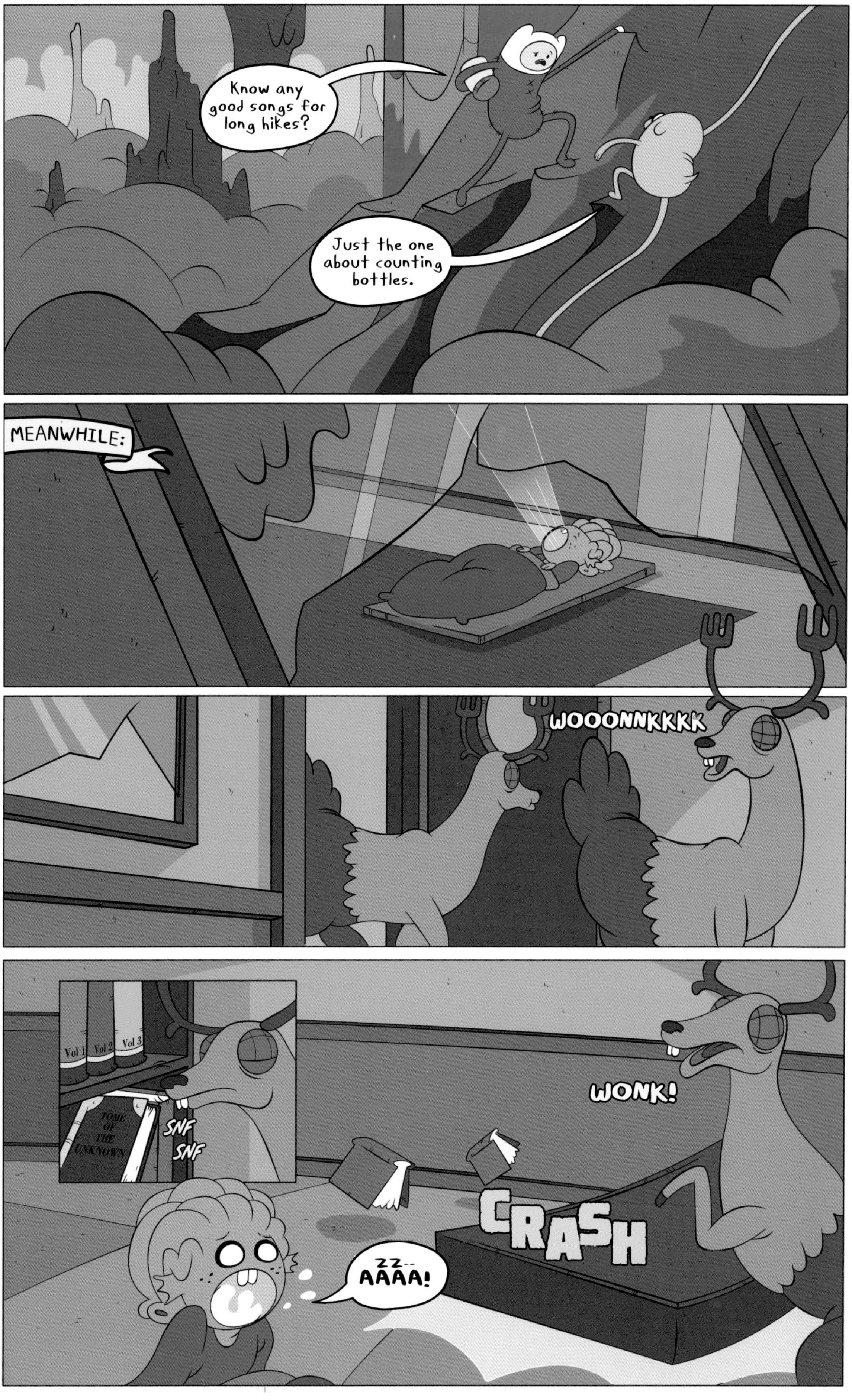
Know any good songs for long hikes?
Just the one about counting bottles.
MEANWHILE:
WOOONNKKKK
Vol 1
Vol 2
Vol 3
TOME OF THE UNKNOWN
SNF
SNF
WONK!
CRASH
ZZ-- AAAA!

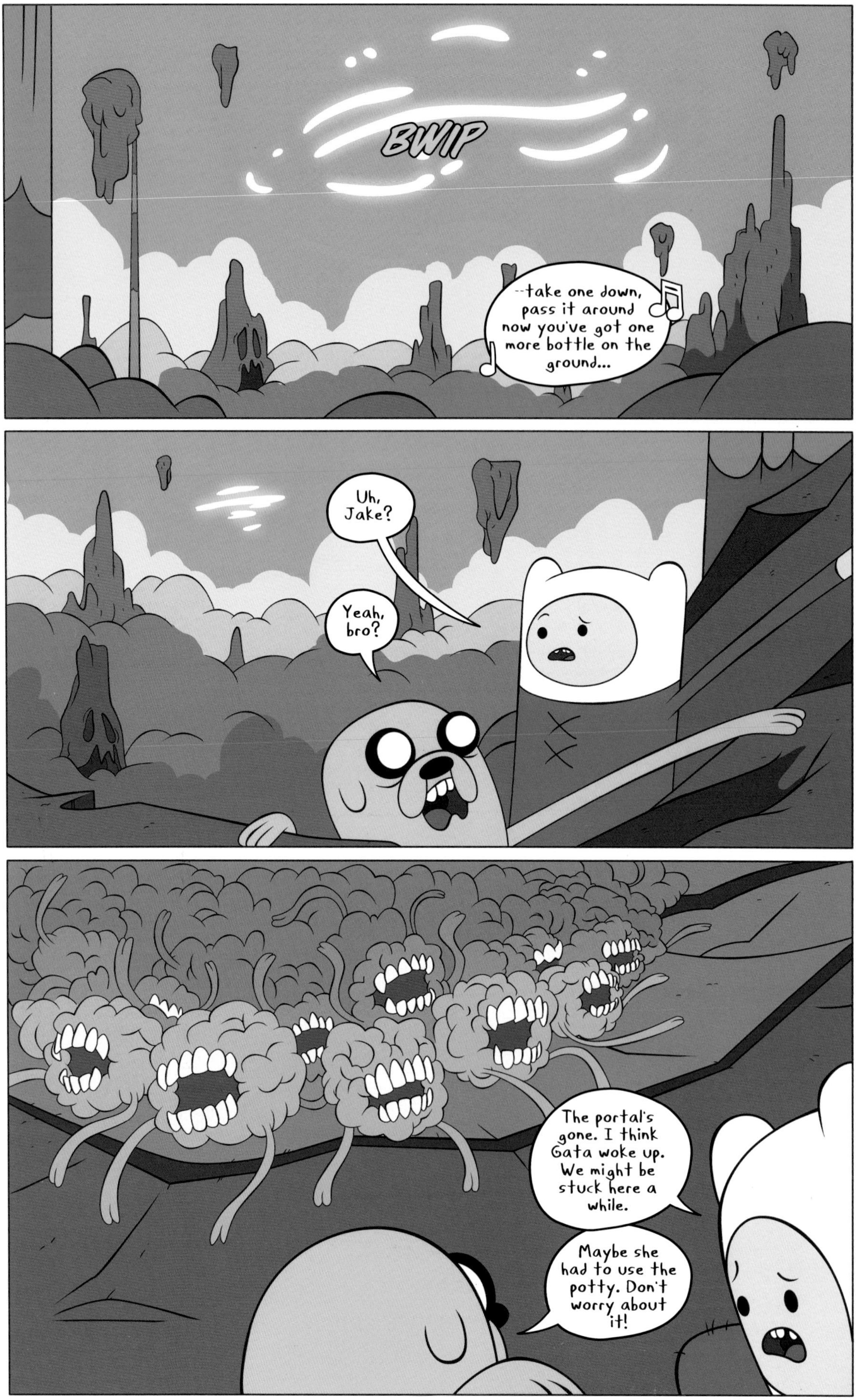
BWIP
--take one down, pass it around now you've got one more bottle on the ground...
Uh, Jake?
Yeah, bro?
The portal's gone. I think Gata woke up. We might be stuck here a while.
Maybe she had to use the potty. Don't worry about it!

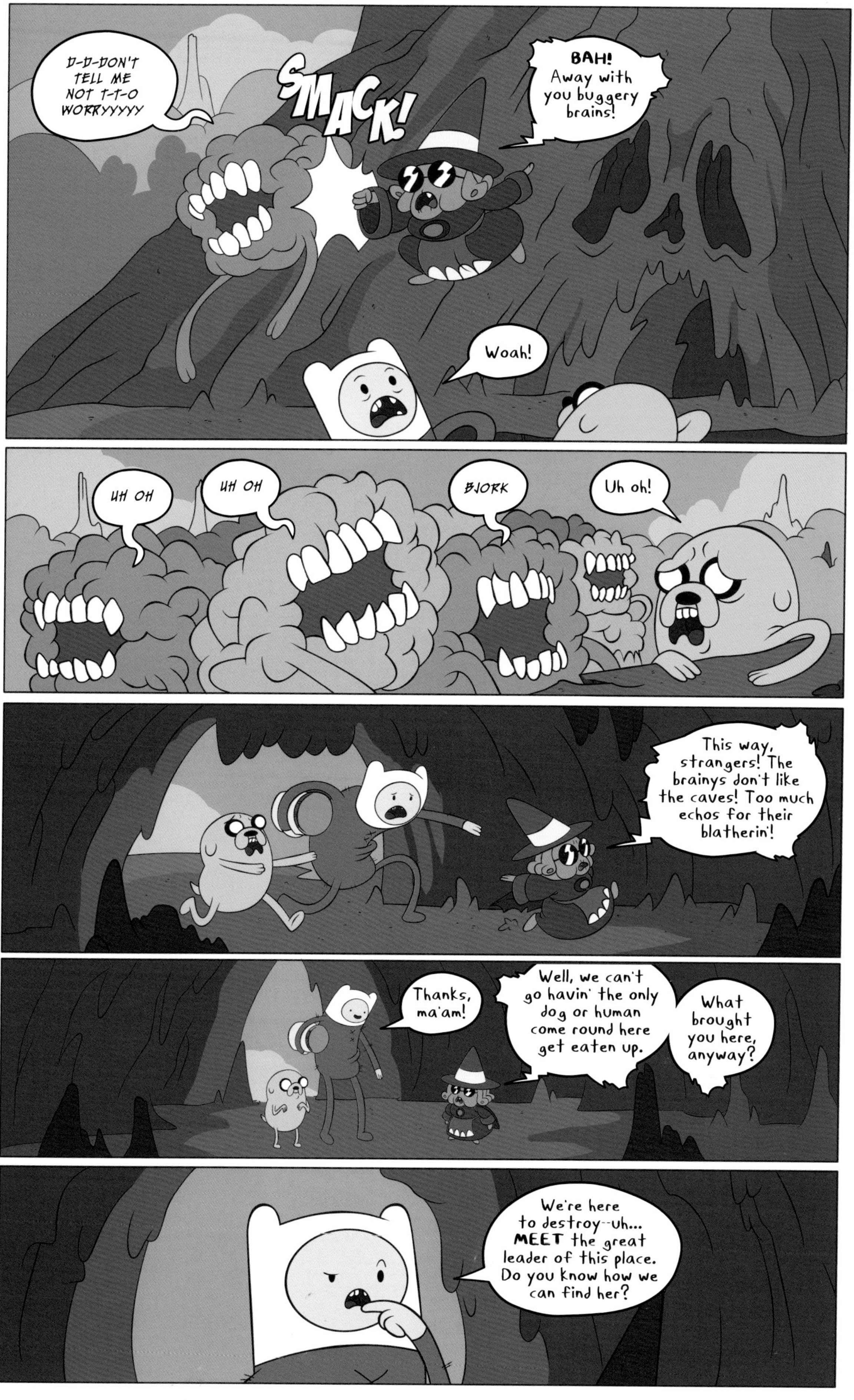
D-D-DON'T TELL ME NOT T-T-O WORRYYYYY
SMACK!
BAH! Away with you buggery brains!
Woah!
UH OH
UH OH
BJORK
Uh oh!
This way, strangers! The brainys don't like the caves! Too much echos for their blatherin'!
Thanks, ma'am!
Well, we can't go havin' the only dog or human come round here get eaten up.
What brought you here, anyway?
We're here to destroy--uh... MEET the great leader of this place. Do you know how we can find her?

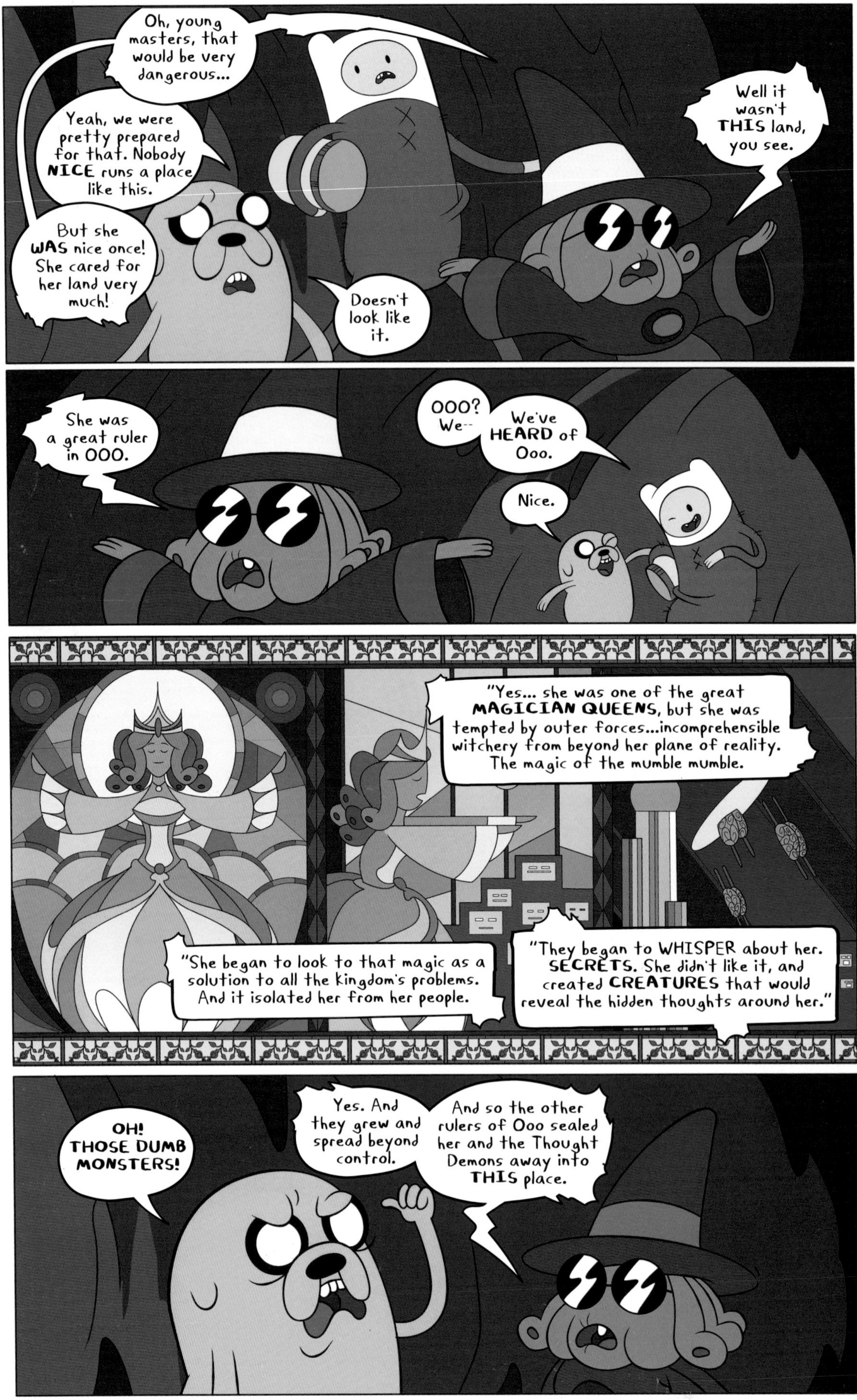
Oh, young masters, that would be very dangerous...
Yeah, we were pretty prepared for that. Nobody NICE runs a place like this.
But she WAS nice once! She cared for her land very much!
Doesn't look like it.
Well it wasn't THIS land, you see.
She was a great ruler in OOO.
OOO? We--
We've HEARD of Ooo.
Nice.
"Yes... she was one of the great MAGICIAN QUEENS, but she was tempted by outer forces...incomprehensible witchery from beyond her plane of reality. The magic of the mumble mumble.
"She began to look to that magic as a solution to all the kingdom's problems. And it isolated her from her people.
"They began to WHISPER about her. SECRETS. She didn't like it, and created CREATURES that would reveal the hidden thoughts around her."
OH! THOSE DUMB MONSTERS!
Yes. And they grew and spread beyond control.
And so the other rulers of Ooo sealed her and the Thought Demons away into THIS place.

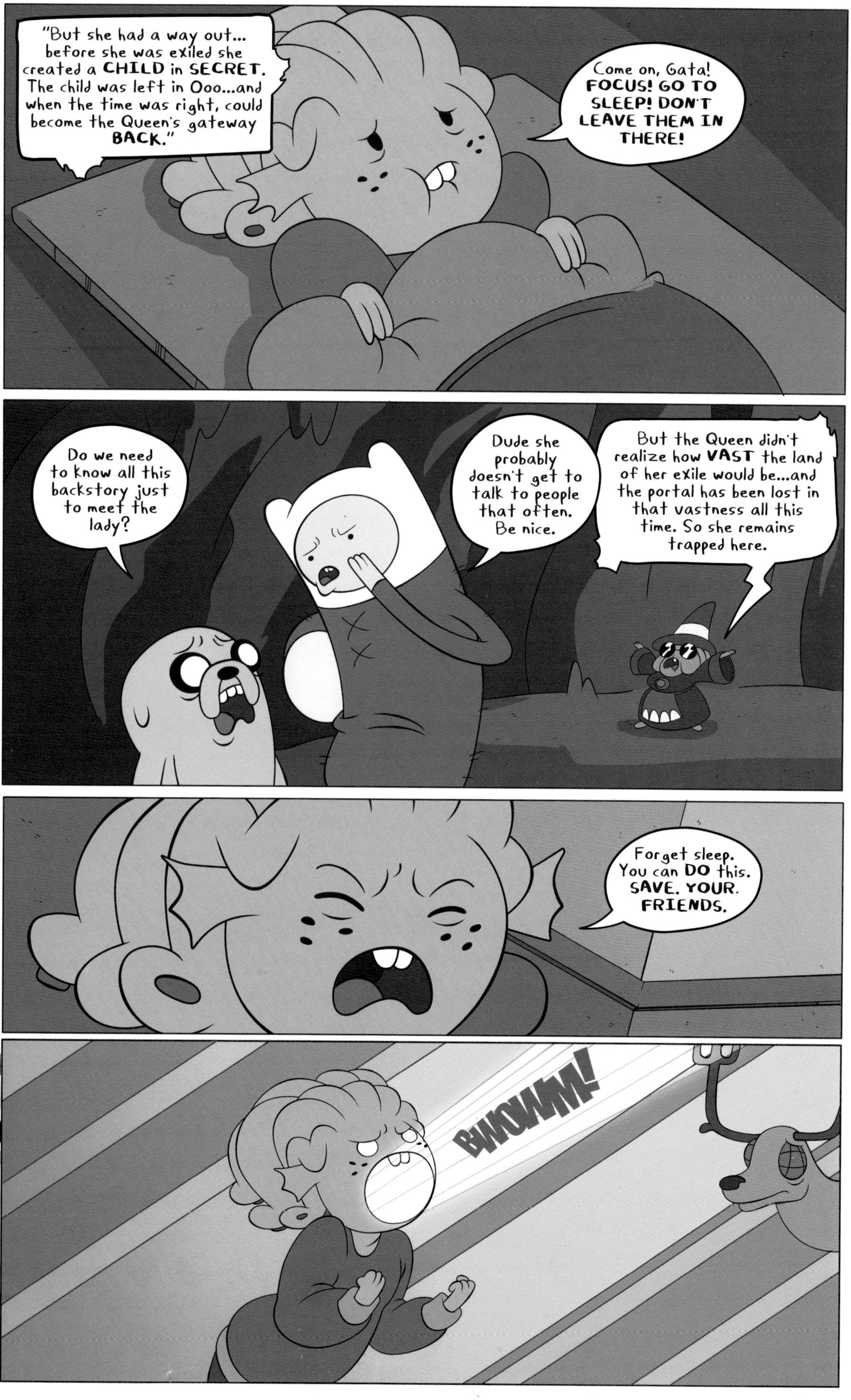
"But she had a way out... before she was exiled she created a CHILD in SECRET. The child was left in Ooo...and when the time was right, could become the Queen's gateway BACK."
Come on, Gata! FOCUS! GO TO SLEEP! DON'T LEAVE THEM IN THERE!
Do we need to know all this backstory just to meet the lady?
Dude she probably doesn't get to talk to people that often. Be nice.
But the Queen didn't realize how VAST the land of her exile would be...and the portal has been lost in that vastness all this time. So she remains trapped here.
Forget sleep. You can DO this. SAVE. YOUR. FRIENDS.
BWOWM!

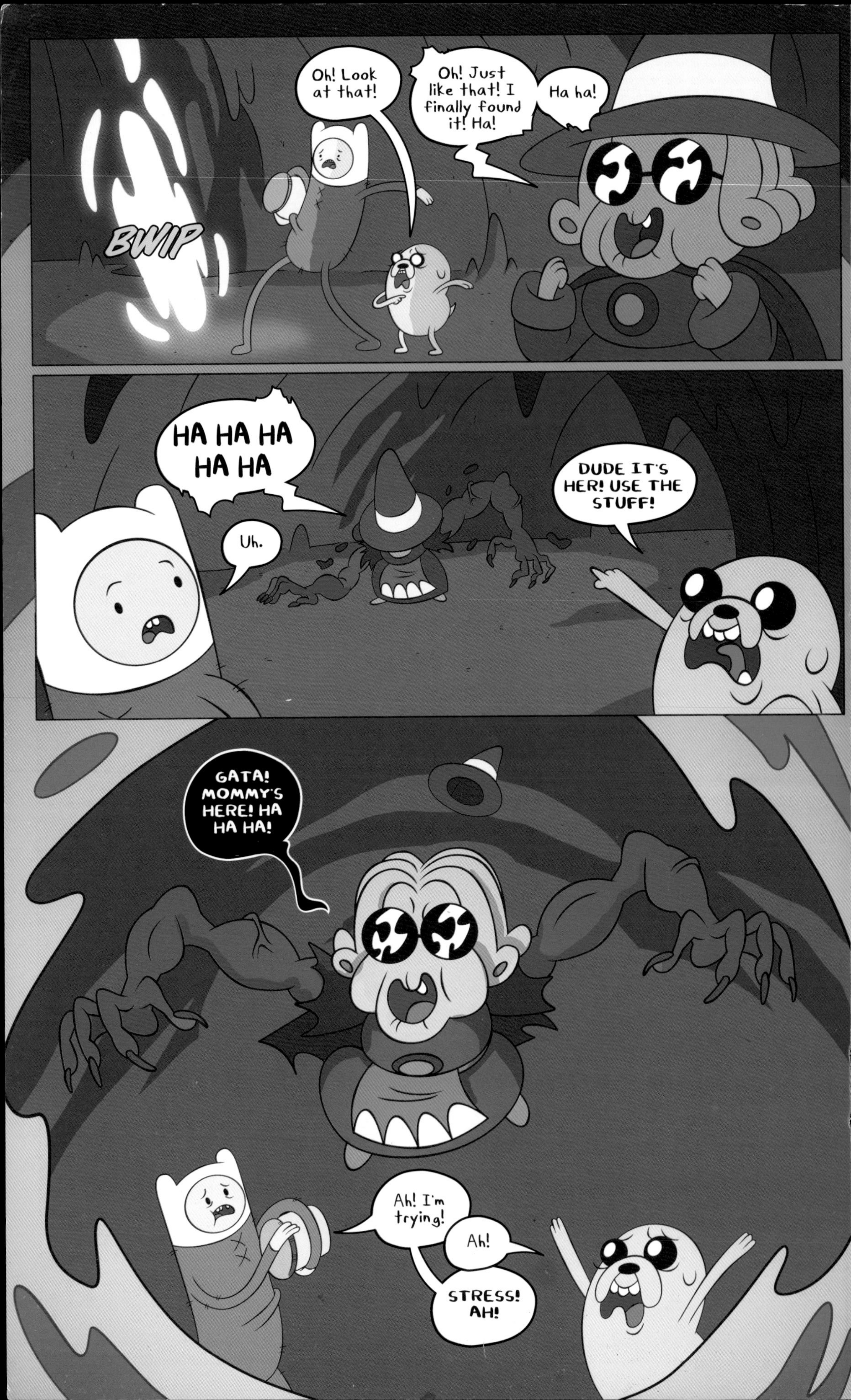
BWIP
Oh! Look at that!
Oh! Just like that! I finally found it! Ha!
Ha ha!
HA HA HA HA HA
Uh.
DUDE IT'S HER! USE THE STUFF!
GATA! MOMMY'S HERE! HA HA HA!
Ah! I'm trying!
Ah!
STRESS! AH!

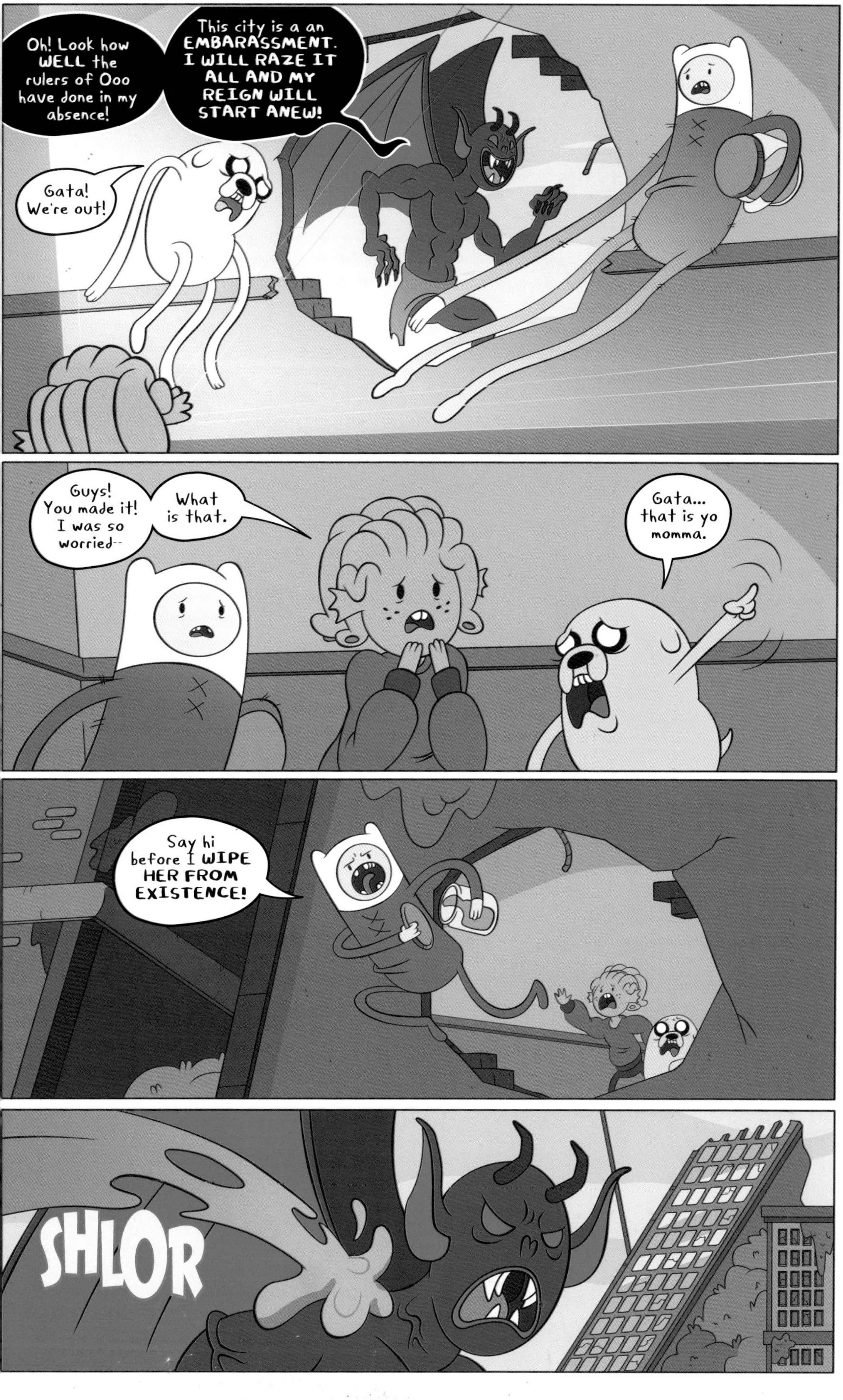
Oh! Look how WELL the rulers of Ooo have done in my absence!
This city is a an EMBARASSMENT. I WILL RAZE IT ALL AND MY REIGN WILL START ANEW!
Gata! We're out!
Guys! You made it! I was so worried--
What is that.
Gata... that is yo momma.
Say hi before I WIPE HER FROM EXISTENCE!
SHLOR

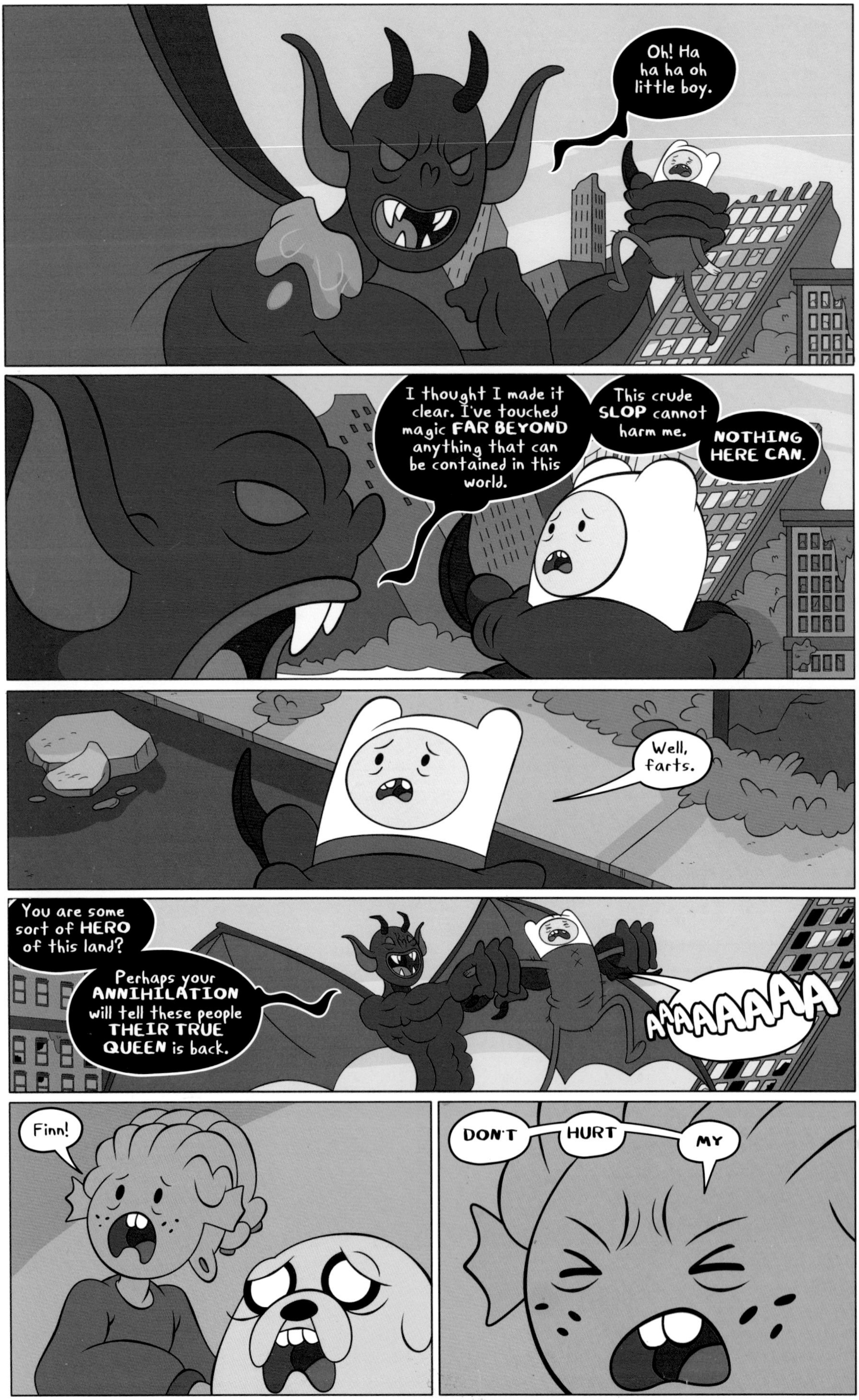
Oh! Ha ha ha oh little boy.
I thought I made it clear. I've touched magic FAR BEYOND anything that can be contained in this world.
This crude SLOP cannot harm me.
NOTHING HERE CAN.
Well, farts.
You are some sort of HERO of this land?
Perhaps your ANNIHILATION will tell these people THEIR TRUE QUEEN is back.
AAAAAAAA
Finn!
DON'T
HURT
MY

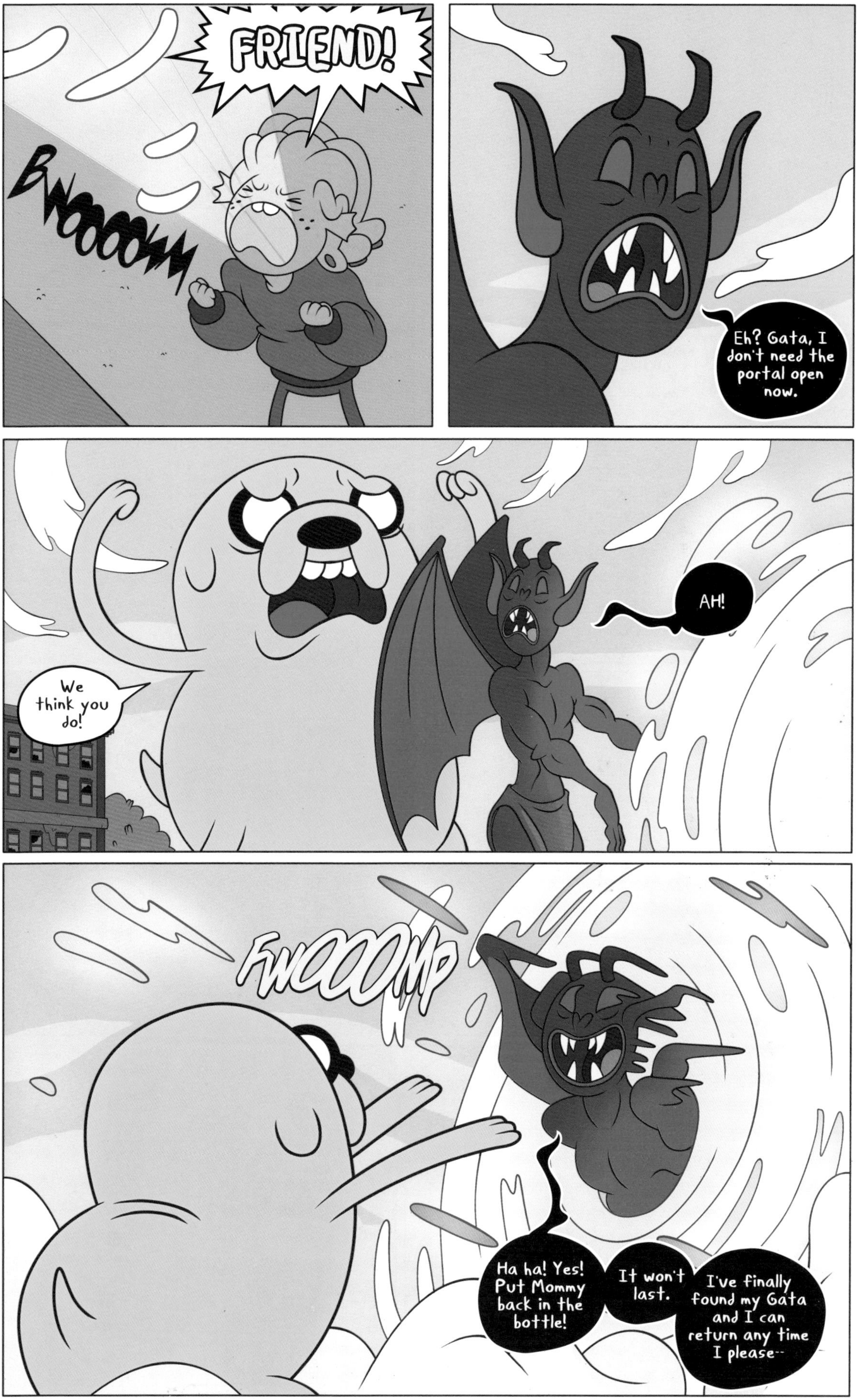
FRIEND!
BWOOOOWM
Eh? Gata, I don't need the portal open now.
We think you do!
AH!
FWOOOMP
Ha ha! Yes! Put Mommy back in the bottle!
It won't last.
I've finally found my Gata and I can return any time I please--

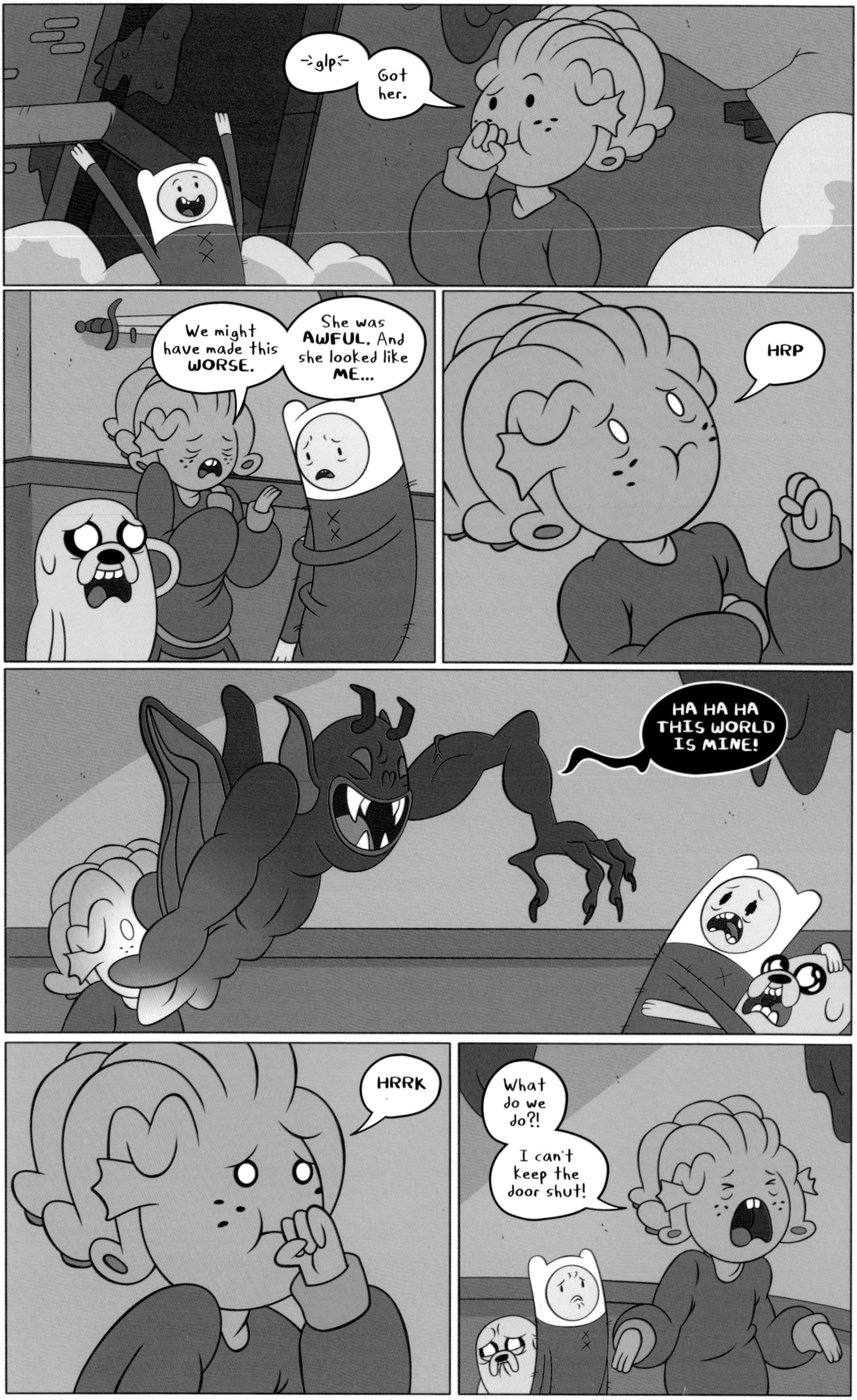
glp
Got her.
We might have made this WORSE.
She was AWFUL. And she looked like ME...
HRP
HA HA HA THIS WORLD IS MINE!
HRRK
What do we do?!
I can't keep the door shut!

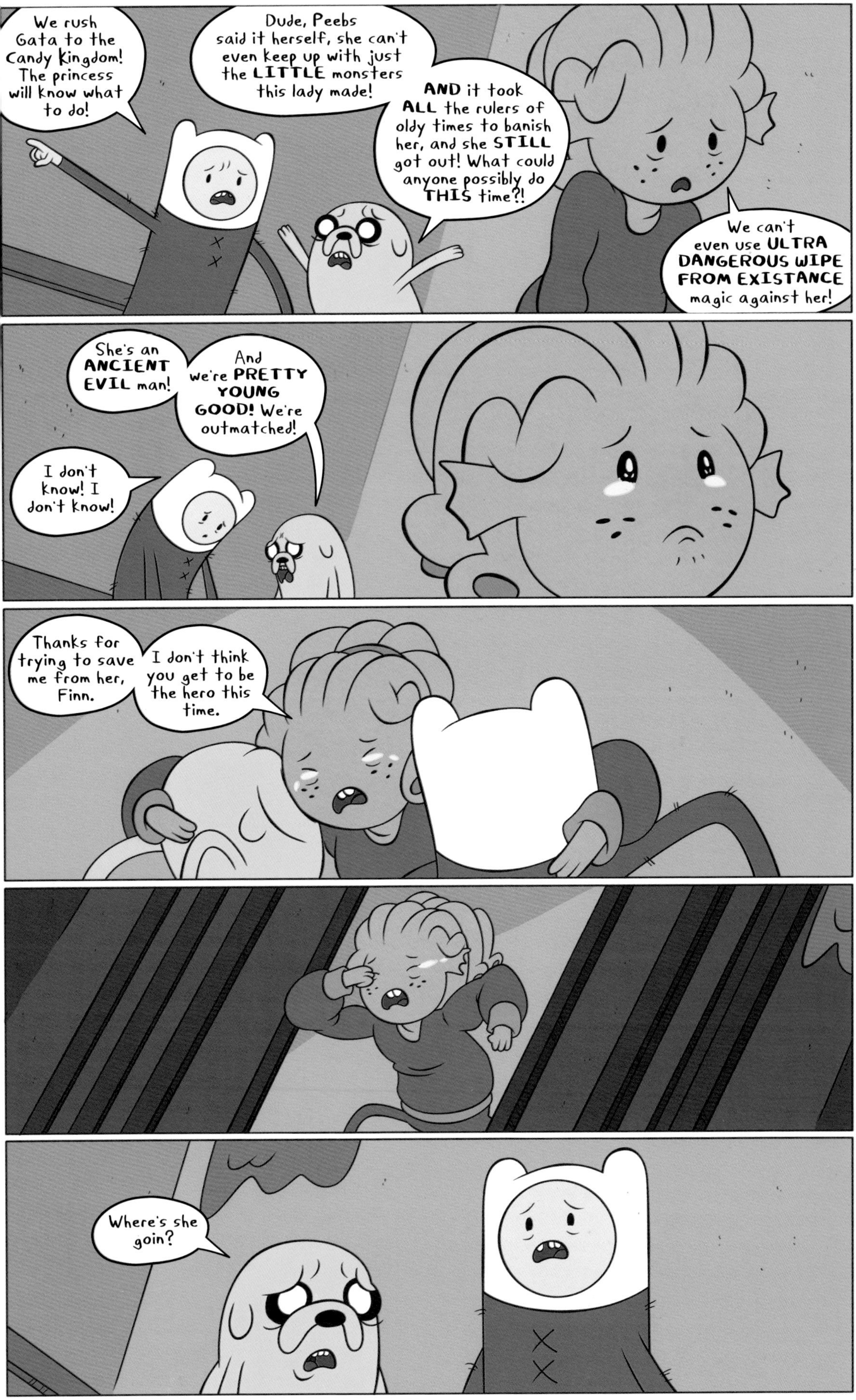
We rush Gata to the Candy Kingdom! The princess will know what to do!
Dude, Peebs said it herself, she can't even keep up with just the LITTLE monsters this lady made!
AND it took ALL the rulers of oldy times to banish her, and she STILL got out! What could anyone possibly do THIS time?!
We can't even use ULTRA DANGEROUS WIPE FROM EXISTANCE magic against her!
She's an ANCIENT EVIL man!
And we're PRETTY YOUNG GOOD! We're outmatched!
I don't know! I don't know!
Thanks for trying to save me from her, Finn.
I don't think you get to be the hero this time.
Where's she goin?

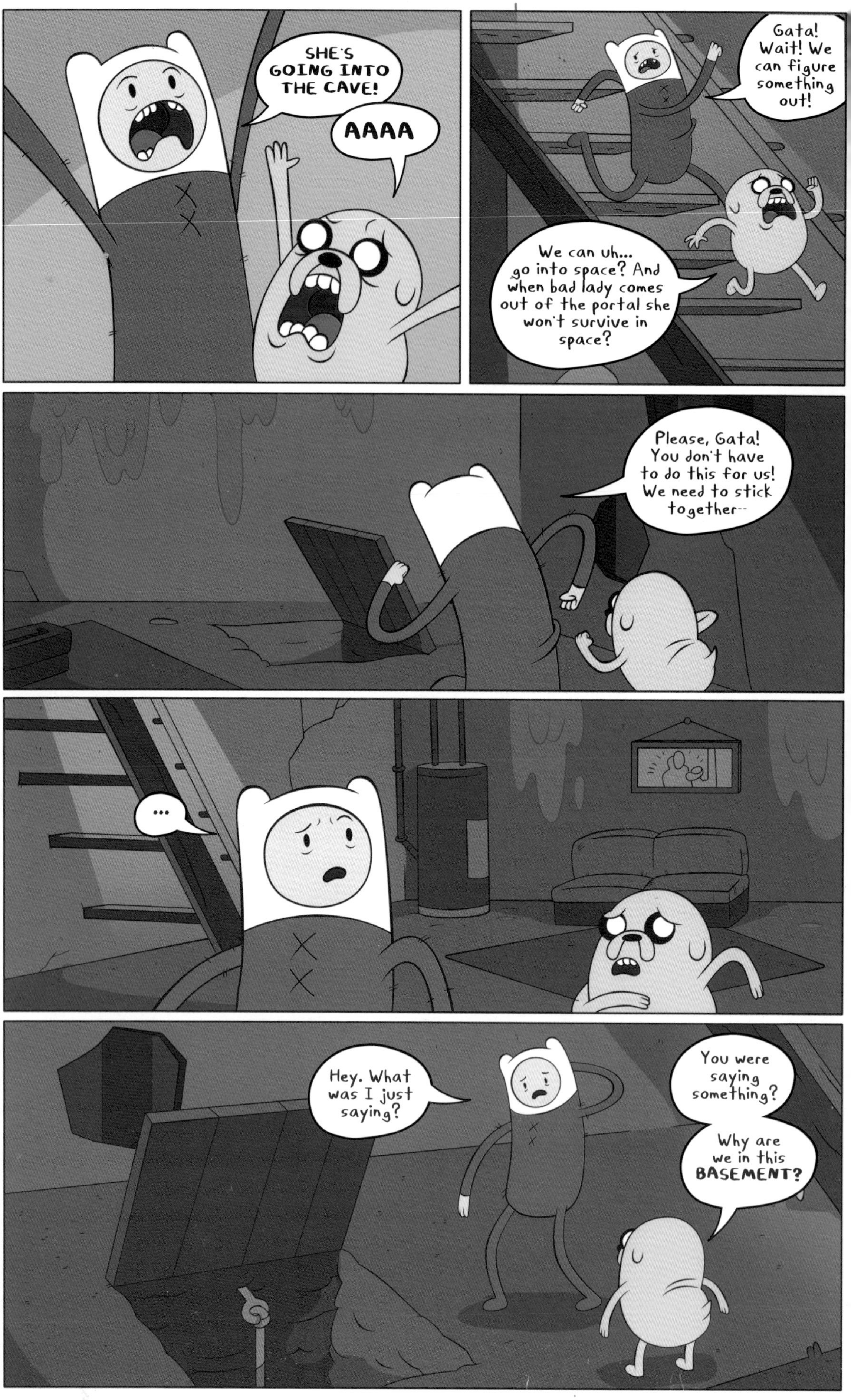
SHE'S GOING INTO THE CAVE!
AAAA
Gata! Wait! We can figure something out!
We can uh... go into space? And when bad lady comes out of the portal she won't survive in space?
Please, Gata! You don't have to do this for us! We need to stick together--
...
Hey. What was I just saying?
You were saying something?
Why are we in this BASEMENT?

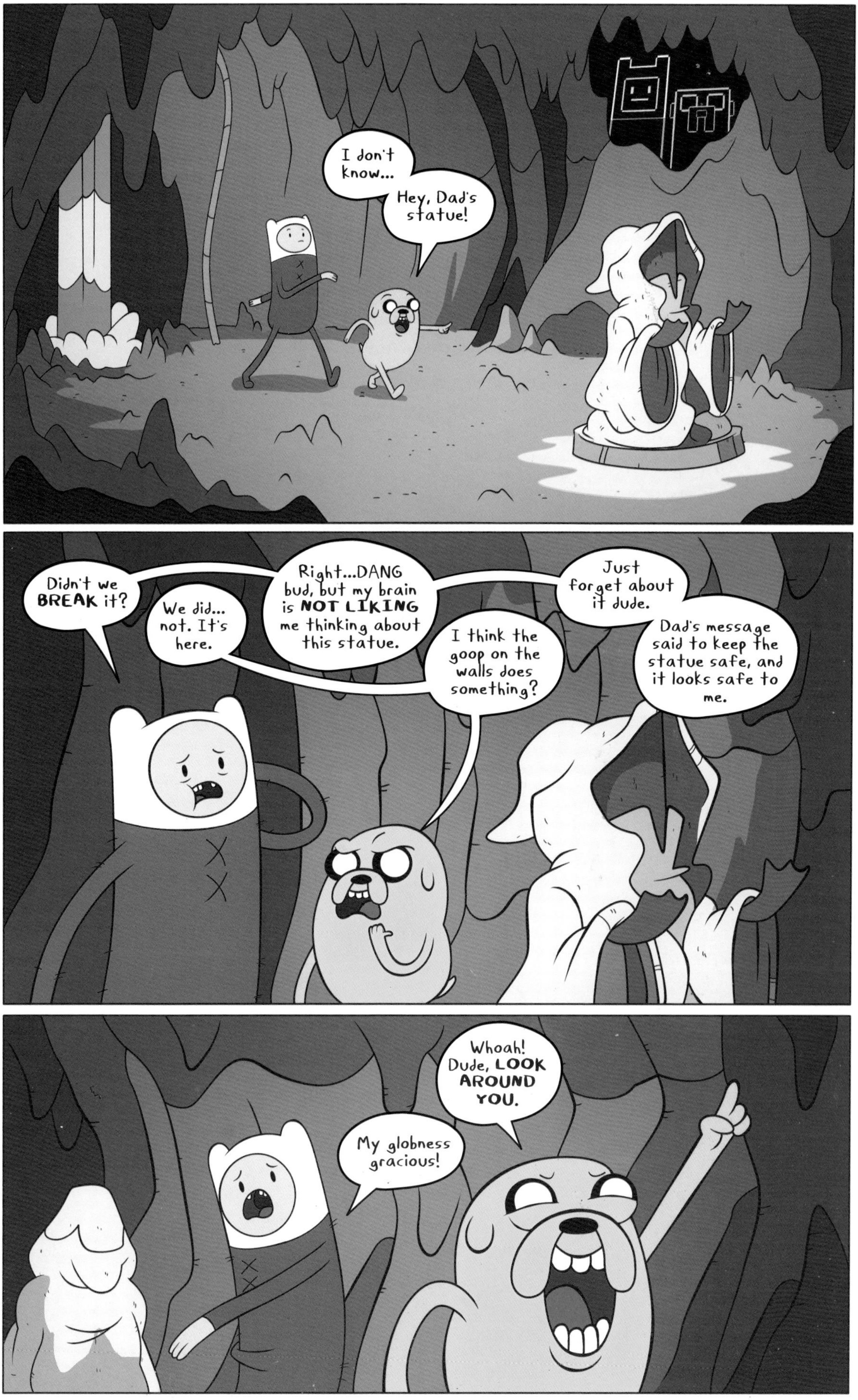

I don't know...
Hey, Dad's statue!
Didn't we **BREAK** it?
We did... not. It's here.
Right...DANG bud, but my brain is **NOT LIKING** me thinking about this statue.
I think the goop on the walls does something?
Just forget about it dude.
Dad's message said to keep the statue safe, and it looks safe to me.
Whoah! Dude, **LOOK AROUND YOU.**
My globness gracious!

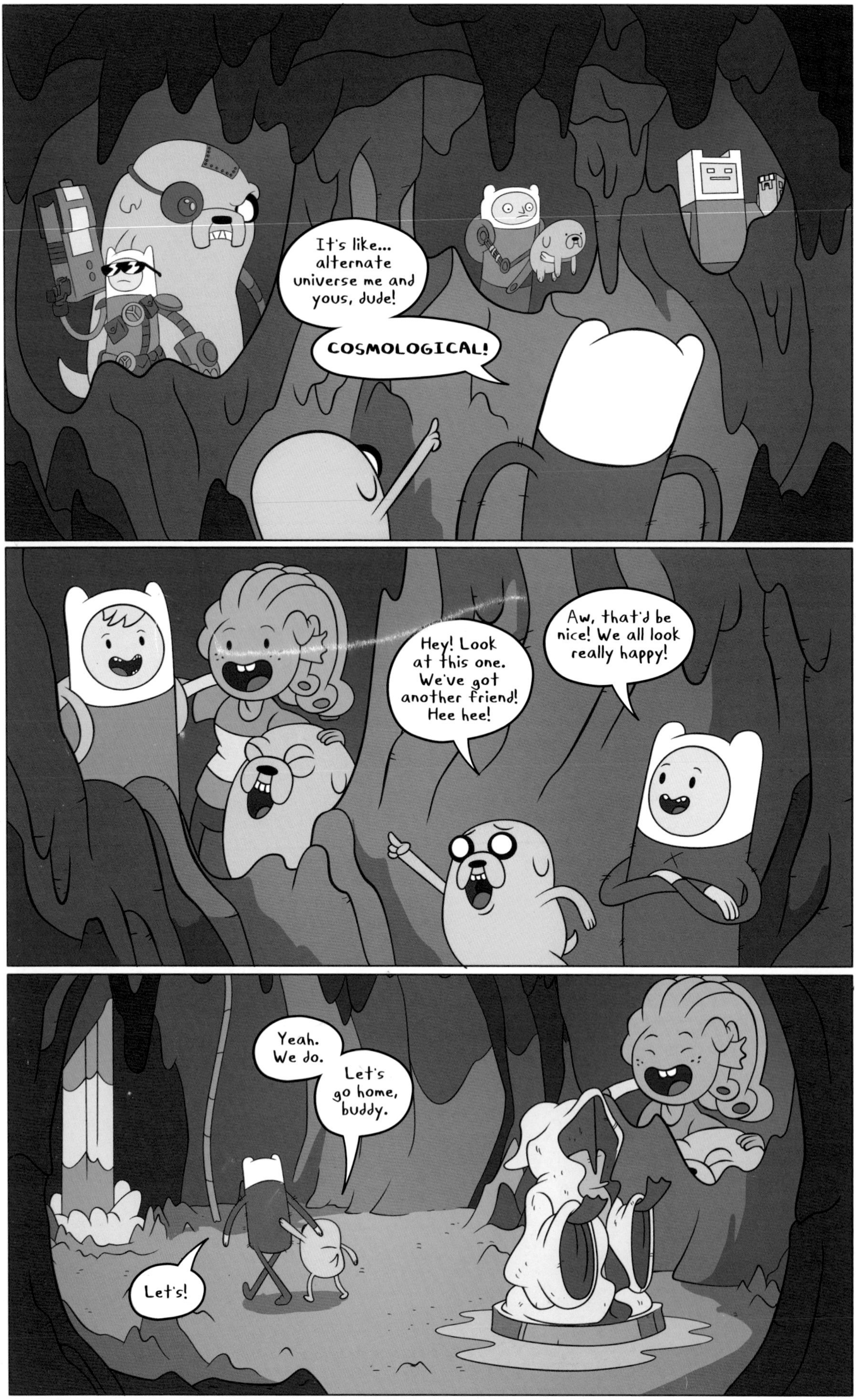
It's like... alternate universe me and yous, dude!
COSMOLOGICAL!
Hey! Look at this one. We've got another friend! Hee hee!
Aw, that'd be nice! We all look really happy!
Yeah. We do.
Let's go home, buddy.
Let's!

COVER GALLERY

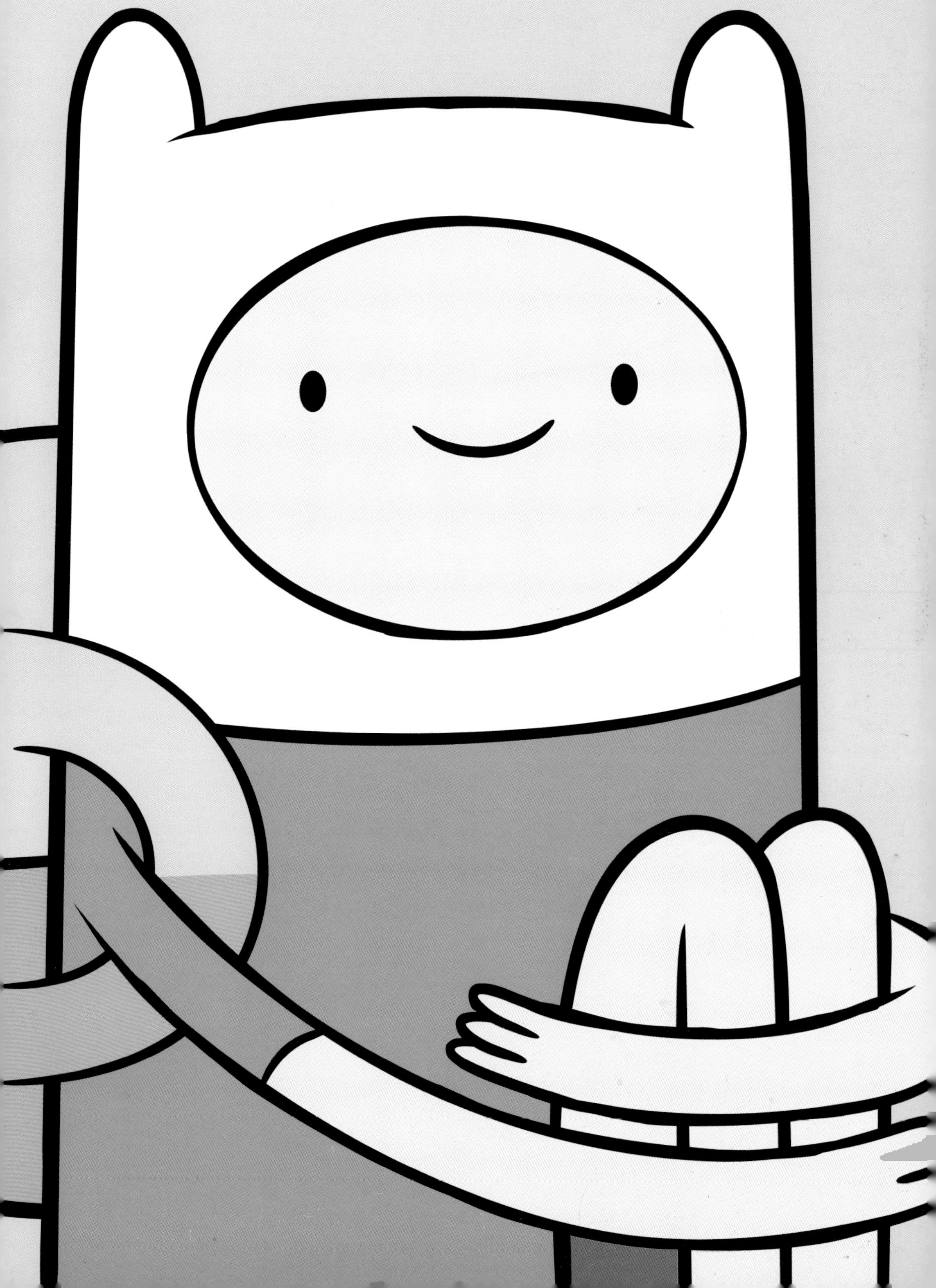

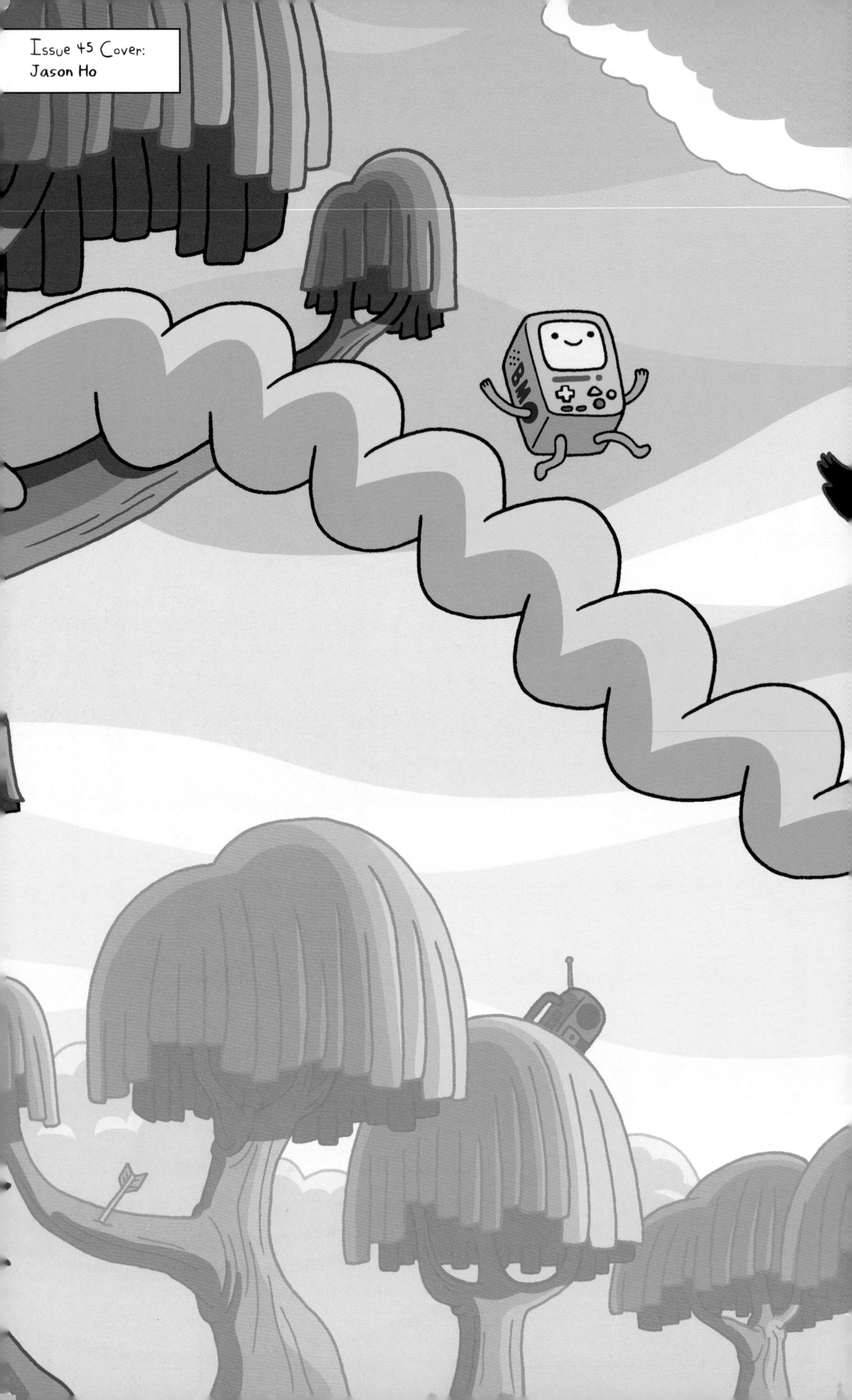

Issue 45 Cover:
Jason Ho

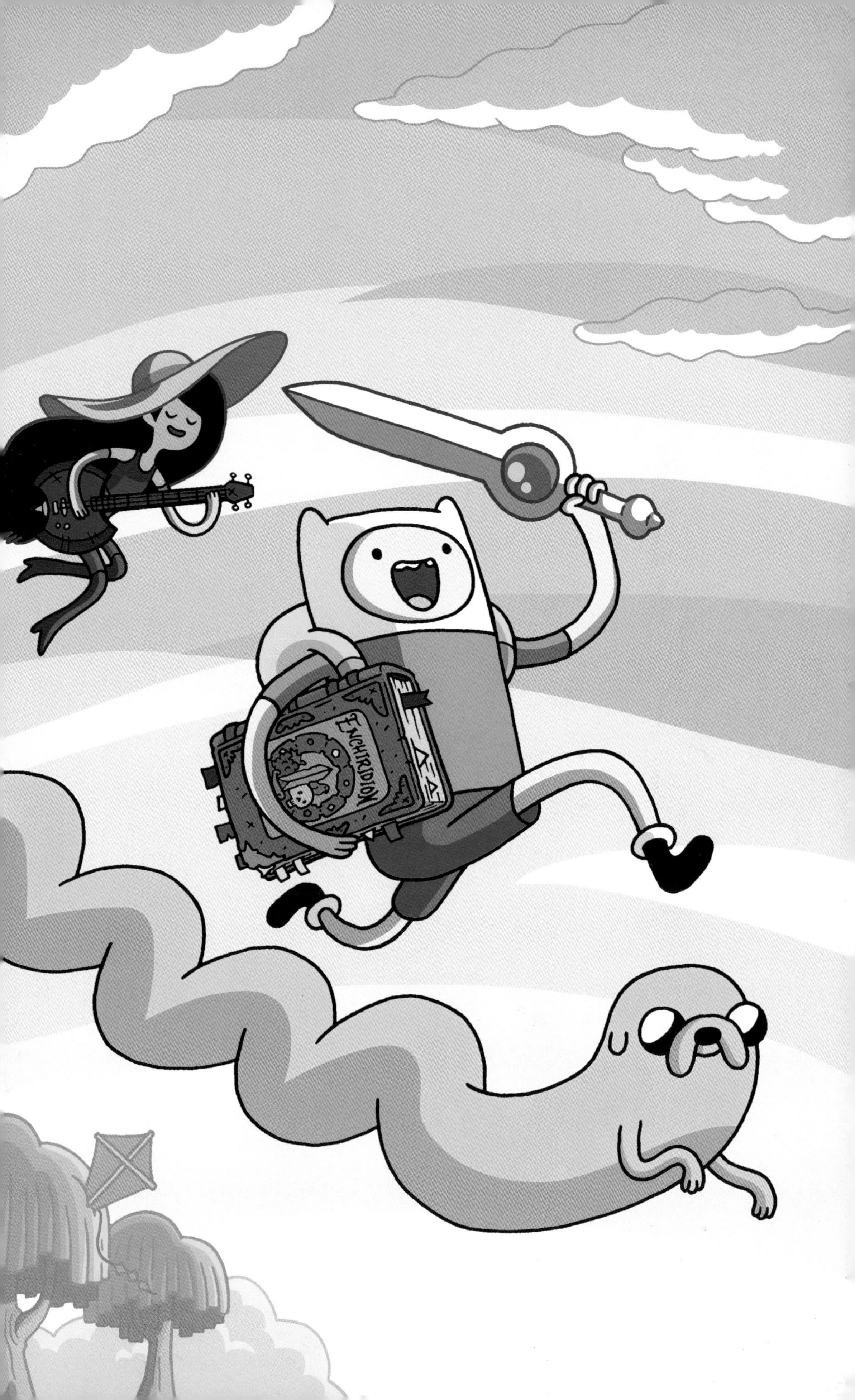
ENCHIRIDION

Issue 45 Subscription Cover:
Andre

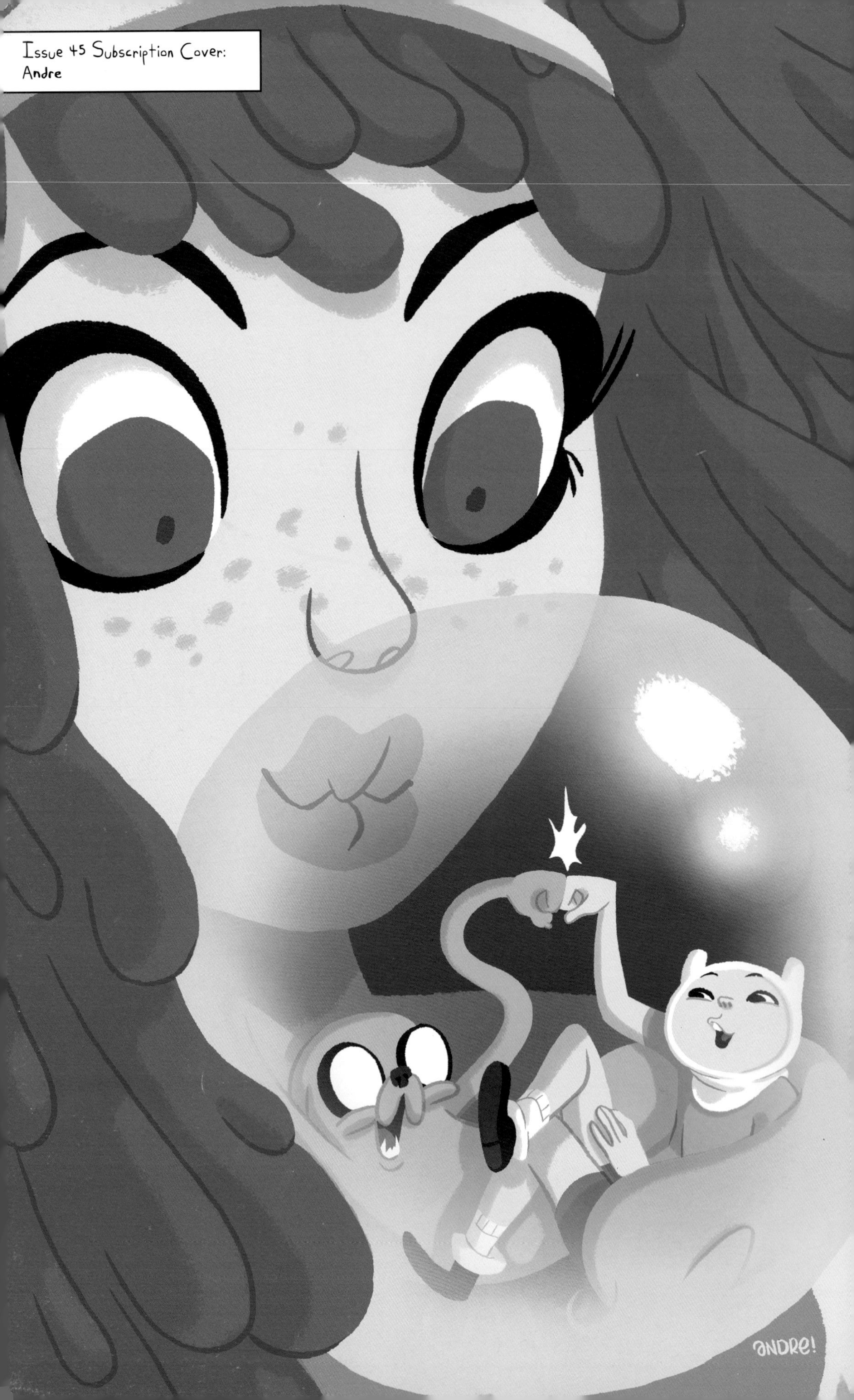
ANDRE!

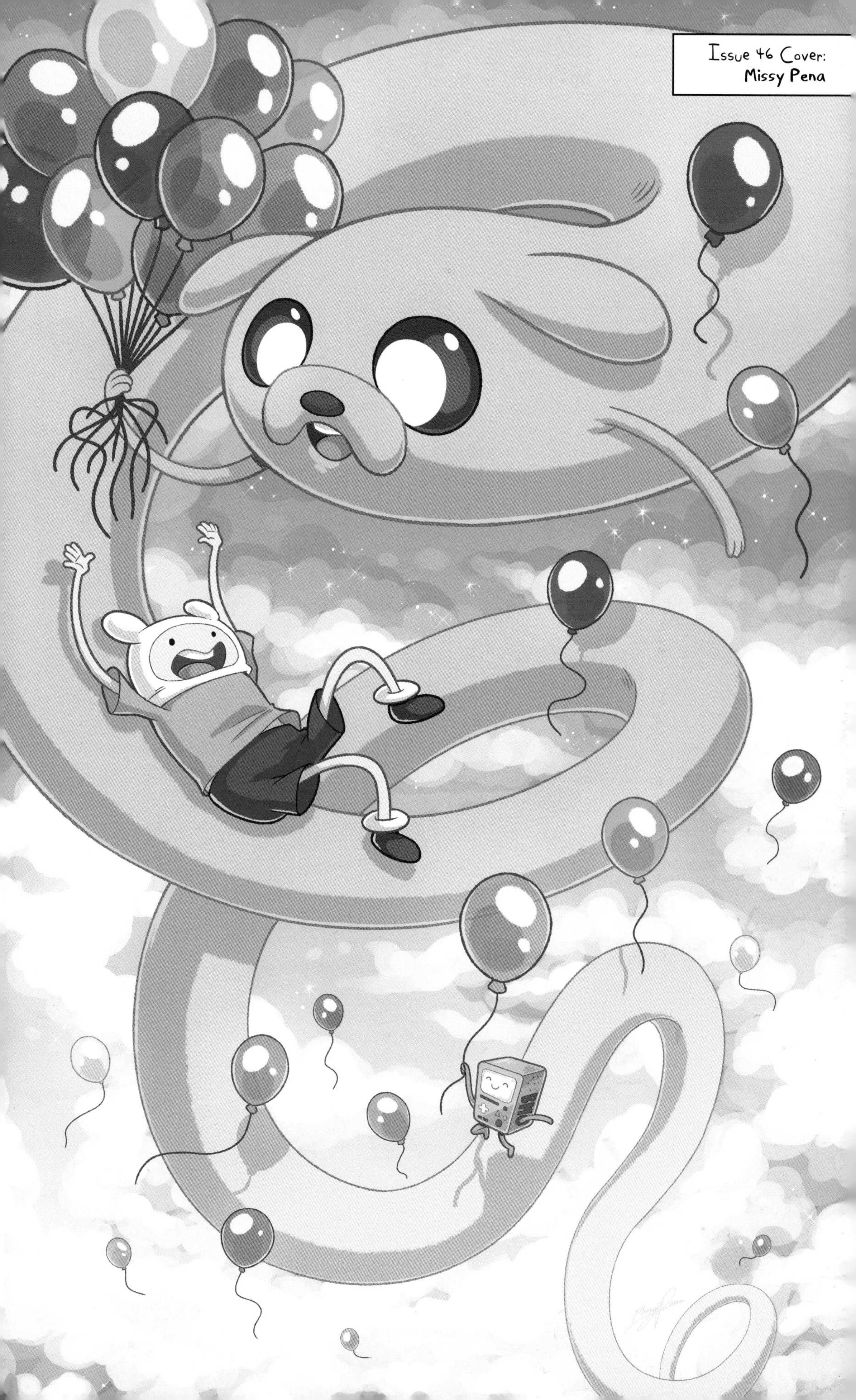

Issue 46 Cover:
Missy Pena

Issue 46 Subscription Cover:
Vivian Ng

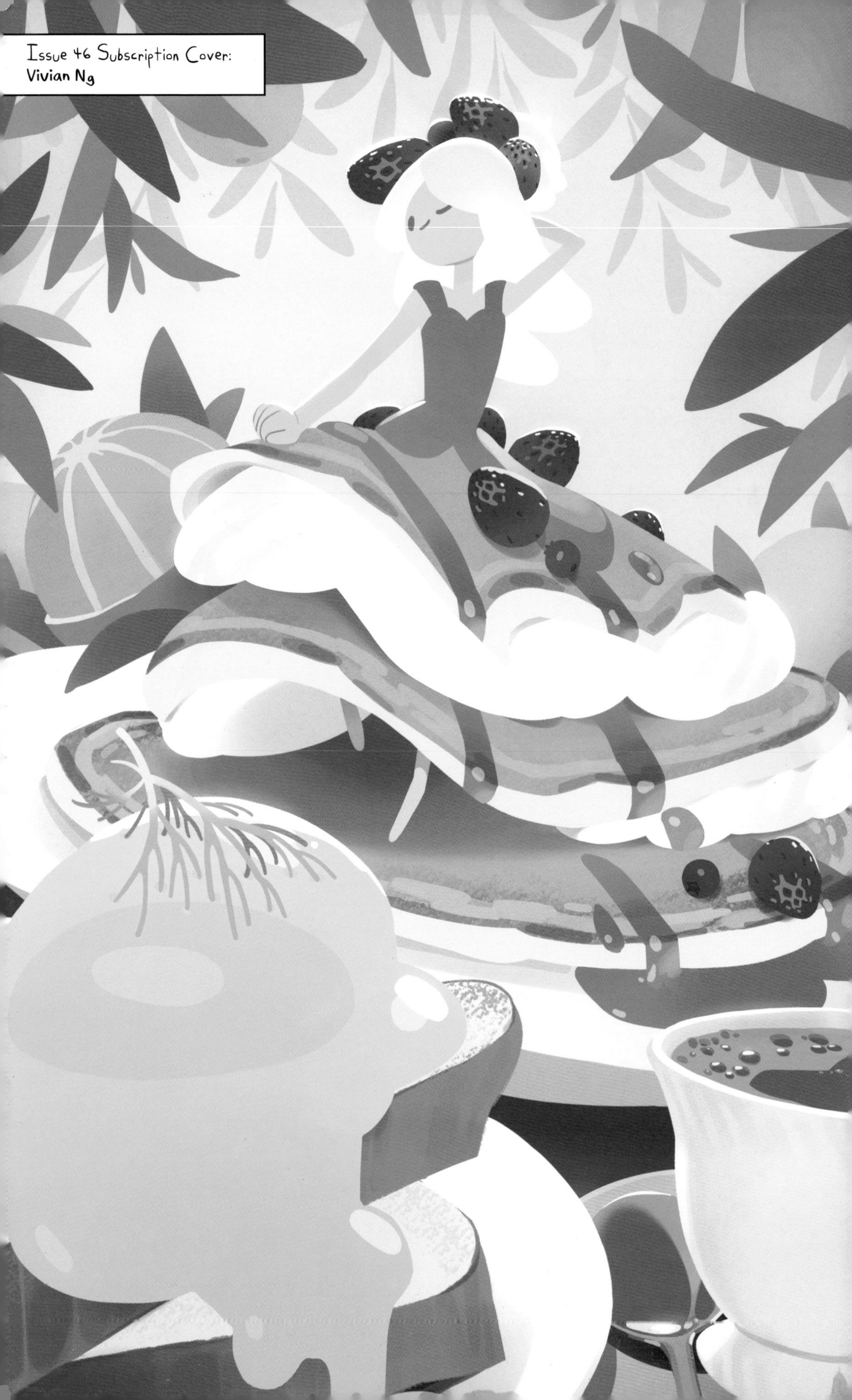

Issue 46 Eugene Comic Con 2015 Exclusive Cover:
Gashi Gashi

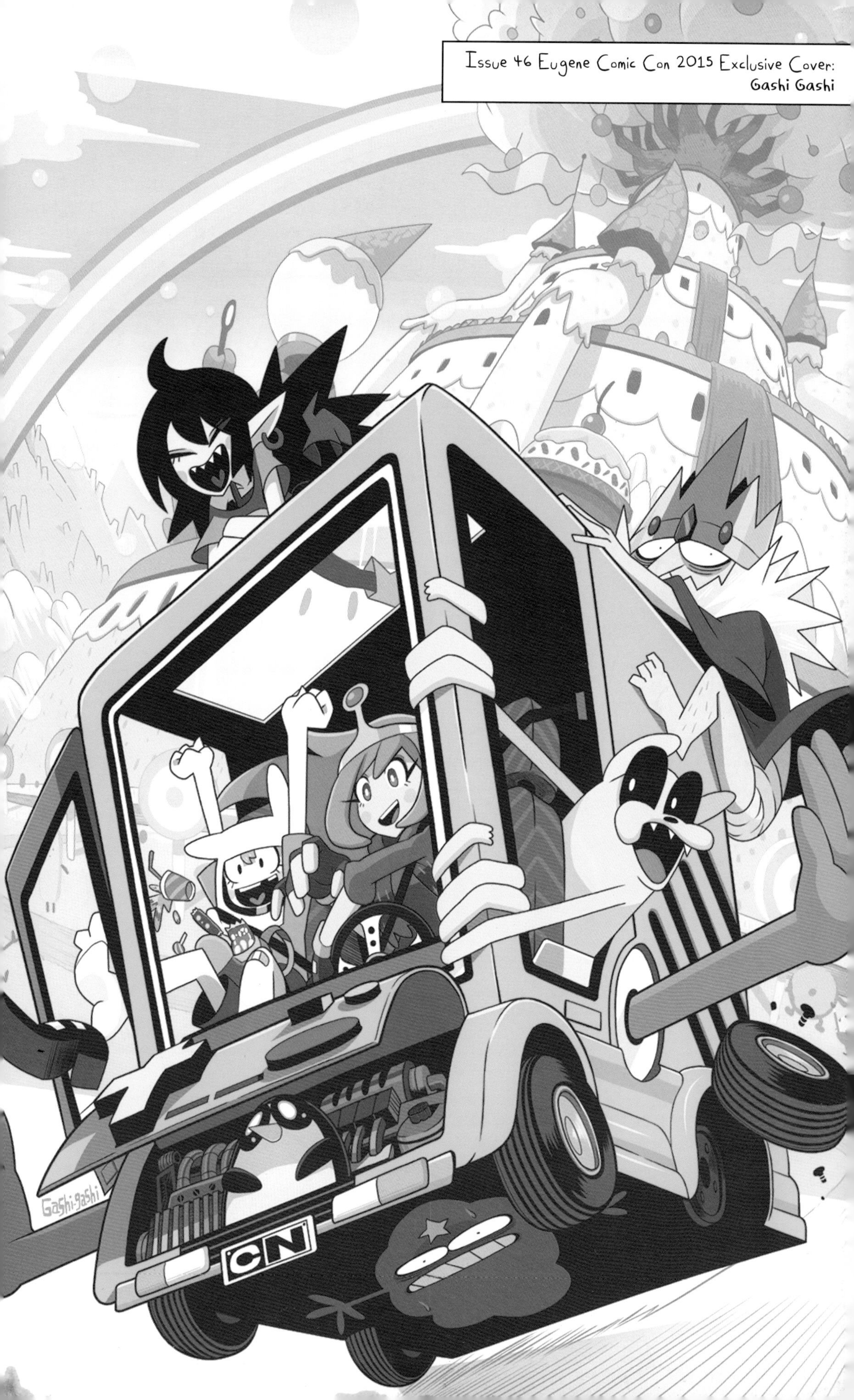
Gashi-gashi

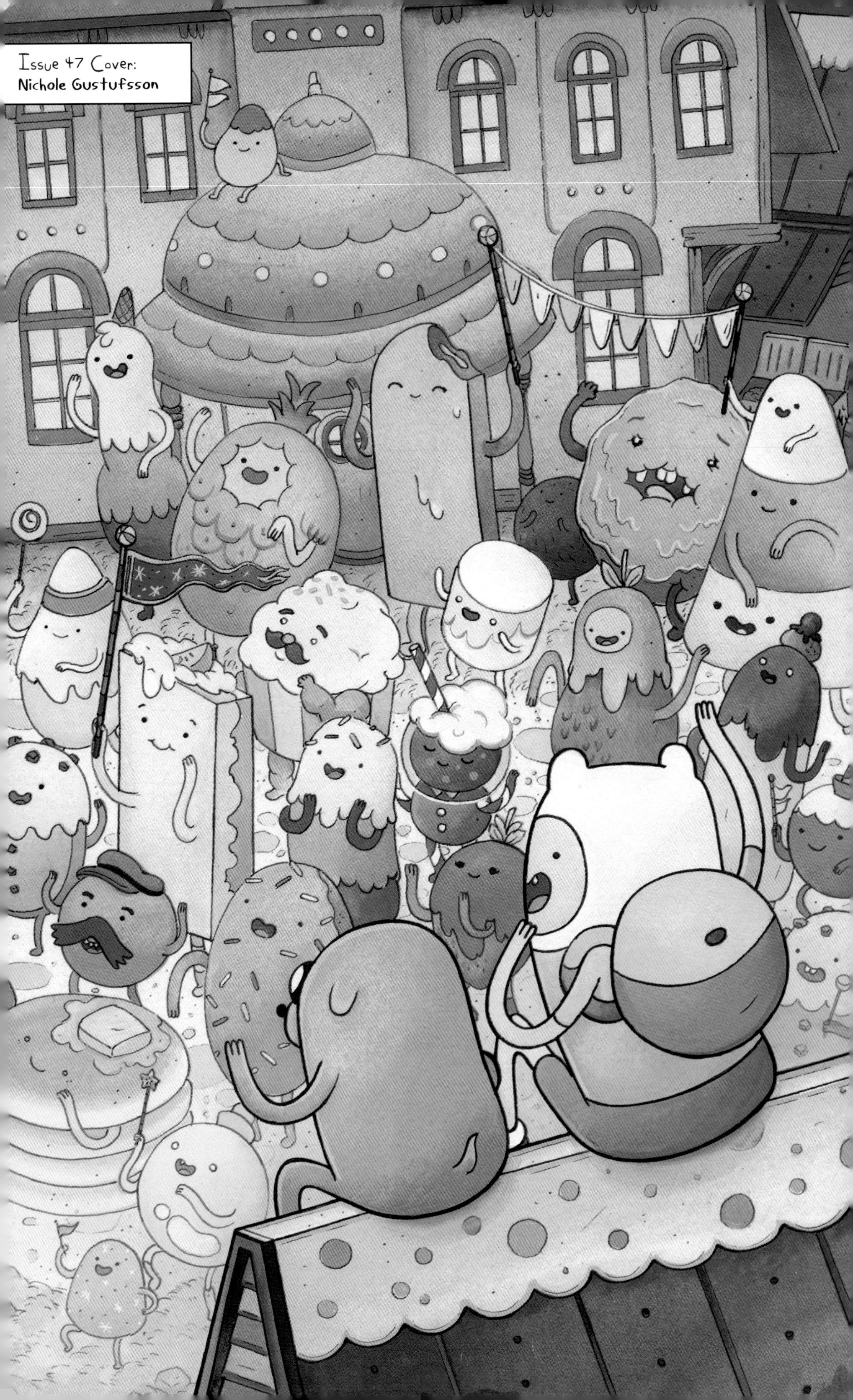

Issue 47 Cover:
Nichole Gustufsson

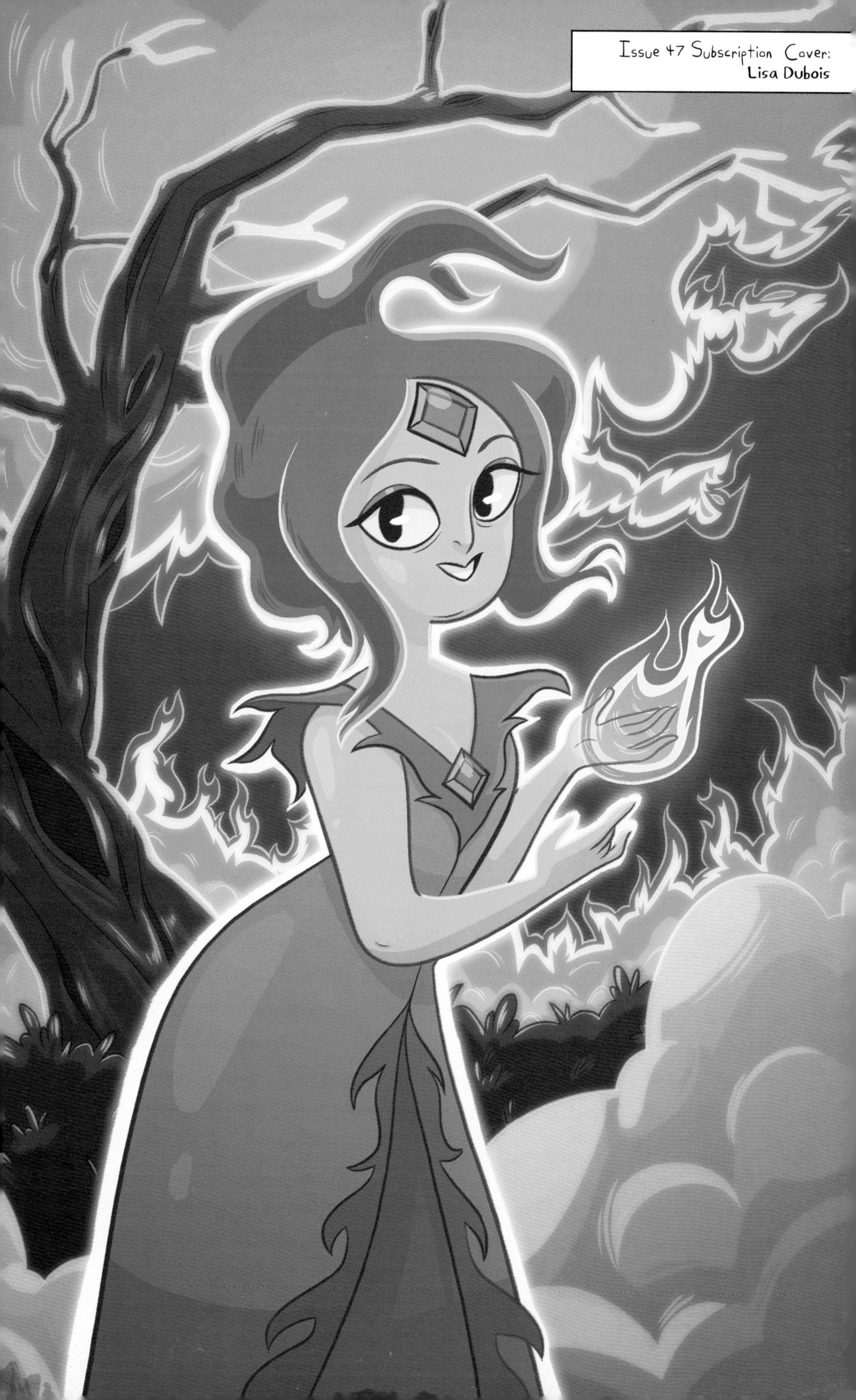

Issue 47 Subscription Cover:
Lisa Dubois

Issue 48 Cover:
Maya Kern

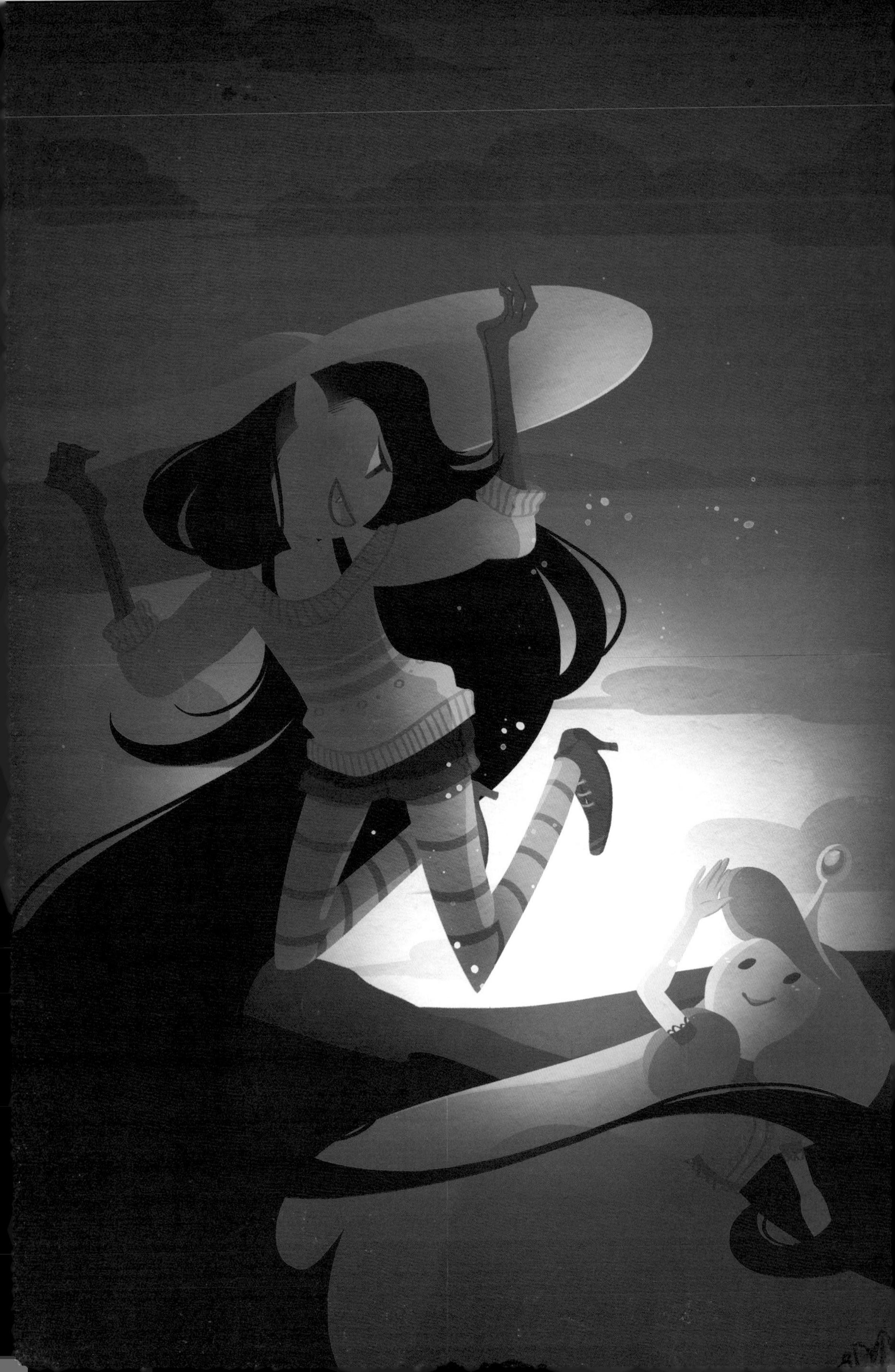

Issue 48 Subscription Cover:
David Ryan Robinson

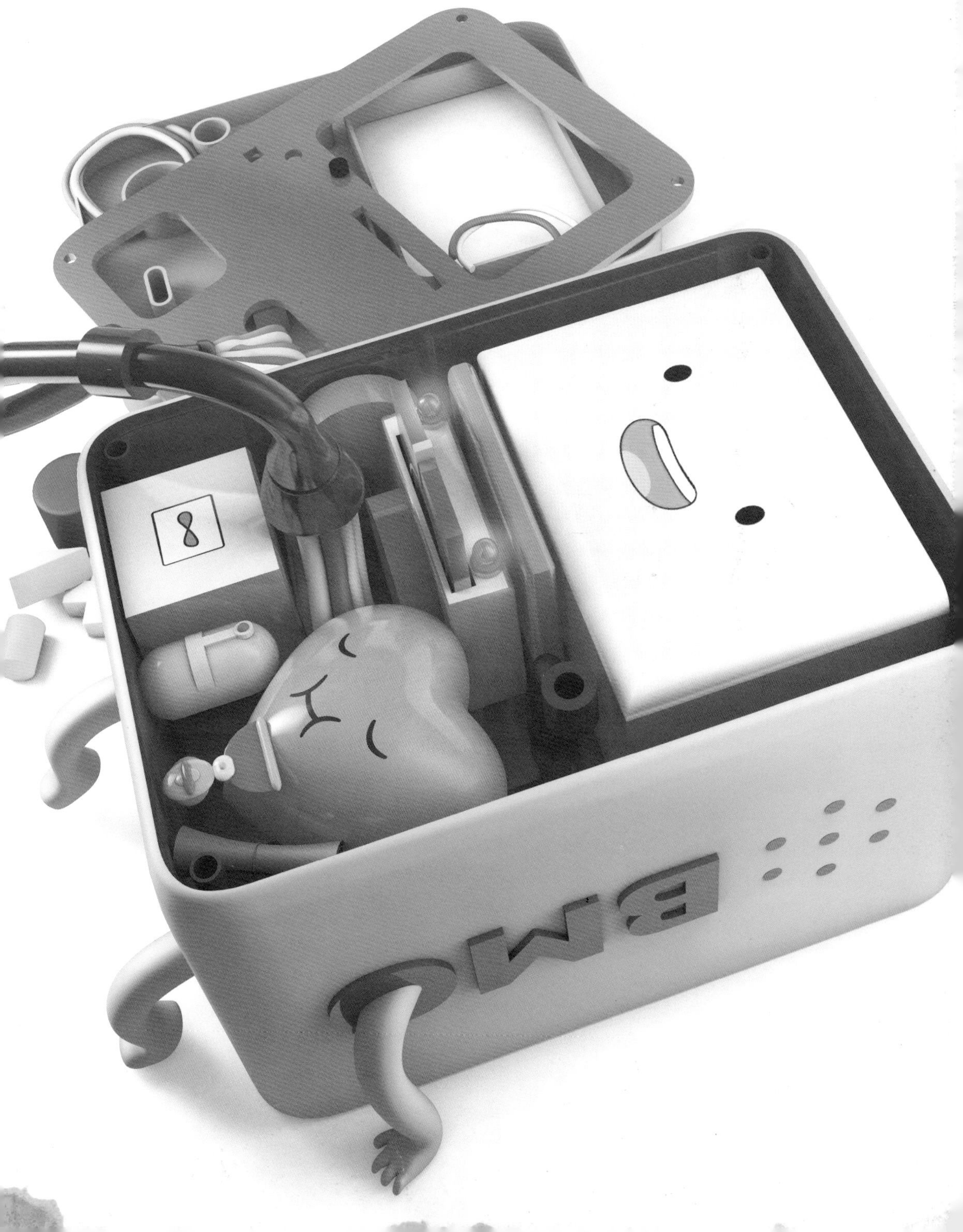
BMO

Issue 49 Cover:
Asia Kendrick-Horton

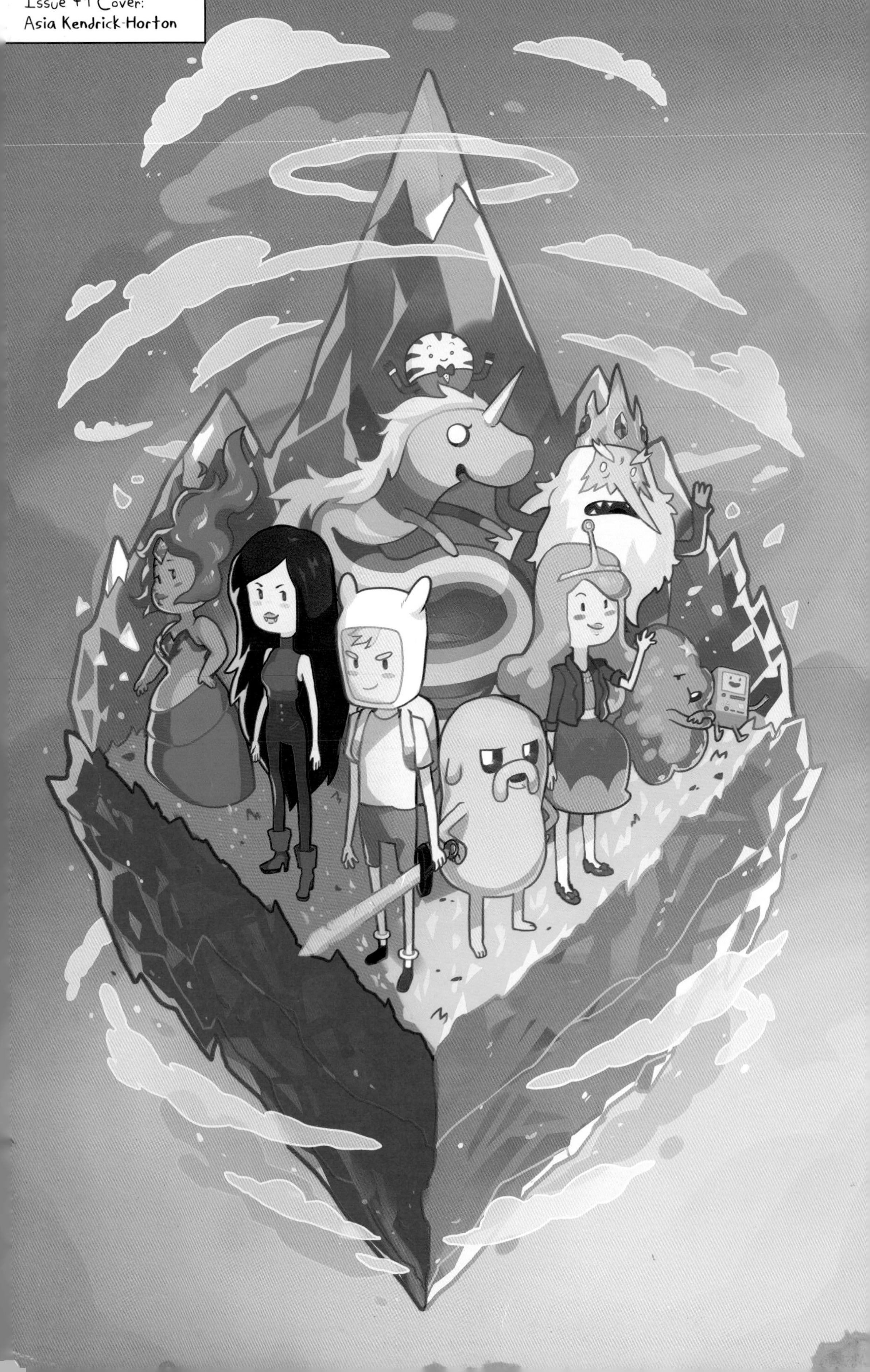

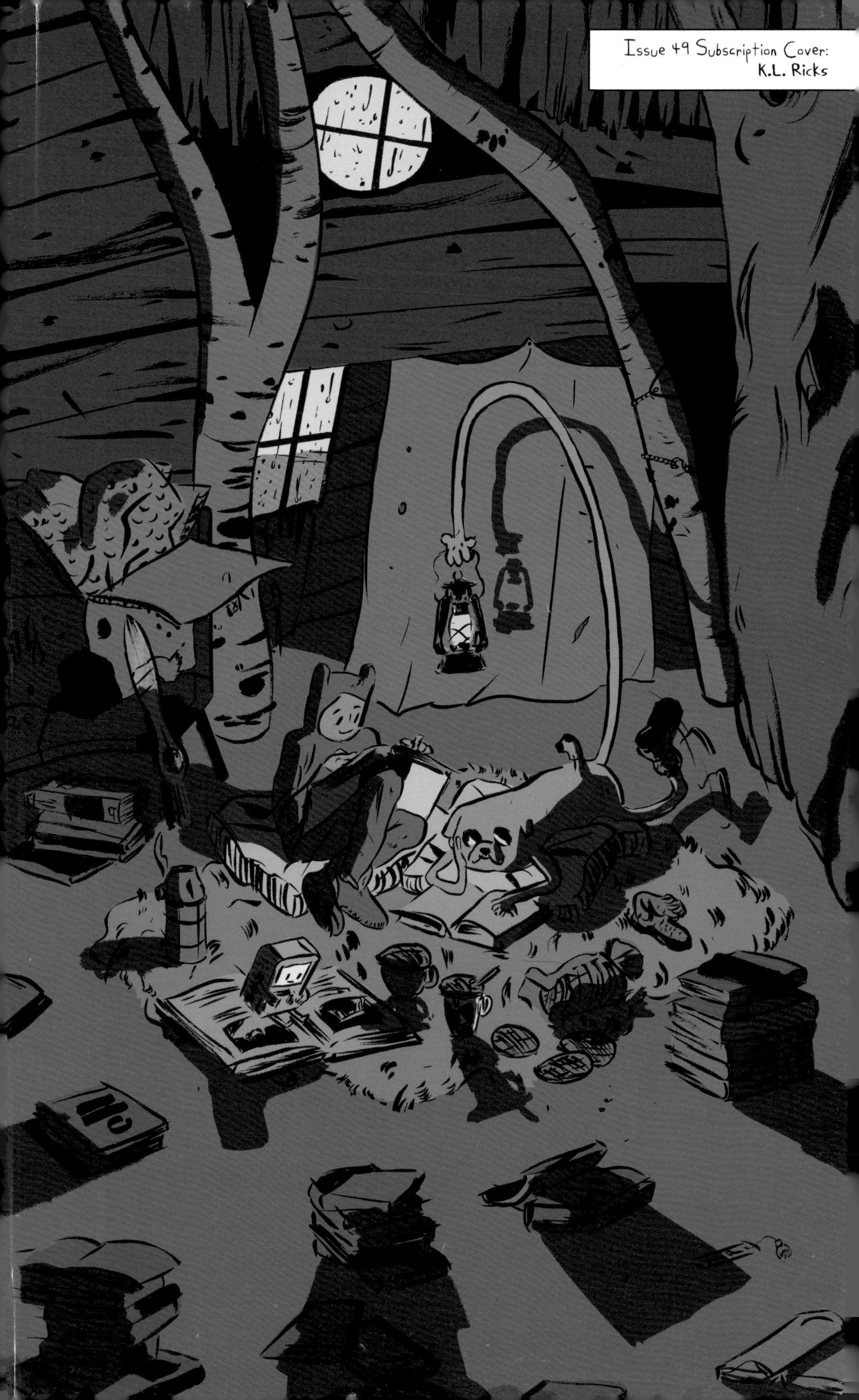

Issue 49 Subscription Cover:
K.L. Ricks